Praise for the Novels of
Elizabeth Thornton

Shady Lady

"Lively, brimming with marvelous dialogue, wit, wisdom, and a pair of delightful lovers, *Shady Lady* is a joy . . . A book to treasure!"—*Romantic Times*

"*Shady Lady* is an exhilarating Regency romantic suspense . . . fans will gain plenty of pleasure from this fine historical."—Harriet Klausner, Book Reviewer

Almost a Princess

"Well written on many levels as a murder mystery, a historical romance, and a chronicle of women's rights—or lack thereof—this book will appeal to fans of Amanda Quick, Candace Camp, and Lisa Kleypas."—*Booklist*

"A fabulous hero, a nicely brainy heroine, one red-hot attraction, and a believable plot make for one great bathtub read."—*Pittsburgh Post-Gazette*

The Perfect Princess

"Steamy sex scenes, fiery repartee, and strong characters set this romantic intrigue apart from the usual Regency fare."—*Publishers Weekly*

"An exciting historical romantic suspense that never slows down until the final page is completed."
—*Midwest Book Review*

Princess Charming

Also by *Elizabeth Thornton*

Shady Lady
Almost a Princess
The Perfect Princess
Princess Charming
Strangers at Dawn
Whisper His Name
You Only Love Twice
The Bride's Bodyguard
Dangerous to Hold
Dangerous to Kiss
Dangerous to Love

The Marriage Trap

Elizabeth Thornton

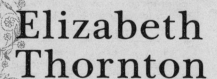

BANTAM BOOKS

THE MARRIAGE TRAP
A Bantam Book / July 2005

Published by Bantam Dell
A Division of Random House, Inc.
New York, New York

Bantam Books and the rooster colophon are
registered trademarks of Random House, Inc.

ISBN 0-553-58753-6

Printed in the United States of America
Published simultaneously in Canada

www.bantamdell.com

OPM   10   9   8   7   6   5   4   3   2   1

For my husband, Forbes.
Remember Paris?

The Marriage Trap

Chapter 1

Ellie's ears pricked the moment she heard Jack's name. It seemed that she wasn't the only female whose ears pricked. Ambitious mamas with young daughters to marry off broke off their conversations and scanned the crush of elegant guests in the embassy's grand salon. This was Paris, six months after Waterloo, and the ambassador was hosting the first ball of the new year.

And, thought Ellie, a glittering affair it was, too. Handsome soldiers in their dress regimentals, gentlemen of fashion, and ladies in their high-waisted, diaphanous ball gowns ringed the dance floor as they watched couples form sets for the next dance.

She wasn't really a part of this glittering crowd. As a paid companion-cum-chaperon, she had to dress modestly and try to look invisible. That wasn't difficult. She was no beauty and was past the age of attracting masculine attention, assets that she took pains to cultivate. Beautiful young women rarely found employment as governesses or companions.

Her gaze came to rest on two gentlemen who had just

entered the salon. They were both tall and dark-haired, both very elegant in their English tailoring and satin breeches. But only one of those gentlemen was known to her—Jack Rigg.

She was probably prejudiced, but she could not help thinking that, even in that glittering crush, he was a formidable presence. Part of his appeal was that he was quite unconscious of the impression he made, either that or he did not care. He was darkly handsome, with beautiful, lustrous eyes the color of the luxurious French chocolate she sipped every morning to slowly bring herself awake. A look from Jack's eyes had the same effect.

She smiled at her fanciful turn of mind.

Though she remembered him very well, he wouldn't remember her. As a young man, no more than a boy, really, he'd been rusticated from Oxford for wildness and truancy and his irate father had sent him to the local vicar for tutoring. Her father just happened to be the local vicar.

She could still see traces of that reckless boy in the grown man, but tempered now by a soldier's discipline. Not that Jack was still a soldier. She'd heard that he'd resigned his commission when he'd come into the title. She supposed she should think of him as Lord Raleigh now and not as plain Jack Rigg.

When he brushed back a lock of dark hair, a fleeting smile softened her expression. She recognized the gesture, as well as the glint in his dark eyes and the slant of that sculpted mouth in his tanned face. He'd had the same expression as a boy when he couldn't get his mind around Greek grammar, and was impatient to get out of the schoolroom and go riding on the downs or flirt with the local girls.

No one denied that Jack had a way with women.

Her father never claimed that he had turned Jack into a

scholar, but he'd imparted the rudiments of Latin and Greek, enough to gain the boy readmittance to Oxford's hallowed halls. Papa had always maintained that though Jack was a little wild, he was sound in the things that mattered, and he expected him to turn out well.

She wondered, if her father were alive, what he would think of Jack now.

Her thoughts scattered when she heard her employer's voice, thin and nasal, pitched above the noise as she addressed her daughter. "Look, Harriet," exclaimed Lady Sedgewick, "there's Lord Raleigh with his friend. Now there's a gentleman I hope your papa will cultivate. Next to Devonshire, he is the most eligible bachelor in Paris."

She fanned her hot cheeks as she gazed avidly at the gentleman in question. Lady Harriet, a tall, willowy girl with blonde curls and a pleasant rather than a pretty face, followed the direction of her mother's gaze. "There are two gentlemen there, Mama. Which of them is Lord Raleigh?"

Her mother frowned. "Not the dandy with the quizzing glass! That is Lord Denison, and everyone knows he has to marry money." Her ladyship flicked a glance at Ellie. "I expect *you*, Miss Hill, to keep a sharp lookout for fortune hunters and keep them away from Harriet."

"Naturally," replied Ellie meekly.

Lady Sedgewick need not have worried about fortune hunters. Harriet was in love with a young soldier who had been posted to Canada, so she was safe from everyone, even from her mother's stratagems to marry her off.

"Mama!" Harriet protested. "He's too old for me. He must be thirty if he's a day."

Thirty-two, to be exact, but Ellie kept that piece of information to herself. She knew her place.

Her ladyship made a *cluck*ing sound. "Stuff and

nonsense! And what has that to do with anything? He must be worth at least thirty thousand pounds a year."

One could never, thought Ellie, accuse the upper classes of delicacy when it came to discussing money and marriage. It was a different story when it came to discussing servants' wages. In her own case, her wages were two months in arrears, but it would never occur to Lady Sedgewick that her daughter's chaperon would need money when her employer paid all her expenses. As her ladyship had pointed out when she'd offered Ellie the position, though the wages were small, it was the chance of a lifetime for a young woman with no money and few connections to see a little of the world.

And so it had proved. Paris was supposed to be their first stop, but they'd been here for a month, and no one was in a hurry to leave, least of all Ellie. Lady Harriet was a good-natured girl and her attachment to the young soldier who had been posted to Canada made her easy to chaperon. Ellie didn't have to discourage suitors. Harriet did that quite well on her own. And Paris was an exciting city. It seemed that half of England's aristocracy had come for an extended visit now that the war with France was over. Every night there were parties, balls and receptions, or visits to the theater and opera.

All the same, she still felt like an outsider looking in on the world. Her place wasn't to offer opinions or share what she was feeling. She was there to listen, to fetch and carry, and smile through it all. She wasn't unique. All young women who served as chaperons or companions led solitary lives.

There was something else that troubled her. She needed money badly, and two months' wages wasn't nearly enough to cover her expenses, even if her ladyship could be hinted into opening her purse.

She sucked in a breath when Jack's gaze passed over

her, then let it out slowly when he gave no sign of recognizing her. *What did you expect?* she chided herself. Jack had been her father's pupil for a mere six months. After that, he'd returned to Oxford, and by the time he came home for the holidays, her father had become the vicar of St. Bede's, a good ten miles from the Raleigh estate.

Fifteen years had passed since she'd last seen Jack. Naturally she remembered him. He'd been seventeen and full of himself. She'd been a tiresome adolescent who had hoped to impress him with her extensive book learning. After all, that's what impressed Papa. Someone should have told her that the way to a man's heart was not through book learning.

Lord Sedgewick joined them at that moment. "Arthur," said his wife, "don't waste a moment or Lady Oxford will steal him from under our noses for one of her girls."

"Eh?" said his lordship, mystified.

"Lord Raleigh!" She used her fan as a pointer. "Invite him over to meet Harriet. How will she ever meet eligible gentlemen if she's not introduced to them?"

Lord Sedgewick, tall and lean, with a perpetual bloodhound expression, studied the crush that was beginning to form around Lords Raleigh and Denison. He shook his head. "It's like a veritable fox hunt. Give the fox a sporting chance is what I say."

And to all his wife's commands and pleas, he turned a deaf ear.

When the orchestra struck up for a waltz, Jack deftly detached himself and his friend from the group that hemmed them in and made for the cardroom. Lord Denison, "Ash" to his friends, and a former comrade in arms, was the gentleman whom Lady Sedgewick referred to as a "dandy," largely because a quizzing glass hung from a black ribbon around his neck, and his neckcloth was done in a series of intricate folds and bows.

Just as they reached the cardroom, their hostess, Lady Elizabeth, exited it with two young hussars in tow. "Come along, Edward, Harry." Her voice was friendly but firm. "This is a ball, remember? I expect you to do your duty. There will be no wallflowers at my ball. If you won't choose a partner, I'll choose one for you."

Before Lady Elizabeth could catch his eye, Jack turned aside and steered Ash toward a stand of potted palms beside a Grecian pillar. From this vantage point they had a good view of the dance floor, and the fronds of the palms gave them some privacy. There wasn't much to see. Only a few couples were dancing, but Lady Elizabeth obviously wasn't going to tolerate that state of affairs. Gradually, more couples joined them.

"I don't suppose," said Jack, "we can slip away unseen?"

Ash looked at his friend with a mixture of amusement and curiosity. "I know you don't mean that because I know you wouldn't dream of offending Sir Charles and Lady Elizabeth. Besides, you're not usually a boor, so what's the problem?"

Jack opened his mouth to defend himself, then thought better of it. Ash was right. He was behaving like a sulky schoolboy. He was irritated because he didn't want to be here, but one did not decline the personal invitation of the British ambassador without serious consequences. He wasn't thinking only of the prime minister, but also thinking of his grandmother, whose friend happened to be the ambassador's aunt. Grandmamma would blister his ears if he slighted her friend's favorite nephew.

He gestured to the dancers on the floor. "It's this cursed ritual. This isn't a ball, it's a hunt, and all those steely-eyed matrons are really a pack of bloodhounds in full cry. And guess who their quarry is?"

"You?" asked Ash, his lips twitching.

"Oh, I don't flatter myself that it's me they want. It's my fortune. That's what is so offensive." He felt in his pocket for his snuffbox, offered it to Ash, then took a small pinch and inhaled. After savoring the aroma, he went on. "Nobody spared me a second glance until I came into the title."

He fell silent as he remembered the drastic change in his circumstances when his brother, the earl, suddenly died, leaving a widow but no male issue to inherit. As his grandmother never stopped pointing out, it was his duty to marry and, in short order, produce the next crop of Riggs to carry on the family name.

He had become resigned to his fate, more or less, until he'd found himself besieged by a horde of ambitious matrons and their equally ambitious daughters. He'd come to Paris for a respite from the hunt, only to meet the same fate here. Ash, whom he'd known since they were at school together, had offered to come with him. It had seemed like a grand idea at the time. Paris represented gaming, drinking, wenching, and dueling. That was the real draw—the dueling. In England, men still called each other out for some slight, imagined or otherwise, but it had become a ritual with no passion behind it. Pistols had replaced swords and no one ever got hurt. It was different in Paris. Frenchmen knew how to wield their small swords to devastating effect. It was an honor and an education to cross swords with them, not to mention a risky business. Not everyone put up his sword when the first blood was drawn.

Ash said, "Cheer up, Jack. Just think—once you've shackled yourself to some eligible girl, you'll be out of the race and the pack will turn on fresh prey."

Jack turned his head slowly and stared at his friend. "I don't know why you're laughing. We're both in the same quandary. In fact, you're a bigger matrimonial prize than I am. One of these days, you'll be a marquess."

"Ah, but I'm not a marquess yet, am I? That's the difference between us. All I have to offer are expectations. You, on the other hand, are a belted earl with a fortune at your disposal."

A spark of amusement glinted in Jack's eyes. " 'Expectations' be damned! You're wealthy in your own right. It suits your purposes to pretend to be a pauper."

Ash's brows lifted. "Can you blame me? I've no wish to be hounded like you or Devonshire. You see, Jack"—a satirical smile touched his lips—"I want to be loved for myself." He raised his quizzing glass and made a leisurely appraisal of the dance floor. "Is that too much to ask?"

Jack lounged against the pillar and eyed his friend with interest. "Careful, Ash, or you'll find yourself snagged by some dewy-eyed damsel with marriage on her mind."

Ash grinned. "But that's my point. Marriage is payment for services rendered. Love should be free. That's why I prefer to remain a single man."

" 'Love should be free'?" Jack made a small sound of derision. "Try telling that to the fair Venuses who hang around the Palais Royal. Haven't you noticed that they swarm around the man who has made a killing at the gaming tables? Wife or courtesan, it's hard to tell the difference."

Ash turned his quizzing glass upon Jack. "You're in an odd humor," he said. "I've never heard you complain of the Venuses at the Palais Royal. What's brought this on?"

Jack shrugged. "I miss my dog. She, at least, loves me unconditionally."

Ash laughed. "She's a slut. You told me so yourself.

You never know who has been bedding her until the pups arrive."

"Ah, but I know it's me she really loves." His smile faded and he said in an undertone, "Don't look now, but our host has discovered our lair and is coming this way."

Ash lowered his quizzing glass. "Well, Jack," he said, "what is it to be? Shall we do our duty and partner one of those dewy-eyed damsels you mentioned, or shall we hide under that table over there and, if we're discovered, pretend to be looking for a priceless ring one of us has lost?"

"Ever the humorist," murmured Jack. "I prefer to meet my fate head-on."

"Better you than me. Ah, look who has just arrived, Lady Pamela Howe. Excuse me, Jack."

Jack was amused. Lady Pamela was an heiress, and his friend's strategic pursuit would only reinforce the fiction that Ash was in need of a rich wife to fill the family's empty coffers. Cautious fathers did not encourage their daughters to court fortune hunters. He wondered why he had not devised a similar ploy to save himself from the huntresses.

The answer came to him unbidden. Because, of course, Ash's grandfather, the marquess, lived in the wilds of Scotland. No one really knew him. His family, on the other hand, lived in Sussex, and there was also a town house in London. As a result, everyone knew their business. If he pleaded poverty, no one would believe him.

He sighed when he felt the hand on his shoulder. Resigned, smiling faintly, he turned to acknowledge his host, the ambassador.

Sir Charles said, "Can't have you standing around, Jack, setting a bad example to all the young sprigs. Allow me to introduce you to any lady of your choosing." In a humorous vein, he added, "One dance is all I ask, then you're free to leave and enjoy all the dissolute attractions of the Palais Royal."

Did everyone know that that's where he and Ash had taken rooms? "Thank you," he replied and added graciously, "but I am quite content with the company here."

Sir Charles grinned at him. "Are you, indeed? Then things must have changed drastically since I was a young man. But let's not quibble. Show me the lady who has taken your fancy and I shall introduce her to you."

Jack lifted his shoulders in a negligent shrug.

He'd hesitated too long.

"Come along, Jack," said Sir Charles. "I know just the lady for you."

With a weary sigh, Jack followed his host to Lady Sedgewick and her party. Her ladyship was one of the hounds he wished to avoid. She was a large, silly woman who loved the sound of her own voice. There was a daughter whose name he couldn't remember, a girl just out of the schoolroom, but she wasn't one of the group, and that puzzled him. Surely Sir Charles didn't expect him to dance with Lady Sedgewick?

Some pleasantries were exchanged, then Lady Sedgewick began to extol the virtues of her daughter who, unfortunately, had just agreed to dance with Captain Tallman and was somewhere on the dance floor. Sir Charles nodded benignly, but when Lady Sedgewick continued to rattle on, he cut her off by remarking as to himself, "Is that the young Duke of Devonshire I see?"

"Where?" she cried.

When she turned to scan the salon, Sir Charles addressed Jack. "You have yet to meet Miss . . ."

"Hill," supplied the lady he brought forward. "Miss Elinor Hill."

The ambassador inclined his head. "Of course, Miss Hill it is. How could I forget?"

Jack's brows rose. Miss Hill was hardly what he had had in mind. This was no schoolroom miss, but someone nearer his own age. She was dressed in gray from head to toe, except for her long white gloves and the lace cap that proclaimed her past the age of marriage. The one thing in her favor was a pair of fine, hazel eyes that briefly met his before she curtsied.

Lady Sedgewick, suddenly realizing she had been tricked, turned on her companion. "I feel chilled," she said. "You'll find my wrap in the cloakroom. Bring it to me at once, if you please."

So the lady is a paid companion, thought Jack. *What game is Sir Charles playing?*

If Miss Hill was aware of Lady Sedgewick's deliberate slight, she gave no sign of it. "Certainly, Lady Sedgewick," she replied in a small, colorless voice.

Jack was offended on her behalf. He was about to offer to escort Miss Hill to the cloakroom when Sir Charles took command.

"That won't be necessary," he said with a charming smile. Sir Charles's charm was legendary. "One of my footmen will be happy to fetch it." He raised his index finger and a footman was at his elbow in a matter of seconds. "Her ladyship wants her wrap," he said. Then to Lady Sedgewick, "Perhaps you would be good enough to describe it to him."

As her ladyship began to describe her wrap, Sir Charles turned his back on her, excluding her from the conversation.

"Miss Hill is cousin to Lord Cardvale," he said. He looked over his shoulder. "That reminds me. I want a word with him."

The lady blinked. "A distant cousin," she corrected.

Jack didn't like the sound of this. He had nothing against Lord Cardvale. In fact, he hardly knew the man.

They had a nodding acquaintance because they belonged to the same clubs in London and attended some of the same functions, but that was all. He hoped that Sir Charles wasn't establishing the lady's credentials as a suitable candidate for his hand in marriage.

Minding his manners, he replied, "I have the honor of being slightly acquainted with Lord Cardvale. He seems...ah...very agreeable."

Miss Hill's only response was a straight look from those striking, hazel eyes.

Sir Charles nodded. "But I've known Ellie since she was a child. Her father was the vicar of our parish church for a time."

Jack grew restless. This was going from bad to worse. Surely Sir Charles wasn't pushing this dowd at him with the hope of a match between them? A vicar's daughter? That was hardly his style.

Was the woman dumb? Why didn't she say something? The thought made him feel mean-spirited. He shouldn't blame the girl. From what he'd seen of Lady Sedgewick, he guessed that she would be a hard taskmistress. Miss Hill's cousin, her *distant* cousin, should have done more for her. Paid companions were only a cut above servants.

A penetrating look from Sir Charles recalled him to his duty. The dissolute attractions of the Palais Royal were growing more appealing by the minute.

"Miss Hill," he began, treating her to a disarming smile, "may I have the pleasure of the next dance?"

He had surprised her. He could see it in the flare of her eyes and the way her hand fluttered to her bosom. And a very fine bosom it was, too, though it was decorously covered by a gray chiffon scarf.

"How very kind you are," she said, and dipped him a minuscule curtsy. "Thank you, but I must decline. Lady

Sedgewick's daughter, Lady Harriet, is in my care. I'm her chaperon, you see."

He thought he caught an ironic inflection, but he saw only a clear, steady gaze and a docile smile. He must have been mistaken, for he could not imagine a lowly lady's companion making sport of a belted earl.

His quick intelligence was beginning to add things up. Sir Charles had known the girl since she was an infant and was obviously fond of her. Her cousin, Cardvale, had failed in his duty toward this impoverished gentlewoman. Her employer, Lady Sedgewick, was a tyrant. He had no doubt now that the ambassador had singled him out to bring a little excitement to Miss Hill's dull life. All he need do was partner her for one dance and her credit would rise considerably among her peers.

She was looking up at him, solemn-eyed, waiting to be dismissed. When the need arose, he could demolish a precocious chit with a word or a look. This mousy little woman who asked for nothing, expecting nothing, inspired him to act with chivalry.

He kept his eyes on hers. "Lady Sedgewick," he said, "won't you use your influence to persuade Miss Hill to dance with me?"

The solemn look was gone. Now she looked startled. Sir Charles, meantime, had turned aside to say a few words in Lady Sedgewick's ear. A moment later, *tsk*ing between smiles, she scolded Miss Hill for giving everyone the wrong impression.

"Of course you must dance," she cried. "I can't think what gave you the idea that you're to play nursemaid to Harriet." She smiled into Jack's eyes. "My daughter never wants for partners, you know. Sometimes I think that girl is too popular. I'm told that I should not be surprised, for she has the sweetest, most biddable disposition. Is that not so, Ellie?" Ellie was not given a chance to respond, for her ladyship gushed on, "And so accomplished, too. If you were to hear her play the piano..." Her eyes brightened. "You must come to dinner. We're staying at the Hotel Breteuil in the rue de Rivoli. Every Thursday we host a dinner party for a few friends, all very informal. Do say you will come."

Alas, Jack was already engaged on Thursday, he said, and before her ladyship could catch her breath, he captured Miss Hill's hand and led her to the dance floor.

The waltz, one of the newfangled dances, had become all the rage. Some called it the "wicked" waltz because of the intimate proximity of the partners as they whirled around the floor. It belatedly occurred to him that Miss Hill might not know the steps. Dull little chaperons would not have much occasion to take to the dance floor. He need not have worried. She was light in his arms, light and slender and supple.

He looked down at the woman in his arms and gave her a warm smile. "You dance very well," he said.

Her head came up and he found himself looking into a pair of eyes that were vivid with anger. He was taken aback. He'd expected to see gratitude, admiration, or, at the very least, he'd expected the lady to be overcome with blushes. He'd chosen to dance with her when he could have had any girl he wanted. All eyes were on them. He'd made her the belle of the ball.

Bosom quivering, she said in a low voice, "Am I supposed to be flattered? I told you I didn't want to dance, but did you listen? Oh no. You wanted to thumb your nose at all the girls who, you suppose, are hanging out for a rich husband. *You*, in fact. Your conceit is outrageous."

Her ungrateful onslaught ignited his own temper. Through his teeth, he replied, "Had I known my attentions were unwelcome, I would not have asked you to dance."

Her tone was arch, "You mean, you *wanted* to dance with me?"

Since she was brutally honest, he saw no need to treat her with the deference due a lady. "I had no wish to dance with anyone, but our host made it impossible for me to refuse. He practically pushed you at me. What was I to do? If you didn't want to dance, you should have made your wishes patently clear."

She gave a disbelieving smile. "I'm only a chaperon, Lord Raleigh, as you knew very well when you asked me to dance. My wishes count for nothing. I hope you realize that you have placed me in an intolerable position. Tongues will be wagging, debating why you singled me out like this. I think you can imagine what people will be saying."

His eyes narrowed unpleasantly. He had a good idea where this was leading. His voice like silk, he said, "Speak plainly, ma'am. What do you think people are saying?"

Without the least hesitation, she replied, "That you're in need of a wife who is biddable and complacent, someone who will turn a blind eye to all your indiscretions." Her voice lowered to a whisper. "And who better to fill the slot than a little nobody like me?"

If he was taken aback before, now he was astonished. This girl was little better than a servant and she was taking him to task. Did she know who he was? Did she realize that one word from him could have her turned off without a character reference? What made her so reckless?

After a moment, the heat in his eyes cooled and he chuckled. "You must be joking," he said.

She looked up at him with clear, clear eyes. "Why? Because I'm only a paid companion? Believe me, my lord, stranger things have happened."

She gasped when he suddenly executed an intricate

turn, so he did it again if only to show the wench that she had better watch her step with him. There was no more conversation until the dance ended. Breathless and flushed, she curtsied. He thanked her, then stalked off.

Having done their duty, he and Ash slipped away and struck out along the rue Sainte-Honore and the short distance to the Palais Royal. Ash did most of the talking, while Jack brooded on Miss Hill and her outrageous behavior. He had tried to be chivalrous and look where it had got him! She was a frump. No one in his right mind would think he had designs on her virtue, hallowed or unhallowed.

Stranger things have happened.

It sounded like a challenge.

No, it sounded like a threat, a warning that he could not trifle with her with impunity.

The poor woman must be demented! Who would want to?

He started to laugh.

"What did I say?" demanded Ash.

Jack shook his head. "What do you say, Ash, to a stroll around Tortoni's before we retire for the night?"

Tortoni's was a café where all the most celebrated duelists gathered, looking for a fight. Ash's eyes lit up. "I'm game if you are."

"And afterward, a champagne breakfast at the Palais Royal."

Ash said satirically, "You do realize that if we win, we'll be swarmed by girls?"

"I'm counting on it."

Chapter 2

On the short drive back to the hotel, Lady Sedgewick lost no time in explaining the hard facts of life to her daughter's chaperon.

"I hope, Ellie," she said, "you have not allowed Lord Raleigh's attentions to turn your head." As ever, she didn't wait for a response, but continued to babble like a river in spate. "You should know better. You are not a green girl though, to be sure, you are innocent of men and their ways. Mark my words, nothing will come of it."

When her ladyship paused momentarily to marshal her thoughts, Ellie said, "I am not such a fool, ma'am, as to—"

"You may think that with his fortune, Lord Raleigh may marry at will, but you are sadly mistaken. A man in his position will look for a girl with bloodlines, even though she is without a dowry."

"I assure you, ma'am—"

"And have you considered how you would feel should his relations reject you, as I'm sure they would? You may not have heard of his grandmother, the dowager countess, but I have, and let me tell you she is a stickler for what is due her name and rank. No, it will not do, Ellie, it—"

"Mama!" cried Harriet, her patience at an end. "This is so unjust! In my opinion, Ellie is too good for Lord Raleigh. I heard things about him tonight that would bring blushes to your cheeks."

"Oh, that!" said her mother disparagingly. "A sensible girl knows when to look the other way. Every young man has his peccadilloes."

Ellie ventured to say, "It was only one dance, ma'am, and he wouldn't have asked me had Sir Charles not insisted on it."

"Then Sir Charles should have known better!" declared her ladyship. "It doesn't do to encourage young women to have ideas above their station."

Harriet gasped, but her father, who had until that moment appeared to be dozing in a corner of the coach, roused himself to say in a languid tone, "Hush, woman. You don't know what you're talking about. Ellie comes of good stock. I met her cousin tonight, the earl of Cardvale. Sir Charles introduced us."

Lady Sedgewick's jaw dropped, Harriet stared, and Ellie sat up a little straighter. "A distant cousin on my mother's side," she replied in a choked tone. "Ah... he is well, I hope?"

"Oh, very well. Unfortunately, he had to leave early because his wife was feeling the heat. They are putting up at our hotel, by the way. Oh, and Cardvale asked after your brother."

"'Brother'?" interjected Lady Sedgewick.

"Yes, ma'am," replied Ellie. "You may remember I mentioned I had a younger brother, Robbie? He's eighteen and a student at Oxford."

Her ladyship nodded. "Yes. I have a vague recollection.

But I know for a certainty that you never once mentioned a relative who was an earl."

Ellie shrugged. "I did not want to embarrass him by admitting the connection. We lost touch over the years and it did not seem right to me to claim the relationship."

"Very commendable," said his lordship. "At any rate, since we're all putting up at the same hotel, I suggested that he and Lady Cardvale join us tomorrow for luncheon."

"I can hardly wait," replied Ellie, summoning a smile.

As soon as she entered her room, Ellie closed and locked the door, shrugged out of her coat, then collapsed into the upholstered armchair by the fireplace. Neither the fire nor the candles were lit, but her room overlooked the Tuileries, and the light from the lamps filtered through the small panes of her bedchamber window, casting a warm glow.

She was thinking that of all the times to make an entrance into her life, her Cousin Cardvale had chosen the worst. She'd known for over a week that he and his wife, Dorothea, were guests at the hotel. Dorothea was hard to miss. The very day of her arrival, she'd caused a commotion because the room she had been assigned was number 13. Everyone heard of it. Not that it made a bit of difference. The hotel was full and number 13 was all that was available.

Having been forewarned, she'd tried to keep out of their way. Cardvale, she knew, would want to acknowledge the connection, not realizing that it would complicate her position. She'd changed her last name from Brans-Hill to Hill, simply because a double-barreled name was too grand for someone who was little more than a servant. She hated to be treated as a curiosity.

Much good her little deception had done her. She hadn't expected Sir Charles to recognize her. The last time she had seen him was ten years before, at her father's funeral. At least he'd had the presence of mind to follow her lead and address her as "Miss Hill." Perhaps that's why he had wanted a word with Cardvale, to warn him to keep her secret. Certainly, Lord Sedgewick gave no sign that he knew her real name.

It was becoming too complicated. Nothing like this had happened before, because no one knew her. She'd lived most of her life in the country.

She decided then that it would be better to reveal her full name first thing in the morning, before her employers found out from someone else.

She could just see it. Lady Sedgewick would be annoyed at having been kept in the dark, but that wouldn't last. Soon, she'd be crowing to anyone who would listen that Lady Harriet's chaperon was no less a person than Miss Brans-Hill, Lord Cardvale's cousin, and wouldn't that be a feather in her cap?

Ellie sighed. Lady Cardvale would not be amused. She was highly conscious of her position in society. That she should be related to a mere lady's companion wasn't something she would wish anyone to know.

Cardvale was quite different from his wife. He was a quiet, well-meaning man who had taken Robbie and her into his own home when their father died. It was a generous act, for they were cousins three or four times removed, and there was no necessity for him to feel responsible for them. But that was his way. Things had changed after he married. Dorothea had made things so unpleasant for them that Ellie had felt compelled to take Robbie and strike out on her own. Dorothea had waved them off with a smile on her face. Cardvale was bewildered and was persuaded to let them go only when Ellie confided that she and Robbie had come into a little money.

And so they had, in a manner of speaking, enough to provide for Robbie's education and tide her over until she found employment. It was better than being the poor relations who were expected to be grateful for the crumbs off Lady Cardvale's table.

Not that Lady Sedgewick was much of an improvement. And now that Jack had singled her out, there was no telling what her ladyship's suggestible mind would make of it.

He wouldn't have asked her to dance if Sir Charles had not practically forced him into it.

It was the first time she'd danced the waltz with a man. The only other partners she'd had had been her charges, young girls like Harriet who needed the practice before they made their bows to society. Nobody expected a paid companion to take to the dance floor in public.

And she shouldn't have. It was no good pretending that she didn't have a choice. She was wise to the ways of the world and knew how to decline an invitation without giving offense. The trouble was, Jack had offended *her* and she'd let her hurt pride lead her into an indiscretion.

When Sir Charles brought Jack over, her heart had flip-flopped against her ribs. Her first thought was that Jack had not forgotten the awkward, adolescent girl who had worshiped him all those years ago. Her hope was dashed by his weary smile and the cynicism in his eyes. But it was his condescension that hurt most. He was no different from all the others. She was a nobody in his eyes, a drab little nursemaid to the rich and famous. He thought he was doing her a favor by asking her to dance. And just as though she were that adolescent girl, she had punished him with her acid tongue.

She groaned as she remembered how she had

upbraided him. Had he been anyone else, she would have kept her tongue between her teeth. That's what she was paid to do. But she was crushed, first because she didn't want him to see how far she had fallen, and then because he had to be prodded into asking her to dance.

The cynical, arrogant man wasn't the boy she remembered.

Pictures formed in her mind—Jack, riding hell for leather over the downs as she clung in terror to his back. Jack, drying her tears when old Sal, whom she'd raised from a pup, expired in her arms. Jack, letting her down lightly when she solemnly promised that she would wait for him forever the day he left to go back to Oxford.

And that was the last she'd seen of him until tonight.

Laughing, high-spirited, responsive, sensitive—that was the boy she remembered. The man he'd turned into was a sad disappointment.

Much the same could be said about her. She cringed to think what Papa would say if he could see her now.

How had it come to this? Why was she eking out a living as a companion to one of the silliest women in Christendom? Why was she forever bailing Robbie out of one scrape after another? This wasn't the kind of life she had imagined for herself when her parents were alive.

An image of her mother came to mind—Mama with her long russet hair, loose upon her shoulders, as she tucked her in for the night. Mama, practical and down-to-earth, relieving Papa of every household responsibility so he could devote himself to scholarship and the needs of his parish. *The Lord will provide* was the rule he lived by.

Mama was more worldly. *The Lord helps them that help themselves,* she used to say, and she lived what she preached. She had a little business on the side to earn money for the extras that a vicar's stipend did not cover. From her own herb garden, Mama found the ingredients to make lotions and potions, which she sold to the ladies of the county far and wide. Papa knew about the lotions and potions and treated them with amused tolerance. What he did not know about was the exorbitant profit Mama made on each little bottle.

There was no doubt that she took after her mother.

Swallowing hard, she got up and went to the window to look out. It was foolish to look back. The present was what mattered and this was the present, here in this room, at the Hotel Breteuil. Outside her window was the rue de Rivoli, as busy as Piccadilly on a Friday night. Streetlamps were lit and carriages were coming and going, rattling over cobblestones. In spite of the frigid temperatures, pedestrians were sauntering along the pavement as they went their various ways. The hotel was in the hub of Parisian life, or so it seemed to her. The Tuileries, the Louvre, and the Palais Royal were only a five-minute walk away.

The Palais Royal, that was her present.

She was going to the Palais Royal, that well-known nest of immorality, to honor a deathbed promise she had made to her mother—she would look after her younger brother and see that no harm came to him. It was no hardship. Robbie was the apple of her eye, but that did not mean she was blind to his faults or that he would escape the sharp edge of her tongue when she met up with him. He wasn't supposed to be in Paris. He should have been in Oxford studying, having failed an important examination. And tomorrow or the next day, when his debts were paid, she would see him off personally, with suitable threats of retribution if he should fail her again.

Until the next time.

She let out a long sigh. She supposed that Robbie was no worse and no better than young men the world over.

She looked at the clock. There was an hour to go before

Robbie's friend, Milton, came to fetch her. That gave her plenty of time to get ready. Robbie, of course, dared not show his face in public because his creditors were after him.

Creditors. That was a polite way of saying that the thugs who worked for the moneylender who had loaned Robbie the money to pay off his debts were demanding their pound of flesh.

After stripping off her gloves and throwing off the hated lace cap, she removed the pins that held up her long russet hair and let it fall to her shoulders. The next thing to go was the unflattering crepe dress. When she had tidied everything away, she washed her hands and face in cold water. This small ritual removed every vestige of the powder she used to make herself look older and wiser and eminently suitable as companion to a young girl.

Invisible, in fact.

Before she could wallow in self-pity, she went to the closet and removed the gown she had pressed earlier. It was an ivory silk that was so fine she could have squeezed it into a ball and stuffed it in her pocket. It was so fine that she gentled her hands as she draped it over a chair. This done, she took a step back and studied the gown critically.

The trouble with fashionable gowns was that they were never in fashion for more than one season. Over time, she'd had to alter it here and there. The waists were shorter this year and the hems were higher. Frills and furbelows were the order of the day, but those were too fussy for her taste. This was more than a gown to Ellie. It was an investment, her costume for the part she was about to play. Her employers knew nothing of the gown's existence and if they had known, they would have been staggered. No ordinary lady's companion could have afforded a gown of this quality.

Only the direst of circumstances could have compelled

her to put it on. Those dire circumstances always revolved around a desperate need for money. She had to transform herself from plain Ellie Hill, lady's companion, into the ravishing gamester, Madame Aurora. Only Madame Aurora could gain admittance to the kind of establishment Ellie had in mind, the kind of establishment where the stakes were high.

The right clothes and a judicious use of powder and paint were all that was needed to make the transformation. There was one other thing that was essential. Money.

She kept enough money in her satin pochette to stake her bets, money that she always replenished from her winnings. If she wanted to, she could have turned her nest egg into a small fortune. She'd always resisted the temptation, first of all because she was Papa's daughter, and secondly because money couldn't buy the things she wanted.

With only minutes to spare before she went to meet Milton, she took a last critical look in the mirror. She felt like a soldier in dress regimentals. The ivory silk was complemented by a cutaway emerald-green overdress with a quilted hem that matched her quilted pochette. Her satin gloves, which reached above her elbows, and her mask and shoes were also in emerald green. Her only jewelry was a pair of silver combs that had once belonged to her mother.

So far, so good. Now all she need do was think herself into the part of the dazzling, mysterious Madame Aurora. She'd done it before; she could do it again.

There was one last ritual before she left Ellie Hill behind. She sent a little prayer to Mama's brother, Uncle Ted, thanking him for passing on to her his vast store of knowledge about gaming and gamesters.

When she slipped out of her room, she stopped to look and listen. There were a few candles in wall sconces to give her light, but she had no wish to meet anyone on the stairs. Not that anyone would recognize her in her getup, but they might start asking questions if they saw her using the key to let herself out. After midnight, the doors were all locked, and only the porter had the key to admit guests. He wouldn't allow Aurora, a stranger, to pass in or out. She wouldn't let that stand in her way. Clutched in her hand was the spare key she had "borrowed" from the manager's office.

Not a soul was in sight. Hurrying now, she descended the stairs and made for the side door. The key made a grating sound as she turned it, then she was through the door and into the chill night air.

Milton was right where he'd promised to be. She whispered, "It was harder to open than I thought it would be."

Without a word, in his gentlemanly way, he took the key from her and locked the door. When he handed it back to her, she dropped it in her pochette and smiled up at him. He really had the nicest manners.

He was Robbie's best friend and, like Robbie, a student at Oxford. Unlike Robbie, however, it was fine for him to take a jaunt to Paris between terms. He was bookish. Things came to him easily. Ellie had never heard of *him* failing an examination.

Milton offered her his arm. "No one saw you leave?"

She smiled. "No one. Don't worry, Milton. If anyone had seen me, I would have turned around and gone back to my room. All they would think is that the porter had let me in. You worry too much."

"Yes. I know."

He was standing there, staring at her as though he'd never seen her before. She'd told him what she would be wearing, but his look of surprise told her that he hadn't expected such a complete transformation.

Flattered and amused, she said, "Well, where is the hackney?"

He blushed. "Ah...'the hackney'? Oh, it's waiting for us in the rue de Rivoli."

"Splendid."

She waited until they were in the hackney and on their way before she voiced something that was troubling her. "When am I going to see Robbie?"

He looked away. "I don't...that is...when things have quieted down, I suppose."

She really liked this well-mannered boy. He was tall, with curly black hair and a face that was, though not quite handsome, open and easy to read. The fact that his expression was now closed and he seemed ill at ease gave her pause for thought.

There was something he wasn't telling her.

All she knew was that Robbie had got in with a bad set, had run up gaming debts and spent lavishly with money he did not possess. And the more he ran up debts, the more he gambled, hoping to win so that he could pay off what he owed.

She was partly to blame. All he was doing was taking her as his example. When she was in desperate straits, she made for the nearest gaming house and invariably made a killing. Robbie rarely won, but he always hoped his luck would turn. Time out of mind, she'd told him that luck had nothing to do with it. Hazard, vingt-et-un, rouge et noir—these were games of chance. She rarely played them except when the odds were in her favor. She had a mathematical mind and could calculate the odds without even trying. As a result, the only time she bet on dice was when she had money to spare, and only as a flamboyant gesture.

What it came down to was that she had a gift that few

people possessed, and Robbie least of all, if only he could be made to accept it.

She touched a hand to Milton's sleeve, bringing his gaze back to her face. "That's not good enough," she said. "He has been in Paris for almost a month. Why doesn't he want to see me?"

"Oh no. You have the wrong idea. It's not that he's avoiding you. It's the moneylender's agents he is trying to avoid."

She might have believed him if he had not avoided her eyes. As severe as she could be, she said, "I'm his sister, Milton. I'm not likely to betray him to the authorities. Now, where is he?"

He hesitated one moment more, then said, "Meurice's hotel in the rue de l'Echiquier. But it's a shabby place, not fit for a lady."

"I'll be the judge of that."

The Palais Royal was lit up like a beacon. This magnificent former royal palace had a courtyard Roman charioteers would have envied, and galleries on three sides that looked like cloisters. During the daylight hours it was quite respectable, its fine shops and restaurants a drawing card for visitors and the elite of society. When night fell, the gaming houses, theaters, and houses of ill repute opened their doors and the demimonde took over—actresses, birds of paradise, soldiers, gamblers, and idlers looking for trouble. And trouble was obviously what the authorities expected if the number of redcoats entering the courtyard was any indication. Paris was still a city under occupation, and British soldiers were always at hand to help keep the peace.

In one of the arcades, beside a bookshop, there was a door that led to the upstairs floors. Milton led the way.

She was glad of his escort, because she wasn't in the know about gaming houses in Paris. A woman on her own could easily run into trouble. Even in England she had to watch her step. If she'd been taller, she would have disguised herself as a gentleman of fashion. Men were always taken more seriously.

When they pushed through the door to the gaming house, Ellie's pulse quickened. She was used to her pulse racing when she entered such an establishment. Once she had her cards in her hand, however, she always forgot everything but the game.

In one room, there was the rouge-et-noir table. She took a peek inside, then hurried past as a group of gentlemen got up to leave. She recognized a face or two, though she couldn't put names to them. They were staying at the same hotel as she. She'd bet her last farthing that their wives and daughters didn't know where they were.

When she entered the cardroom, she allowed her gaze to drift. She'd expected something better than this dingy room with its haze of tobacco smoke. There were other ladies present, but none as elegant as Madame Aurora. All the same, they had their own kind of allure. Their attractions were laid out like sweets in a confectioner's shop. They were not gamblers. They were demireps, or "ladies of easy virtue," as Lady Sedgewick called them. What they were interested in were the men who won the largest sums of money.

Her gaze sharpened and became more searching. It did not take her long to discover who among the patrons were employed by the house. There were the puffs who acted as decoys, the flashers, the ushers, the dunners, and waiters whose only aim was to make sure that the gambler and his money were soon parted.

Her uncle had taught her well.

A director came to meet them, well dressed in a black

coat and trousers, all smiles because, she supposed, he thought she and Milton were pigeons ripe for plucking.

"*Monsieur,*" he said, "*que voudriez-vous jouer?*"

Milton replied in broken French, as they'd rehearsed beforehand, "*Je ne jouer pas. Mon... ma soeur...* my sister is the gambler."

The director's eyes slowly measured her, then gleamed in appreciation. His experienced eye would have summed her up as a lady with money to burn. To reinforce that impression, she opened her pochette so that he could see the banknotes. "I have five thousand francs here if you care to count it," she said. "And my brother has a letter of credit from our bank in London."

She had the five thousand francs, but not the letter of credit. It was a small deception. If it ever came down to it and she lost her nest egg, she would quit the table. It had never happened yet.

The director smiled and nodded. "What is your pleasure, madame?"

"Cribbage," she said at once. "I'm told I'm very good at it." She looked up at Milton, who nodded in confirmation of her boast. There was nothing a director liked better than an eager gambler. Eager gamblers made easy pickings.

"Then cribbage it is," he said.

Still beaming, he motioned her to a table for two. The operator, the man who would play against her, was already seated. As she took her place, she looked up at Milton. He knew what to do. He was to keep watch behind her so that no one could look over her shoulder and see her cards.

After the cribbage board and pegs were set out, the director, who would supervise the play, handed the operator a fresh pack of cards. Everything was graciously done and civilized. No one would expect such kindly-looking gentlemen to resort to cheating, unless they had an Uncle Ted to put them wise to the ways of the world.

As the operator began to deal the cards, two flashers decked out as patrons began a loud conversation on the actress who had been done to death on New Year's Day at the theater on the west side of the building. That was only four days ago. Ellie had read the story in the newspapers and had heard it talked about in hushed tones among her employers' friends, but knowing that this was a ploy to distract her, she kept her eyes fixed on the operator's fingers. When his fingers slowed, she looked up.

He wasn't smiling quite as broadly as before. She had to watch her step. She mustn't appear too confident. Gamblers who betrayed that they knew how to use the system to their advantage were soon hustled out the door.

"That poor woman," she said, suppressing a shudder. "Have they found who did it?"

"*Non,* madame, not yet, but they will. They think it was her young lover and that he is hiding out in the Palais Royal."

Since she knew that he spoke only to break her concentration, she played her part. Shuddering again, she said, "I hope they catch him!"

"Don't look so frightened." His fingers became nimble as he dealt the cards. "You're quite safe here. Our ushers are armed and are crack shots."

She tried to look gratified.

She would lose a little to begin with, to establish how innocent she was. And she wasn't going to break the bank. She wasn't greedy. When she had enough for Robbie's needs, she would collect her winnings and retire gracefully.

It was time to discuss the stakes.

Chapter 3

The cards were the least of her worries. She wasn't conscious of memorizing which cards were played or discarded. Her brain seemed to work automatically, systematically slotting cards into various combinations that she could use to her advantage in the next play.

Her most pressing problem was how to conceal from her opponents that she was their worst nightmare, what Uncle Ted called a "virtuoso." The only way they could beat her at cards was if they cheated or found another virtuoso to play against her, and the odds of that happening were too remote to consider.

It helped that she wasn't greedy or addicted to gaming. Most gamblers with her gift couldn't help themselves. They had to show everyone how clever they were and went on to break the bank. All this achieved was that someone, usually an employee of the house, accused them of cheating. As a result, their winnings were confiscated and they were thrown out on their ears.

Her strategy was simple: lose a little, win a little, and leave everyone happy and smiling.

Her game began well enough, but she soon lost ground, deliberately, of course, and was back where she started. The operator and director were all smiles. Very soon, however, her luck changed and she was on a winning streak. When she had forty thousand francs to her credit, Milton started to cough.

"Aurora," he got out between gasps, "I'm . . ." He shook his head and steadied himself with one hand against the back of her chair. "We should go home. I don't feel well."

This was what they'd arranged beforehand, that when she had forty thousand francs to her credit, Milton would feign illness. It was a ploy to get them out of the gaming house just in case the director took exception to losing a large sum of money with no chance of winning it back.

The temptation to go on was almost irresistible, and that had never happened before. At one stroke, she could solve all her problems. If she played for another hour, she would have enough money to set herself up for life, not in luxury, but modestly. She was tired of being humiliated by employers who took her for granted, and tired of living on the fringes of other people's lives. She wanted a life of her own.

"Not *now*, Milton." She glanced at her cards, then looked up at him with an appeal in her eyes. "I'm on a winning streak. I feel lucky. You can't ask me to go home yet."

This was unexpected and his expression showed it. "Aurora?"

She wavered. A glance at the director steadied her. He was beginning to look suspicious. One of Uncle Ted's precepts belatedly came back to her. A gamester who did not follow the strategy he'd set for himself could find himself playing with the devil.

Papa could not have said it better.

She breathed deeply, then pushed back her chair. "Just one more hand?"

That's what she was supposed to say, the cue for the next part of the charade.

Milton seized on it before she could change her mind. He coughed again, felt in his pocket, produced a large white linen handkerchief and proceeded to cough into it. Everyone could see that there was already a red stain on the handkerchief and assumed, wrongly, that it was blood.

With a show of reluctance that wasn't entirely feigned, Ellie got to her feet. "I suppose we must go," she said. She looked at the director. "But I shall be back the first chance I get."

The director gave her one of his measuring stares, then nodded. His manner was a little stiff. "I shall look forward to it," he said.

The same flashers who had tried to distract her with their loud conversation about the actress who was done to death, now talked over the other patrons about the lady who had won handsomely at the card table. The hum in the room faded as people stopped to listen.

Ellie was aware that this was another of the house's tactics. It went to show that the house was honest and it was possible for the ordinary patron to win at the tables.

After bringing Ellie her winnings, the director escorted them to the door. She smiled and offered him her hand. When he bid them both *au revoir,* he was effusive and meticulous in his attentions.

On the way downstairs, Milton said, "What brought that on?"

"I passed him a banknote for a thousand francs."

Milton stopped and looked up at her. "Why?"

She patted him on the shoulder. "Always leave a place so that you will be welcomed back. It's a precept I learned from my favorite uncle, and it's stood me in good stead."

Alarmed, Milton said, "You're not thinking of coming back here?"

"No. I'm glad it's over. I just want to go home to my bed."

When they came out of the door, they halted. Though it was closer to dawn than midnight, the arcades and courtyard were thronged with people, but not as orderly as they had been when Ellie and Milton had entered the building. There was a great deal of drunkenness and rough play. Ellie could see now why so many redcoats and gendarmes were posted in the courtyard. They were there to keep order or haul away the miscreants who refused to obey them.

Milton's hand closed like a vise around her arm.

"What is it?" she cried.

"The moneylender's messengers, and I think they've seen me."

She followed the direction of his gaze. "You're not saying that Robbie is here somewhere?"

"No, but *I'm* here and they know I can lead them to Robbie."

"What do you mean to do?"

"I'm going to lose them, then I'll come back for you."

This didn't make sense to her. "What if I pay them the money Robbie owes? I have it right here."

He drew her behind one of the arcade pillars. "That won't do. They're gladiators sent to find Robbie and teach him a lesson. We have to pay the money directly to old Houchard, then we'll be free of them."

"Houchard being the moneylender, I suppose?"

"Yes. There isn't time to debate the point. Just do as I say."

He sounded very masterful for an eighteen-year-old, and not at all like the Milton she knew. "But—"

He was done debating. With his hand cupping her elbow, he steered her to one of the cafés in the arcade. "Wait for me here," he said. "Speak to no one. I'll come back as soon as I can."

She was thrust unceremoniously through the door of the Café des Anglaises and left to fend for herself. It was crowded, boisterous and smoky, and patronized, for the most part, by gentlemen. A few were in British uniforms, and that was reassuring. All this registered in one comprehensive glance, then she turned her back on the room and gazed searchingly out the window.

She scanned the crowds, trying to find Milton, but the task was impossible. There were too many people.

She gave a start when a masculine voice spoke at her back.

"Madame est solitaire? Isolée?"

She turned slowly. A Prussian soldier, no more than Robbie's age, was gazing at her with an intoxicated smile. She could smell the drink on his breath.

Hoping to discourage him, she shrugged and said, "I'm sorry. I don't speak French."

His intoxicated smile grew broader. As though translating each word carefully inside his head, he replied, "I don't speak French, either, but my English is quite good."

She flashed him a neutral smile, neither provocative nor aloof, brushed by him, and took a chair by a table for two against the wall. When he sauntered over, she affected an interest in the other patrons. She wasn't alarmed. If the young Prussian soldier became a nuisance, she would simply appeal to the British soldiers for their protection.

She suffered a small pang when she began to take stock of the other ladies present. They were just like the ladies in the gaming house, expensively turned out, but as unsubtle as concubines in a harem.

The objects of their fawning did not escape her notice, either. Two gentlemen, whom she recognized immediately as English by the cut of their clothes, were holding court at the table in the far corner of the café. The light was too dim to see their faces clearly, but one seemed to be the life and soul of the party. The other gentleman was quietly sipping from a glass, his eyes studying her reflectively.

She blinked to dispel the foolish fancy that flitted through her mind. It couldn't possibly be Jack . . . could it?

Flustered now, she looked up at the Prussian soldier whose conversation she had missed. He was lonely if she was not, he'd said. That much she remembered. Her long silence was all the encouragement he'd needed to start taking liberties.

Seating himself on the opposite chair, he reached for her mask. She instinctively slapped his hand away.

It was the wrong thing to do. His smile vanished and his expression turned ugly. Reaching for the mask again, he tore it from her face. His words were slow and slurred. "I want to see what I am buying before I put down my money."

She was ready to bolt for the door, then she looked into his young, young face and felt her confidence return. She spoke to him as she would to her brother. "That's no way to speak to a lady. What would your mother say if she could hear you?"

His brows knit in a befuddled frown. "If you were a lady, you wouldn't be here. So—"

His words were choked off when a strong, masculine hand hauled him up by the collar. It was no flight of fancy. Her rescuer was none other than Jack Rigg. She took a shaky breath and swallowed hard.

His voice soft with sarcasm, Jack said, "You have something that belongs to the lady, I believe. If you know what's good for you, you'll return it at once."

A silence had descended at every table as all waited to see what would happen next. Ash Denison got to his feet and slowly sauntered over. Between sips from the glass in his hand, he said in a conversational tone, "Now, Jack, what's this all about?"

Jack said, "This jackanapes insulted the lady."

Ellie sat there frozen in silence, her nerves on edge, expecting at any moment to be recognized by Jack or his friend. If it ever got back to her employer that she'd visited the Palais Royal when she was supposed to be in her bed, she would be ruined.

Her confidence crept back when it dawned on her that no one recognized her. She wondered how long that would last and began to think how she could get out of there unscathed.

To Ellie, Ash said, *"Permettez-moi d'instruire ce jeune homme ici des manières."*

Having already told the young soldier that she did not speak French, Ellie thought it prudent to keep up the pretense. She lifted her shoulders in a tiny shrug. "I'm sorry, I don't speak French."

Jack said, "If anyone is going to teach this lout some manners, it will be me."

The young soldier suddenly wrested himself out of Jack's clasp and turned to face him. "You have insulted me," he gritted out. "I demand satisfaction."

"You mean, a duel?" Jack sounded incredulous. "I don't duel with boys."

Ellie decided it was time to make her move. She rose and gestured to the door. "I really must go. My husband will be looking for me. I was supposed to wait for him here, but I think he must have mistaken the time he said he would return." She was rattling on as she tried to inch past him with no clear idea of what she was saying.

Jack smiled. "What time did he say he would return?"

"Ah—what time is it now?"

He looked at his watch. "A little before four o'clock."

"That's the time he said he'd come and fetch me."

Jack's smile widened into a grin. "Then what's your hurry? He's not late. Why don't we sit down and have a little conversation until he turns up?"

She picked up her mask and put it on. There was no smile now. "You're too kind, but I must decline."

Ash now spoke to Jack in fluent French, which Ellie had no trouble understanding. "Leave her alone, Jack. She's not for you. I'd say she already has a protector, and a rich one at that. Just look at the clothes she is wearing. She's a pretty piece, I grant you. But do you really want to fight another duel this evening just to bed her? I'd be surprised if you're able to unsheathe your sword, let alone keep it up."

This was obviously a huge joke, because both men laughed.

Jack's French was as fluent as his friend's. "You always think the worst of me. I swear on my honor that my intention is not to bed the lady, but to rescue her from a boor. Didn't your mother ever teach you anything about chivalry, Ash?"

"I'm chivalrous, after a fashion."

Ellie was tempted to blast them both with a few choice words in any language they cared to name. They wouldn't be talking like this if they thought she could understand them. Jack, she absolved. He was more truly the gentleman, then he spoiled the impression with his next words.

"You're right, Ash. She is 'a pretty piece.' Chivalry be

damned! I may not have my usual stamina, but I believe I can keep the lady happy for an hour or two."

The young soldier was becoming restive. It was obvious that he had not followed the conversation. "You, sir," he said, addressing Jack, "are a coward."

"And you, sir, are drunk. Go home and sleep it off."

Ellie was edging toward the door when it opened and a gust of cold air rushed in along with a boisterous group of Prussian soldiers. Their laughter died when their young countryman called out to them that the English were spoiling for a fight.

What shocked Ellie was that it seemed to be the signal everyone was waiting for. Within seconds, in every corner of the café, men were out of their chairs and closing with whomever they took exception to; women were screaming; glasses and chairs went flying. She had never seen anything like it. The English and the Prussians were supposed to be allies. No one would have known it from the brawl that ensued.

Her one aim was to get out of there with her precious hoard of banknotes intact. The door to the courtyard was blocked, but there had to be a back door leading into a lane or the street behind. On that thought, she began to push and elbow her way down the length of the café. There were others with the same idea, and she followed where they led. All went well until a gun went off and someone shouted, "Militia!" Then it was every man for himself and the devil take the hindmost.

Ellie was pushed hard against the wall as panic took over. Her precious pochette was knocked out of her grasp and fell on the floor. She didn't care about the stampede. Nothing was going to part her from that pochette.

She dropped to her knees and began to crawl toward it. Someone else got to it first. With an almighty lunge, she dived toward it. She was too late. The pochette disappeared. Gasping, sobbing with rage, she came up for air. One of the patrons helped her to her feet, and she found herself gazing into the smiling eyes of Jack Rigg. She wasn't interested in his smiling eyes, only the pochette he held aloft.

"Stay close to me and I'll get you to safety," he said.

He turned and began to shoulder his way through the crush, the pochette still in his hand.

What choice did she have? Ellie went after him.

His rooms were only one floor up. That's why he chose to dine at the Café des Anglaises—for the convenience. He'd told his manservant not to wait up for him, but Coates had banked the fire in the salon and left a candle lit.

"By the way," he said, "my name is Jack. And yours is?"

"Aurora," she replied.

He was fascinated by the way her eyes followed the satin evening bag he held in his hand. On their way up the stairs, he'd taken a quick look inside and was astonished to discover that it was stuffed with banknotes. It led his mind to make all sorts of conjectures about the lady.

"Good," he said. "No last names. I like that."

She was waiting to see what he going to do with her bag. Biting down on a smile, he tossed it carelessly on the armchair by the fire. If she wanted it, she would have to ask him to move.

Evidently, she was too canny to betray herself. No mention of the bag. She simply turned, walked to the window overlooking the courtyard, and looked out. As he poured himself a neat brandy, his mind began to speculate.

He was sure of one thing. She was no ordinary demirep, for sale to the highest bidder. No ordinary demirep made the kind of money she had in her bag. Moreover, this woman had quality, style, confidence. He could see her presiding in a lady's drawing room. On the other hand, no lady of quality would risk her reputation by showing her face in the Palais Royal.

She'd worn a mask, but so did many ladies, not so much to conceal their identity, but as an accessory, to add an air of mystery.

Who was she, and what was she?

He thought Ash must be right, that she was the mistress of some wealthy English gentleman who had taken her to Paris to see the sights. That would account for the large sum of money in her bag. Maybe she was keeping it for her protector and they'd become separated. If that was the case, her protector should have known better than to leave her alone in such a place and at such an hour. He was tempting some stray gentleman, such as himself, to make the lady a better offer.

It was a reasonable explanation, but it did not satisfy him. Which was she, a lady of quality or a rich man's mistress? He knew which one he wanted her to be.

When he reached for the decanter to top up his brandy, he winced. That trifling wound he'd taken earlier that evening in the duel outside Tortoni's was beginning to sting like blazes. It shouldn't have happened. He'd drawn the first blood and relaxed his guard. He should have known better. Frenchmen took their dueling seriously. That's why they were so good at it. A little blood didn't put them off. So though they were both scratched, the duel had continued till he'd wrested his opponent's sword away from him.

She spoke to him over her shoulder. "What on earth is going on down there?"

He joined her at the window and looked out. All was pandemonium in the courtyard below. Groups of men were fighting. Red-coated soldiers were dragging people away. Gendarmes were buzzing around like angry hornets.

"The guards," he said, "have been called out to help the gendarmes keep order."

"They're clubbing people."

"That's one way of keeping order."

Her hair was loose upon her shoulders, kept off her face by silver combs. She was still wearing her mask, so her eyes were in shadow. The temptation to touch and take had to be severely resisted. He wasn't a callow youth like the boy soldier who had molested her. He knew the value of patience.

Looking up at him, she said, "How long is this likely to go on?"

"An hour. Maybe less. Does it matter?"

Her eyes were huge and dark behind her mask, so he wasn't sure whether he was caught in *her* stare or she was caught in *his*. She reminded him of someone—he couldn't think who—but it was someone from the past, someone he had once liked and admired. He supposed he was transferring some of the softer feelings he'd felt for the woman he could not remember to the woman who was looking up at him with uncertain eyes.

He wanted to see her without her mask and wondered what she would do if he reached out to take it. The mask wasn't the only thing he wanted to take from her.

He must have betrayed what he was thinking, for her breasts began to rise and fall and her breathing quickened.

"It matters," she said. "I was supposed to meet my husband in the café. He must be worried out of his mind, wondering what has happened to me."

"Aurora," he said gently, "I know there's no husband. You don't wear a ring."

She held out her left arm with the glove that sheathed

it to well above her elbow, then looked up at him. "You can't know that!"

He gave a helpless shrug. "My chivalry is only skin-deep, I'm afraid. When I took your hand to help you up the stairs, I took the liberty of feeling for a ring. There wasn't one."

Her eyes glittered up at him. Her voice was cool. "And would a ring make a difference, Jack?"

He nodded. "Regrettably, yes."

" 'Regrettably'?"

"There is nothing that dampens my ardor more than the sight of a wedding ring on the finger of a beautiful woman."

She tilted her head to one side as she gazed up at him. "Well, here is something else to dampen your ardor. I'm not interested. Now what do you have to say to that?"

There it was again, that feeling of déjà vu. The way she tilted her head, challenging him, reminded him of... The memory wouldn't come to him.

Maybe if he removed her mask, all would become clear.

"Allow me," he said, and before she could prevent it, he had the mask in his hand.

Her eyes were green. Or were they gray? "We've met before, haven't we?" he said.

"Have we?" Her voice was shaken, breathless.

He reached out to remove the combs from her hair and let out a choked gasp when she gave him a hard shove. Clutching the wound under his armpit, he staggered to the nearest chair and slowly, carefully eased himself down.

"What did I do?" she cried.

"Nothing." His teeth were clenched. "It's only a trifling wound that I got dueling. I think my shirt must be stuck to it."

She gave a soft gasp when he removed his fingers from

under his armpit and she saw the blood. Moving quickly, she crossed to him and knelt down. "Let me see," she said.

There was no need for alarm. In fact, now that he'd adjusted his position, the pain had gone. He knew that all he had to do to stanch the bleeding was keep his arm close to his side. But he decided that he liked the anxious look on her face, liked the soothing touch of her fingers as she eased the edges of his jacket aside.

She shook her head. "This won't do. I can't see anything. Let's get your jacket off, then your waistcoat."

He wasn't one to argue with fate. She wanted to get his clothes off, and he was happy to oblige. Besides, he liked being fussed over. Fawning, pursuit, lures, and snares—that was his usual treatment at the hands of women. No woman had ever looked at him with such sweet concern.

At the gentle pressure of her hands, he edged forward in the chair. She went behind him and, murmuring soothing words of encouragement, eased his jacket off. This done, she kneeled in front of him and began on his waistcoat. Her fingers could not work the buttons free. *Tsk*ing, she removed her gloves, inch by slow inch, and set them aside.

The unconscious feminine gesture evoked lurid pictures in his mind, and warm pleasure rose in him. Breathing harshly, he spread his legs to give her easier access. The position was highly suggestive. She must have been aware of it, too, because her fingers trembled as she undid each button. The air between them was becoming charged.

He could hear the soft sound of her breathing, smell the faint fragrance of flowers. "Aurora." His voice was husky.

Her fingers stilled and she looked up at him.

Her eyes were huge and dark in her pale face. He brushed the back of his fingers against her cheek and smiled when her lids grew heavy. His fingers moved on, gently tracing the line of her jaw, her ears, her neck. When he felt the frantic pulse in the hollow of her throat, he took her fingers and pressed them to her own throat, then to his.

"See what you do to me?" he murmured. "See what I do to you?"

What was she thinking, feeling? He had to know.

He used his good arm to draw her closer. There was no resistance, and when his mouth took hers, she twined her arms around his neck. His lips parted over hers, not demanding, but hungry for the taste of her. Everything about her was unfamiliar, her taste, her flavor, her fragrance, the feel of her in his arms, yet he couldn't shake off the impression that she wasn't a stranger. They'd known each other from before.

A shadow of doubt crossed his mind. He could not make up his mind about her. She seemed too innocent to be a woman of the world, and too worldly to be an innocent. Who was she? What was she?

Raising his head, he gazed down at her. Her eyes were closed, her breasts were rising and falling with each labored breath. His body was aching to take her, but he wouldn't seduce her. This had to be what she wanted, too.

She opened her eyes and gave him a sleepy smile. Cupping his neck with one hand, she brought his head down and kissed him slowly, voluptuously, thoroughly.

Everything was going to be all right.

When he cupped her breasts, she responded by pressing herself into his embrace. She was soft and womanly and so sweetly giving. The smallest pressure of his hands on her breasts brought little whimpers of pleasure from her throat. As she became pliant in his hands, he became hard. He gritted his teeth until he had himself under control, then he began to think of logistics.

He couldn't take her here in the chair. He wanted to take his time with her, explore her intimately, thoroughly. Instinctively, he brushed his fingers along her shoulders, her throat, her neck, reassuring her even as he enticed her to accept more.

He said hoarsely, "Aurora, I want to make love to you."

She sucked in a breath and pulled back a little.

"Aurora?"

She breathed and crooned, "It's what I want, too." She covered his lips, face, and throat with fiery kisses. Her arms slipped around his waist.

He groaned with pleasure as her hands moved over him. But in the space of a single heartbeat everything changed. In her ardor, her hands pressed against his wound and his body clenched in pain.

Gasping, gritting his teeth, he sank back in the chair.

"I'm sorry," she cried softly, her hands fluttering to her throat. "I should have remembered your wound. Oh, God, what have I done?"

He unclenched his teeth. "It's all right. I'm fine. It's not your fault."

She got to her feet and studied him for a moment. "This is hopeless," she said. She waited until her breathing had evened before going on. "We shouldn't be doing this. It's a doctor you need."

"I don't need a doctor." He was pressing his hand to his side, waiting for the pain to ebb. "My manservant can take care of me."

"You have a manservant?"

He didn't want to talk about menservants or doctors. He wanted them to resume where they'd left off. If she was careful, they could manage.

One look at her convinced him it was too late. Her arms were folded across her breasts; her brows were knit in a frown. He'd missed his chance. But there would be other chances, he promised himself, and next time there would be no more dueling before he came to her.

Resigned, he said, " 'Coates' is his name. Perhaps you'd be good enough to call him. His room is at the end of the hall."

"Yes," she said. "I can do that."

To his great surprise, she kissed him swiftly, then she quit the room.

He heard her knocking on Coates's door. He didn't need a doctor. A wadded towel bound tightly under his arm and across his chest would do the trick. Ash had already taken care of the wound before they went to the café, so there was little chance of infection setting in.

The minutes dragged by and at last Coates appeared. Jack looked over his manservant's shoulder. "Where is the lady?" he asked.

"She left."

Jack knew that she would not leave without her bag of money and that was in the very chair in which he sat. He felt behind him. There was no bag. He slowly hoisted himself to his feet. The bag wasn't there or anywhere else he looked, nor were her gloves or mask.

It took a moment for him to grasp the situation. The witch had tricked him! She'd slipped the bag from the chair when she was taking off his coat, then had concealed it on her person before she kneeled in front of him. Her passion was a sham! So sweetly giving, so soft and pliant, be dammed! The only thing on her mind was money. Wasn't that just like a woman? She'd probably thought that he would steal it from her!

Coates coughed.

"What?" asked Jack, none too civilly.

"She left you a note, my lord."

Jack took the proffered piece of paper. It was no ordinary note, but a banknote in the sum of one thousand francs.

"She wrote something on it," Coates ventured to say, "after I gave her your old cloak to wear."

Jack went to the candle and read aloud, "For services rendered, thank you. Aurora."

He stared at the banknote long and hard, then his shoulders began to shake. He looked at Coates. "At least we know she's not a fortune hunter."

"She told me to bring bandages and a towel to bind up your wound."

"In a moment."

He crossed to the window and looked out. Things had quieted down. It took a moment for him to find her.

As he watched, she turned and gave him a little wave. Then she disappeared through the gate to the rue de Rivoli.

She shouldn't be too hard to find. A few discreet inquiries about the beautiful English girl who went by the name of "Aurora" would soon track her down.

Chapter 4

One of the gendarmes stationed at the entrance to the courtyard hailed a hackney for her after she explained, in her flawless French, that she was an actress employed at the theater. She told the driver to drop her off at the Tuileries, climbed in, then sank back against the banquette with her evening bag tucked tightly under her arm beneath her borrowed cloak.

All things considered, she thought she'd got off lightly. Her garments were crushed, but a warm iron would soon take care of that. The main thing was, she still had her money. She was lucky. The ruse she'd used to get her money back had almost cost her her virtue. That's what came of playing with fire. She hadn't realized, hadn't known, how a man's touch could addle the brains of an intelligent woman.

She removed one glove and touched her fingers to her lips. Her lips felt swollen, her body was still humming, her skin was hot. She was beginning to understand what made some women lose their heads over men. They weren't wicked; they were beguiled. Perhaps, like her, they'd been surprised by their first taste of passion and hadn't understood its power. Now that she did understand it, she'd make sure never to behave so recklessly again.

She rested her head against the banquette and closed her eyes. It had started innocently enough. Her one thought was to get her pochette and leave. But something else was at work in her. The thought that Jack saw her as a desirable woman had gone to her head and, just as though she were that silly schoolgirl again, she'd acted out her favorite fantasy.

Her gloves had saved her. In the heat of the moment she'd put her full weight on them as she kneeled in front of him and the pressure from one tiny glass button had made her flinch in pain. That's what had brought her to her senses. That's when she had deliberately pressed her hand to Jack's wound.

At least she knew now that kissing Jack Rigg was everything she'd imagined as a girl and more.

A smile flickered at the corners of her lips when she felt her toes curl. Every woman should have a kiss like that to remember. She was taking the kiss one step further in her mind when the hackney hit a pothole and brought her out of her reverie. She was thankful for the interruption. It was foolish to indulge in memories that were best left undisturbed. Memories led to dreams, and those dreams were out of her reach.

Her dreams were modest. She had to earn her living until Robbie was settled in some profession, then she'd keep house for him. Naturally, she expected him to marry. If she got along with her sister-in-law, well and good. If not, she'd go back to earning her own living.

The prospect was daunting. This was not how she'd imagined her life would unfold. She'd dreamed of having her own home, a husband, children. She'd had suitors in her younger days, but their interest had waned when they realized that they were taking on not only a wife but her brother, as well.

It was no wonder that she was tempted, occasionally, to let Aurora have her head.

The moment her coach pulled up outside the Tuileries, she knew something was wrong. Across the road, the hotel blazed with lights. She'd never been out this late before, but she knew that it was too early for any of the guests to be up and about. Yet there were lights at all the upstairs windows. The ground-floor windows were shuttered, but even there lights glimmered.

Heart thudding against her ribs, she paid off her driver and walked to the corner of the next street, cut across the rue de Rivoli and made her way to the side door. She had the key ready to insert in the lock when the lock turned from the inside and the door swung open. The porter was waiting for her. She slipped her key into her pocket before he could see it, then sailed by him with a cheery, "*Bonjour, Georges,*" as though there was nothing unusual in her arriving home at this unearthly hour.

"*Arrêtez!*" His tone was threatening.

"Don't you recognize me, Georges? It's Miss Hill, Lady Sedgewick's companion."

He nodded. "They're waiting upstairs for you."

She hoped she'd misunderstood his dialect. While he watched her with eagle eyes, she sedately mounted the stairs, but when she turned the corner, she ran like a hare.

The key to her chamber was at the bottom of her pochette. She dug around, found it, and whisked herself inside her room the moment she had the door open.

For a few moments, she stood with her back pressed against the door, waiting for her breath to even, trying to calm her chaotic thoughts. *They're waiting upstairs for you.*

She'd been found out. Something dreadful must have happened in her absence, and they'd discovered she wasn't on the premises. Dear Lord, what could she say?

Georges's warning spurred her to action. The first order of business was to light a candle. That done, she took the money from her pochette and stowed it in the traveling box where she kept her stationery. Then, she began to strip out of her clothes. She could hear voices coming from a room farther down the corridor, and that made her hurry all the more.

She was undoing the buttons on her gown when someone knocked at her door.

"Miss Hill? I know you're there!" The voice belonged to Staples, Lady Sedgewick's elderly abigail. "The porter told me. Her ladyship wants to see you at once."

Ellie took a deep breath and let it out slowly. Miss Staples had the instincts of an English bulldog. There was no escaping her, so she tried a little prevarication.

"What is it, Miss Staples? What's wrong?"

Miss Staples snorted. "It's no good pretending you don't know. At once, Miss Hill. Those are her ladyship's orders."

"Give me a few moments to get dressed."

"*Now,* Miss Hill. Or shall I fetch her ladyship?"

Ellie ground her teeth together. There wasn't time to get out of her dress and put on her nightgown. Reaching for her dressing robe, she shrugged into it. The rest of her costume—her overdress, gloves, shoes, pochette, along with Jack's cloak—were hastily deposited in her closet. At the last moment, she remembered to remove her silver combs and put on her embroidered slippers. When she opened the door, her stomach was in a knot.

Miss Staples's experienced eyes took her in at a glance, then she sniffed and led the way down the carpeted corridor to Lady Sedgewick's private parlor. At least, thought

Ellie, the abigail wasn't spiteful to her in particular. She was like this with all Lady Sedgewick's employees. Having served her mistress before her ladyship's marriage, she thought she ruled the roost.

When she walked into her ladyship's parlor, she came to a sudden stop. Not only were the Sedgewicks there in force, but so were her Cousin Cardvale and his wife, Dorothea.

Cheeks flushed and bosom heaving, Lady Sedgewick jumped up from her chair beside the fire and crossed quickly to confront Ellie. Her voice quivered in outrage. "Lies won't serve you now, my girl. Only the truth will do. Where have you been? What have you done with Lady Cardvale's diamonds?"

It was the second question that set Ellie back on her heels. " 'Lady Cardvale's diamonds'?" she said faintly.

"Her diamond necklace!" retorted her ladyship.

Ellie's mind raced this way and that as she tried to make sense of what was happening. She knew about the diamonds. They'd been in the family for generations. Dorothea never lost an opportunity to show them off.

She shook her head. "I don't know where the diamonds are."

She glanced at Dorothea. For someone whose diamonds had just been stolen, she looked remarkably pleased with herself. Her beauty was dark and dramatic, but spoiled, to Ellie's way of thinking, by shades of malice.

Harriet ran to Ellie and took her by the hand. She cried passionately, "Nothing will ever convince me that Ellie is a thief."

Ellie was beginning to feel light-headed. As she swayed on her feet, Lord Sedgewick came quickly to her side and led her to a chair. "I'm sure," he said in his calm way, "that Miss Hill has a reasonable explanation for her absence from the hotel tonight." He ignored his wife's disbelieving snort. Looking directly into Ellie's eyes, he said gently, "You see how things are, my dear. Lady Cardvale's dressing room was broken into. Her maid was attacked and her diamonds stolen. Lady Cardvale awoke and raised the alarm."

"The maid?" she cried.

Dorothea said hotly, "It might have been me! I practically surprised the fiend in the act."

Ellie pressed a hand to her heaving stomach. "Don't say the maid is dead?"

"No, no." Sedgwick spoke soothingly. "She'll be fine in a day or two, but she took a nasty knock on the head. We sent for the gendarmes and they searched the hotel. Everyone has been accounted for but you. You must see how bad this looks. The authorities will want to question you. You must tell us where you were and who can vouch for you."

She returned Lord Sedgewick's direct look and said earnestly, "I did not steal Lady Cardvale's diamonds. I swear it."

She looked at her cousin, who had yet to speak to her. He was sitting with his hands clasped loosely in front of him, studying his fingers with an abstracted frown. Though he was only in his late thirties, he looked much older. His brown hair was thinning; his shoulders were stooped. A "milksop" was what Uncle Ted used to call him. Marriage to Dorothea had not improved him. She was another one who liked to rule the roost.

"Cardvale," Ellie said softly, "I swear I did not take the diamonds."

He looked up with a smile. "I don't doubt you, Ellie, not for a moment." Then to his wife, "Can you really see Ellie forcing the door? She hasn't the strength."

"How did it happen?" she asked him quietly.

"The thief used the staff's staircase and forced the

door into the dressing room. There was a scuffle with the maid and he went off with the diamonds, or at least, with the jewelry box containing the diamonds. We found it just outside the door. Ellie, I know you didn't do it."

The alarm that seemed to have settled in her throat eased momentarily and she thought that this was the strangest conversation between cousins who had not seen each other in years.

"Thank you," she said simply.

This exchange between her husband and his cousin did not please Lady Cardvale. Her voice was cold with dislike when she spoke to Ellie. "And why have you changed your name to 'Hill'? Only someone with something to hide would do such a thing."

"I haven't changed it." Ellie was as cold as Dorothea. "I dropped 'Brans' because I wanted something less pretentious when I had to earn my living. I've been known by 'Ellie Hill' for some years now, and that's how I want to keep it, plain and simple."

Cardvale said, "If that's what you want, Ellie, then of course you shall have it." His voice was gentle, but the look he gave his wife was razor-sharp.

Dorothea either did not see it or ignored it. She was still on the attack. "We are still waiting to hear where you have been all night and who can vouch for you. We know you weren't in the hotel, so it's no good pretending you've just risen from your bed." As she spoke, she rose and went to stand in front of Ellie. Her eyes made a slow appraisal, missing nothing. "Well? What have you to say for yourself?"

As though she were playing a game of cribbage, Ellie's mind began to sort through various possibilities. She dared not mention Milton and the gaming house. As for being with Jack Rigg in his rooms at the Palais Royal—

that was even worse. She was thinking of pleading sleep-walking or loss of memory when Dorothea gasped.

With a shaking finger, she pointed to the hem of Ellie's gown that dipped below the edge of her warm robe. "There is blood on her nightdress!" she cried out. "My maid's blood! See now, Cardvale, how your favorite has repaid us after all we did for her."

The silence was profound. All eyes were on Ellie. The prospect of being charged with attempted murder loosened her tongue. "I was with the Earl of Raleigh," she said. "He will vouch for me."

In his rooms at the Palais Royal, Jack was roaring like a caged lion as his manservant held him down while Ash Denison tipped a bottle of brandy over the wound in Jack's armpit.

"You really ought to rest in your bed," said Ash. "The wound is in an awkward place. Any slight movement will open it again."

Jack threw off his manservant and sat up. "God, you two belong in the Inquisition! It was only a scratch! Now you've made it start bleeding again. You should have warned me you were going to douse me in brandy." To Coates, he went on, "One more trick like that and you'll be looking for another position."

Ash winked at Coates. "Is he always such a baby?"

Coates's only answer was a prudent smile. "If you're done here, my lord," he said, "I shall make breakfast."

As Coates withdrew, Jack reached for a pad of folded linen and shoved it under his arm. "Now bind me up," he said, "with enough pressure to keep the damn thing from slipping."

Ash did as he was told. "My, my," he said, "you are in a

foul humor this morning. What happened last night between you and our lady of mystery?"

"Nothing happened." Jack reached for the clothes Coates had laid out for him and began to dress. "I started to bleed like a pig. She left. That's all there was to it."

Ash grinned. "That explains the foul temper." He lounged against the table, arms folded across his chest. "Who is she, Jack?"

"Aurora. That is all she told me." He was buttoning his shirt and his fingers stilled as a memory came back to him—the catch in her breath just before his lips covered hers, the warm glow in her eyes when he handled her intimately. He was well aware that she'd tricked him to get to her bag, but he had the experience to know that her passion wasn't a sham. The lady had been caught in her own trap.

Ash said, "Now what am I to make of that smile?"

Jack erased the smile, but traces of it lingered in his eyes. "It's been a long time since I've liked a woman half as well."

"'Liked' or 'lusted after'?"

"Liked," responded Jack emphatically. "Oh, the lust was there, on both sides, but I started to bleed like a pig, and that was that."

"I hope you rewarded her for her trouble."

"Just the opposite. See for yourself. There's a banknote on the sideboard."

Ash walked to the sideboard, rooted around for a moment or two, and came up with the thousand franc banknote. Holding it up to the window, he read, "For services rendered." He looked at Jack. "What 'services'?"

Jack sat on the bed and carefully pulled on his boots. "She went off with my cloak, so it could be payment for that, or because I rescued her during the riot."

"Well, I'll be damned! You're smitten, aren't you?"

"'Smitten'?" Jack sighed. "I said I *liked* her. She has a sense of humor." He was remembering the jaunty wave she had given him on her way out of the courtyard. "Don't read more into it than that."

"Well, I think it's a shame."

"What is?" Jack was attempting to tie his neckcloth and not doing a good job of it. "Help me?" he said. "I can't raise my arm for that cursed bandage."

Ash took over. His face all innocence, he said, "If it weren't for the fact that she's a demirep, my nose would be smelling orange blossoms."

Teeth bared, Jack replied, "Go on in that vein and I'll put your pretty nose out of commission. Besides—"

"What?"

He'd been about to say that it was quite possible that Aurora was not a demirep, but he knew that such a declaration would only add coals to the fire, so he said instead, "I don't know who she is or where she came from."

"And you're not going to try to find her?"

"I'm thinking about it."

"Well, don't leave it too late, or I may find her first. You see, Jack, you've made Aurora sound intriguing. Do you suppose she might be interested in a penniless lordling such as myself?"

"On my estate," Jack said pleasantly, "we don't prosecute poachers, we shoot them."

They were both laughing when Coates announced a visitor, Lord Sedgewick, who wanted to speak to Jack in private. "I put him in the salon," said Coates.

Jack looked at Ash, shrugged, then left the room. He remembered Lord Sedgewick from the embassy ball. What he remembered best was that he was married to that ghastly woman with the galloping tongue.

Lord Sedgewick greeted him stiffly, refused the offer of coffee, and remained standing.

"How may I help you?" asked Jack. The older man's stiffness made him wary.

"I'm here on behalf of my daughter's companion, Miss Hill," said Sedgewick.

Jack nodded. "The lady I danced with at the ball last night." He refrained from adding *the lady with the venomous tongue*. "What about her?"

"She swears that she was with you in your rooms at the Palais Royal late last night."

It was the last thing Jack expected to hear and he was momentarily speechless, but as the significance of Sedgewick's words sank in, he said violently, "That's a lie! I was with another lady whose name I prefer to keep to myself."

"'Aurora'? That's what Miss Hill told me you would say. That's the name she gave you."

Jack stared at his lordship, then said harshly, "I don't know what game Miss Hill is playing, but she's way off the mark if she thinks I would confuse her with the woman I was with last night. There's no comparison."

Sedgewick's bloodhound eyes were not unsympathetic. "Yes, she said that, too, and asked me to give you this."

Over his arm, he carried a folded cloak. As he handed it to Jack, he said, "I believe this belongs to you."

Jack accepted it automatically. "All this proves," he said doggedly, "is that Aurora and Miss Hill know each other. Aurora must have given her my cloak."

"It's possible," his lordship said without conviction. "But there's more at stake than you realize. I'll tell you about it on our way to the hotel where we're putting up."

A sleety rain was falling, so they took a hackney to the hotel. In short, precise sentences, Lord Sedgewick apprized

Jack of the salient facts. What it amounted to was that Miss Hill was in need of an alibi for the precise hour of four o'clock that morning, when Lady Cardvale was awakened by her maid's scream.

"Someone broke into Lady Cardvale's dressing room and was discovered by the maid," Lord Sedgewick said. "That's where the maid sleeps, you see. The poor girl was knocked on the head and the thief got away with the Cardvale diamonds."

Jack was incredulous. "And you suspect Miss Hill?"

"Not I," responded Lord Sedgewick. "But she was nowhere to be found when a search was made of the hotel, and when she did turn up, there was blood on her gown. Lady Cardvale is an excitable woman and, I'm sorry to say, my wife is not much better. They jumped to the conclusion that it must be the maid's blood. That's when Ellie, Miss Hill, told us she'd been with you at four o'clock this morning."

Jack felt as though a noose had tightened around his neck.

He'd looked at his watch at four o'clock when he was with Aurora. If Miss Hill and Aurora were the same person, some lunatic might expect him to do the honorable thing and offer to marry her. Not that he would. He'd rather renounce his estates and title than marry a woman who had deliberately set out to catch him in her net. And if Aurora was Miss Hill, that's what it would amount to.

He thought he was wise to every feminine trick....

He stopped right there. The thought was preposterous. There had to be some other explanation. It was true that Miss Hill wasn't nearly as docile as she appeared at first glance. He'd discovered that when he danced with her, but she wasn't anything like Aurora.

Aurora was feminine, intriguing, captivating. From the moment she had walked into the Café des Anglaises, he could hardly stop staring. Part of her allure was that she wanted to be left alone, and he had resolved to change her mind.

When he tried to picture Miss Hill, he couldn't quite bring her into focus. Before she'd opened her mouth, he remembered thinking that she had a trim little figure under her frumpy gown. But a trim little figure couldn't make up for that viper's tongue.

If Aurora and Miss Hill turned out to be the same person, they could hang, draw and quarter him before he would marry such a deceiving jade.

Chapter 5

Ellie's head was beginning to ache. She'd been up all night, without a wink of sleep, and now the maids were serving coffee and rolls. She was nervous, waiting for the moment when Lord Sedgewick would appear at the door with Jack. She was sure that Jack would support her alibi—that went without saying. But that wasn't the same thing as supporting *her*. No man liked to be duped. What she feared was losing his good opinion, but that was Aurora speaking. He already disliked Ellie Hill, and she didn't know why it mattered to her.

They'd had a short respite to wash and dress for the new day, then they'd returned to Lady Sedgewick's parlor to wait for Lord Sedgewick and Jack. Cardvale, who was sitting in the chair closest to the fire, was lost in his own private thoughts. Dorothea and Lady Sedgewick were on the other side of the fire, heads close together, conversing in whispers, and Harriet, whom Ellie considered her staunchest ally, had been sent away, as though she were too innocent to hear the salacious details of Ellie's adventure with Lord Raleigh. And that's what Ladies Sedgewick and Cardvale were hoping for—a salacious scandal to titillate their appetite for the seamier side of life.

They would be disappointed. Nothing much had happened, and Jack, she knew, would not elaborate on the simple facts. Not that it mattered. Alibi or no alibi, her reputation was in tatters. No respectable young woman would show her face in the Palais Royal at night, let alone accompany a man of the world to his rooms. The fact that she'd gone with him to escape the riot did not signify, not with these two ladies. They would have been happier if she had allowed herself to be trampled to death.

She'd kept Milton's name out of it and she hoped he had the good sense to stay away. For one thing, she was with Jack at the crucial time, and for another, she didn't want to be accused of corrupting the morals of the young. Milton was, after all, only eighteen years old.

Dear Lord, she had a lot to answer for, dragging a blameless young man into a salacious scandal. She should never have allowed him to act as her escort.

She knew what was in store for her. She would lose her job without a reference, and the knowledge made her defiantly determined not to show how desperate she felt. Having nothing to lose, she hadn't bothered to dress with her usual care. She'd left off the powder that made her look older, left off the lace cap, and had covered her plain gray crepe gown with a crimson stole. It wasn't all bravado. Though she wasn't nearly as elegant as Aurora, she wanted Jack to see that there was more to Ellie Hill than the nondescript lady's companion he'd met at the embassy ball.

She was doing it again, trying to impress Jack, and that made her impatient with herself.

When the door opened, she looked up. Lord Sedgewick entered first, then Jack. He paused on the threshold and let his gaze roam over each of them. He dominated the room, not because of his dark good looks, or because he projected an air of confidence, but because he held himself with the stillness of a predator selecting its prey.

When that pitiless gaze came to rest on her, she controlled a panicked shudder. She'd seen his face softened with charm and good humor, but that was last night, when she was playing the part of Aurora. This morning, his high cheekbones and the line of his jaw were all angles and planes.

He was livid, and she couldn't understand it. She'd expected him to be annoyed, though she'd hoped he would be amused. This excess of emotion, banked though it was, seemed out of proportion to her offense.

He sauntered over and took the chair next to hers. He spoke through his teeth. "I hardly recognize you, Miss Hill. Or should I call you 'Aurora'?"

"'Miss Hill' will do," she replied, her eyes not quite meeting his.

"Well," said Lord Sedgewick, who had yet to sit down, "is Miss Hill the lady you entertained last night? Can you give her an alibi for four o'clock this morning?"

"Not so fast," said Jack. "I want to know exactly what's going on."

"I told you," said Sedgewick. "There was a robbery—"

"Before that," Jack interjected. He looked at Ellie. "What were you doing at the Palais Royal?"

She had no intention of telling anyone about the gaming house, so she told him exactly what she'd told the others. "I had heard so much about the Palais Royal at night that I wanted to see it for myself. I never imagined that it would be dangerous. Had there not been a riot, I would have come straight home."

She could see that her answer did not satisfy him, and

was vastly relieved when he went off on another tack. "What exactly was stolen?"

Lord Sedgewick shrugged and sat down. "Cardvale can tell you about that."

Lord Cardvale took a mouthful of coffee before responding. "The Cardvale diamonds—that's a necklace that has been in the family for generations and was the only thing of real value."

His wife interjected, "What about my betrothal ring? The thief took that, too, a ruby set in gold."

Cardvale nodded. "And some smaller items: a silver pin with the Cardvale crest. What else, Dorothea?"

"A leather purse with fifty gold guineas!"

"What about banknotes?" asked Jack.

At the mention of banknotes, Ellie straightened. Jack was watching her with an ironic twist to his lips. He must have known that her pochette was stuffed with banknotes. Did he think she'd stolen them before the robbery?

Cardvale shook his head. "No banknotes."

Sedgewick said, "We are still waiting to be told whether Miss Hill is the lady you know as 'Aurora.' Was she with you at precisely four o'clock this morning?"

In a languid tone, Jack replied, "Oh, I don't think there is any doubt about that, so you will have to look elsewhere for your thief."

Ellie went weak with relief. At least she wouldn't be charged with robbery or attempted murder.

Jack's assurances did not placate Lady Sedgewick. "Is that the only explanation we are to have? That Miss Hill was with you when someone broke in and stole Lady Cardvale's diamonds?"

"My man will confirm the time if you need another witness."

"That's not the point." Her ladyship's ample bosom

quivered with the tumult of her emotions. "What I want to know is how that blood got on her gown."

Jack looked bored. "I have no idea. Why don't you ask Miss Hill?"

For a moment or two, Ellie was mystified. What difference did it make how the blood got on her dress? The important thing was that it was not the maid's blood, could not be the maid's blood because she'd been with Jack when the diamonds were stolen. As the thought revolved in her mind, a wave of heat spread through her. *Virgin blood*—that's what they were thinking, though they were too refined to say it. They thought Jack had dishonored her, and if Cardvale came to believe it, he might challenge Jack to a duel.

Her hands clenched. "I told you," she said fiercely, "it was all very innocent. There was a riot. Lord Raleigh rescued me and took me to his rooms. He was bleeding. It's *his* blood on my gown." She looked at Jack. "Tell them!"

He turned an inscrutable expression on her. "What difference will that make, do you suppose? You've said it all, and not one word can be taken back."

"I don't want to take back anything I've said." Her tone was still fierce. "All I want is to clear my name. I was with you when Lady Cardvale's diamonds were stolen. You rescued me from the riot. Nothing happened. I've done nothing to be ashamed of."

Cardvale got up. "Of course you haven't, Ellie. No one believes you have. But you must see that you've been compromised. There is only one way to restore your good name. You and Lord Raleigh must marry at once."

"Ah," said Jack, "I was wondering when we would get to that."

Now that her hopes for an advantageous alliance between her daughter and Lord Raleigh were crushed, Lady

Sedgewick turned bitter. "Well, I think that's a shabby trick you played on Lord Raleigh, Ellie, to pretend to be one sort of woman, then turn out to be another. I suppose you saw your chance when you learned that Lord Cardvale was here. Of course he would see that right was done by you."

"Naturally," replied Cardvale. "Ellie is a blood relative."

Ellie felt like the captain of a sailing ship who had escaped a whirlpool only to run smack into a hurricane. She hadn't foreseen this new peril because gentlemen of Jack's rank and fortune did not marry penniless nobodies just because they were compromised. And no one would have expected it of him if her cousin had not come upon the scene. It was her connection to Cardvale that made the difference.

She appealed to Lord Sedgewick, who had always been a good friend to her in the past. "Won't you stop this, please, before it gets out of hand?"

He shook his head. "It's not my place to interfere. Cardvale is the head of your house. You must be guided by him. However," he got to his feet, "I think you and Lord Raleigh need a little time to get used to the idea. We'll leave you in private to talk things over, shall we?"

Cardvale looked doubtful. Lady Sedgewick protested that she wanted to remain. Dorothea demanded to know what steps they were going to take to get back her diamonds. In his imperturbable but relentless way, Lord Sedgewick ushered them out.

Ellie sat there, gathering her thoughts, while Jack went to the sideboard and poured himself a cup of coffee. She didn't know whether she should begin by thanking him for saying only enough to clear her name—for their time together wasn't entirely innocent—or whether she should apologize for the ludicrous demand her kinsman had placed on them both. Maybe they could have a good laugh about it? She heard the rattle of cup and saucer as he put them down, and she looked up at him.

"You're to be congratulated," he said abruptly. "I swallowed your bait, hook and line, but don't imagine you're going to reel me in. Better women than you have tried— and failed. You see, Miss Hill, I'm an old hand at evading the marriage trap, no matter how cunningly it's baited."

His words stunned her. This was the last thing she expected to hear. Even a man of his standing—no, his conceit—must see that she was the victim of circumstances as much as he.

Before she could answer, he went on, "Don't come the innocent with me, Aurora. I've tasted your kisses, remember? Yes, and a lot more besides. When I offer my hand in marriage, it will be to a lady whose reputation is spotless."

She was furious. The only reason she had kissed him was to get to her pochette, as he must have guessed by now. She wanted to rage, rant, slap the cynical smile from his face. What stopped her was that small voice inside her head, reminding her that she was Papa's daughter. The thing to do now was make a dignified exit and show him how badly he had misjudged her.

The trouble was, she didn't have Papa's temperament, but Mama's. She would make that dignified exit, but only after she had taught this overbearing oaf a lesson.

Concealing her seething emotions behind a smile, she said archly, "Come now, Jack. That's no way to start our marriage. Let's be civil about this."

Anger made his voice harsh. "How can I say this more plainly? I won't have you at any price."

She looked down at her clasped hands. "You do realize that they'll turn me off without a character? Then how shall I live? Who will support me?"

He smiled grimly. "Stop playacting, Miss Hill. I liked you much better as Aurora."

"Ah, but there is no Aurora. She's a figment of my imagination. Miss Hill has to make her own way in the world."

"Then I suggest you elope with your present protector! I'm sure the life of a lady's companion is too tame for you now. And beggars can't be choosers."

"My 'present' protector?" Her brow wrinkled. She remembered, then, that Lord Denison had put forward the idea that she had a rich protector when he spoke to Jack in French. It took all her control not to start foaming at the mouth. "And who might that be?"

A muscle twitched in his cheek. "You tell me. All I know is that your bag was stuffed with banknotes. Oh yes. I looked. How else would you come by such a sum of money if not from a rich protector?"

There was a pause as she tried to read his expression. She had the strangest notion that her answer mattered to him. Then the look in his eyes was gone, and the ironic smile became more pronounced.

"Do you deny it?" he asked.

"Why should I? But you see, Jack, money doesn't mean all that much to me. I have always dreamed of becoming a ... countess."

His eyes narrowed on her, weighing, measuring, as though he were not quite sure how to take her. Finally, he said, "How did you know I would be at the Café des Anglaises?"

"I didn't know. I was waiting for ..." she flashed him another arch smile, "for my protector when you came to my rescue. The first thing that popped into my head was—here is an earl for the taking. *The Countess of Raleigh*. Can you imagine what that means to a poor girl like me? I'd be presented at court; I'd take precedence over viscountesses and lesser-titled ladies." She went on rapturously, "I can see it now."

He said dryly, "You have a vivid imagination, but alas, not much common sense. It will never come to that, though I must applaud you for trying. You certainly played your cards right."

This time, her smile was genuine. "If you knew me better, Jack, you'd know that I always play my cards right."

A reluctant smile tugged at the corners of his mouth. He shook his head and folded his arms across his chest. "Except that you missed a better prospect. Lord Denison, who was with me in the café, is heir to a marquess."

"Perhaps you'd be good enough to introduce us? I mean, the marquess, of course. Not his heir."

He raised a brow and studied her for a moment. "I was right about you," he said slowly, reflectively. "You do have a sense of humor."

This had gone on long enough. It was time to make that dignified exit. When she got up, so did he. She managed a low, throaty chuckle. "Don't worry, Jack. You're safe and so is your friend. You see, I'm not the marrying kind of woman. I like my freedom too much. You need not worry about Cardvale. I'll make things right with him."

He was silent, watching her as she adjusted her stole. As she turned away, he said, "What will you say?"

"Oh, that you offered to marry me and I turned you down. Then I shall elope with my rich protector and live happily ever after. Good-bye, Jack. I wish you well."

She was at the door when he called, "Aurora!" commanding her to stop.

"What is it?"

Relaxed, his dark eyes bright with amusement, he said, "If it's a protector you want, look no farther. I think we would suit very well."

The thrust slipped under her guard and found a mark he had never intended. Pride kept her head high and her temper at bay. She managed a creditable laugh. "Aurora wouldn't suit you, Jack. She's an intelligent, cultured woman. All you know is dueling and horses. You're practically illiterate. You'd be out of your depth."

On that crushing snub, she left the room and managed to refrain from slamming the door behind her.

Her most pressing concern was Robbie. As she packed her belongings, she tried to keep the chills at bay by concentrating on how they would manage. One thing was certain. She could no longer stay in Paris. She could not face all the titters and sideways glances of people who believed she was a fallen woman, and word of her escapade was bound to get out.

That left the problem of how she would earn her living.

Aurora could never be the permanent solution to their problems. For her own peace of mind, she could not continue to resurrect Aurora every time she got into difficulties. She would have to find another position and impress upon Robbie that he must return to university to prepare himself for a profession. Once Robbie was settled, she'd feel easier in her mind.

The chill that gripped her began to thaw. Robbie was her reason for living, or, at the very least, he gave meaning to her existence. He was easy to love but hard to discipline. That's what happened when boys had no father to guide them.

She had to be strong for Robbie's sake.

It did not take her long to pack. After that, there were the inevitable interviews, first with her employers, then with Lord Cardvale. She was polite, reserved, and adamant. She would not marry Lord Raleigh. She would not remain in Paris, not even for another day. Her one wish, she told them, was to return to England where she had friends who would help her until she got settled.

Only the gentlemen tried to change her mind. Cardvale was kindness itself. There was a cottage in Hampstead she could have, he said, until she found other employment. She wasn't even tempted, knowing what Dorothea would make of that. The ladies said very little, but their eyes betrayed them. They thought that she was a fallen woman and had got just what she deserved. When she asked about Harriet, she was told that Harriet had come down with a cold and was confined to her room. That was the unkindest cut of all.

Her last interview was with a soft-spoken gendarme who questioned her about her alibi. Cardvale was there to smooth things over. It helped when he implied that Lord Raleigh was a relative. After that, she was free to go.

A calèche was hired to take her to Calais. There was no one to chaperon her except the coachmen, but, as she pointed out, a chaperon had no need of a chaperon. She then retired to her room to await the arrival of her hired coach.

Here she allowed the facade she'd kept up, of a woman in control of her life, to slip a little. She felt utterly alone and friendless. The friends she'd alluded to in England did not exist. No one was to blame. It was what came of moving around from one employer to the next, never being settled in one place for long. And one did not make friends of one's employers, although some of them were kinder than others. Thousands of women were in the same position as she—governesses, chaperons, ladies' companions. It was depressing. It was frightening. If they could not find work, they had few choices. The specter of the workhouse was always there in the background.

Cardvale handed her into the coach and before she could stop him, he'd slipped a fat leather purse into her muff. She knew it would be full of guineas. Then he gave the coachmen the order to move off.

They had not gone far when she ordered them to stop. She had an errand to run, she told them, and gave them directions to Meurice's hotel. She was going to pick up her brother, possibly Milton, as well, pay off the moneylender, and get them all safely home to England.

There was another shock waiting for her at the hotel. Robbie had been stabbed in the shoulder in some brawl he'd become involved in during the New Year's revels. That was his story, anyway, and all her questions were answered with wide-eyed innocence, which made her wonder what he was keeping from her. She did not have the heart to scold him, not after her own reckless adventure with Jack.

Milton arrived soon after, and when he began to apologize for leaving her unescorted the night before, she waved him to silence. Then she related her own reasons, giving only the sketchiest details, for why she had to leave Paris.

They were as eager to leave as she, but she was worried about Robbie. Though the wound was healing, and he had seen a doctor, he did not look well enough to travel. Her misgivings were overruled. They'd both had enough of Paris, Milton said, and were eager to get back to Oxford and their studies.

Getting Robbie back to Oxford was the one argument that could persuade her.

While she helped Robbie pack, Milton went off with Aurora's winnings to pay off the moneylender. Half an hour later, they were on the road, but it was a somber party inside the calèche. All were absorbed in their own thoughts.

Chapter 6

The news of Ellie's disgrace did not take long to circulate among the English visitors. No one believed that Lord Raleigh had offered for her, a mere lady's companion. They were avid to know all the intimate details, but with Ellie having left Paris and Jack as hardmouthed as a slab of Aberdeen granite, they were left to speculate. Imaginations ran wild, aided and abetted by the darkling looks and oblique hints of Ladies Sedgewick and Cardvale.

As far as Jack was concerned, Paris had lost its luster. He was disgusted to find himself more sought after than ever, while Ellie's character was torn to shreds. He saw then that he had misjudged her. If she'd really wanted to ensnare him, she would have persevered, cried rape, appealed to Lord Cardvale to protect her good name. She had done none of those things. In a matter of hours, she had packed her bags and was on her way home to England. Everyone was shocked at the suddenness of her departure, and none more than he.

During the week that followed, thoughts of Ellie

occupied his mind. He knew what people were saying and that pens would be busy carrying tales about the scandal across the English Channel. Nothing he said would make a difference. People liked to think the worst.

He might have been more uneasy had he not known that she had sufficient funds to support herself until the scandal had blown over. But where had the money come from? That question continued to tease his mind, as did the mystery of why she had played the part of Aurora.

He'd dismissed the notion that there was a rich protector waiting in the wings. If that were the case, she would hardly have returned to the hotel to take up her old life. There was nothing there for her but a life of drudgery.

What amazed him was that he had not seen the resemblance between Aurora and Miss Hill until he'd been summoned to the hotel to support her alibi. And he should have seen it. They had the same sculpted features, the same molded mouth, and eyes that spoke volumes without a word being spoken. The difference was, Aurora's unspoken messages were oddly erotic. Miss Hill's were as sweet as vinegar.

Maybe she had cause. He'd got off unscathed, while she paid the toll for her reckless, though quite innocent, escapade. He wished he could make amends, but feared that anything he tried to say or do would only make matters worse.

Having made up his mind to do nothing, he surprised himself by proposing to do the opposite.

On the day before they were to leave Paris, while walking in the Bois de Boulogne, Jack confided his thoughts to Ash. "So when we reach London," he said, "I thought I might call on her just to make sure that she is all right. You need not look at me like that. I'd do as much for my gardener or my butler if I felt I had a hand in their downfall."

Surprise etched Ash's voice. "Now what brought this on?"

Jack kicked a pebble and sent it rattling along the path. "As I said, I feel responsible."

"Leave that to Cardvale. As her nearest relative, he should be looking out for her interests."

"But that's the point. As far as I can see, he isn't the least bit interested, except to mouth a few platitudes to ease his conscience."

And that's what rubbed him. There ought to be someone who felt responsible for the girl. Had he been the girl's nearest male relative, he would have challenged Jack Rigg to a duel.

Ash was shaking his head. "Leave well enough alone. That's my advice. Besides, didn't you tell me that Aurora's bag was stuffed with banknotes? Sounds to me as though she knows how to take care of herself."

"You're not saying anything that I haven't said to myself. I hope you're right. But what if you're wrong? For my own peace of mind, I have to find out."

"In that case, I won't try to dissuade you. But how will you find her? Not through the Cardvales or the Sedgewicks?"

"No. They might read more into my object than I intend."

"Then who else is there?"

Jack was remembering the embassy ball and how the ambassador pressed him to ask Miss Hill to dance. "Sir Charles Stuart seems to know the family quite well. If anyone knows her whereabouts, it's Sir Charles."

Ash squinted speculatively at his friend. "Does this mean that you won't be taking Brand up on his offer for a little shooting and hunting at his hunting lodge?"

Brand Hamilton was the third member of their

fraternity. At one time they'd been inseparable, but the war had changed that, the war and Brand's unswerving determination to make himself a force to be reckoned with in the newspaper world. He rarely took time off from building his little empire, but he always managed to escape for a week or two's shooting at his hunting lodge in Leicestershire to be with his friends.

"No. This should only take a few days. I'll still make it to Brand's place."

"Mmm. So you say, and I'm sure you mean it, but these things have a way of unraveling. Watch your step, that's all I'm saying. Don't get caught in the marriage trap!"

"As if I would."

He wasn't certain that he would be welcomed at the embassy, and was pleasantly surprised when he was kept waiting for only ten minutes before an attaché showed him into Sir Charles's private office. His welcome was not warm, but not as frigid as he might have expected, considering that the ambassador was Miss Hill's friend, or a friend of her family.

There were no pleasantries. After waving Jack to the chair on the opposite side of his commodious desk, the ambassador said, "I was hoping to have a word with you before you left Paris. And before you ask, yes, I know what happened between you and Ellie. Cardvale told me." He lounged back in his chair, fingers steepled, and made a *tsk*-ing sound as he shook his head. "Jack, Jack, I thought better of you."

"Indeed." Jack controlled his annoyance at Sir Charles's presumption, but his mouth flattened. "I do not think Cardvale can have told you the whole story."

"What—that little Ellie decked herself out as a woman of the world and embarked on a little adventure?" Sir

Charles chuckled. "You should know as well as anyone that there's a strong streak of recklessness in that girl. This is not the first time she has led you astray, and I had that from my aunt who had it from your grandmother."

There was a silence. Every sound in the room faded as Jack tried to make sense of what the ambassador had told him. Finally, sinking back in his chair, he said, "You must be confusing me with someone else. I assure you, I never met Miss Hill before you introduced us at the embassy ball."

"You mean..." Sir Charles shook his head. "I was sure you recognized her."

"No. Who is she?"

"Her father was your tutor for a time—Dr. Austen Brans-Hill? Ellie is his daughter."

"Miss Hill is Ellie Brans-Hill?" He was shocked.

"So, you do remember her."

What Jack remembered was a family that was so unusual, so "fey," as his grandmother put it, that they might have come from another world. The father could never remember to tie his shoelaces, but he was renowned for his scholarship. He spent hours in his study, poring over those obscure Greek particles, signifying nothing, and could wax enthusiastic for hours to anyone who showed the slightest interest.

He always made it a rule to beat a hasty retreat whenever the vicar got started on his favorite subject.

The mother was no less an original in her own right. He remembered an ethereal lady whom nothing could fluster, floating about her herb gardens in pale muslins and stout leather boots. She was too innocent for her own good, and was frequently taken advantage of. He never knew who would be sitting next to him at dinner—a beggar, a serving girl who had been turned off for licentious behavior, a family that had been turned out of their cottage because they could not pay the rent. The list was endless.

Then there was Ellie. A halfling, a brat, a precocious child-woman who alternately shamed him because her knowledge of the classics was far superior to his—and didn't she love to lord it over him—and who also strained his patience to the limits by attempting to seduce him. Not that she knew what she was doing. To her, it was a game.

The incident Sir Charles referred to was a case in point. He'd received the warmest letters, anonymously, from, he deduced, the miller's widowed daughter. Becky was every-thing a randy seventeen-year-old youth, eager to shed his virginity, could hope to encounter. But when he'd finally met his mystery lady in the gardener's shed behind the vegetable plots, it was Ellie who was waiting for him. He would have blistered her backside if she had not set her dog on him.

How on earth had his grandmother got to hear about that?

Ellie Brans-Hill was Ellie Hill. Ellie Hill and Aurora. Now he could see it.

And she was still up to her old tricks.

He looked at the ambassador. "Why did she change her name?"

"I suppose because she thought a hyphenated name was too grand for a lady's companion."

"'A lady's companion'! Ellie Brans-Hill! I'm amazed. The little girl I knew was too headstrong, too independ-ent to fit that mold."

What didn't surprise him was that Ellie had been forced to earn a living. Her parents were good, decent peo-ple, but too openhanded with anyone in need, when they should have been conserving the little they had for Ellie's future.

"Dr. Brans-Hill," he said, "should have done better by Ellie."

Sir Charles was in the act of pouring out two sherries from a decanter he'd produced from the bottom drawer of his desk. "Austen didn't leave Ellie penniless if that's what you think. There was a small annuity for her, and a little laid by for Robbie's education." He handed Jack the glass of sherry. "That's where the money went—to the son. There were scholarships from the church, of course, but that wasn't enough to cover all Robbie's expenses. So Ellie took care of the rest."

"'Robbie'?" Jack thought for a moment, then nodded. "I'd forgotten about him. He was only an infant when I stayed at the vicarage. Where is he now?"

"That's what I wanted to talk to you about."

The ambassador settled himself more comfortably in his chair and took a moment to gather his thoughts. It seemed to Jack that the atmosphere was warmer. He sipped his sherry as he waited for Sir Charles to begin.

Sir Charles said, "Only this morning I was informed, as a courtesy by French authorities, that an English subject, Robert Brans-Hill, is suspected of murdering an actress at the Théatre Français in the Palais Royal."

Jack felt the shock of the ambassador's words all through his body. When the shock subsided, he said emphatically, "No one will ever convince me that a son of Dr. Brans-Hill could deliberately murder anyone."

Sir Charles smiled. "I agree with you. Now drink your sherry while I tell you how things stand.

It was a familiar story—a young man, no more than a youth, really, diverging from the straight-and-narrow path laid out for him first by his parents and then by his sister, and freed of restraint, indulging in all the dissolute pleasures that Paris had to offer.

"The young scapegrace," Sir Charles said with feeling, "should have been poring over his books in Oxford, not gallivanting in Europe. What is known now is that almost a month ago Robbie arrived in Paris and, within hours of his arrival, attended a performance at the Théâtre Français, where he fell under the spell of one of its leading lights, Louise Daudet."

Jack nodded. "I remember reading about it. The murder happened, what, two weeks ago? Why have they taken so long to bring it to your notice?"

The ambassador shrugged. "I got the impression that they have more important cases to solve, and actresses don't rate as highly as sober-minded, industrious French citizens. I, of course, have no authority over the French police. It's only because Robbie is a British subject that they told me anything at all."

Jack was puzzled. "Why do they suspect him? There's nothing unusual in young men making fools of themselves over opera dancers and actresses. I did my share of fawning when I was a stripling. It doesn't mean anything."

"Ah, but this *is* unusual. You see, out of legions of admirers, Mlle. Daudet chose him, a young, penniless Englishman, to be her lover. He was there at the theater every evening. Their affair was no secret."

"You must be joking!" Jack exclaimed. "I read the papers. Louise Daudet was at the peak of her profession. She was greatly sought after. Why would she take a callow youth to be her lover?"

Sir Charles shrugged. "Who can say? At any rate, her interest did not last long. She told her manager that she was retiring from the theater and was going to live abroad. He did everything he could to make her change her mind, but she would not budge. When he asked her whether she was going off with Brans-Hill, she laughed at him. Someone else had replaced Robbie in her affections, some older man, but she wouldn't say who."

"And the authorities think that the boy found out and killed her in a fit of jealousy? I can't believe it! What does he have to say?"

Sir Charles shrugged again. "He cannot be found. What is known is that the day following the murder, Robbie was treated by a doctor at one of the local hospitals for a knife wound that he claimed he had sustained in a brawl. Hear me out, there's more to tell. What looks bad for him is that Mlle. Daudet seems to have put up a fight before she was stabbed to death. A chair was overturned; there was blood on the wall. No knife was found, so the murderer must have taken it with him."

"That means nothing," said Jack. "That doesn't place Robbie at the scene of the crime."

"I know, but what is damning is that he seems to have gone into hiding."

Jack considered for a moment, then said, "Wouldn't he go to Ellie for help?"

"More than likely, but she is not here and cannot be questioned."

"What about Cardvale? Would Robbie turn to him?"

Sir Charles replied dryly, "I see you have not followed the history of the young Brans-Hills since their father died. Cardvale is all right in his way, but his wife is a Tartar. She was no sooner married to Cardvale than she practically turned them out of the house. There's no love lost there, so you see, Robbie might well become the prime suspect in the burglary of the Cardvale diamonds, as well. So far, the authorities don't know of his connection to Ellie, but if it becomes known, you can see how they will add things up, and she may be incriminated, too."

Everything within Jack rejected this line of reasoning. Certainly there was a mystery here that was more complex than he had first realized, but nothing would convince him that the girl he knew in that long-ago summer could be involved in a criminal act.

The ambassador went on, "You are no doubt wondering why I am telling you all this. Well, the fact of the matter is, I think Robbie did turn to Ellie for help. I think she spirited him out of harm's way when she left Paris. They'll be in England now, friendless and alone. My responsibilities keep me here, or I would go to them."

A sinking feeling settled in the pit of Jack's stomach. He knew where this was leading. The ambassador wanted him to take both Ellie and Robbie under his protection when he returned home. This was far more involved than he'd anticipated. It was no longer a simple case of looking up a woman he hardly knew.

He leaned forward slightly in his chair. "What is the legal position?" he said. "Can Robbie be forced to return to France to stand trial if it comes to that?"

"It's quite possible, especially in these sensitive times when we are trying to prove to the French that we are their friends."

"But he is a British subject. Doesn't that make a difference?"

"I know what you're thinking, that Wellington is commander of the army here and can decide Robbie's fate. But whether he will choose to intervene is debatable. All that aside, the boy cannot go through life with this infamy hanging over his head. He must clear his name."

Sir Charles set down his glass and rested his linked fingers on the flat of his desk. "Don't look so bleak. There are other suspects besides Robbie—Louise Daudet's other lover, for instance, the one who wanted to take her abroad. There is also her dresser, a young woman named Rosa, who, like Robbie, has disappeared without a trace. There may be others. All the same, it seems to me that Bertier—he is the chief of police—has already made up his mind that the lad is guilty. I don't see him exerting himself to chase down the other suspects. However, I have my own corps of men who can investigate the case— discreetly, of course. But I need to know what only Robbie can tell me. I need someone to question him, someone who knows the family well, someone like you, Jack."

"Easier said than done," replied Jack. "And with all due respect, sir, I don't think you understand how things were left between Ellie and me."

"Indeed?" Sir Charles sat back in his chair. The warmth in his smile had faded. "I understood you were coming here today to get her direction so that you could make your peace with her."

There was only one person who could have told the ambassador that, and that was Ash. "Lord Denison was here?"

"To take his leave of me before he returned to England. He has only just left."

Sir Charles got up. "However, if I'm asking too much of you—"

"Sit down, Sir Charles!" Jack rudely ordered.

There was a silence, then Sir Charles obeyed. "Yes," he said, "you feel the obligation as keenly as I do, don't you, Jack? Austen Brans-Hill and his wife Mariah were exceptional people. We can dismiss them by saying they were too unworldly to be of earthly use, but we know better."

Jack's tone was dry. "It was a privilege to know them, I'll give you that."

"They touched many lives for good."

"As I am well aware."

"Were it not for Dr. Austen Brans-Hill, I would never have made anything of my life. Correct me if I'm wrong, but I believe you could say the same."

Jack ignored the bait. "Just tell me," he said, "where I can find Ellie and what you want me to do."

In his rooms at the Palais Royal, Jack stood at the window that overlooked the courtyard. It was well past midnight, but there was still a throng of pedestrians below his window, coming and going, pleasure-seekers for the most part. The trouble with pleasure was that it was fleeting. There had to be more in life.

He made a small sound of self-mockery and, with glass of brandy in hand, ambled over to the chair in front of the fire. He was allowing Sir Charles's flowery eulogy of Dr. Brans-Hill to color his thinking. It made him wonder what the good vicar had done for Sir Charles to earn such high praise.

His own case was different. He'd failed his examinations. The good vicar had tutored him, then he'd passed with flying colors. There was nothing unusual in that. It happened to many young men at university.

Except in his case, passing his examinations had been a turning point. After that, there was no holding him back. Not that he had the makings of a scholar. It was something inside him that changed. He expected to succeed when he set his mind to something, and he did.

Dr. Brans-Hill had told him how it would be.

Yes, he felt the obligation, though not perhaps as strongly as Sir Charles. Now Robbie was the same age as he had been when he'd come under the vicar's influence.

Who was there to influence Robbie? Who would look out for the boy's interests?

Ellie?

Himself?

He didn't think he was up to it, but if he didn't do it, no one else would.

Chapter 7

London

Lord Cardvale was wishing that he'd ignored his wife's summons and escaped to his club. Her lovely features had hardened unpleasantly as she studied her reflection in her dressing-table mirror.

"When I told you," she said, "to rent a house in town, naturally I was thinking of Mayfair. Hans Town is home to lawyers and doctors and people of that class. I'd be ashamed to have my friends call on me here. The house is too small. The upholstery is shabby. As for the furniture, it belongs in a museum. Have you no taste, Cardvale?"

He replied mildly, "This was the best my man of business could find at such short notice. And it's only for another month, until the workmen are finished with our own house." The dull ache behind his eyes became more intense. "There was no pressing need to come home. We should have stayed in Paris until the house was ready."

She threw down her comb and swiveled to face him. "We couldn't stay and you know why. We became laughingstocks. My diamonds gone! And my betrothal ring! We know who the thief was, but did you take steps to have her arrested? Oh no. Your cousin Elinor can do no wrong."

"She had an alibi! Raleigh vouched for her. The authorities were satisfied."

"Well, I'm not satisfied!"

She pushed to her feet and stood before him, a beautiful woman, he conceded, but one who left him unmoved. That was the source of all their problems. They'd married for the usual reasons, he because he had a duty to his House, and she because she wanted security and a position in society. Neither was satisfied with the result.

He touched his fingers to his furrowed brow. "What are you saying, that you don't accept Raleigh's word?"

"I'm saying that your cousin may have had an accomplice. What if someone else stole the necklace and hid it where she could find it?"

"The hotel was searched and nothing was found."

"That doesn't mean anything. Maybe the search wasn't thorough. What we *should* have done was search Ellie's boxes before she left that last morning. Instead"—she threw him a withering look, then sat down at her dressing table and turned her back on him—"you gave her a purse stuffed with gold coins."

"It's the least I could do. She *is* my kinswoman."

"And I am your wife. Your first loyalty should be to me."

It seemed pointless to argue the merits of Ellie's character, that he'd known her all her life and knew she was innocent, so he merely remarked that he didn't know why she should bring this up now.

"I'll tell you why." Her eyes glowed with triumph. "I know something now that I didn't know then. Your other precious cousin, Robert, was in Paris at the same time. Ellie never mentioned it to Lady Sedgewick. Don't you think that's odd?"

"Who told you about Robbie?"

"Lady Sedgewick. I met her by chance the other day in Bond Street. They left Paris shortly after we did, and for the same reasons. They couldn't go anywhere but they were besieged by people asking them questions about the theft." Her quick smile was edged with malice. "Lady Sedgewick was telling me about her friend, Mrs. Dailey, whose nephew was in Paris recently with a friend. She asked Lady Sedgewick whether their paths had crossed. The nephew's name is Milton and his friend's name is—can you guess?—Robbie Brans-Hill! Of course, Lady Sedgewick had not met them, but she distinctly remembers Ellie saying that her brother was in Oxford at the time."

He was amused. "Young men don't go to Paris to mingle with their mother's friends. And I'd be surprised if Ellie knew Robbie was there. She would have sent him straight back to Oxford."

"I disagree. I think it adds weight to my suspicions. Robbie and Ellie could have been in this together."

He rarely lost his temper with her, and not only because he didn't like scenes. He was indifferent, and that made him immune to both her dislike and her temper tantrums, but this attack on Ellie was going too far.

In a voice that left her in no doubt of his resolve, he said, "I'd advise you to keep your suspicions to yourself. I mean it, Dorothea. If I hear one word from anyone about Robbie and Ellie being behind the thefts, we shall leave London at once and spend the season at Broadview."

Satisfied that he'd made his point, he walked to the door. "Don't expect me for dinner," he remarked casually, as though there had been no harsh words between them. "I'll dine at my club."

She waited until she heard his steps recede along the corridor before she vented her temper. Her silver brush was at hand. She reached for it and threw it hard against the wall. From the corner of her eye, she caught her reflection in the mirror. She hardly recognized herself—the hard eyes, the shrewish set to her mouth and features. This was what marriage to a man like Cardvale could do to a woman.

She'd learned the trick of mastering her emotions. All she had to do was bring past triumphs to mind. She closed her eyes and let her thoughts wander. The happiest day of her life was the day she had married Cardvale, not because she was wildly in love with him, but because she was the envy of her peers. It wasn't every day that a country squire's daughter ensnared an earl. She'd achieved everything she'd ever wanted—a position in society, a husband who gave her a free hand, and all the luxuries that came with marriage to a wealthy man.

Her little exercise wasn't working. The tension was still tight across her shoulders. Her neck was stiff. If she opened her eyes and gazed at her reflection, the same discontented woman would stare back at her.

She felt betrayed, displaced by Ellie Brans-Hill. Cardvale would not hear a word against his dear cousin. What did people see in her? She was a frump. She was eccentric. And she was a deceiving witch.

Vicar's daughter be damned! She was a born actress. Aurora. What decent woman would tart herself up and go gallivanting in the Palais Royal? A clever woman. She had almost snared herself a rich husband.

Even as a bride, she'd had to put up with Cardvale's cousins. He'd taken them into his own home before he married. She'd clothed them, fed them, provided for all their needs. No one could say that she had not done her duty. And what thanks had she got? None whatsoever. Ellie had soon come to see that there could not be two mistresses in Cardvale's house, so she had left with her crest lowered.

He wasn't the same man she had married. Once, he'd been putty in her hands, now, he was revealing a core of steel she hadn't known existed.

Perhaps if she'd had a child things would have been different. Her hold over him would have been absolute. But she had never wanted children and had taken steps to make sure that she never had any. Now he never came to her bed, and it was too late to change her mind.

The thought of children made her shudder. Her own mother had borne eight children, and she wouldn't wish that on any woman. Mama was old before her time. When she was in the family way, she couldn't go anywhere, couldn't receive visitors. She'd lost interest in her looks and in her life outside the walls of her own little domain. Her children grew up despising her.

No. The lack of children was not something she regretted. What she regretted was befriending a conniving young woman who had managed to turn her husband against her. Ellie Brans-Hill had been a thorn in her side from the start.

She thought about Ellie for a long time. Gradually, the knot of tension across her shoulders relaxed.

When she had finished with Ellie, Cardvale would despise his cousin. No one would have a good word to say about her. At last, people would know her for what she was. Her eyes glittered in anticipation of Ellie's downfall, and not only Ellie's, but her brother's as well.

But before that happened, she had things to do, plans to make.

She'd learned more about Cousin Ellie than she'd told Cardvale. Ellie had lodgings somewhere in the district of Marylebone. But Robbie's whereabouts remained a mystery.

On that thought, she got up and walked to the bellpull.

The young maid who answered the summons was small and slender. Her color was dark and her eyes oddly blank. Cardvale had brought Morri into their home when he found her half-starved and roaming the countryside. She was slow-witted and spoke little. Cardvale suspected that she'd escaped either from the workhouse or from a cruel master, and hoped to place her in service in a suitable home. However, when Dorothea discovered that her credit had risen considerably among her acquaintances because she'd given a home to a half-wit, she'd kept the girl on.

Morri's duties were not onerous. She fetched and carried for her mistress. She ran errands. Her most valuable asset, in Dorothea's eyes, was that Morri served her with slavelike devotion.

"How nice you look in your uniform, Morri." Dorothea's smile was warm and inviting, the gracious mistress. It had taken some persuading to get Morri into a bath and away from the rags she wore. "I told you that you would get used to it in time and I was right."

Morri's eyes warmed a little and she dipped a curtsy. "Yes, ma'am."

"Are the other servants treating you well?"

The maid bobbed her head.

"Good. Good." Dorothea lowered her voice. "Has his lordship left the house?"

"Yes, madam."

Dorothea smiled encouragingly. "You know Mr. Derby, don't you, Lord Cardvale's man of business?"

Morri nodded.

"I want you to tell me when he comes in. But don't tell the other servants I want to see him. It's our secret, Morri, yours and mine. Understood?"

Morri's eyes glowed. She loved secrets. "I won't say anything."

"Good girl. I knew I could count on you."

Five minutes later, Morri returned. "Mr. Derby is in his office," she whispered.

Dorothea allowed another five minutes to pass before she left her dressing room.

Paul Derby was young for the responsible position he held, only in his mid-twenties, and had stepped into the job when it was vacated on his father's death. The elder Derby had been a slow, plodding fellow and cautious to a degree. Paul was the opposite. He was ambitious and eager to advance his career.

His rise to power was matched by an equal decline in his regard for his master. In Derby's opinion, Cardvale was incompetent not only as a master of a large estate but also in his role as a husband.

Since all Derby's actions were governed by self-interest, he had cultivated the favor of the real master of the house, Lady Cardvale. In the last several months they had become lovers.

His temporary office in this rented house was at the back, a small room that was not much bigger than a broom closet. There was a desk, two chairs, and a stack of ledgers on the floor. His sleeping quarters, until the house in Cavendish Square was ready, were with the servants in the attics, which made it difficult for the lovers to carry on their affair—difficult, but not impossible for two determined people.

"Paul," said Dorothea as she entered his office, "I want to talk to you about the renovations to the Mayfair house."

"Yes, your ladyship."

The bold, crooked grin made her breath quicken. "Shut the door," she said.

He did as she asked, then turned to face her, his bold eyes raking over her.

Now that no one could hear them, she dropped the pretense of discussing renovations. "I've learned," she said, "that Cousin Ellie has taken lodgings somewhere in Marylebone. If we find her, she'll lead us to her brother."

She did not bother to elaborate. He wasn't stupid. He knew what to do.

He nodded slowly. "Leave it to me."

She trembled in sudden arousal. Here was a man who knew how to be a man. She sensed danger, power, and a will to match her own. He didn't disappoint her. He locked the door.

His hands dragged her skirts up to her thighs. His voice was low and thick. "I can't think when you look at me like that."

"Then don't think." She held his head steady with both hands and nipped his bottom lip with her sharp teeth.

When she released his lip, he said hoarsely, "What about your husband?"

"Morri will tell me when he comes in. Don't worry, Paul. I've thought of everything."

Cardvale did not remain long in his club. There were too many interruptions, too many acquaintances eager to hear about Paris and the theft of the diamonds. All he wanted was to be left alone with his thoughts.

He walked for a time, through St. James's Park then along the riverbank, uncaring of the cold or the chill wind whipping at his coat. By chance, he came to a livery stable. He knew then where he wanted to be. Though he had horses in his own stables nearby, he rented a mount and set out for Hampstead. This way, Dorothea need never know where he'd been.

The cottage had been in his family for generations. "Cottage" didn't do it justice. It was a two-story brick building, unpretentious but pleasing in its proportions, set in an acre of grounds. In the summer, the gardens would burst into bloom and the air would be fragrant with the scent of honeysuckle, roses, lilacs, and flowers he could not name. On this wintry day, the bare branches and black earth seemed to reflect the barrenness of his own life.

After stabling his horse, he entered by the front door. There were no servants. The caretaker was a man from the village who kept an eye on the place and came in every other day to check on things. Everything looked clean and tidy, at least to Cardvale's uncritical eye. Unlike his wife, he was not troubled by a little dust.

This was the cottage he had offered Ellie just before she left Paris. It was a house that would suit a doctor's family or a vicar's family and was more to his taste than the palatial grandeur of Broadview, the family seat in Hampshire. That he preferred this house should have told him, he thought, something about the kind of girl he should have chosen to be his wife. One made choices and one paid the consequences.

The fire was set in the grate in the front parlor. He lit it after procuring a glass of brandy, then pulled a chair close to the fire and let his thoughts drift.

It occurred to him that he should sell the house. He had no use for it now. There were no younger brothers to provide for, no sisters and no children. But the thought of selling it was almost frightening. The house was his sanctuary.

He dwelled on that thought and his reflections

brought him to a decision. He wouldn't sell the house. He would open it up and find someone congenial to share it with.

His thoughts shifted to Ellie. For his peace of mind, something would have to be done about her.

Chapter 8

All that Sir Charles could tell Jack before he left Paris was that Ellie kept on rooms in a lodging house in Henrietta Street and whenever she was between jobs, that was where she stayed. That wasn't far out of his way, thought Jack, because Henrietta Street was on one side of the Oxford Road, and Park Street, where his town house was located, was on the other. He could walk the distance in less than thirty minutes.

He might have chosen to go on to Oxford, no great distance from town, to talk to her brother first, but on thinking it over, he decided that that would only raise Ellie's hackles or, at the very least, alarm her. It would be better for all concerned if he won her over so that she would be on his side when he talked to her brother. She must see, or be made to see, that Robbie had to clear his name.

Win Ellie over? He had no idea how he was going to do that, in spite of Sir Charles's confidence in his powers of persuasion. If charm and sincerity didn't work, he might be forced to resort to threats. But that had never worked with her in the past. Why would it be different now?

His thoughts were fanciful, but at least they amused him on the five-hour drive from Dover.

He made it to London in good time, and arrived in Park Street just as his grandmother and his half sister, Caro, were returning from a trip to the shops. He was surprised to see them, because they were supposed to be fixed in the country until the London season got under way in another month. This was an event that Caro was looking forward to, having just turned seventeen, and she would be making her comeout, with all its attendant parties and balls. He wondered whether the anticipation had been too much for her to contain, or whether there was another reason for this change of plan.

After the customary kisses and greetings, he asked about Frances, his late brother's widow, and learned that she was visiting her parents in Wales and wasn't expected to return for another fortnight. This was a great relief. Frances in town, especially during the season, was a trial. She expected him to dance attendance on her at every event.

As soon as the coats and packages were put away, his grandmother led the way to her private parlor where a cheery fire was burning in the grate. The dowager told the footman to bring the tea tray, and as soon as he'd shut the door on them, Caro weighed right in.

Dark eyes glinting, she said in her mischievous way, "Well, where is the bride? Oh, don't say you are still a bachelor! A lady's maid! That's just what this family needs!"

Jack's smile was a tad thin. "It never ceases to amaze me how gently bred ladies delight in wallowing in slime. I should have washed your mouth out more often when you were a child."

"That's no answer!" protested Caro.

His grandmother, whom he usually counted on to

keep Caro in check, was gazing at him with the same avid interest as his sister.

Jack's lids lowered. "So, that's why you've come up to town, to quiz me about an unfortunate incident that's been blown out of proportion. What have you heard?"

His grandmother answered. "That you and Ellie Brans-Hill spent the night in your rooms at the Palais Royal."

"I rescued her from a riot." One shoulder rose in a negligent shrug. "That's all there was to it."

Caro said, "Well, at least you had the good sense not to offer for the woman."

There was something in Caro's voice, something about her words, that did not sit right with Jack. "Let me correct any misunderstanding that may have arisen. Miss Brans-Hill is not a lady's maid but a respectable lady's companion."

Caro pounced on that. "If she is respectable, what was she doing at the Palais Royal when she should have been in her bed?"

"Caro!" remonstrated the dowager. "You must not believe everything your friends tell you. I'm sure there is a reasonable explanation for this storm in a teacup." To Jack she said, "Caro's friend is with her parents in Paris right now, you know, the Courtney girl? That's how your sister knows so much. I'm sure most of it is nonsense and you can clear up any misunderstanding."

"Thank you," said Jack, "but I have nothing more to say except that the reason you need not wish me happy is that the lady would not have me at any price."

The dowager and Caro were shocked into silence. Her ladyship recovered first. Her voice was as dry as scorched paper. "I hope that was a lesson to you! There are, thank the Lord, a few women who have more in their heads than the desire for wealth and position. It's no more than I would expect of Ellie. Even as a girl she was sensitive to any act of condescension. I don't say it's a good thing, but—"

Caro burst out, "Grandmamma, are you saying you *know* the girl?"

The dowager's lips flattened for a moment, then she smiled. "I knew her before she was born, and that's all you're going to get out of me until I have a chance to talk to Jack. Caro, you must have things to do to get ready for tonight?" To Jack, she elaborated, "I'm hosting a musicale for a few of Caro's close friends and their parents. My friends will be there, too. This will be something of a test for your sister, to see how she acquits herself among so many distinguished people. General Baird will be there and—"

"General Baird," said Caro with feeling, "is an old fogy. All he ever talks about are battles. I never know what to say to him."

"Try flirting with him," replied her brother unsympathetically. "That always works with old fogies like me."

Her ladyship said, "I hope you'll join us tonight, Jack?"

"Unfortunately," he said, glad of a genuine excuse to avoid the boredom of listening to Caro and her friends sing and play the evening away, "I shall be otherwise engaged."

"With Miss Brans-Hill?" Caro enquired coyly.

"Caro!" Her ladyship pointed to the door. "At once."

With a soulful sigh, Caro got to her feet. "There's more than one way to skin a cat," she said darkly, and left the room just as the footman returned with the tea tray.

"Set it down here, Simpson," said the dowager.

As his grandmother poured the tea, Jack relaxed against the back of his chair and studied her. He thought that, for a woman approaching her eightieth birthday, she looked remarkably youthful. As she was the first to admit, however, her girlish complexion was an illusion and came from the pots and bottles on her dressing table. But no art supplied the intelligence in her vivid blue eyes or her supple frame. The dowager believed in keeping both her mind and body active to stave off old age and, in her case, it seemed to work.

He automatically accepted the cup and saucer she offered him. Though he wasn't partial to tea, the ritual was familiar and brought back many happy memories. He had often shared his grandmother's tea tray when he was a boy. Her rooms had always seemed warmer than any room in the house, a place of refuge where he could speak his mind without fear of scorn being heaped on him. He used to think that Grandmamma was his mother's mother, and so unlike his father that even yet he could detect no resemblance, either in looks or manner.

When his mother died, Grandmother had moved into the ancestral home to fill the void, but not for long. His father remarried, a cold woman made in his own image, and any warmth in the house quietly evaporated. They had a daughter, Caroline, but her birth hardly made a ripple on his father's life. He, Jack, was in much the same case as Caro, except that he came under a harsher discipline. But the harshest discipline of all was reserved for the firstborn, Jack's brother, Cedric.

"What are you thinking?" asked the dowager.

"What?"

"You looked quite grim for a moment there."

"I was thinking of Cedric." He took a sip of tea. "I went to war and came home unscathed. It hardly seems fair."

"Cedric was never very strong. He had a weak chest, just like your mother. In fact, he was like your mother in many ways." A fleeting smile touched the dowager's lips. "He tried so hard to be what your father wanted. It never works, you know. You can't change nature."

Her blue eyes dimmed and she gave a soft sigh. Look-

ing up, she went on, "Your father was his own worst enemy. He was a lonely man and had no one to blame but
himself. But enough of this. I know you did not come
into my parlor to satisfy *my* curiosity. So, what is it you
want to know?"

No fool, Grandmother Rigg. He couldn't help smiling.
"I want to know as much as you can tell me about Ellie
Brans-Hill and her family. And don't get your hopes up,
Grandmamma. I didn't tell Caro everything. Not only will
Ellie not have me at any price, but the feeling is mutual."

The dowager's look sharpened. "You wouldn't care to
elaborate on that remark?"

"No, I would not!"

"I wouldn't like to think Ellie's feelings were hurt."

"Grandmamma..."

"Oh, very well. But at least you can tell me why you
want to know. I mean, if you're not going to marry the
girl, why bother?"

He didn't want to mention Robbie's troubles, so he
told her as much of the truth as he thought was prudent.
"I feel obligated to make sure that she doesn't suffer hardship because of that foolish adventure." His grandmother
looked surprised, so he explained. "For old time's sake,
you might say."

"What will you do?" The dowager took a mouthful
of tea.

"I shall call on her this afternoon."

And promptly choked on it.

"If I can discover where her lodgings are."

When she could find her breath, her ladyship said irri-
tably, "That won't help, just the reverse. I'm delighted to
see that you have a conscience, but let someone else act
for you, for Ellie's sake. It's all right for a man. The rules
don't apply to him. But a woman's reputation must be

blameless, and Ellie's reputation is already tarnished, except to those who know her."

The point was well taken, but there was no way he could get out of it, even if he wanted to, which he did not. His mission was to take Robbie Brans-Hill under his protection until Sir Charles had time to investigate the case. Ellie's help was crucial.

"I'll be discreet," he replied.

She gave him a look that told him his credit had fallen by several notches in her estimation, then she gazed into space as she gathered her thoughts. "What can I tell you about Ellie and her family? Not a great deal. You should know them as well as anyone. You stayed with them for a summer, did you not?"

"Whose idea was that?"

"Mine, of course. Your father was looking for someone to tutor you, and I suggested Dr. Brans-Hill, and not only because of his reputation as a scholar. I thought it would do you good to get away from your father and stepmother for a while. Cedric was different. He never argued or defied your father."

Jack remembered those days very well, but only when someone brought them to his attention. He'd done too much in his life to give those painful memories more than a passing nod.

"You once told me that the Brans-Hills were all fey," he said.

"Did I? Well, I must have meant it as a compliment. I thought you enjoyed your time at the vicarage."

"I did."

"And your father was happy with the result. Dr. Brans-Hill gave you the confidence to master Greek and Latin grammar. He said that that was all you needed—confidence in your own ability."

It was on the tip of his tongue to say that what gave

him the will to master Greek and Latin grammar was the strong desire to put a know-everything, precocious chit in her place.

There was a spark of speculation in his grandmother's eyes, so he replied easily, "Yes. Brans-Hill was a remarkable man. What happened to him?"

"He died when Ellie turned twenty. I remember it well because I was at his funeral. Her mother died some years before. Now, that *was* a shock, because Mrs. Brans-Hill was so much younger than her husband. He married late in life, you see. Shortly after his death, Ellie and her brother went to live with a distant cousin on her mother's side, Lord Cardvale. He is a sad case, bullied first by his mother and now by his dragon of a wife. Ellie didn't stay there long."

"Your memory is very sharp."

"Yes, for an old fogy, I do very well."

Jack laughed. "What about the son? What can you tell me about him?"

"Robert? Not very much. He was a well-mannered child, but not so clever as his sister. Ellie is devoted to him, or so I hear. In fact, she spoils him."

"Grandmamma, you're a fount of information. How can you possibly know all this?"

She gave a tiny shrug. "I have friends with whom I keep up a correspondence. You may remember Agatha Lyle? Her youngest grandson attends Oxford and knows Robbie quite well. Then there's Lady Elizabeth Stuart, the ambassador's wife. She keeps me abreast of the latest news, too."

Jack's interest sharpened. "Lady Elizabeth knows Ellie?"

"Through Sir Charles. Ellie's father was his godfather and took a keen interest in him when he was a boy. In fact, they were very close. I think he would do more for Ellie and her brother, but she's too proud to accept charity."

That explained a point that had been puzzling him. Now he understood why Sir Charles took such a keen interest in the Brans-Hills.

What was wrong with the woman? Everyone wanted to help her, but she would have none of it.

His grandmother said gently, "No one likes to be the poor relation, Jack, as you should know as a younger son."

After a moment, he smiled. "There's not much gets past you."

"Oh, I wouldn't say that. You still haven't told me what happened between you and Ellie."

He said pleasantly, "Nothing happened, Grand-mamma. As I told you, I rescued her from a riot. I have no idea what she was up to at the Palais Royal."

His grandmother nodded. "I believe you, dear, but I doubt if the world will."

He sighed. "Just tell me where she lives."

Ellie adjusted the flame of the lamp to help her read better. Even during the daylight hours she was forced to light a candle. In her basement lodgings, no rays of the sun ever penetrated the small windows.

She didn't regard these lodgings as her home, but as a temporary stop between jobs. It was cheap, it was convenient, and a place to store the few pieces of her mother's furniture that she wished to keep. And whenever she felt the walls close in on her, Hyde Park was only a short walk away. She did a lot of walking in Hyde Park, but not today. After reading the letters that had come by the second post, the spark had gone out of her. So she'd made herself a cup of medicinal tea and had a good cry.

She couldn't stop reading those letters. Even now, she

sat down at the table, smoothed them open, and read them again. Each said much the same as the one before it. The position for which she had applied was no longer open, thank you very much, et cetera, et cetera. And this without ever having interviewed her.

Her name said it all, though she'd changed it back to Elinor Brans-Hill. It was uncanny how, in less than a fortnight, word of her disgrace had spread far and wide.

"At least," she said aloud, "to the wealthy families in London who can afford to pay for a lady's companion."

She was doing it again, talking to herself. What she longed for was a little dog. She could speak her thoughts aloud then, and not feel that she was losing her mind.

She would have to start over, only this time she would look for a position outside of London, where no one had heard the name of Ellie Brans-Hill. But not too far away. She wanted to be close to Robbie.

Sighing, she spread open that morning's newspaper and ticked off anything that was of interest.

There was an advertisement for a housekeeper for a doctor with a growing family in Hampstead.

Hampstead. That jogged her memory. Her cousin had offered her a cottage in Hampstead after that dreadful debacle in Paris. Had Dorothea been a different kind of woman, she might have been tempted to accept. But Dorothea was not going to be given another chance to make her life miserable. Poor Cardvale.

She read the advertisement again.

A growing family. That meant she would be part housekeeper, part nursemaid. It was not up to the standing of her former positions, but it would be better than this dismal place.

Or she could become Aurora again. One night as Aurora would solve all her problems.

Or it could turn into a fiasco like the last time.

Before she was carried away on that train of thought, she put a mark with her pencil beside the advertisement for Housekeeper in Hampstead. It had much to recommend it—fresh country air and it was close to London.

The kettle on the hob started to whistle. She got up and made a fresh pot of tea. When the tea was infused, she poured out a cup and added a teaspoon of a home-brewed cordial—her mother's recipe—to calm the nerves. This potent brew was intended for her landlady, who had trouble sleeping at night. A healthy young woman should have no need of such aids.

The thought only added to her depression.

She sat in front of the smoldering fire, warming her toes, sipping the hot tea. The hearth was the warmest spot in the house. Her bedroom-alcove, concealed by a curtain, was as cold as a tomb.

She sighed and sighed again. She'd been down before, but never this low. Aurora's money was gone, all used up on Robbie's debts. And Robbie wasn't the boy he'd been before that trip to Paris. He'd told her that he'd been attacked in a brawl. What he had not had the courage to tell her until they were England was that he'd been *suspended* from Oxford for failing that Greek examination. That's why he'd embarked on a jaunt to Paris. Silly young fool! Now he had to work like the devil to pass that examination or he'd be sent down, expelled, and that would be the end of his university education. Meantime, he was convalescing with Uncle Freddie in Chelsea. She'd visited him once, but the visit was anything but satisfactory.

She sipped her tea slowly, reliving in her mind the conversation she'd had with Robbie on the journey home to England. Milton had vouched for everything her brother told her. But they were both ill at ease and evasive. They'd told her the truth up to a point, but it wasn't the whole truth.

What in heaven's name was going on?

Maybe she was imagining things. Living like a mole in this underground tunnel didn't help. This was her permanent residence and, when she'd first found it shortly after leaving Cardvale's protection, she'd been delighted. It was cheap; it would do to store all her mother's furniture. But best of all, these rooms had a door that led directly outside to a flight of stone steps that came out on Henrietta Street. It was quiet and private, and her comings and goings need concern no one but herself.

Now her lodgings seemed too close to the street for comfort. No doubt it was her imagination acting up again, but she was beginning to hear footsteps late at night, coming and going on those stone steps. She was so unnerved that she'd taken to leaving a candle burning in front of the grate after she had gone to bed, hoping that the light would scare off intruders.

Her hand jerked. She heard them now, footsteps descending her stairs.

There was a rap on the door. "Ellie?" Her landlady's voice. "There's a gentleman to see you. Your solicitor."

She put down her cup and sucked air into her lungs. At this rate, she'd end up in Bedlam. Rising, she hurried to unlock the door. The darkly handsome gentleman who filled the doorway was not her solicitor.

"Jack!" She was astonished. "What brings you here?"

He bowed, prompting her to mind her manners. She curtsied.

"Forgive the intrusion," he said, "but I have a letter here that urgently requires your attention." To the landlady, he said, "I usually conduct business at a more civilized hour in my chambers but, as I said, the matter is urgent."

This little speech amused Ellie. Mrs. Mann would not care how late a gentleman called or whether the proprieties were adhered to. She mothered all her lodgers, and her one ambition for Ellie was to see her settled with some nice young gentleman. She would be only too happy to relax the rules of propriety.

Jack was looking over her shoulder, taking inventory of her dingy, cramped quarters. She wasn't ashamed, but her cheeks burned all the same. She had the strangest urge to shut the door in his face, but Mrs. Mann would be shocked. Even now, she was making faces at her, telling her to smile, be nice to the gentleman.

The decision was taken out of her hands. Jack dismissed Mrs. Mann with a charming bow, advanced into the room, forcing Ellie back a step, then he closed the door. His stillness unsettled her, and she wondered what he was thinking.

He was trying not to let his feelings show. He'd heard of genteel poverty, but this was pitiful. It was also unnecessary. For one thing, she had good friends who would have been happy to help her out. Sir Charles was one. Cardvale was another. All that aside, he knew that she'd had a large sum of money at her disposal before she left Paris.

He caught the unguarded look in her eyes and saw something he had never expected to see. She looked beaten.

As though reading his mind, she straightened her shoulders and lifted her chin. "I'm just getting over a cold," she said, then she dug in her pocket, found her handkerchief, and blew her nose.

He spoke gently. "You should have told me in Paris who you were. I would have helped you, Ellie, both you and Robbie. I don't know why I didn't recognize you."

She had to blow her nose again. "Thank you, but we don't need your help. We can manage."

His gentler feelings evaporated. "Oh yes, I can see how

well you manage. What happened to the money you had in Paris? Obviously you did not spend it on yourself, so what did you... ah, it would have to be Robbie."

Her face tightened. "You are not my solicitor. I owe you no explanations. So why are you here?"

"Shall we sit down?"

"Not until I know why you are here."

Her tone did not improve his temper. As curt as she, he replied, "I am here at the request of Sir Charles Stuart. He has asked me to intercede on your brother's behalf." He removed a letter from his pocket. "This letter from Sir Charles will explain everything."

He held the letter aloft, just out of her reach. "Now can we sit down?"

She huffed when he took her by the elbow and led her to a chair. Only when they were both seated did he hand over the letter. She broke the seal and began to read. Before she got to the end, all the color had washed out of her face.

"Well?" he said finally.

She was staring blankly at the letter. Her voice was faint. "I knew Robbie was in some kind of trouble, but I never imagined anything like this." She looked up at him. Color surged back into her cheeks and she said fiercely, "It's not true! It can't be! Robbie doesn't have it in him to hurt anyone. He's a good boy." Her voice cracked, but that did not stop her. "Sir Charles says that the evidence against him is circumstantial. Well, I say they should look elsewhere for their murderer!"

"I'm sorry. I should have realized your brother wouldn't confide in you."

"There's nothing to confide! He's innocent."

"I believe you. So does Sir Charles. We are not your enemies. We want to help you."

She raised the letter and read it again. "The actress,"

she said. "I remember now. They were looking for her lover." She lifted her eyes to his. "That couldn't be Robbie."

"Are you sure?"

No. She wasn't sure of anything except that her brother wasn't a murderer. She said, "Sir Charles says that you'll explain what must be done. What does he mean by that?"

He shifted slightly, edging forward in his chair. "I must see Robbie and take a statement from him, a deposition that will be notarized by my attorney. In the meantime, Sir Charles is making his own inquiries into the death of Louise Daudet. Robbie isn't on trial. There are other suspects in the case, and, all going well, the deposition I send Sir Charles will clear your brother's name."

She said quietly, "You won't send him back to France?"

"Absolutely not. I give you my word on that."

When she sniffed again, he reached over and took her hands in his. "There's no need for such anguish," he said. "Robbie will be under my protection, do you understand?"

She nodded, but kept blinking.

He looked at her hands and frowned. "You're as cold as ice."

She tried to tug her hands away. "It's my own fault. I let the fire burn too low. If you give me a moment, I'll fill the coal scuttle."

"Where is the coal kept?"

"In the coal cellar, of course." She sounded cross. "It's no hardship."

He knew that the coal cellar would be in one of the outhouses and was about to offer his services when he had a better idea. He wanted to take her away from this depressing little house to a place where there was light and warmth, a place where they could have a bite to eat and a glass of wine to wash it down.

He got up. "There's an inn just off the Oxford Road, the Windsor Arms. It's warm and comfortable and only a short walk away. We can talk there."

When it looked as though she might argue, he added, "I'm hungry, Ellie. Starved, in fact. And I don't suppose you have any strong spirits in the house. Beer would do."

"Certainly not!"

"Not even a medicinal brandy?"

"I can offer you a medicinal cup of tea."

He grinned. "Thank you, but tea brings me out in a rash."

A grudging smile curved her lips. "Oh, very well." She got up. "But you do realize that if people see us together, there will be more talk."

"They won't see us. It's dark outside, and the Windsor Arms is in a quiet cul-de-sac. Now get your coat."

She gave him a speaking look, picked up a candle that she lit from the lamp, and took the few steps to the curtained alcove that served as the bedchamber. He noted that Sir Charles's letter was still in her hand and surmised that she would want to read it again without him looking over her shoulder.

His grin faded the moment she disappeared behind the curtain. He found the gloom in this little dungeon that Ellie called "home" too chilling to shake off. He had promised Sir Charles that he would do what he could for both Ellie and her brother, and he was more resolved than ever to keep his promise. And the first thing he would do was move Ellie into more congenial surroundings. In his mind's eye, he saw a room with light streaming through long windows. There would be a French door leading into the garden, and an apple tree . . .

His lips twitched when it came to him that the room

he was thinking about was the front parlor of the very house where Ellie grew up, the vicarage. A happy house, as he remembered.

She shouldn't have to live like this.

There was an open newspaper on the table. He picked it up, curious to see what had caught her interest. It was opened at the section that displayed advertisements. Several were marked, all of them for positions as governess or lady's companion, with one exception. It was for a housekeeper in a busy doctor's house in Hampstead.

His face was grim when he set the paper aside.

On the same table were several letters neatly stacked. He hesitated for a moment, but his conscience was easily soothed. His only motive was to serve Ellie's best interests. With that in mind, he picked up the letters and began to read them one by one.

They were short and to the point, but the tone adopted by each writer made his temper burn. He scanned the signatures, memorizing names, resolving that should any of these hapless people ever cross his path, he would teach them the manners they so evidently lacked.

When he heard her step, he quickly put the letters back as he had found them.

The first thing she looked at when she entered the room was the stack of letters on the table. The last thing he wanted was to crush her pride, so he nudged the newspaper as though he'd just set it down.

"I see Amherst has been appointed ambassador to China," he said. "Poor Amherst. That's what comes of slighting the Prince Regent." More seriously, he added, "Things aren't hopeless. You're not alone now, Ellie. I promised Sir Charles I would help you and your brother, and I keep my promises."

Her air of fragility vanished and a spark of amusement

lit her eyes. "Careful, Jack," she warned. "We both know what happened the last time you promised to help me."

"Ah, but that last time you kept secrets from me. Had I known then that you were the insufferable little show-off who once lectured me on the difference between gerunds and gerundives, I would have dunked you in the water trough as I did then. Aurora, indeed!"

She smiled. "You remember that day?"

He nodded. "Precocious brat!"

"I wanted to impress you. I just went about it the wrong way."

"Well, you can impress me now. No more secrets, Ellie. You must tell me everything."

She said quickly, "I haven't agreed to anything."

"No, but you will."

Her head came up, but after one glance at his unsmiling face, she did no more than heave a sigh. "Shall we go?"

As he followed her up the stairs, his thoughts were far from pleasant. There was the problem of Robbie, but for the moment it was the problem of Ellie that disturbed him more. As a boy, he'd teased her mercilessly, but in spite of it, there had been a casual kind of affection between them. It was still there, which was why he wanted to see her settled in a nice, comfortable home of her own, not barely subsisting in a place like this.

That was something else that disturbed him—the tone of the letters she had received from prospective employers. It was only now that he was coming to realize how steep a price she had paid for her jaunt to the Palais Royal. No. Not the Palais Royal so much as the time she had spent alone with him. News had traveled fast.

The thought that turned in his mind was how he could put things right for her.

Chapter 9

The proprietor of the Windsor Arms was well-known to Jack. McNaught had served under him in the Spanish Campaign. It was Jack who had loaned McNaught the money to put a down payment on the inn. He wasn't a regular, but from time to time he dropped by to compare notes with his former comrade and was always assured of a warm welcome.

As a result, he and Ellie were shown to the inn's coziest private parlor, and dined on the finest the Windsor Arms had to offer. Ellie ate sparingly at first, but as she sipped from her glass of wine—a glass that Jack kept topping up—she began to relax and her appetite returned.

This was better, thought Jack. A roaring fire in the grate, plenty of candles lit, and that scared-rabbit look gone from Ellie's eyes. She had color in her cheeks and seemed genuinely pleased to be with him. He felt the same about her. The wine had mellowed them both.

An unbidden picture flashed into his mind: Aurora—or was it Ellie?—her body soft and pliant beneath his hands and mouth.

He suppressed the image, looked at his glass of wine and set it aside. Ellie didn't notice the gesture. Her eyes were half closed as she savored the last spoonful of her dessert, a creamy syllabub flavored with brandy and sherry. Fascinated, he watched the tip of her tongue lick the vestiges of flavor from her lips.

He closed his mind against the next erotic image and concentrated instead on the mission Sir Charles had given him. His train of thought was broken when Ellie thrust her empty glass under his nose and asked for more. He obliged, but sparingly.

He'd just learned that Robbie was not attending university, that he had, in fact, been rusticated for a term. She seemed happy to have someone to confide in, except that she still hadn't told him where Robbie was hiding out.

He left that for the moment and focused on what her brother had told her to explain away the wound he had to have doctored in Paris.

"So," he said, "Robbie told you that he'd been in a brawl?"

She nodded. "I saw the wound myself. He is lucky to be alive. There is no way he could have returned to university even if he hadn't been rusticated. Only ..." She swallowed a mouthful of wine, "Only, I suspected something was wrong before you gave me Sir Charles's letter." She added quickly, "That doesn't mean I think he is guilty of murder!"

"Then what do you think it means?"

"Now that I've read the letter, I think he's frightened. That's why he's in hiding." She blinked as a thought came to her. "That's why he won't come to town to see me. He doesn't want to be found."

This was the opening he had been waiting for. "Which is why it is imperative that I see Robbie at once. He must clear his name. And he'll feel much better knowing that he has powerful friends."

She nodded doubtfully.

"So where is he, Ellie?"

The words seemed to be dragged out of her. "He's staying with Uncle Freddie in Chelsea." Then hurriedly, "And that's all I'm going to tell you until I speak with him myself."

She touched his hand briefly. "Don't think I'm ungrateful. But I'm all Robbie has. He doesn't know you as I do. I don't want him to think I've betrayed him."

She fell silent for a moment and stared blindly at the wine in her glass. Heaving a sigh, she went on softly, "Our parents died when he was very young, so he missed all the advantages that I had. He can hardly remember our mother. If he is a little wild, I'm to blame. Whenever he got in a scrape, I was there to bail him out of it. I should have been harder on him when he was a child. But he is all I have. I can't fail him."

There was a discreet knock on the door and the waiter entered to clear the table. "Take the wine away," said Jack, "and bring us coffee."

Ellie held on to her wineglass. "Thank you," she said. "The meal was delicious."

The waiter beamed. "Mr. McNaught will be pleased to hear it, miss."

This small exchange brought a memory to his mind. Jack remembered Ellie as a child, rebuking him for taking the servants for granted. He'd made game of her by thanking the vicarage maid-of-all-work for every small service she performed until the poor woman wouldn't enter a room if he were in it.

When they were drinking their coffee, Jack said, "Do you trust me, Ellie?"

She replied casually, "I've always trusted you, Jack."

Her answer pleased him. "Good. Tell me, then, how did you come to have such a large sum of money when I rescued you from the mob?"

She chuckled. After a careful sip of wine, she said, "Aurora is a gamester, Jack. She made a killing at the gaming tables at the Palais Royal."

His patent disbelief made her laugh. "I assure you, it's true. I'm surprised you didn't work it out."

He retorted, lecturing her, "I find it incredible that a daughter of the manse, a daughter of Austen Brans-Hill, would stoop to play cards, much less enter a gaming house."

Her smile faded. "I had to have the money to pay off Robbie's debts, don't you see? Oh, I know gaming is wrong and Papa would be scandalized, but it would be more wrong to abandon Robbie to his creditors, wouldn't it? He would have been locked up in a French prison with no hope of returning to England. I couldn't let that happen."

Her answer did not placate him. "What if you had lost? You would be in the same position as Robbie."

"Oh, I never lose." Her glass was empty and she was looking around for the wine bottle. "I'm a virtuoso."

"What the devil is a 'virtuoso'?"

"Someone who never loses at cards." Not finding the wine bottle, she contented herself with the cup of tepid coffee. "Like my Uncle Ted. My mother's cousin. He was the black sheep of the family, but he was fun." She gazed into space with a dreamy smile on her face. He was beginning to wonder how much wine she had ingested.

"What became of him?"

"Mmm? Oh, he was barred from playing at all the respectable gaming houses because he always won, so he started patronizing gaming dens. That's where he was cheated out of everything he owned. No honest gambler, however good, can beat a cheat. He never played again, except with me."

"An 'honest gambler'!" He wasn't amused. "I tremble for you, Ellie. You're too innocent for your own good. What if someone had tried to take your winnings away from you? It does happen."

She retorted, "I know it's risky, but it's a risk I'm willing to take. Besides, I never go alone. This time Milton was with me. He's Robbie's best friend."

"Where can I find Milton?"

She blinked at his harsh tone. "He's gone back to Oxford. Why do you want to know?"

He felt his jaw tightening. "I should like to ask him why he left you unattended in the Palais Royal."

She replied loyally, "He was gone for only a few minutes when the riot erupted. You can't blame Milton for the riot."

"He shouldn't have taken you gaming in the first place."

"Don't blame Milton. He did it as a favor to me. Anyway, it's not as though I go gaming every week. I only do it out of necessity, when Robbie is in trouble or I can't find work."

"As now?"

She shrugged. "I have a little to tide me over, but it may come down to it yet. You need not look at me like that. If you have a better solution to my problems, I'd like to hear it."

Evidently, she meant to go on in the same old way for a boy who, in his opinion, deserved a whipping. "The solution to your problem was staring you in the face. You should have married long since, then your brother would have had the benefit of your husband's hand to guide him." He kept the rest of his thoughts to himself, that the boy would have benefitted from a swift kick to his backside.

She glared at him. "And where was I to find a husband? They do not grow in flower gardens, you know, ripe for a lady's plucking. I'm proud to say I work for my living. I've been a governess, a chaperon, a lady's companion, a tutor in Greek and Latin, and I may take up a position as a housekeeper-cum-nursery maid. This is not the way to meet eligible gentlemen, I mean, the kind of men who would marry a girl with no dowry and the burden of a brother to raise."

She put her cup and saucer down with a *thunk*. Her nose wrinkled. "Besides all that," she said, "I find the thought of marriage for such mundane reasons singul..." She couldn't get her tongue around the word, so she went on seamlessly, "...unattractive." Humor kindled in her eyes and she rested her chin on her linked fingers. "You, of all people, should understand how I feel. I don't see you hurrying to the altar, yet you have more reason to marry than I. You have to secure the succession by producing the next generation of the House of Raleigh. Thankfully, that's your burden, not mine."

She looked at him with a question in her eyes.

He didn't share the novel idea that had just passed through his mind, that if they married, his problems would be solved and so would hers.

Frowning, he said, "You won't be accepting any offers of employment unless I give you permission."

Her eyes glinted with hostility. "And what am I going to live on?"

"I'm coming to that. I want you and Robbie to live with me until this business is cleared up. I gave Sir Charles my word that I'd protect you both, and I mean to keep my word."

Her voice was like a squeaky wheel. "Have you lost your

mind? Live with you? Oh, wouldn't that give all the fat tabbies something to talk about!"

"I don't mean without a chaperon. My grandmother and sister will be there. Their presence will put a stop to the gossipmongers."

"Hah! That shows how little you know! I can't afford to get into any more trouble."

His words came slowly, deliberately, making his point. "There's something here that makes me uneasy. I can't put my finger on it. But my instinct tells me we're not out of the woods yet. I'd be happier if you were both under my roof."

That got her attention. She stared at him for a moment, then said, "I thought when Robbie sends his statement to Sir Charles, that would be the end of it. Do you think he's in danger?"

"I don't know, but until I do, I want you where I can keep an eye on you."

She pressed a hand to her eyes. "I don't know what to do for the best."

"Ellie!" There was just enough bite in his voice to get her attention again. When her eyes lifted to meet his, he went on, "You said you trusted me. Did you mean it?"

Her brows rose. "The last time you asked me that, you broke my heart."

He sat back in his chair. "When was that?"

"When you left to go back to Oxford. Don't you remember? In Mama's parlor? I told you that I would wait for you, and you told me that one day I'd meet someone my own age and live happily ever after. *Trust me*, you said. Well, you lied."

His lips quirked. "We're the same age now, more or less."

She yawned behind her hand.

He put down his cup and scraped back his chair.

"Come along, Ellie. Time to go home. We'll talk tomorrow when you're more yourself."

She wasn't drunk, but she was not quite steady on her feet. He smiled into her wine-glazed eyes. "Something tells me you're going to hate me in the morning."

She spoke slowly, getting her tongue around each word. "I promise never to hate you, Jack. Trust me." And she giggled at her own jest.

Because she wasn't fit to walk, they took a hackney to her lodgings. She wanted to doze but couldn't get comfortable, so first she removed her bonnet and tossed it aside, then she sprawled halfway over him, settling herself into him as though he were a lumpy mattress.

At first he was amused, then not so amused as she squirmed in his lap. The cobblestones didn't help. He found himself gripping her bottom to hold her steady. The fragrance in her hair was as delicate as wildflowers. Fresh. Tantalizing. Tempting him to taste her. Erotic images filled his mind. He subdued them by focusing his thoughts on how he would deal with her brother.

There was a thin bead of sweat on his brow when the hackney pulled up outside her door. His hands were not gentle when he hauled her out of the coach. There was a foolish smile on her face.

"Where's your bonnet?" He was as surly as sin.

She pointed to the hackney. Sighing, he reached in and snared it. When he emerged, Ellie was already at the iron railings, feeling her way down the stairs to her door. He paid off the driver and went after her.

He could hardly see his hand in front of his face when he caught up to her. "You should have a lantern outside this door," he said. "It's as black as pitch down here."

"There *is* a lantern, but I keep forgetting to light it. Why are you so cross?"

He shoved the bonnet on her head. "I'm cross because... oh, hell!"

Since she was already using him as a prop to keep herself from keeling over, it took very little pressure to draw her into his arms. She didn't struggle; she didn't say a word. Their breath mingled, their lips touched. That's all he wanted, one little taste.

Oddly enough, one little taste wasn't enough for him. The flavor of wine slipped from her lips to his, filling his mouth, stealing his breath, his reason. He couldn't help himself, he wanted more. His hand slid onto her nape, dislodging her bonnet. His thumb felt a pulse. The beat of her body found an answering beat in his own.

When she made a small incoherent sound, he raised his head. His breathing was difficult. Between breaths, he got out, "You're a dangerous woman, Ellie Brans-Hill."

Her response was to loop one arm around his neck and drag his head down to renew the embrace. His arms clamped around her. Their lips clung. The leap to raw passion was instantaneous.

He used his weight to pin her against the wall. Since she wasn't protesting, he unbuttoned her coat and took his fill of her, handling her possessively. Her breasts were small and plump, their crests hardening as he brushed the pad of his thumb over each one in turn. Her mewling sounds drove him on. His hands traced the flare of her hips, splayed wide on her abdomen and moved lower. She was pliant in his hands, pliant and receptive...

And inebriated.

He groaned in protest. He didn't want to think about that now. He was so close to taking her. He was hard and hungry, and she was soft and willing.

And innocent and inebriated.

With a savage curse, he dragged himself away from her. His breathing was ragged. She was panting. Gritting his teeth, he said, "I think you had better go in before I do something we'll both regret."

It took a moment for her breathing to even. "Oh, my" was all she said, and she began to slide down the wall.

Though he was afraid to put his hands on her again, he had no choice. He hauled her up and steadied her with his hands on her waist. "Did you hear me, Ellie?" His eyes had adjusted to the dark, but all he could make out was the shape of her face. He couldn't read her expression or tell what she was feeling.

He could feel her stiffen under his hands. "Don't worry, Jack! I won't tell anyone! You won't be caught in the marriage trap."

"That's not what I was thinking. And if you knew what was in my mind, you'd get yourself into your house and lock the door on me."

Another lengthy silence, then she said with a lilt in her voice, "That's the nicest compliment I have ever received."

"You're tipsy, Ellie. Foxed, in fact. You've had too much to drink."

"No." She yawned. "It's Mama's cordial. It's quite powerful."

"What 'cordial'?"

"My medicinal tea. I did offer you a cup."

"Medicinal—? What's in it?"

"The usual, and Mama's secret ingredient."

Now he was beginning to understand why she was so affectionate and confiding, so much like Aurora.

"Where is your key?"

It was in her reticule, which, along with her bonnet, had fallen to the flagstones in the heat of the moment. He unlocked the door and ushered her inside.

"I'll get a candle lit," she said.

"No, I'll do it."

Her voice fairly crackled. "I am perfectly capable of lighting a candle."

"Fine, but watch your step."

He wasn't going to stay for more than a few minutes, just long enough to see her settled. As he carefully edged his way toward the table, he heard flint strike iron as she tried to get a spark going to light the candle. The room smelled of mold, but there was another scent that was familiar, yet out of place.

Brandy.

The instant the thought occurred to him, Ellie screamed and something fell heavily to the floor. Jack started forward and launched himself at a shadow that was moving toward the door. He was checked by a blow from a heavy object that caught him hard across the shoulder. As he stumbled to his knees, the shadow vanished through the door. He could hear the tread of feet racing up the stone stairs.

"Ellie!" he cried out.

"I'm all right ... just ... I can't get up. I think I've sprained my ankle."

He felt his way to Ellie. "Where is the tinderbox?"

"On the floor somewhere. I dropped it when he slammed into me."

He found the tinderbox and got a candle lit. Ellie let out a soft cry. Someone had ransacked the room. Every drawer was open. Books and papers littered the floor. The curtain to the bed alcove had been torn down and clothes were tossed in a heap on the bed.

"Maybe I wasn't imagining things after all," she said. "Maybe someone *was* trying to break into my house."

He looked at her. "When was this?"

"Not long after I got back from Paris. I'd hear footsteps

at night on the stairs, so I'd leave a candle on the hearth to scare them off."

Jack's face was stern. With candle in hand, he examined the door, then the window. "The window has been forced," he said. "That's how he got in."

He found the instrument he'd been struck with. It was the poker. After returning it to its nook beside the grate, he turned his attention on Ellie who, by this time, was sitting in a chair. Kneeling down in front of her, he examined her ankle. She could wiggle her toes, but winced when she tried to put her weight on her foot.

"Stay right there," he told her. "This won't take long."

He took the stairs to the street. Though it was late, Henrietta Street wasn't exactly a backwater, and there were a few pedestrians there, but no one he recognized, and no one who looked suspicious. It's what he'd expected.

He was in luck. A hackney drew up beside him. "Looking for a ride home, guv'nor?"

"I am. Give me a minute and I'll be right back."

He returned to Ellie. "We're leaving," he told her. And to convince her, should she need persuading, "It's too risky to leave you here. He may come back."

Her eyes went wide and she pressed a hand to her chest. "Why would he do that?"

"He was looking for something, Ellie, and I don't think he found it. I think he was waiting for you."

She shook her head mutely.

He was losing patience. "I'm not taking 'no' for an answer."

Suiting action to words, he swooped down and hoisted her up in his arms. A searing pain tightened the shoulder his assailant had struck, but he ignored it.

As he moved toward the door, she cried out, "I'll need my night things."

He didn't stop. "I'll take care of that."

"And . . . who is going to tell my landlady?"

"I'll take care of that, too."

"But . . . where are you taking me?"

"To my house in Park Street."

That stopped the flow of questions. Smiling grimly, he maneuvered her through the door.

Lady Raleigh, the dowager, along with her granddaughter, Lady Caro, paid their departing guests the compliment of seeing them off in person. Her ladyship wasn't sorry to see them go. She was well aware that the curious among them had delayed their departure in hopes of coming face-to-face with Jack. It seemed everyone knew about the unfortunate episode in Paris, and wished to know all the salacious details. It was only when she ordered her footmen to stop dispensing wine and brandy that her guests had taken the hint.

There was a crush of people in the spacious marble hallway, laughing and jostling one another while they waited for their respective carriages to be brought round. All things considered, her ladyship was pleased with Caro's first party. Her musicale had given her granddaughter and her friends the opportunity to practice the social graces in a small, intimate setting before the rigors of the season were upon them. That was something she was at some pains to impress upon her granddaughter. There was more to the season than the pleasure of being with one's friends. The old biddies, such as herself, had to be won over, because the old biddies were an influential lot. They were the ones who sent out the gilt-edged invitations or whispered a word in a hostess's ear to ensure that someone's name was added to the invitation list.

Or they could do the reverse.

Caro had not neglected her duty to her grandmother's friends. Even General Baird had come in for his share of attention. As for the veiled questions about Jack and the Brans-Hill girl, Caro had followed her grandmother's advice and replied to every question with words to the effect that Miss Brans-Hill was a friend of the family. They'd known her as long as Caro could remember. It was all a misunderstanding.

This was not to protect Jack's reputation so much as Ellie's. The dowager had always had a soft spot for Ellie and regretted now that she had not kept up with the family. That would be put right, for she had made up her mind to seek Ellie out and use her influence not only to restore Ellie's character, but to find a suitable candidate for her hand in marriage.

She was ticking off in her mind young clergymen of her acquaintance who might do for Ellie, when the front door was thrown open and Jack strode in with a young, disheveled woman held high in his arms. There were a few gasps from guests who did not immediately recognize Lord Raleigh in the disreputable gentleman who stared at them with hard eyes.

"What the devil!" He made a small sound of impatience, then went on rudely, "I thought you'd all be gone by now."

The woman in his arms was more polite. "How do you do?" she said. "I am Miss Brans-Hill and it's not what you think. I was attacked in my own home, and if Jack had not been there to rescue me, I don't know how things would have turned out."

This little speech evoked a few titters and one guffaw from a gentleman whom Jack silenced with a look.

Ellie? Thought the dowager. *Of course. It has to be Ellie.*

As though they were spectators at a play, all followed

Jack with their eyes as he carried Miss Brans-Hill to the stairs and began to climb them.

General Baird edged closer to the dowager and whispered in her ear, "All a misunderstanding, eh, Nell? So what do you say now?"

The dowager's lips curved in a complacent smile. "What I say," she said, "is that all young, eligible clergymen can go to the devil."

Chapter 10

Ellie was hoping it would turn out to be a bad dream, but when she opened her eyes and saw the strange room, she knew it was all true. Not only had she embarrassed herself horribly by practically forcing herself on Jack, but she'd also embarrassed his grandmother in front of all her guests.

How on earth could she live this down?

She couldn't. All she could do was follow Mama's advice. Put it out of her mind. Pretend it had never happened. But Mama was referring to social gaffes—when a lady tipped over her glass or used the wrong spoon at a formal dinner. She'd never anticipated a situation like this.

The *clink* of a glass had her hauling herself up. Her stomach swam, her head churned. A kindly-looking maid with a big white apron covering her ample frame was smiling down at her.

"Good morning, miss," she said. "Her ladyship said I should persuade you to drink this before you get up."

Ellie automatically took the glass the maid offered

and put it to her lips. The potion was milky and tasted like chalk. She knew what it was. Her mother used to make it up for the blacksmith's wife to give to her husband when he'd drunk himself stupid every Saturday night.

"It was Mama's cordial," she told the smiling maid. "I think I must have made a mistake with the recipe." She tried to hand the glass back.

The maid nodded but refused to take the glass. "Drink all of it," she said, her sympathetic smile at odds with her words.

Ellie accepted her fate meekly, knowing that this was only the beginning of her penance.

When the maid pulled back the drapes, Ellie blinked rapidly. It took her eyes a moment to adjust to the sun's rays. The clock on the mantel told her that she'd slept half the day away.

"Time to get up," said the maid cheerfully. "There's a bath waiting for you in the dressing room."

No one had ever waited on Ellie before, not even when she lived with Cardvale. She'd had servants bring her tea or bring messages from her employers, but no one to fuss over her as though she were a fine lady. She wasn't sure that she enjoyed the experience, but she gave in without a murmur. She didn't want to cause any more trouble.

The servant's name, she learned, was Webster. Ellie had been around enough stately homes to know what that meant. When a servant's surname was used, he or she was high up in the hierarchy. Scullery maids, boot boys, and stableboys went by their Christian names. In her own home, Webster would have been addressed as *Miss* Webster as a mark of respect. Since this wasn't her home and she wanted to leave it without causing a ripple to mark her presence, she remained uncharacteristically mute. Mute and thoroughly miserable.

As she listlessly soaped herself, the maid gave her a running commentary on what had been happening while she slept. The master had reported the burglary to the authorities. They were to make enquiries, but were not hopeful of finding the culprit. Meantime, her boxes with all her clothes and toiletries had been brought round and she wasn't to worry about a thing.

Her boxes had been brought round? She didn't like the sound of that. She didn't want to accept anyone's charity, and she doubted that the dowager would welcome her with open arms, not after the spectacle she had made of herself last night.

She remembered Jack's grandmother quite well. *A character*, Papa had called her ladyship, but he'd said it with a smile. She'd been liberal with her purse and liberal in her views. But she might not be so liberal in her views when she realized she had taken a lady with a slightly tarnished reputation into her home.

"Her ladyship," Ellie said. "Does she know that my boxes are here?"

"I don't rightly know." Webster paused as she held out a warmed towel to wrap Ellie in. "She said nothing to me about boxes before she and Lady Caroline went out."

"Her ladyship went out?" This sounded ominous.

Webster smiled. "To the linen drapers, to buy muslins and cambric for the gowns that a young lady requires for her first season. They should be home soon."

"And Lord Raleigh? Did he go with them?"

"No. As soon as you're ready, you are to meet with him in the library."

It didn't sound as though Lady Raleigh had taken umbrage or left in a temper. That was a good sign. On the other hand, she'd been left alone with Jack, without a chaperon. Did that mean her ladyship thought her reputation was beyond repair?

In her present frame of mind, nothing satisfied her.

When Ellie was dressed and had partaken of a little thin gruel to settle her stomach, the maid pulled the bellrope to summon a footman to take her to the library. As she waited, she took stock of her surroundings.

Not only was this a lovely room, done in yellow and gray, but it had a splendid vista over Hyde Park. There were two long windows, and she stood at one looking out.

Park Street was right below her window. This was, she knew, one of the most prestigious streets in Mayfair. There were no houses on the other side of the street to obscure her view of the park. The winter landscape of trees denuded of their leaves had its own stark beauty. But there was more than nature to admire. There were carriages of every description, pedestrians, riders—most of them fashionable people—who had come to see and be seen. This was the time of day she usually avoided when she walked in the park. She wanted to avoid meeting anyone she knew. She wanted to shield herself from pitying glances or the other sort.

When the footman arrived, she took a last look at her reflection in the cheval mirror. She was wearing her best wool gown, a green twill with buttons to the throat and long sleeves. Her fiery mane was tamed into a knot and pinned to the crown of her head. She was the picture of decorum. No one looking at her could possibly mistake her for the wild woman of last night, who had to be carried up the stairs.

As she followed in the footman's steps, she repeated her mother's litany. *Don't make a fuss. Put it out of your mind. Pretend it didn't happen.*

He was standing by the window, looking out on the park. He turned at her entrance and motioned her to an armchair by the fire, then took the chair next to hers.

She found his scrutiny unsettling, and his closed expression daunting. The thought that he was deliberately trying to intimidate her stiffened her spine.

"Thank you, yes," she said, "I slept very well. And you?"

A swift smile crinkled the corners of his eyes. "I'm not surprised you slept well. Tell me, Ellie, how much laudanum did you add to your mama's cordial?"

So much for Mama's litany. "Just a few drops. How did you know there was laudanum in it?"

"I found your cup of medicinal tea when I went to your rooms this morning. Don't you know that wine and laudanum don't mix?"

"I do now. I can't think why Mama set such store by that cordial. It's a recipe for disaster." Not wishing to explain her unguarded remark, she went on quickly, "The maid tells me that there's little chance of catching the man who broke into my house."

"That's what the authorities think."

"And you? What do you think?"

He took a moment to stretch out his legs. "I'm not convinced," he said quietly, "that the attack on you was a random burglary gone wrong."

She spoke slowly, trying to make sense of his words. "Not random? Why do you think that?"

"A number of reasons." His shoulders lifted slightly. "Tell me, Ellie," he went on, "what would you expect to be missing after your house was robbed?"

"Well, everything of value would be in the walnut box I keep on top of the dresser—my mother's silver combs, an Egyptian cameo, a pearl ring with earrings to match. Oh yes, and Cardvale's leather purse with nine or ten guineas still left in it."

"You forgot the silver bracelet with the scroll that says 'Annie.'"

"My grandmother's bracelet." She sat back in her chair. "You mean, you've recovered everything? That's wonderful."

He shook his head. "Nothing was taken. The box was on your bed, with everything turned out on the bed pane."

"Oh." There were shades of meaning here that her aching head couldn't make sense of. "That doesn't say much for my few precious treasures, does it? What did he expect to find—the Cardvale diamonds?"

Something shifted in his eyes and she said quickly, "That was a joke! You know I couldn't possibly have taken them because I was with you!"

A ghost of a smile flitted across his face. "I wasn't thinking of the diamonds. As you say, you were with me when they were taken. Could there be something else?"

"Like what?"

"Anything of value that I haven't mentioned?"

She shook her head. "Nothing that comes to mind."

"Perhaps it's not valuable except to you. At any rate, we'll know more when we go to your rooms and you have a chance to take inventory."

He was watching her with an expression that was oddly calculating. "What are you implying, Jack? What is it you're not saying?"

Again, that tiny, enigmatic shrug. "I thought perhaps that your brother might have given you something to keep for him."

"Robbie?" Her head jerked up. "Are you accusing him of something? And anyway, how would a burglar know that my brother had given me something?"

"You work it out."

She said slowly, "It would have to be someone who knows Robbie and knows me, too. No. I can't believe it. It was a random burglary, nothing more."

"Possibly, but I don't like so many things happening at once." He braced his arms on his thighs and leaned toward her. "First Louise Daudet is murdered, then the Cardvale diamonds are stolen, and now this robbery that isn't a robbery. You see what connects these events? You and your brother. Nothing else, or nothing we know about."

She swallowed a small constriction in her throat. "If you're trying to frighten me, Jack, you're succeeding."

"I hope you mean that."

"I meant afraid for Robbie."

"Now, *that* I can believe. Perhaps now you'll see why I want him here where I can keep an eye on him. And the sooner I question him, the safer he'll be. Agreed?"

She nodded automatically, not sure what exactly she was agreeing to.

"Splendid." He got up. "And now for something to settle your stomach and chase the fog from your brain."

He went to the sideboard and returned with two pewter tankards. "What is it?" she asked doubtfully, as she accepted one of the tankards.

"Jack's cordial." He grinned hugely. "The antidote to Mama's cordial."

Her thoughts were too chaotic to argue with him. She took a sip and wrinkled her nose. "It's bitter." She took another sip, then said, "I know what it is. It's ale!"

He was still grinning. "And you'll feel much better after you drink it. Ellie, among gentlemen, it's a well-known remedy for the morning after a night of dissipation. Drink it."

She didn't want to talk about nights of dissipation, so

she covered her embarrassment by following his example. When she set the empty tankard down, she screwed up her face as though she'd swallowed a lemon.

"Satisfied?" she asked.

"No. But I intend to be." Hands clasped loosely together, he said, "How much do you remember about last night?"

She thought of Mama's litany and said as complacently as she could manage, "I remember the burglary and getting into a hackney, but everything else is...ah... hazy."

His eyes lit with laughter. "Fortunately for you I'm a gentleman, so I won't mention how you tried to seduce me. That's our secret."

Though her cheeks were red, she glared at him. "Thank you."

"But it's what happened next that has landed us in quicksand up to our necks."

She could feel herself sinking into the quicksand. "Go on," she said cautiously.

"You introduced yourself to my grandmother and her guests and implied that you were my mistress."

She was aghast. "I did no such thing."

"Ellie," he said gently, "you told them I was in your rooms when you were attacked. What else were they to think, especially after our history, except that I had set you up as my mistress?"

Her voice rose by several notches. "You could have told them the truth."

He said impatiently, "If we try to defend ourselves, it will only make us look guilty. But you see what a coil we're in? My grandmother is ready to disown me and, I daresay, when Cardvale gets to hear of it, he'll be demanding satisfaction at twenty paces."

Her head ached. Her stomach churned. His cordial

wasn't working. "You can't fight Cardvale," she said weakly. "He'd be no match for you."

"Then there's your brother. I'm sure he will call me out, as well."

She blinked. "A moment ago you were talking about helping Robbie, not dueling with him. Besides, I know you don't duel with boys. I heard you say so to that young Prussian soldier in the Café des Anglaises. So why are you trying to alarm me like this?"

He gave a short laugh. "I hope you *are* alarmed, because this latest imbroglio is not so easily got out of as the one in Paris."

Headache or not, she was beginning to resent the inference that she was entirely to blame for the monstrous muddle they were in. "I did not ask to be brought here! You should have taken me back to the Windsor Arms or, better yet, never have allowed me to leave it."

"Hindsight," he replied laconically, "won't help us, either."

"Then what do you suggest?"

His brows climbed. "Isn't it obvious? We must marry, and the sooner the better."

Her head stopped swimming, her stomach stopped churning, her heartbeat slowed. She was shaking her head as she groped for words. Finally she got out, "Is this a joke?"

"Now why should you think that?"

"Because," she replied waspishly, "the Jack Rigg I met in Paris said that he wouldn't have me at any price. You droned on about better women than I who had tried to ensnare you and failed, yes, and you called me some nasty names, too. You said that nothing and no one could possibly persuade you to marry me. How is this different?"

He spread his hands. "In Paris, I didn't know you were the daughter of my tutor. I thought you had deliberately tried to compromise me. This time around, I'm to blame, and I always pay my debts." He leaned toward her. "Ellie, we must marry. You had better make your mind up to it."

This cold-blooded proposal sent shivers along her spine. Here was another recipe for disaster. When she had command of her voice, she said, "And what if, after we are wed, you meet the love of your life? What will you do then? Thank me for ruining your chance for a happy life?"

"'Love'?" He looked startled. "I don't believe in love, and I wouldn't thank you if you handed it to me on a silver platter."

She looked at him curiously.

"Don't let your imagination run away with you." A glint of amusement shone in his dark eyes. "I'm not talking from personal experience but from what I've observed of the human race."

"Then your observations," she retorted, "are different from mine."

His response was as clipped as hers. "My philosophy is to make the best of things and try to right the wrongs I've done. If there was another way, don't you think I'd take it?"

She was astonished to find that tears were stinging her eyes, and put it down to the effects of her night of dissipation. She couldn't possibly be hurt by anything this jaded cynic said to her. And that's what he had become, a jaded man of the world. It was time to set aside all those girlish fancies she had once entertained about that long-ago romantic figure. That boy no longer existed.

To be fair, cynic or not, he was not without honor. He was trying to make things right. But two wrongs did not make a right.

Striving to be reasonable, she said, "I think you're exaggerating the problem. Our situation is far from hopeless. If your grandmother supports our story and—"

She stopped when he suddenly got up and came to stand in front of her. When he boxed her in with one hand on either arm of her chair, she strained away from him. There was a reckless glitter in his eyes that reminded her of the boy she once knew.

"Now you listen to me," he said. "Our wishes don't matter. It has gone beyond that. I won't have it said that I ruined Dr. Brans-Hill's daughter. I won't have my family ostracized because people believe I've taken my mistress to live with me in my own home. I refuse to put my life in jeopardy by fighting duels with your cousin and your brother. And I absolutely refuse to take responsibility for casting you off to fend for yourself. Oh yes, I know you can't find employment."

This last remark was the most wounding of all. She didn't want him to think of her as a suppliant depending on his goodwill. She wanted . . . she didn't know what she wanted.

Cheeks burning, she said, "You've been reading my private correspondence."

He ignored her response. "I haven't finished yet. Don't you know the kind of insult you're leaving yourself open to? A fallen woman is fair game for any man. If you won't think of yourself, think of your brother. You'd be seriously compromising his chances of success in whatever profession he enters. Is that what you want?"

She felt so battered by his tirade that she could only answer faintly in the negative.

"Well, then, make the best of it."

She wanted to sound aloof, but succeeded only in sounding like a fractious child. "I don't want to marry anyone. I like my single state."

He stared at her for a moment or two, brows furrowed, then straightened. "If that's your only objection, let me set your mind at rest. I have never forced myself on an un-willing woman, as you know very well."

Though her cheeks burned, she met his gaze squarely. "I'm set in my ways. That's what I meant. I don't have to answer to anyone but myself."

That quick smile was back in his eyes, but this time it lingered. "It seems that we shall both have to make sacrifices, doesn't it?"

There was a knock at the door and a footman entered.

"What is it?" asked Jack, annoyance lacing his voice.

The footman cleared his throat. "Lord Cardvale wishes to speak with you, my lord."

Ellie sucked in a breath.

"Well," said Jack, "that didn't take long, did it?" To the footman, he said, "Show him in, show him in."

When Cardvale entered, Jack was at the sideboard pouring out three glasses of sherry. His greeting to Cardvale was effusive. "Come in, come in. I can't tell you how glad I am to see you."

Cardvale, on the other hand, was white about the mouth. He spared Ellie one glance, then advanced toward Jack. Ellie knew exactly what was on her cousin's mind. It was just as Jack had predicted. He was going to challenge Jack to a duel.

She jumped to her feet. "Cardvale," she cried, "you're just in time to wish me happy." She joined Jack at the sideboard, gave him a brilliant smile, and picked up two glasses. Her cousin seemed to have had the wind knocked out of him.

She crossed to him and offered him a glass. "You're the first to know. Lord Raleigh and I are going to be married. Won't you drink a toast to our future happiness?"

Jack joined her and slipped a possessive arm around her waist. "Yes, Cardvale. Wish us happy."

Cardvale seemed unconvinced, so Ellie hastened to

reassure him. "You and Dorothea must come to the wedding."

"And when," demanded Cardvale, "is the happy event to take place?"

Ellie could feel Jack stiffen by her side. The hostility between the two gentlemen fairly crackled.

"As soon as you like," Jack threw out in a challenging voice.

Ellie hardly knew what to say to smooth things over. It was beginning to seem that, marriage or not, a duel was inevitable.

Just then the door opened and a lady whom Ellie recognized as Jack's grandmother entered. Behind her was a dark-eyed young woman with glossy dark curls. The older woman looked radiant; the younger was sullen.

"Well?" said her ladyship, ignoring everyone but her grandson. "Don't keep me in suspense."

Jack laughed. "It's all settled," he said. "Ellie has consented to be my wife."

For the next half hour, Ellie's smile was set like plaster. If she stopped smiling, she knew her jaw would crack. Everyone congratulated Jack and wished her happy. Cardvale seemed to come round and went so far as to propose the toast. But it was her ladyship who added an air of festivity to the occasion. She, at least, was genuinely pleased with how things had turned out.

As she pretended to sip her sherry, Ellie studied each person in turn. The dowager glowed with happiness; Jack was putting on a good face; Cardvale was reserved, and Lady Caroline was as stiff as starch. She wondered about Robbie. How would he greet the news of her impending marriage?

She hadn't meant things to go this far. Perhaps, when she was feeling more herself, she would devise a way out of this dilemma. Meanwhile, she smiled and laughed in all the right places and gave the impression that she hadn't a care in the world.

Cardvale wasn't fooled, as she discovered when he asked if she would show him out. When he had donned his coat, and the porter had retreated to give them some privacy, he turned to her with a smile.

"You know, Ellie," he said, "you're not alone in the world. You and Robbie are the only blood relatives I have left. I want you to know that if ever you are in trouble, you can turn to me."

This little speech brought a tightness to her chest. She knew he meant it. He'd said much the same when her father died. But he was married to a witch. Dorothea would not be as generous or as welcoming as Cardvale.

She touched his hand briefly, trying to convey some affection, though it was hard to show affection to a man who was so reserved. "I shall never forget you said those words to me," she said, knowing that she would never take him up on his offer.

Before she could withdraw her hand, he surprised her by clasping it firmly. "I mean it, Ellie," he said. And just as though he could read her mind, he went on, "I know you would never share a house with Dorothea, and I wouldn't expect you to. But that cottage in Hampstead is still vacant. If you want it, it's yours."

Now she felt guilty. She'd always felt slightly contemptuous because Cardvale would not stand up to his wife. She was beginning to see that he was so generous that it would be only too easy to take advantage of him.

She returned the pressure of his handclasp. "Thank you, Cardvale, but you've got the wrong impression about my marriage to Jack." She wanted to take that anxious look from his eyes, so she stretched the truth. "I think I've loved him since I was an adolescent girl and he was my father's pupil. I can't believe how lucky I am."

On impulse, she kissed his cheek. He looked surprised, but not taken aback. He patted her shoulder, congratulated her again on her good fortune, and left the house.

She remained standing in the hall lost in thought. Cardvale, she was thinking, did not look well. Living with Dorothea was taking its toll. Before his marriage, he was considered a prize in the marriage mart. A handsome young man who was both wealthy and titled could be forgiven his quiet and reserved nature. It had been years since she'd heard him laugh.

She should have kept up with him, in spite of Dorothea. It's what her mother would have done. He seemed... lonely.

Sighing, she turned toward the stairs. Jack was watching her from the gallery, his hands curled around the banister. He was unsmiling.

"What did Cardvale want?" he asked when she came up to him.

"Oh, just looking out for my interests." She smiled to make light of it.

Jack did not smile. He tucked her hand into the crook of his arm. "Too late now," he said. "You have *me* to look out for your interests, and not only yours but Robbie's, as well. Never forget it."

Two gentlemen in one day offering to take care of all her burdens. Things didn't look quite so black anymore.

Chapter 11

She was quiet on the drive to Chelsea, her mind dwelling on first one problem then another, the same problems that had kept her awake for half the night. Jack had been right about the break-in, at least in one respect. Nothing had been taken. This morning, they'd gone to her house so that she could check things over. She had meticulously gone through every drawer and cupboard, and though Jack had put some things back in the wrong places, everything was accounted for, even her mother's letters and recipes and the items in her medicine box.

There was one thing, however, that was not as it should be. One of the candles had burned down to a stump. Her assailant must have been in the house for some time, either searching for something by the light of the candle or waiting for her to return.

Then what? What was she supposed to know or have in her possession that anyone could want?

The murder of Louise Daudet, the theft of the Cardvale diamonds, the break-in at her house—she couldn't forget Jack's words, but she found it hard to believe these events were connected to Robbie or to herself. Either they were random events or the connection must be through someone else.

She flinched when a hand closed over her arm.

"You're shivering," said Jack. He adjusted her shawl to cover her shoulders. "You're not still suffering the effects of Mama's cordial, are you?"

He was attempting to jog her out of the doldrums, so the least she could do was smile. "There's nothing wrong with Mama's cordial. I told you, it was the wine. Taken together, they're a recipe for disaster."

Her smile faded. *Recipe for disaster.* The words were becoming a cliché, she'd thought of them so often in the last little while—Robbie's trip to Paris, Aurora's jaunt to the Palais Royal, Mama's cordial, and now this unholy match with Jack. When would her run of bad luck end?

He was quick to sense her mood. Reaching for her gloved hand, he squeezed gently. "Listen to me, Ellie," he said. "Forget the fact that this marriage has been foisted upon us. When you think about it, it's not such a bad idea, is it?"

The last remark was rhetorical, so she didn't reply.

"Well, then." He let out a breath and smiled. "From a purely practical point of view, this marriage will serve both our interests. You are looking for employment and I'm offering it to you. As my wife, your duties will not be onerous. You'll have a home of your own, plenty of pin money to spend as you will, and a position in society."

Her tone was dry. "And what do you get out of it, Jack?"

"Why, I get you, Ellie, and it so happens that you suit me very well."

She treated this remark with the skepticism it deserved. "I'm all ears," she crooned.

He chuckled. "I mean it. I can talk to you as one intelligent person to another. You won't expect me to whisper sweet nothings in your ear. You won't demand my attendance at every function, or fly into a rage if I as much as look at another woman. You know that I must marry, if only to provide my line with an heir, and, as I've said, I've yet to meet a woman who suits me half as well as you. This marriage is a *fait accompli*, so to speak. Can't we make the best of it?"

She had every intention of making the best of it, but this little speech hardly reconciled her to her fate. In fact, it did the opposite. She said crisply, "Providing you with an heir so that your line may continue doesn't appeal to me." She might have said more, that the role of a neglected wife was even less appealing, but she decided that that would only lead to more baiting.

He patted her hand. "I know. It doesn't appeal to me, either. But I don't think it will be too onerous a duty for either of us, not if past experience is any indication."

She snatched her hand away. "Don't be too sure about that, Jack. I won't be making a habit of drinking Mama's cordial. Besides, we have an understanding and I'm keeping you to it."

He gave her one of his slow, enigmatic smiles. "No more Mama's cordial," he agreed. "I think we can safely leave things up to Mother Nature, don't you?"

Her scowl told him what she thought of that idea.

"And no more long faces. For Robbie's sake," he added.

She nodded. "I'll be the soul of happiness."

Because Jack had not wanted his prize horses to be kept standing in the cold, they'd traveled to Chelsea by hackney instead of taking his coach. The village, though still quite pastoral, had practically become a suburb of London, as with each passing year the western boundary of the city expanded to meet it.

They reached Chelsea by mid-afternoon, passing first the Royal Hospital for Veterans, which now comprised the grounds of the once celebrated Ranleigh Gardens. After that, there was a long row of handsome Georgian houses that commanded a fine view of the river and, beyond them, Chelsea Old Church.

The house they finally stopped at was a two story, modest building a mile beyond the village. Its acreage was small and its orchard, like the house, in good repair. The sun was watery, the ground hard-packed, the lawn was brown, and the only greenery were clumps of holly bushes guarding the front door.

"Smile," Jack murmured as the front door opened.

Ellie smiled.

That brilliant smile was still on her face when the maid ushered them into Uncle Freddie's shabby, though warm and comfortable, parlor. Jack's first impression was that there were enough books here to equal his own library.

Ellie had told him that "uncle" was a courtesy title Frederick Wallace had earned when, as a young man, he'd served as her father's curate. Though their paths had diverged, the ties of friendship had continued. Wallace was retired now, a widower with no children, who devoted himself to scholarship and teaching.

The man who enfolded Ellie in a bear hug did not match Jack's idea of a cleric. Though his longish straggly hair was snowy white, Mr. Wallace possessed the physique of a pugilist, and Jack supposed it came from working outdoors in his acreage of gardens and orchards.

When the introductions were made and they were seated around the fire, Mr. Wallace sent the maid to put the kettle on for tea.

"Robbie shouldn't be long," he said in answer to Ellie's query. "He often goes out for a walk along the riverbank at this time of day, to clear the cobwebs from his mind."

Mr. Wallace's spirits seemed to flag a little, but whether it was because he was thinking of Robbie or for some other reason, Jack could not say. The lapse was momentary. He turned his attention to Jack. His eyes were measuring, but not unfriendly.

"Are you acquainted with Robbie, Lord Raleigh?"

Naturally, the old boy was curious about his presence here. Jack didn't suppose Ellie had brought too many fashionable young gentlemen to meet Robbie's tutor. She should have made their relationship clear from the start, and her failure to do so was mildly annoying. He was supposed to be a matrimonial prize. Not that he had ever wanted to be, but Ellie behaved as though he was just another courtesy uncle.

That would change.

"I know Robbie only by reputation," he said. From the corner of his eye he caught Ellie's glare and softened his observation. "That is to say, Ellie had told me all about him. However, now that we are to be related, I hope he and I shall be friends."

"'Related'?" Wallace looked from Ellie to Jack. He seemed incapable of making the connection.

"Ellie?" prompted Jack.

She rose to the occasion with a finesse that put Jack in mind of Aurora. No mention was made of the circumstances that compelled them to wed. She told the story that they had agreed on, that they'd known each other for years, and having met again in Paris, after a whirlwind courtship, had decided to marry.

Fortunately, not a whiff of the gossip had reached Mr. Wallace's ears, and his pleasure at hearing her news could hardly be contained.

When the excitement had died down, the conversation returned to Robbie.

Wallace smiled dryly. "I'm afraid," he said, "I haven't

been much help with his studies." He gentled his voice. "You see, Ellie, I don't think Robbie wants to return to university. Not everyone is cut out to be a scholar."

Ellie clasped her hands together and looked earnestly into Mr. Wallace's face. "Give him time, Uncle Freddie. He's at a difficult age. And he must get an education or all the professions will be closed to him."

Mr. Wallace sighed. "Now that he is on the mend, he is easily distracted. You may think Chelsea is a quiet backwater, but even here, there are temptations for young men."

Ellie sat back in her chair. "Not gambling!"

"Ah no." Mr. Wallace's cheeks went rosy. "I've said too much already. I don't like to carry tales out of school. You should really talk to Robbie."

Jack was of the opinion that they should really talk to *him*. Now that he and Ellie were about to be married, he had some say in managing her affairs, and that included the affairs of her scapegrace brother.

He adjusted his long length in the upholstered chair. Keeping his voice casual and respectful, he said, "No one could fault you for your care of Robbie, sir. I only hope I am equal to the task. I see that I shall have to exercise a great deal of patience now that he'll be living under my roof."

His words were met by a startled silence.

Ellie stuttered something incomprehensible. Mr. Wallace's eyebrows disappeared into the fall of hair on his forehead. As enlightenment dawned, a smile creased his cheeks.

"Of course," he said. "Now that you are to marry Ellie, Robbie will have to answer to you. That's splendid." As though suddenly aware that this response was less than tactful, he quickly went on, "Well, well, a younger man will probably suit Robbie better, be more of a mentor to him. And I'm sure you'll use your influence to see the boy settled in some...ah...suitable occupation when the time comes."

"You can count on it," replied Jack with a deprecating smile.

Ellie was struggling to find her voice. "I don't care if Robbie becomes a shepherd or...or a coachman," she declared. "An education is never wasted."

"Oh, I think I can do better for the boy than a shepherd or a coachman," replied Jack easily. "But the main thing is to advise him of how things stand since we left Paris."

The veiled reference to the murder charge hanging over Robbie had little effect. "I am aware of that," she said, still bristling. "But it would be a mistake to think that Robbie is in need of a guardian, because he already has one—me."

Mr. Wallace got nimbly to his feet. There was a worried look in his eyes. "I'll see what's keeping Mabel," he said. "I don't think I asked her to bring scones and strawberry preserves. I'll only be a moment."

When the door closed, Jack said, "I think we failed our first test, Ellie."

"What 'test'?" Her brows were down.

"I don't think we convinced Mr. Wallace that we're a couple of lovebirds."

Her nose wrinkled. "I couldn't act like a lovebird if my life depended on it."

He bit down on a smile. "All the same, we made poor Mr. Wallace take to his heels. We'll have to do better than that if we're to convince the world, and your brother in particular, that we're the proverbial happy couple. At the very least, we should be civil to each other."

She gave him a fulminating look, but her voice was surprisingly civil. "I would be civil if you wouldn't provoke me."

He shook his head. "I'm not trying to provoke you. Like it or not, your brother *will* answer to me. How can I make you understand that he is in trouble up to his neck? I gave my word to Sir Charles—who has your best interests at heart—that I'd take the boy under my wing, and I mean to keep my promise."

At this pointed reminder, some of the fight went out of her. "I understand," she said. "And don't think I'm not grateful. But I warn you now, Robbie has a mind of his own. He won't take kindly to being ordered about. He has been his own master, more or less, since he went away to university. All I'm saying is that tact and patience will serve you far better than intimidation."

Barely suppressing the twinkle in his eyes, he said, "Oddly enough, my grandmother used words very like those to my commanding officer when I got my first commission. He'd heard it all before from other fond mamas and grandmothers. Fortunately for England, he ignored their advice."

She began to steam again. "The war is over, and Robbie is not a soldier. He—"

He held up his hand, silencing her. "I think I hear Mr. Wallace's step. Smile, Ellie, and make the old boy happy."

Over tea and scones, they talked about everything but Robbie. The minutes slipped by, then an hour. Ellie was beginning to lose her sparkle. Uncle Freddie kept watching the clock. Finally, Jack could stand it no longer. He got up.

"Where am I likely to find him?" he asked abruptly.

Mr. Wallace heaved a sigh. Flashing an apologetic look at Ellie, he said, "I'm afraid he has got in with a fast crowd. They hang out at the Three Crows on the river beside the old Ranleigh Gardens."

Jack nodded. "We passed it on the way in."

Ellie jumped to her feet. "I'm coming with you."

He drew on his gloves. "I think not. The Three Crows is not the sort of place a lady would wish to enter."

Her chin tilted. "I've been in worse."

"Yes," he replied easily, "but not when you were engaged to marry me. Stay here. This shouldn't take long. In the meanwhile, you can make yourself useful. You can help Mr. Wallace pack your brother's boxes. He'll be coming home with us."

He was aware of her smoldering gaze following him as he quit the room.

The light was beginning to wane by the time Jack arrived at the Three Crows. This was no bustling hostelry as could be found on the main thoroughfares into town, but a quiet country inn whose patrons appeared to be artisans, journeymen, or local shopkeepers who had stopped by for conversation and a tankard of ale at the end of a hard day's work. The members of his own club in London weren't so very different, except that they were dressed by the finest tailors and would have been passing around jeweled snuffboxes instead of puffing on clay pipes. The fog in the taproom was making his eyes sting.

One thing was certain. This was not the haunt of the fast crowd Mr. Wallace had mentioned, the crowd Robbie was supposed to run with. No self-respecting young buck would feel at home in these respectable surroundings. Having once been a young buck himself, he knew that they'd be looking for danger, excitement, rubbing shoulders with pugilists or highwaymen, anything to convince themselves that they were a devil-may-care lot and as different from their sober-sided parents as curry from custard.

Conversation was beginning to flag as the patrons became aware of his presence. He was a stranger and therefore of some interest. He approached the bar and spoke to the man dispensing drinks.

"I'm looking for a young friend," he said. "Robbie Hill or Brans-Hill. Do you know where I can find him?"

The barman looked over the crowd. "He was here a minute ago, he and his friend, Mr. Milton, but I can't see them now." On the next breath, he bawled out, "Has anyone seen Mr. Hill and his friend?"

A patron pointed to a door at the far end of the taproom. "They left in a hurry," he cried out. "Must be something they ate in one of your pigeon pies, Bernie."

Everyone laughed.

The joke was lost on Jack until Bernie, his host, explained that the door by which the two young gentlemen had hastily exited, was the door to the outside privy.

Jack tossed the barman a shilling and went after his quarry.

Failing light or not, it was impossible to miss the privy. The stench of it gave it away. He didn't approach it from the path, but took a detour around a wilderness of scraggy shrubbery that gave him some cover. These two young whelps were trying to avoid him and he was determined to find out why.

When he got to the privy, he listened for a moment, heard nothing, then used his booted foot to break in the door. There was no one there.

He took a moment to think things through. There was only one place Robbie could go, and that was back to Mr. Wallace's. But what about his friend Milton?"

He knew from Ellie that Milton was the friend from Oxford who had accompanied Robbie to Paris and had helped her get Robbie away. He'd had it in his mind to interview young Milton after he'd talked to Robbie, but he'd expected to find him in Oxford, not here. What the devil was going on?

All this hide-and-seek nonsense was beginning to annoy him.

Milton wasn't staying with Mr. Wallace, so where was he putting up? The logical place to look was the local inn.

Just in case he was right and they were observing him from an upstairs window, he wandered down to the river, then, keeping himself out of sight, doubled back. One of the chambermaids gave him directions to Mr. Milton's room, and after tipping her handsomely, he went up the back stairs.

Though the lamps in the inn were lit, there was no pool of light coming from under the door of Milton's room. All was quiet. That didn't deter Jack. He knocked at the door and spoke in the rough vernacular he'd heard in the taproom. "Beggin' yer pardon, Mr. Milton, sir, there's a lady downstairs who wants t'speak t'yer. A Miss Hill, she said her name was."

There was a whispered conference on the other side of the door, the sound of flint striking iron, then the grating of a key turning in the lock.

Before the door was halfway opened, Jack charged inside, using his shoulder as a battering ram. The man at the door gave a grunt and went down like a skittles pin. The one at the window came at Jack brandishing a brass candlestick. He would have used it, too, but Jack feinted to the left and kicked his assailant hard in the gut. The young man made a *whoosh*ing sound, dropped the candlestick, and sank to his knees.

The man behind the door had come to himself. He came at Jack with flying fists. "Run, Robbie, run," he cried.

Jack felled him with a blow to the chin. "I wouldn't advise it, Robbie," he said, and stepping over Milton's inert form, he hauled Robbie to his feet.

"I'm Raleigh, by the way," he said, "and your sister sent me to find you. No need to tell me who you two are. Now, shall we sit down and talk like civilized people?"

No one argued with him when he propelled them with a viselike grip to the nearest chairs.

Chapter 12

Jack didn't give his companions a chance to argue their case. In a few curt words, he told them how things stood in Paris, that if Robbie didn't clear his name, he could quite easily be charged with the murder of Louise Daudet. He concluded by handing him Sir Charles's letter and telling him to read it.

Apparently stricken into silence, Robbie obeyed.

As Robbie read the letter, Jack put the flame of the candle to a rolled paper and lit the fire. When he was sure the kindling had caught, he turned to study his two companions.

Robbie was by far the more handsome, with the kind of good looks that would appeal to females. His hair had a reddish hue, but was several shades darker than his sister's. They had the same expressive eyes and those darting glances from Robbie were telling Jack that the boy was still wary of him.

Mr. Milton was harder to read. He was tall and slender, with a broad brow and angular features. While Robbie was careless about his appearance, Milton was meticulous. Even the scuffle hadn't made a difference to the folds in his neckcloth or the set of his garments. He was the kind of man Jack's valet wished his master would emulate.

"It's as bad as it can be," said Robbie, stricken, and he passed the letter to his friend.

When Milton had read the letter, he carefully folded it and returned it to Robbie. He looked at Jack. "What's your interest in this, Lord Raleigh? Why did Sir Charles choose you?"

Jack plucked the letter from Robbie's fingers. "This belongs to me," he said. "Sir Charles chose me because I've known the family for a long time." To Robbie, he went on, "When I was about your age, your father tutored me in the classics for a while. I was Jack Rigg then."

Robbie shook his head. "I don't recall the name."

"No, you wouldn't," said Jack. "You were an infant when I came to stay at the vicarage."

Milton said, "I know who you are! Robbie, this is the man I was telling you about, the one who compromised Ellie and refused to marry her."

"Did Ellie say that?" asked Jack.

"No," replied Milton. "She said that you gave her an alibi. I heard rumors, though. Are they true?"

"That is between Ellie and me. At any rate, we're to be married at once."

Robbie's face was a study in incredulity, as though he'd just been told that he'd passed his Greek and Latin examinations at the top of his class. Milton, on the other hand, looked as though he'd been told the opposite.

Milton was shaking his head. "Ellie would never marry someone like you," he said. "She wouldn't...she couldn't."

"Now, why would I lie about a thing like that?" Jack asked pleasantly.

"But..." It was Robbie's turn to shake his head. "But Ellie isn't like that. She would never marry anyone just because she was compromised."

"How true," said Jack. "We are marrying because we suit each other."

Milton scowled. "You and Ellie have nothing in common."

Jack let out an exasperated sigh. First Cardvale, now Milton. He could read the signs. It would be an exaggeration to call them lovesick swains, but their interest in Ellie was not entirely platonic, and he was becoming thoroughly peeved by everyone acting as though Ellie's marrying him was a tragic mistake.

"Ellie and I," he told Milton, "are none of your business. Now, can we get back to what is really important? I want to talk to Robbie alone. Take a walk, Mr. Milton. Fifteen minutes should do it. But don't go far, because after I talk to Robbie, I'd like to talk to you."

"I want him to stay!" said Robbie, clearly uneasy at the thought of being left alone with this formidable inquisitor.

Milton got up. "It's all right, Robbie," he said. "Tell him the truth. We have nothing to hide."

To Jack, he said, "I'll be in the taproom," and he sauntered from the room.

Jack took the chair Milton had vacated. "I'm truly puzzled," he said. "Your uncle seems to think that you're hanging out with the local bloods. Now how did he get that impression?"

"Uncle Freddie," said Robbie with feeling, "has a vivid imagination. Yes, I meet my friends here occasionally, but it's only to drink a jug of ale and play a game of cards."

"How odd," said Jack. "I remember saying much the same thing to your father when he smelled strong spirits on my breath. I think on that occasion I was chasing the miller's daughter."

Robbie looked interested. "And did that stop you from chasing the miller's daughter?"

"No. Ellie did that. However, that's another story. So"—he pushed back his chair and folded his arms across his chest—"I want to know why you ran from me and why you subsequently tried to bash my brains out when I entered your room."

Robbie regarded him balefully. "You didn't enter the room, you charged in like a bull on the rampage."

"Who did you think I was?"

Robbie looked at the door as though willing Milton to return. When he got no help there, he looked at Jack. Finally, he replied, "I thought...oh, it's all in such a muddle. I'm not sure what I thought, except that I'd be the prime suspect in Louise's murder." He gave a short, brittle laugh. "We were hoping that the French authorities wouldn't have jurisdiction here, but we couldn't be sure, so we weren't taking any chances."

Jack's voice rose. "And you were prepared to use physical force against an English officer of the law?"

"Of course not! You were the one who attacked us. We were trying to hide from you."

Jack wasn't entirely satisfied with this answer, but he let it go for the moment. His voice was harsh when he spoke next. "For a man whose mistress was brutally murdered, you seem remarkably unaffected. All you seem to care about is saving your own skin."

Robbie blushed to the roots of his hair. He fumbled over his words. "Of course I was affected by Louise's death. I was devastated! But we were not as close as you seem to think. Louise was not my mistress! She's your age, for heaven's sake!" Now he was tripping over his words in his haste to get them out. "She didn't love me and I didn't love her. I admired her. It was an honor to escort her to parties and so on. But that's as far as it went. You know how it is. Your generation fawned over that celebrated courtesan, Harriette What's-her-name."

"Wilson," Jack supplied.

He remembered it very well. He and his friends would cut tutorials and come up to town to attend the opera in hopes of catching a glimpse of London's most sought after courtesan. Occasionally, a favored few would be invited into her private box to pay her homage, but he'd never been one of those favored by an invitation. Worcester had, and the numbskull had fallen head over heels in love with the lady and almost caused his father, the duke, to suffer an apoplexy because his son and heir wanted to marry her. The rumor was that she'd been bought off.

Robbie went on, "And it's not as though I was her only admirer. There were legions of us."

"But she singled you out. Why?"

Robbie shrugged helplessly and looked away. "I don't really know. She said I was amusing."

This answer did not satisfy Jack and he wondered how much money Robbie had squandered on Louise Daudet. That might explain why she had singled him out.

"Tell me about your debts," he said.

An edge of defiance crept into Robbie's voice. "I don't see what that has to do with Louise's murder."

"Humor me."

It was a command, not a request.

Glances locked and held, but Robbie's gaze eventually dropped away. "My debts just grew," he said, "as though they had a life of their own." He gave a forced laugh. "I arrived in Paris with money that I'd won gaming with my friends in London. I know, I know. I'm not supposed to gamble. I promised Ellie I wouldn't. But what's a fellow to do when his friends want to drop into some gaming establishment or other at the end of a night in town? Was I to wait for them outside the door? Was I to tell them I'd promised my sister that I'd be a good boy? You know as well as I what they would make of that. Of course I went with them. I made a small wager. And I won. And I kept on winning. So you see, when I arrived in Paris with Milton, I had a tidy sum of money at my disposal."

Jack understood only too well. There were two camps of students in Oxford, those who had to work hard at their studies to fit themselves for a profession, and the drones, the sons of aristocrats, who would never have to earn a living. Most of the latter had more money than sense and, in the eyes of their less-fortunate friends, led glamorous if rather wild lives. There was no doubt that they were the envy of their peers.

At Oxford, he'd had a foot in both camps. He was the son of an aristocrat, but not the heir. Second sons had to make their own way in the world eventually, hence his stint with Ellie's father to prepare him for his examinations. All the same, it was a matter of pride to appear as devil-may-care as the next fellow. Of course Robbie joined his friends at the gaming tables. And the jaunt to Paris, where he was taken up by a celebrated actress, would have been an adventure to boast about for a long time to come.

Except that everything had gone wrong.

"Tell me about Milton," he said. "Did *he* have a tidy sum of money at his disposal?"

"Hardly. He comes from a long line of university dons, and one day he'll be one, too. They don't make much money."

"Didn't he go gambling with you? In London, I mean."

"No. He's a Fellow and had students' papers to mark that night."

Jack was impressed. A Fellow was an outstanding scholar who was paid a stipend to teach less-academic students. They came and went as they pleased. Some lived in the college and some did not. They all had plenty of time to pursue their own studies. A trip to Paris, he supposed, could be described as educational if one chose one's words with care.

Something else occurred to him. He could see why Milton was attracted to Ellie. How many females could speak intelligently about gerunds and gerundives? How many men would care?

He suppressed a smile. "So you paid the shot?"

Robbie nodded. "We're friends. I wanted him to come with me."

"And, no doubt, squandered your little nest egg on the oh-so-admirable Mlle. Daudet." If his voice was harsh, it was because he was thinking of Ellie and the risks she'd taken to help her brother.

"It wasn't like that," Robbie protested. "Louise never asked for a thing."

"But you did buy her presents?"

"They weren't expensive. Flowers, a lace shawl, dinners in the Palais Royal. Most of the money went to my own expenses, mine and Milton's. I didn't realize . . . I thought I had enough money to cover my debts."

The harshness was still in Jack's voice. "And when you realized you were in tick up to your neck, you came up with the idea of having your sister bail you out."

Robbie looked like a cornered mouse.

Jack said, "You're not betraying any secrets. I know all about Aurora. Ellie has told me everything."

A look of relief that was nearly comical crossed Robbie's face. He heaved a sigh. "It wouldn't be the first time we'd done this, except that this time Milton went with her."

"Because you were hiding from your creditors?"

"It wasn't only that. I was afraid that the French police

might be looking for me." He couldn't meet Jack's eyes. "You know, to ask me about Louise. Everyone believed we were lovers. Who else would they suspect?"

There was much that Jack wanted to say, but railing at Robbie wasn't going to get him the information he wanted, so he strove to bridle his temper. "Let's go back to New Year's Day and the night Louise was murdered. Where were you?"

Robbie thought for a moment, then said, "I hadn't seen Louise for a few days. Well, I was hiding from Houchard's thugs until..." He seemed to realize that any mention of Ellie's part in helping him would provoke Jack's temper, so he stopped and started over.

"I knew that I'd be leaving Paris soon, so I went to the theater to say good-bye to Louise."

"When was this?"

"After the performance."

Jack said slowly, "But that's...that's when she was murdered."

Robbie gulped. "I know. I was the one who found her."

Jack was thunderstruck. He had never imagined anything like this. As far as he knew, Robbie was a suspect largely because he was presumed to be Louise's lover, and had disappeared.

He looked at Robbie's fear-bright eyes and managed to bite back the spate of questions he wanted to ask. He didn't want to alarm the boy. But he did want answers.

"Go on," he said levelly. "You went to the theater."

Robbie nodded. "Milton waited outside while I went upstairs to Louise's dressing room."

"Why did you take Milton?"

"Why do you think?" Robbie raised his head, his expression puzzled. "To watch my back in case the thug who was acting for Houchard was following me."

"I see."

When it looked as though Robbie had become lost in thought, Jack prompted, "So, you left Milton outside among the New Year's revelers and you entered the theater. Then what?"

"I remember thinking that the theater was practically deserted, apart from the cleaners. Well, it would be, wouldn't it, on New Year's Day? Everyone has a party to go to."

He swallowed hard. "When I got to her dressing room the door was open. There was no sign of her dresser, and I supposed she had left early to be with friends or family. Louise was like that, you know. She was generous to a fault. Her servants adored her."

He smiled faintly, then went on, "There was no candle lit, and the only light came from a lamp in the corridor, but I could see that something was wrong. She was at her dressing table, and it looked as though she'd fallen asleep, or that she'd taken ill. She'd put her head down, you see, on the tabletop. I called her name, but there was no response, and when I touched her, she toppled over. I only had time to register that her eyes were staring and my hands were sticky when I sensed something—a movement behind me. I turned quickly, but not quickly enough to save myself from the slash of a dagger. I don't know what happened next. There was a bit of a struggle and my assailant ran off. I don't know how long I lay there before I got to my feet and stumbled down the stairs. You can imagine Milton's shock when he saw the state I was in. I was barely coherent."

He cleared his throat and said roughly, "He got me out of there and into a hackney. I didn't realize we were running away. The next day, Milton took me to a doctor to tend my wound." He pressed a hand to his shoulder, just above his left breast. "When I was myself again, I was afraid the police would think I had murdered Louise and I was too afraid to give myself up."

It was on the tip of Jack's tongue to say something biting, but Robbie's look of anguish halted the rush of words. Still, one question had to be asked.

"Robbie," he said. When Robbie blinked and looked up, Jack said, "Can you tell me anything about the person who stabbed you?"

"No. The light was behind him."

"So, it *was* a man?"

"I think so, but I can't be sure. I was kneeling on the floor, and he was looming over me. All I did was try to defend myself."

Jack kept his voice gentle, unthreatening. "Let's go through this again from the beginning. There are still some points on which I am unclear. You left Milton in the courtyard. Go on from there."

Robbie looked down at his clasped hands and started over.

Jack and Milton were in a quiet corner of the taproom, drinking ale. He had sent Robbie home to wait for him there because he didn't want him correcting his friend if their stories did not tally.

After he'd taken a swig of ale, he studied his companion. Unlike Robbie, Milton wasn't the least bit edgy. When asked what he thought of the whole sorry business, he looked Jack straight in the eye.

"I thought then and I still think," he said, "that Robbie is innocent. Why would he kill Louise? He has no motive. He doesn't fly into jealous rages."

Jack interjected sharply, "Was there a reason for him to be jealous?"

"Only people who don't know Robbie well would think so."

"That's not an answer."

Milton shrugged. "There was a rumor that she'd found a rich protector, but it's ludicrous to think that Robbie was jealous. She was old enough to be his mother, though you would never have known it just by watching her onstage."

Jack almost smiled. No doubt young Milton thought that anyone over thirty had one foot in the grave. "Was she as old as I?"

"A year or two older, I would say."

"Thank you. Now, shall we get back to what happened that night? You were in the courtyard waiting for Robbie. What happened next?"

Jack visualized each step as Milton related it. It was freezing cold that night and Milton had sheltered behind one of the arcade pillars to escape the breeze. He'd only been there a few minutes when Robbie ran out of the theater.

"Did you see anyone leave before that?" Jack asked sharply.

"No one I recognized. A couple of cleaners, maybe. I can't be sure. And there are other doors on the other side of the building. The murderer could have left by one of them."

There was a long silence before he went on. "Robbie said Louise was dead. He was covered in blood. I couldn't leave him. Besides, I knew what the authorities would think, that there had been a lovers' quarrel and that Robbie had wrested the knife away from Louise after she'd struck the first blow. Then he'd stabbed her to death. I didn't believe it for one moment, so I got him out of there as fast as I could. No one gave us a second glance. To anyone watching, Robbie would look like a reveler who'd had too much to drink. I got him out of the court-yard, hired a hackney, and got him away. The next day I took him to a doctor."

"What about the knife that killed Louise?"

Milton shook his head. "I wouldn't know about that."

"I see."

It amazed Jack that he could still sound reasonable when what he wanted to do was tear his hair out. He didn't see how he could edit the evidence to make these two ninnies appear as naive as he believed them to be. His attorney was going to have his work cut out for him.

One thing was certain. Milton would have to make a statement, too. He was a material witness and could corroborate Robbie's story up to a point.

He took a long swallow of ale, hoping to dull the incipient ache behind his eyes. He said, as the thought occurred to him, "What about you, Mr. Milton? Were you jealous?"

There was a silence, then Milton gave a disbelieving laugh. " 'Jealous'? Why should I be? Louise had legions of admirers. To her, it was amusing to favor one, then another. It was a game, that's all, a game."

"Don't you think that the authorities would have worked that out? What you've done is muddy the waters. You've both acted suspiciously. Is it any wonder that Robbie is a suspect?"

Milton shot right back. "What would you have done in our place? We were foreigners in a strange country. I had no idea that Sir Charles Stuart was a friend of the family, and even if I had known, I doubt that that would have made a difference. The connection, at best, is distant. I thought our best bet was to get home to England as soon as Robbie was fit to make the trip."

His voice lost some of its assurance. "Tell me, sir, does Robbie have to answer to a French court? I thought, hoped, that when we returned to England, that would be the end of it."

"It's possible. But that's not the only problem." A waiter was hovering, and Jack waved him away. He didn't want to order another round of drinks when Ellie would be anxiously waiting for his return, and he was almost done here. He went on, "Is Robbie to stay in England for the rest of his life? What happens in the future if he returns to France? He'll be a wanted man. And if it becomes known here that he is suspected of murder, he may find every door shut against him. No. Until he is cleared of this crime, his name will be blackened."

There was a long silence, then Milton heaved a sigh. "Then we had better clear his name." He leaned forward, with one hand on the flat of the table. "You didn't answer my question, sir. What would you have done in our place?"

Jack didn't have to think about his answer. "Probably what you did. But that doesn't make it right."

When Milton smiled, his features softened and he looked almost handsome. All the fine lines he'd acquired while studying had disappeared. It was quite a change.

"And now that we've got that out of the way," Jack said, "is there anything else I should know? It need not be evidence. Something odd you can't explain? A suspicion that someone or something was in the wrong place at the wrong time? Anything at all?"

Milton shook his head slowly. "No. Nothing. I've told you all I know."

There was something critical he had meant to ask Milton but, for the moment, it had slipped his mind. It would come to him eventually.

Jack pushed back his chair and got up. "Where can I find you if I need you?"

"I'll be returning to Oxford tomorrow."

"Good. I'll be in touch."

They made the return trip to town in a hackney, the three of them squeezed together like peas in a pod. Jack did most of the talking, but it was small talk and sporadic, an attempt to lighten the gloom that gripped his companions.

Robbie appeared chastened, as well he should. When Ellie heard what had happened in Paris, she'd turned deathly pale and said hardly a word. Her dejection had worked on Robbie to better effect than a sisterly lecture.

Hence, there was no argument about taking up residence in Jack's town house in London, and no sullen looks when Jack assured Robbie that he would continue his studies in London with a new tutor.

He wondered how long Robbie's willingness to please would last.

As for himself, he had the oddest sensation that he'd stepped through a door into an alien land. He could hardly credit that he was sitting in a hired hackney, squeezed against the side to give Ellie more room, all his thoughts absorbed in how he could make life easier for two people who were practically strangers to him.

Chapter 13

Two days later, they were married by Special License in St. James's Church on Piccadilly. It was a cold January morning, but everyone was dressed for the weather, including the bride. Ellie was wearing her finest winter ensemble, a long-sleeved, high-necked gown in gray crepe with a fitted pelisse to match. Her outfit was subdued, but so was everyone else's. This was not exactly the wedding of the year.

Outside of the immediate family, only Cardvale and Dorothea were present. In fact, the Cardvales had graciously offered to host the wedding breakfast in their own home. It was more than a gracious offer. Both Cardvale and his wife had insisted on it since, they said, they were the bride's nearest relatives and the privilege belonged to them.

As the meal progressed around Dorothea's beautifully appointed table, Ellie became more relaxed. Her fears were proving to be unfounded. The episode in Paris, when Dorothea had accused her of stealing her diamonds, might never have happened. Dorothea was all charm.

Cardvale was less effusive but was obviously pleased with the way things had turned out, as was Jack's grandmother. Robbie seemed preoccupied, but that was to be expected. He, Milton, and Jack had an appointment with the attorney the following day. Caro was more sullen than preoccupied, and Ellie wondered if it was because she was disappointed in her brother's choice of a wife.

Maybe that's what the trouble was. There hadn't been a choice, not for Jack and not for herself. This wasn't the best way to start a marriage.

A light touch on her arm gave her a start. She turned her head to look up at Jack. His smile was grave, but humor lurked in his eyes.

He spoke in a soft undertone. "I'm glad you waited for me, as you promised you would, all those years ago."

It took her a moment to make the connection. He was teasing, of course, trying to put her at her ease. She replied tartly, "Don't let it go to your head. I waited for all of two weeks, and when you didn't return, I promptly fell in love with the baker's boy."

His bark of laughter had all heads turning in their direction.

"Do share the joke," said Dorothea, and the refrain was taken up by the others.

Jack shrugged. "We were reminiscing about the past, when Ellie's father tutored me in Greek and Latin." He flashed Ellie a smile. "Even then, she made quite an impression on me."

"Childhood sweethearts?" intoned Dorothea with a stiff smile.

Ellie swallowed her response when Jack reached for her hand, hidden by the tablecloth, and gave it a hard squeeze.

"We couldn't agree on a single thing," he replied easily, "so I suppose it must have been true love even then."

Laughter erupted around the table, then the conversation moved on to other things—Ellie's bridal clothes (or, more precisely, her lack of them); the honeymoon that had to be postponed because this was Lady Caro's first season and, naturally, the family had to be there to support her; whether or not Ellie would be refurbishing the house in Park Street; Robbie's plans for the future, and so on and so on. Dorothea's curiosity was insatiable.

In the coach going home, which Jack and Ellie had to themselves, Ellie's mind was still on the reception. Jack had answered most of Dorothea's questions, which was just as well, because Ellie wouldn't have known what to say. She hadn't discussed any of these things with Jack.

"I think," said Jack, "that went off rather well, don't you?"

Ellie shook her head. "Dorothea loves to know everybody's business. She can't help herself. I think she was born a gossip. Before the week is over, she will have broadcast everything she has learned about us to all her friends."

"Like what, for instance?"

She didn't want to mention her lack of bridal clothes or the delayed honeymoon, in case he thought she wanted them, which she certainly did not, so she said instead, "Well, that story you concocted about us being childhood sweethearts. Soon everyone will have heard it and everyone will be gossiping about us."

"And that bothers you?"

"Doesn't it bother you?"

He shrugged. "Hardly. I've been the object of so much gossip in my time, I've become used to it. However"—he gave her the smile calculated to melt a lady's heart—"it will be a change to have people think well of me. The world admires a constant lover."

She blew out a derisory breath. "No one will believe it."

"Why not?"

Because he was a matrimonial prize and she was an old maid who had been withering for years on the shelf—or so the world thought. "Because," she said, "I was only thirteen to your seventeen when we first met."

"Juliet was only thirteen when she met Romeo."

He had removed his gloves and his bare thumb brushed her cheek. Ellie, who was never at a loss for a quick retort, couldn't find a thing to say. His expression became serious, searching. She knew where this was leading.

And she felt completely out of her depth.

Dragging her eyes from his, she said lightly, "Let's not get carried away, Jack. I'm not Juliet and you're not Romeo. We're both too long in the tooth to play these parts convincingly."

He linked his fingers through hers. "You're too modest. When you make the most of yourself, you're ravishing. Don't forget, I've seen you as Aurora."

The compliment left something to be desired. She spoke in a bantering tone. "If you're trying to win me over, you're not succeeding."

"'*Win you over*'?" He unlinked his fingers from hers. "I wouldn't dream of it."

She could see from his expression that she'd given offense. But so had he. She was searching in her mind for a way to make amends, when the carriage pulled up outside their front door.

As soon as they alighted, he snagged her wrist and led the way inside the house. She had to move quickly to keep up with him. The servants who were about wished them happy, but Jack's only acknowledgment was a grim smile.

Up the stairs he led her, to her new chamber, the one that was reserved for the master's wife. A maid came out of Ellie's dressing room, shaking out Ellie's garments. She took one look at Jack's face, bobbed a curtsy, and quickly left them.

"This," said Jack, walking to a door opposite her dressing room, "is the door to my chamber."

There was a key in the lock. He turned it, locking the door, then slapped the key into Ellie's open palm. Her fingers curled around it automatically.

In the same harsh tone, he went on, "I won't come through that door unless I'm invited. Oh, and be careful Aurora doesn't get hold of that key. She doesn't have to be won over."

Stupefied, she watched him walk to her bedchamber door. On the threshold, he turned to face her. The grimness had gone and he seemed to be quietly amused.

"I almost forgot," he said. "There's something I want to show you. Dress warmly and wear boots. I'll meet you downstairs in, oh, say half an hour? We're driving to Kensington."

And on that annoyingly cryptic note, he left her.

She had barely removed her coat and bonnet when someone knocked at her door. It was Wigan, the butler, come to offer her his best wishes for her future happiness, and to enquire if it was convenient for her ladyship to meet some of the senior staff.

She'd got off on the wrong foot with her new husband. She wasn't going to make the same mistake with the servants.

They were waiting for her in the hall: Mrs. Leach, the housekeeper, who was as gaunt as one of the winter trees in the park; Mrs. Rice, the cook, whose ample proportions seemed to suit her profession; and Webster, whom Ellie had already met.

Wigan was the most senior, not only because of his position, but also in years. Ellie judged him to be fiftyish. He wasn't reserved so much as punctilious in his manner, not unlike Milton. She warmed to him at once.

It was otherwise with the housekeeper. Mrs. Leach was stiff and unsmiling and her manner was chilly to the point of being uncivil. Ellie's heart sank. Did everyone have to be won over in this household?

Mrs. Rice's kind eyes met Ellie's as she bobbed a curtsy. *At last, a friendly face,* thought Ellie. The same could be said for Webster, who, Ellie learned, was the head housemaid.

Things could be worse.

They soon were. The introductions were hardly over when Wigan, Cook, and Webster melted away, leaving Ellie to the tender mercies of Mrs. Leach.

"This way, my lady," said Mrs. Leach. "You'll want to inspect the domestic quarters."

And like a little lamb, Ellie followed her captor into the bowels of the house.

The domestic quarters were impressive. Servants' Hall, three separate kitchens, laundry rooms, drying rooms, and rooms she couldn't name, all were as neat as a new pin. Ellie was effusive in her praise, but she might as well have spoken to a block of wood. Mrs. Leach was doing her duty, nothing more.

At the end of the tour, Ellie said, "Thank you, Mrs. Leach. I'm sure we're going to get along famously. If you have any problems, my door is always open."

The housekeeper's thin eyebrows arched. "Thank you, my lady," she said, "but Lady Frances is mistress here. I take my orders from her."

"Of course," Ellie replied at once. She felt as though someone had punched her in the stomach. Lady Frances was Cedric's widow. Naturally she'd had oversight of the servants. And, Ellie told herself fiercely, she wouldn't have it any other way, though by rights this was her house now.

But it was galling to have been snubbed by a servant. She whisked herself around and made her escape.

Ellie dragged herself from her gloomy reflections when Jack told her why they were in the coach and on their way to Kensington.

"That's where Cloverdale Stables are," he said. "We're going to buy a mount for you."

After her humiliation at the hands of his housekeeper, she was more than willing to salvage what was turning out to be a sorry wedding day. "I always wanted a horse," she said.

"All the females in my family ride, and I remember you were a fair rider yourself at one time."

"Middling to fair," she replied modestly. His memory was faulty. She'd ridden pillion with him once and had been terrified out of her wits. Since then, she'd learned to ride, but only at a snail's pace.

"I'm out of practice," she elaborated, answering the question in his eyes.

"We shall soon fix that."

Her hackles began to quiver. "Is there anything else about me you'd like to fix?"

"Since you ask," he said pleasantly, "your wardrobe. Don't get that look in your eyes, Ellie. I'm not finding fault. I'm sure your garments were more than adequate for your position as a lady's companion. But you have a new position now. And you'll be escorting my sister to various functions. This is her first season. Like it or not, you'll both be on display. If I'm not ungenerous with my sister, I most certainly will not be ungenerous with my wife."

That made sense. She never shriked a duty, and just because she would enjoy the experience of dressing up didn't make it a sin.

"I'll try not to bankrupt you," she said lightly.

"Oh, I'll make sure of that."

He smiled. She smiled. Harmony reigned.

It was a pleasant drive to Kensington and, before long, their coach drew to a halt inside Cloverdale's gates. It was an impressive establishment. Two long rows of stables faced each other across a cobbled yard. There were grooms coming and going, some with harnesses or saddles, others mounted and walking their mounts to a circular exercise track outside the paddock gates. There were others, like themselves, who had come to look over the stock with a view to buying.

The owner, Jack said, was Augustus Rider, and his family had bred horses for generations. Many of the thoroughbreds at Newmarket came from Rider's stud. The old man was a bit of an eccentric. He looked over his buyers as carefully as they looked over his stock, and if he didn't like what he saw, he wouldn't sell to them.

A groom in his mid-fifties, small and whiplash lean, with blue eyes made all the bluer by his weatherbeaten face, tipped his cap as he came up to them.

"Mr. Rider is in his office, your lordship," he said, and he moved off to speak to another gentleman.

Ellie breathed deeply, savoring the scent of horses and leather. She could not detect even a whiff of a midden, which told her that the owner kept his stable in pristine condition.

She looked up to see Jack studying her. Shrugging helplessly, as though caught in the act, she said, "I'm a country girl at heart."

He chuckled. "That's an odd thing for Aurora—" He stopped.

The moment of harmony was lost. Her voice chilled. "Let's not keep Mr. Rider waiting."

After touring the stalls with Mr. Rider, Ellie selected two horses that were then led into the paddock so that they could examine them more closely. Jack favored a two-year-old gelding. He praised its confidence, its proud stance, none of which found favor with Ellie.

"Jack," she said, mildly remonstrating, "I said I could ride. I didn't say I had served with the cavalry."

He threw up his hands. "You're the one who chose him."

"I know, but I'm having second thoughts. Brutus—is that his name?—has a mean look about him. He'd have me reduced to a shivering jelly before I got settled in the saddle."

She'd chosen him because she wanted to please Jack, to be the dashing kind of woman he seemed to want. But Brutus terrified her.

The groom stroked Brutus's neck. "Her ladyship is right," he said. "Brutus needs a firm, experienced hand on the reins. Now Blackie, he has a sweet temper."

"He looks older than the other horses," she said to the groom.

"Aye, that he is," he replied. "He's not one of ours, you see. He was a colt when he came here. Famished, he was, and scared of his own shadow. Mr. Rider took him in." Pride laced his voice. "And now look at him. Why don't I saddle him and you can take a turn around the track?"

"Thank you. I'd like that."

As the groom sent a stableboy to fetch the saddle, Ellie approached Blackie. He looked at her curiously, but he didn't shy away or appear nervous. He nibbled her outstretched fingers and blew through his nose.

Jack watched with a smile on his face, then moved away to some acquaintance who had hailed him. When Jack moved away, a gentleman who had been leaning on the fence approached Ellie.

"I wonder if you remember me, Lady Raleigh?" he said.

She looked up to see someone about her own age, with hair the color of ripe wheat, a handsome young man of moderate height, with bold eyes and a crooked smile.

"I'm Paul Derby," he said, "Lord Cardvale's man of business. Perhaps you remember my father. He was Lord Cardvale's man of business until he died."

Ellie's expression cleared. "I remember you both. But I met you only once or twice. You were at university when I lived with my cousin. How are you, Mr. Derby?"

The conversation that followed seemed ordinary on the surface, but Ellie didn't feel comfortable. Mr. Derby seemed very curious about Robbie—where he was, when he would be returning to university, what college he attended. She replied vaguely to all his questions. It reminded her of the conversation she'd had with Dorothea at her wedding breakfast that morning. She'd been vague about Robbie's plans then, too.

The boy returned with the saddle, and after tipping his hat, Mr. Derby moved away. When she was mounted on Blackie, she forgot about Derby.

They went once around the circuit, then made for the paddock.

"Who trained Blackie?" she asked the groom.

"Mr. Rider did, ma'am. No one as thought it could be done, but he proved them wrong. Patience and persistence, that's old Rider's motto. I never thought as he would part from Blackie. His lordship must have been very persuasive."

Ellie was puzzled. "You mean, my husband *chose* Blackie for me?"

"Bought and paid for," replied the groom.

Now she was astonished.

When they returned to the paddock, Jack helped her dismount. "You're a better rider than you know," he said.

"Thanks to Blackie! But you know all about that."

His eyes measured her. "So, the groom has a loose tongue. Fine. If you don't like Blackie, we'll choose another mount for you, but not Brutus. He's all show and temper. You'd never know what he'd do next."

"The point is…"

"Yes?"

The point was, she didn't like to be tricked or managed. She was used to making her own decisions. One day of marriage and she was reduced to the level of a witless child.

His eyes gleamed knowingly. "Tell me," he said, "who was that gentleman who was talking to you a moment ago, the one with the toothsome grin? I don't recall meeting him."

His lightning change of topic had her confused for a moment. "Oh, that was Paul Derby, Cardvale's man of business. The oddest thing, Jack. He was asking a lot of questions about Robbie, the same questions Dorothea asked this morning." And she went on to tell him about her vague sense of misgiving, ending with, "Am I being too sensitive? Does he know something we don't know?"

He patted her hand. "It pays to be careful," he said. "I think I'd like to get to know Mr. Derby a little better. But his presence here could be quite innocent. Perhaps he's settling one of Cardvale's bills."

Ellie was silent, but she was thinking that it was time she got to know her brother a little better.

She didn't see Robbie until it was time for bed. He'd been pressed into service as escort for the dowager and Caro, and they'd spent the evening at the theater taking in the revival of one of Sheridan's plays. Ellie was well aware that the dowager had planned this little outing so that the newlywed couple could have time to themselves, but the newlywed couple soon exhausted every topic of conversation and the silences between them were becoming longer and more strained.

Dinner was long over and they were sitting in front of the fire in the drawing room, waiting for the others to come home. Her head was bent over a cushion cover that she was embroidering and Jack was sitting opposite her, reading a book, sipping from a glass of brandy. Her relief was palpable when she heard the front door open and not long after, the sound of voices on the stairs.

She set aside the embroidery. Jack put down his book and glass. When he rose and crossed to her, she looked up at him with a question in her eyes.

He tipped her chin up with one hand and bent over her. Against her lips, he said, "Let's make this convincing, Ellie. For the family's sake."

If there had been a spark of amusement in his eyes, she would have found a ready retort. But his expression was intensely masculine, the way a man looks at a woman he wants.

At the first brush of his lips, she froze, but as his lips sank into hers, the familiar wave of pleasure rushed to every sensitive spot in her body, and just like the last time, her bones turned to jelly. Her hand closed around his arm in a vain effort to steady herself. The dowager, Caro, and Robbie were momentarily forgotten as she gave herself up to his kiss.

It was over in a moment. He straightened and said with a laugh, "We've got company, my love."

When he moved aside, Ellie had a clear view of the people who had just entered the room. The dowager's smile was brilliant and Robbie was grinning from ear to ear. Caro's expression was more difficult to read, but one thing was certain, she was not happy to have witnessed that kiss.

Except for Ellie's blushes, there was no awkwardness. No one mentioned the kiss. Everyone began to talk naturally of the performance they'd just come from, or whom they'd seen at the theater. Caro's contribution to the conversation was to remind everyone that Frances would soon be home, and she, for one, could hardly wait.

Frances, thought Ellie, Jack's sister-in-law, whom she now displaced as mistress of the house. Is that why Caro was so sullen? She need not be, for Ellie had no desire to displace anyone. Mrs. Leach had brought that lesson home to her.

At last, they all began to drift off to bed. As was his habit, Jack went downstairs to make sure every window and door was locked. Ellie walked Robbie to her own door and halted.

"All set for tomorrow morning?" she asked. In the morning, he and Milton were to meet with Jack's attorney.

He shrugged. "I can't help feeling nervous."

"That's natural." She patted his arm. "Jack knows what he is doing. You can trust him."

"Oh, I do."

When he would have turned away, she put a hand on his sleeve. "Robbie," she said, "are you making any plans you haven't told me about?"

He looked puzzled. "What kind of plans?"

"I don't know. I happened to meet Cardvale's man of business today, and something he said made me think you might be leaving us."

" 'Leaving'? I don't know what gave him that idea. No, Ellie, I'm doing exactly what we agreed upon. I'll cram for my examination, then, if I pass it, I'll return to Oxford. Who is Cardvale's man of business, anyway? Do I know him?"

"Paul Derby. His father was Cardvale's man of business before him."

Robbie shook his head. "The name means nothing to me."

"Could you have met him in Paris? Could he have been one of Louise's admirers?"

"A man of business?" He sounded incredulous. "What would he be doing in Paris?"

She spoke from sheer frustration. "I find it just as incredible that you were in Paris and that a beautiful actress, who could have had her pick of any man, chose a boy who was hardly out of the schoolroom to be her lover."

"I wasn't her lover! How many times do I have to tell you?"

"Then explain to me why she favored *you*."

He blushed and shuffled his feet. Finally, he said, "It was my name, Brans-Hill. She recognized it. She said that our parents sheltered both her and her mother when they were stranded in England a long time ago." He grinned sheepishly. "That's why Louise singled me out. She wanted to hear all about our parents and how our family had fared in the intervening years. Don't tell Milton. I let him think that Louise took me up because she thought I was a charming fellow."

"So you were never in love with Louise or she with you?"

He screwed up his face. "Don't be daft! She was older than you! Of course, Louise knew how to dress and make the most of herself..." He saw something in his sister's face that made him hasten to add, "Not that you've ever been interested in such frippery things. And Louise didn't have your book learning. Few ladies do."

"Thank you for the compliment," she said, scarcely mollified.

This encouraged him to elaborate. "Louise wasn't a highflier, you know. Most people had the wrong impression about her, just because she was an actress and she was beautiful." He shrugged. "I don't know how to explain it except to say I'm sure you would have liked her."

Ellie was looking at him thoughtfully. "And she wanted to hear all about our family?"

"Yes. I was surprised, too. You don't remember her or her mother?"

"No. But it may come to me."

"Well," he said, "I'll just toddle along. Nice wedding. You looked lovely. Raleigh is a lucky man."

She stared after him, her mind absorbed in what he had just told her.

Her parents had helped Louise Daudet and her mother when they were stranded in England a long time ago. It was quite possible. Her parents were always taking in strays. But she had no recollection of a French girl and her mother.

It wasn't relevant anyway. A murder in Paris could have nothing to do with her parents helping two French émigrés many years before.

As for Paul Derby, it was obvious to her now that she'd made too much of what was, after all, a kindly curiosity about a family he once knew. Cardvale had probably mentioned them to his man of business and the rest followed naturally. Isn't that what had happened with Louise Daudet and Robbie?

Alice, who occasionally worked as lady's maid, was waiting for her in her chamber. The girl was extremely shy, and Ellie could hardly get a word out of her. She conversed with her just the same, but it was a one-sided conversation and she was relieved when she was alone.

She looked at the locked door that separated her room from Jack's. He'd told her that he would never enter her chamber uninvited and she believed him.

A sensitive man would realize that behind the bravado, she was shy, inexperienced, and totally ignorant of men. A sensitive man would make allowances and overlook her odd humors. The trouble was, he was used to women fawning over him. He'd never had to court a woman. All he had to do was crook his finger and they came running.

The very thought of it made her want to strangle him.

Sniffing, mumbling under her breath, she climbed into bed.

Chapter 14

"Naturally, when we received your momentous news, we dropped everything and posted up to town, fearing you had taken leave of your senses."

"What Ash means," elaborated Brand Hamilton, "is that we wanted to be among the first to congratulate you. This calls for champagne."

"Thank you," said Jack. "It's not every day a man gets married."

When Ash sighed theatrically, Jack grinned. In their longstanding friendship, they had perfected these skirmishes with words, and rather enjoyed them.

To the waiter who was hovering, Brand said, "Champagne." There was no need to add "well chilled," or "the best the house has to offer." They were in a private parlor in Watiers's club, and only the best was ever served here.

When the champagne was poured, Brand gave the toast. "To the fair Elinor and our comrade, Jack. Long life and happiness to you both."

Of the three men, Brand was the darkest. His skin

seemed to have a perpetual tan. His hair, cropped at the collar, was ink-black and his eyes were the true blue of a Cornishman's. With the right clothes, and in a different setting, he could easily have passed himself off as a gypsy. Among friends, he could relax, as at present. For the most part, however, he was an intensely private person and shared his inner thoughts with only a select few. Jack and Ash were among the select few, but even with them he could be reserved.

They made allowances. Though Brand was the son of an aristocrat, he'd been born on the wrong side of the blanket. He'd met prejudice in his time and had developed a thick shell to protect himself.

There was no reserve now as he quizzed Jack about how the fair Elinor had stormed the citadel. "I know," he went on, "there must be more to your capitulation than Ash told me," and he raised his brows drolly, inviting a response.

Jack removed a speck of lint from his sleeve, then looked up with a smile. "Ellie and I got off to a shaky start," he said, "but that's behind us now. The important thing is, I couldn't be happier with the way things have turned out," and in as few words as were necessary, he disabused them of the suspicion that he'd been forced into a marriage he did not want.

He was bending the truth a little. Circumstances *had* forced him to do right by Ellie, but now that they were wed, he didn't regret it. What he regretted was that the marriage was still in name only.

If he told his friends, they would laugh themselves silly, or they would bombard him with advice. He knew what he would say if Brand or Ash were in his shoes. *A man should be master of his own woman.* Whoever coined that old saw didn't know Ellie.

He didn't want to master her. For the first time in his

life, he'd found a woman whose opinion mattered to him. He had to exert himself to please. And she was hard to please.

His friends were looking at him expectantly. Where was he? "I couldn't be happier with the way things have turned out," he repeated, "and that's all I have to say on the matter. Now, can we order luncheon? I have a series of appointments this afternoon with prospective tutors for Ellie's brother and there's something important I want to discuss with you first."

Brand and Ash exchanged a quick look, then Brand called the waiter over and gave their order. When the waiter left, he looked at Jack. "We're all ears," he said.

"I presume," said Jack, "that Ash told you about the commission I was given by Sir Charles Stuart?"

Brand nodded. "Your wife's brother is suspected of murder. You were to take a statement from him and send it to Sir Charles."

"That has already been done. I also had to take a statement from his friend, Milton, because he can verify Robbie's account of things." He paused, marshaling his thoughts. "I'd best begin at the beginning, when things started to go wrong for Ellie."

Though he tried to keep his account brief and to the point, he told them everything, beginning with Robbie running up debts, Ellie raising the money to pay them off by gambling at the Palais Royal, and ending with the statements Robbie and Milton had made to his attorney.

After a prolonged silence, Ash said, "Ye Gods! I'd no idea that Miss Hill would turn out to be so interesting. A virtuoso, you say? I've heard about them. If I really were a fortune hunter, I'd marry her on the spot."

"Except that she's already married," Brand interposed. "Can we return to what is really important? Jack, tell me more about the attack on Ellie. You're not satisfied that it was a random break-in?"

"No." Jack raised his glass of champagne and took a small swallow. "What self-respecting burglar would break into her modest lodgings?"

Ash offered, "A burglar of 'modest' ambitions? Maybe all he wanted was the price of a tankard of ale."

"But nothing was taken. Her rooms were ransacked and he was lying in wait for her."

"Perhaps," Brand intervened, "he was after the Cardvale diamonds, and when he couldn't find them, he waited for her to return, with some idea of forcing her to tell him where they were hidden."

"That won't do," said Ash. "Jack gave her an alibi for the time the diamonds were taken. It's common knowledge. And at the time, he had nothing to gain by it. Ellie was practically a stranger to him."

"I wonder," said Brand. He took a sip of champagne before continuing. "For the sake of argument, let's say the thief wasn't looking for the diamonds. You see what this means?"

Jack had thought about this so often, he had his answer ready. "That Ellie has something in her possession that is valuable to the thief, without her being aware of it."

"What, for instance?" asked Ash, not bothering to hide his skepticism.

"I haven't the least idea," replied Jack. "I've searched her rooms, but have yet to find anything valuable or out of place. Incidentally, I've kept on the rooms for the time being, in the hope that the thief will return and we'll apprehend him." To Brand's questioning look, he nodded. "I've hired Bow Street Runners to keep an eye on the place."

Ash was astonished. "Don't you think you're making mountains out of molehills?"

Jack shrugged. "I sincerely hope so."

Brand was shaking his head.

"What?" asked Ash.

"Too many misadventures for one slip of a girl." He enumerated them on his fingers. "Someone who is close to Ellie, her brother, discovers the body of Louise Daudet and is himself attacked. Four days later, Lady Cardvale's diamonds are stolen and Ellie is implicated, until Jack gives her an alibi. Two weeks later, Ellie's lodgings are ransacked and the thief is still on the premises, possibly lying in wait for her." He looked at Jack. "Have I left anything out?"

Jack smiled ruefully. "You'll think I'm delusional, but the other day, quite by chance, or so it seemed, Ellie ran into Cardvale's man of business. His name is Paul Derby and she remembers him from when she once lived with her cousin. Derby, she told me, was very curious about Robbie, his domestic arrangements, his plans for the future, that sort of thing. His questions made her feel uneasy."

"Sounds to me as though he was being excessively polite," said Ash.

"There's something else." Jack went on, "When Robbie and Milton made their statements to my attorney—separately, mind—their accounts matched practically to the letter. Even my attorney said that their answers were too pat to be credible. They're hiding something, but I haven't the least idea what it is."

"Good Lord!" exclaimed Ash. "And we thought dueling was risky. These Brans-Hills could teach us a thing or two about living dangerously."

The humorous comment was just what was needed to

lighten Jack's mood. It did seem incredible that his former tutor's offspring should have become embroiled in some sinister plot. In another month, if there were no more incidents, he would look back on this and laugh at his fanciful turn of mind.

In the meantime, however, it gave him a good feeling to know that he had two good friends whose support he could count on. Ash was like himself, an amateur. Brand was different. He was a newspaperman. He was used to investigating plots and conspiracies and blazoning his findings on the front page of his newspapers. He would enjoy solving a good mystery.

A newspaperman. That was a misnomer. He was master of his own little empire and owned a string of newspapers in all the major cities of the southern counties.

When their smiles died away, Jack said, "I told you that Robbie isn't the only suspect in the case. French authorities are also looking for Louise Daudet's dresser and the man of mystery."

"The rich protector for whom she is supposed to have given up Robbie?" said Brand.

"Yes. But I can't help feeling that Ellie, through her brother, has become inadvertently involved, and that's the assumption I'm working on."

"I think that's a fair assumption," said Brand. He added quietly, "How can we help?"

Jack drained his glass. "I thought we'd begin in a small way, by investigating anyone who knew Ellie in Paris and is now back in town. You see what I'm getting at? This person must have been in Paris when Louise was murdered and then in town when Ellie's house was ransacked. Frankly, I don't know where else to begin."

"We'll need a list of names," said Ash.

Jack grinned. He fished in his pocket and withdrew a piece of folded paper. "I anticipated your request. There are only a few names here. I'm sure it's not a complete list, but at least it's a start." He offered the list to Brand. "I added Paul Derby's name. He may not have been in Paris when the murder took place, but he is connected to Cardvale."

"Thank you." Brand's tone was dry. "You think of everything."

Jack left immediately after they had eaten. Brand ordered coffee for two and he and Ash went over everything they'd heard from Jack. Ash was of the opinion that they were "tilting at windmills," as he put it, but Brand was keeping an open mind until he'd dug a little deeper. One thing they agreed on. The former Ellie Brans-Hill had well and truly caught their friend.

"What is she like?" Brand asked at one point.

Ash shrugged. "I hardly know. I only saw her twice, once at the embassy and once at the Palais Royal. As a paid companion, she was exactly as you would expect, an aging spinster who dressed modestly. As Aurora, she was a taking little thing."

"A schemer?"

"I think not or Jack would never have married her. I think she's as innocent as they come. She is, after all, a vicar's daughter." Ash shook his head. "And now she's a countess, poor girl."

"Yes," said Brand. "She may have been elevated to the rank of countess, but that doesn't entitle her to any privileges. Those society matrons can be vicious. They won't let her forget that she was once little more than a servant."

He understood prejudice only too well. He was a duke's illegitimate son, and though he'd been well provided for and had attended the best schools and universities, the taint of his birth had followed him like a dark cloud. One good thing had come of it. He'd been driven to succeed, and now, as the owner and publisher of several influential newspapers, he was cultivated by the very people who had once scorned him. No one in society or in the public eye wanted to make an enemy of Brand Hamilton, not when he could so easily destroy their reputations.

Jack and Ash had been his closest friends since they were at Eton together. In fact, they'd been his only friends. They had no idea how much that friendship had meant to him as a boy. How much it still meant to him.

He looked up to find Ash studying him. "What?" he asked.

Ash said, "You're smiling, and that doesn't happen very often. So what's on your mind?"

That observation wiped the smile from Brand's face. "Only idiots smile all the time," he remarked. "As for what's on my mind, I was contemplating the pleasures of taking in the season. I shall have to ask my valet to shake out my evening clothes. Perhaps a visit to my tailor wouldn't hurt."

Ash cocked his head to one side. "You never take in the season," he said. "You despise polite society and its hollow modes and manners. I've heard you say so more times than I can remember."

Brand let out a patient sigh. "That was before our comrade wed his Elinor. It's our duty to lend our support. And she'll need it, if I know anything about human nature. They'll never forgive or forget that she was once a lady's companion. Are we going to let her fend for herself?"

"What can we do?" Ash sat back in his chair. "Call everybody out?"

"No. But you're a popular fellow. A word from you in the right ear could help ease her way in society."

"Consider it done. And what about you, Brand? What will you do to help Jack's wife?"

Another fleeting smile. "Anyone who snubs her or makes her life difficult will find themselves lampooned in my newspaper."

"And if they won't mend their ways?"

"I'll ruin them."

Ash suppressed a shudder. "I'd hate to have you for an enemy, Brand."

Ellie was upstairs in the drawing room, arranging flowers from the hothouse in two exquisite crystal vases, when she heard the commotion downstairs. She ignored it. Jack was in the library interviewing a Mr. Barrie for the post of tutor and he could investigate much more quickly than she. Besides, she felt like a guest in this house, and was reluctant to interfere in any domestic matter. Only when Jack's grandmother stood behind her, in person, did she have the confidence to take charge, but the dowager and Caro were making calls, leaving the newlyweds to amuse themselves.

What Grandmamma expected them to get up to did not bear thinking about. All the same, she was glad of any excuse to delay the inevitable bridal visits she would be expected to make soon. She understood polite society only too well, having lived on its fringes for a number of years, and she did not expect to receive a warm reception.

"Jack! Jack! Where are you?"

The voice was feminine. Curious now, Ellie put down her scissors and made her way to the gallery, where she halted and looked over the banister.

"Where is everyone?" cried the lady who stood in the hall, removing her coat and bonnet while footmen carried her boxes upstairs. "Jack? Caro? I'm home."

This could only be Frances, the widow of Jack's brother. Ellie had heard a great deal about Jack's sister-in-law from Caro, all of it complimentary. Caro had not exaggerated the lady's beauty. Pale blonde ringlets framed a heart-shaped face. She was small and feminine. Even her voice was feminine, not girlish, but soft with a hint of huskiness. Her garments marked her as a lady of fashion.

Pinning a smile to her face to cover her nervousness, Ellie began to descend the stairs. She was halfway down when the library door opened and Jack appeared.

"Frances," he said. "This is a surprise. We weren't expecting you till next week."

Frances laughed. "Caro wrote me and told me the good news. So, you're caught at last! I can scarcely believe it."

Crossing to Jack, she lifted her face to his and pursed her lips, inviting a kiss. There was something intimate and wifely about the gesture that made Ellie feel like an intruder, and she wondered whether she could slip away unseen. This seemed cowardly, so she stood her ground, waiting to be noticed.

Jack ignored the pursed lips and brushed a careless kiss on Frances's brow. Disentangling himself from the lady's arms, he looked toward the stairs. "Ellie," he said, "come and meet my sister-in-law, and yours, too, now that we are wed."

Keeping her smile in place, Ellie descended the stairs and crossed to Frances. The formal introductions were never made. Frances enfolded her in her arms and hugged her.

"You," said Frances, "shall be the sister I never had." She held her at arm's length and spoke to Jack. "She's lovely, Jack, but I should have expected it. You always had an eye for beauty."

"I've always wanted a sister," said Ellie.

Frances was beautiful, sweet and friendly, and Ellie disliked her on sight. It was natural, she supposed, after the housekeeper's set down and Caro's effusive praise for dear Frances, who had all the attributes Ellie seemed to lack. But it was unfair to Frances to dislike her for that. Surely she wasn't so childish!

"But red hair?" Frances laughed. "I distinctly remember you telling me that you couldn't abide red hair."

"Ah, but that was before I met Ellie," replied Jack with an adeptness that Ellie could only admire.

Frances linked her arm through Ellie's. "Come along," she said. "You can talk to me while I change. I suppose Grandmamma and Caro are out making calls?" As she spoke, she steered Ellie to the stairs. "Why aren't you with them?" she shook her head. "Silly me! You're afraid that the tabby cats will tear you to shreds. Well, now that I'm here, that won't happen. I am not without influence, and any unkindness to you will be repaid in full by me."

Ellie chanced to look back at Jack. He was standing in the center of the spacious hallway, arms folded across his chest, watching them as they mounted the stairs. She couldn't tell what he was thinking.

The woman was perfect. Another reason why she could not warm to her, Ellie mused as she watched Alice dress her sister-in-law. Frances's figure, though not voluptuous, was nicely rounded. The gown she had chosen to wear, an aqua silk that brought out the aqua in her eyes, was the kind of gown Aurora would be happy to wear.

But Frances wasn't like Aurora. She wasn't dashing and devil-may-care. She was intensely feminine. Her smiles, her laughs, her fluttering lashes and sidelong glances were pure coquette.

After seating herself at her dressing table, Frances selected an opal pendant from the jewelry box that Alice held out to her, then she angled her head so that the maid could fasten it around her throat.

Even her choice of jewelry was perfect.

When it occurred to Ellie that she was seriously looking for flaws, she gave herself a mental shake. This was nonsense. She couldn't dislike Frances just because she felt inadequate. Surely, she was more mature than that?

Her train of thought was interrupted when Frances gave a sudden shriek. Ellie's heart leaped to her throat.

Her lovely features twisting in fury, Frances slapped the maid's hand away, and turned to snarl at her. "You caught my skin in the clasp, you...you ball of fat. Go back to the laundry where you belong! Send Meghan to me."

Tears flooded the little maid's eyes. Biting down on her lip, she bobbed a curtsy and hurried from the room.

Ellie hardly knew where to look, but there was no awkwardness on Frances's part. She held out the pendant and smiled at Ellie as though nothing had happened. "Help me, Ellie?"

Help her? Ellie wanted to strangle her! In her time as a lady's companion, she'd been the recipient of slights and snubs, but no one had ever called her names. Had they done so, she would have left their employ.

She fastened the clasp without incident, but could not bring herself to smile. "I should change, too," she said, not wanting to spend another minute with this woman, "before the others come home."

To her own ears, it was a feeble excuse, but Frances's mind was obviously on something else. She got up and linked her arm through Ellie's as she walked her to the door.

"Ellie," she said, her tone, like her smile, dulcet and confiding, "I don't know what you may have heard about Jack and me, but I promise you, you have nothing to worry about. It's true that I was engaged to Jack once, but after I met Cedric, there was no one else for me. I had to break my engagement to Jack. You do see that, don't you?"

Her mind in a whirl, Ellie could only nod. No one had ever told her that Jack and his sister-in-law were once engaged to be married.

Frances shrugged gracefully. "Naturally the family blamed me when Jack went off to become a soldier. But if he suffered, so did I. I don't have it in me to hurt a fly, much less someone who loves me."

She opened the door. "His marriage to you makes me hope that he is finally over this youthful infatuation. After all, nothing can come of it. As the law stands, we can never marry."

Lucky, lucky Jack! Ellie thought.

She felt herself being gently propelled into the corridor. "All I ask," Frances went on, "is that you make him happy. And I promise I shall do everything in my power to make you comfortable. I know you have never had to manage a household of this magnitude. Well, don't give it another thought. I shall continue in my role as chatelaine. Just enjoy yourself, Ellie."

A moment later, Ellie found herself staring at a closed door.

Once in her own chamber, she sat on the bed and let her mind roam through Frances's monologue, and that's what it was, a monologue. All that was required of her was to be silent and biddable, just as though she were still a lady's companion.

It didn't take her long to come to the conclusion that

she had been mauled as badly as Alice. She felt inadequate as a wife and a countess. Alice was plump. Had Frances divined their weaknesses and used them to humiliate the two women?

On that thought, she jumped to her feet and went in search of Alice. She wasn't going to let Mrs. Leach get her teeth into the little maid.

She found her with Webster, going through one of the linen closets. She had stopped crying and was listening intently to what the head housemaid was saying.

"Yes, my lady?" asked Webster.

Ellie said, "I just wanted to make sure that Alice was all right. I thought she looked rather pale in Lady Frances's room."

Miss Webster's eyes had a knowing glint. "She does get nervous around Lady Frances, so I thought it would be best to assign Alice to other duties for the next little while."

So, thought Ellie, *Miss Webster tries to protect the little maid, too.* She was beginning to like the head housemaid more and more.

"I think that's a splendid idea," she said.

Miss Webster nodded. "She'll be a great help to me with mending the linens. Alice is accomplished with a needle. Her stitches are always invisible. And in the laundry, there's not a stain or mark Alice doesn't know how to get out. One of these days, she'll make a fine lady's maid."

"That's good to know."

Alice was emboldened to say, "My mother was a lady's maid."

"Well, then," said Ellie, "when your duties allow, you must look through my garments and give them a good turnout."

She made the offer knowing that none of the maids would feel that Alice was encroaching on her territory.

There were no abigails as such, but the maids with senior-
ity were expected to drop everything and fill in as lady's
maid as required.

Alice's blue, blue eyes were filling up with tears again.
"Thank you, my lady. I'll do my best."

Ellie and Miss Webster exchanged a gratified smile.

Chapter 15

In the following weeks, Ellie's fortunes took a turn for the better. It began when Sir Charles wrote to say that the prime suspects in the case were now the dresser and her lover. It seemed that Louise Daudet had withdrawn a large sum of money from her bank. Not only was that missing, but so were some especially fine pieces of her jewelry, and someone remembered seeing the dresser wearing a broach belonging to the actress on or near the date of the murder.

Ellie and Robbie were in Jack's study when he read the ambassador's letter to them. When he came to the end, he folded it and locked it in his desk. "I need not tell you," he said, "that this settles nothing. The dresser is only suspected in the murder. She has not been found guilty."

Robbie shook his head. "But why has she become the prime suspect? They must know from the statement we sent to Sir Charles that I was at the murder scene. If I were an officer of the law, I would think that far more incriminating than a broach the dresser wore. For all we know, Louise might have made the girl a present of the broach."

"True," said Jack, "but the difference is, the dresser and her lover have disappeared. No one has seen them since the night of the murder. You may have run away, but eventually you came forward and made a statement of your own accord. That is in your favor. Then there is Sir Charles. He is on your side, so they know they have to come up with more than circumstantial evidence to prove their case. Sir Charles carries a great deal of influence with Wellington."

Suddenly it was too much for Ellie. Her eyes became teary. Robbie patted her awkwardly on the shoulder. "There, there, Sis. Don't take on so. This will all come out right in the end." He forced a laugh. "With Sir Charles and Jack on our side, how can we not succeed in proving my innocence? Tell her, Jack."

"I prefer to say," said Jack with a smile, "that with Ellie on your side, you have nothing to worry about."

Ellie gave a watery laugh.

Robbie got up. "I want to thank you, sir, for all that you've done for me. And if there is anything I can do for you, you have only to ask."

"Just listen to your tutor and concentrate on that Greek examination that is coming up."

"I'll do my best."

When she and Jack were alone, Ellie said, "This is good news, isn't it, Jack?"

"It would seem so."

This noncommittal answer left her less than satisfied. "Your friend, Brand Hamilton, won't have to go on with his investigation, will he? I mean, what would be the point?"

The faint frown in his eyes vanished. "There never was much evidence to suggest that either you or Robbie was in any danger. It was all speculation on my part. It seems I was wrong."

"That's a relief!" She got up. "Any words of wisdom for me?"

He steepled his fingers, then looked up at her. "As a matter of fact, I have. It's time for you to make your bows to society. Don't look so stricken. It's no worse than Robbie facing a Greek examination. And I've found the perfect tutor for you, too."

After she left, Jack sat at his desk, gazing into space, his fingers idly drumming out a tattoo. In spite of what he'd said to Ellie, he wasn't satisfied that they were in the clear yet, but he had nothing to substantiate that view. In fact, everything contradicted it. There were no more break-ins, no more attacks, no one spying on her or Robbie. A reasonable man would accept the obvious.

On the battlefield, an officer who too readily accepted the obvious could lead his men into a trap. He wasn't prepared to take that chance with Ellie.

It was better to err on the side of caution. The investigation would go forward.

The perfect tutor for Ellie turned out to be Jack's friend, Ash Denison. Ash was a member of the dandy set. He knew how to bring a lady up to snuff and launch her in society. At first Ellie was wary, thinking she would be snubbed at every turn, but when Ash introduced her to one of *his* friends, Beau Brummel, who made a point of promenading with her during one of the intermissions at the King's Theater, and the trickle of people who stopped to chat became a flood, she realized how lucky she was to have Ash as her mentor. Beau Brummel, for some odd reason, wielded immense influence. A word from him could bring a lady into fashion or do the opposite. She was one of the favored few.

Try as she might, however, she couldn't completely

overcome her anxiety. As the Countess of Raleigh, she was expected to be a fashion plate. People were watching her every move. Some, she knew, would be hoping to see her fall on her face. It was her desire not to shame Jack that made her determined to succeed.

This wasn't only her pride at work. She was coming to see that, with Jack, actions spoke louder than words. When she catalogued all the ways he'd helped Robbie and her since they'd crashed into his life like a fiery comet, she felt guilty for snapping at him just because he was inept with words. He wasn't inept so much as too frank for comfort.

She wished they could start over. Then there would be no locked door between them. All she had to do was invite him in. She was working herself up to it, trying to show him with *her* actions what she found so hard to put into words. She'd unlocked the door a long time ago. Why wouldn't the stupid man turn the doorknob?

One thing she knew that would please Jack was if she and Caro could become friends. This was easier said than done, for Caro made no secret of her preference for Frances. Daunted, but not entirely without hope, Ellie invited Caro to come driving with her and Ash in the park.

They were on the stairs, and Ellie was dressed to go out. Caro drew back as though she'd been stung.

"Go driving! With you?" Caro's voice was quivering.

"Well, Ash will be driving, so you'll be quite safe."

"What about Frances?"

"What about her?" asked Ellie, her heart sinking. She was wishing she had let well enough alone.

Caro was a pretty girl with a clear complexion, large, expressive eyes, and dark glossy hair that curled naturally. She didn't look pretty to Ellie at that moment. She looked like a fledgling witch.

"You'll never displace her," Caro declared, "not in

Jack's affections or as mistress here. You may have tricked my brother into marrying you, but don't expect me to like it."

Ellie adjusted her gloves. "Is that a 'no'? What a pity! Beau Brummel was hoping to meet you when we were out driving. Perhaps another time."

She went down the stairs to meet Ash as though she hadn't a care in the world.

It did not take long for Ash to see through her forced gaiety. "Don't tell me Frances has been up to her old tricks," he said.

"What tricks are those?" she asked archly.

"She must be the queen bee. They always sting their rivals to death. It's in their nature."

She turned her head to look at him. "Now, that is very acute of you. But it's not Frances who has stung me."

"Then it's Caro."

She sighed. "She is devoted to Frances and seems to think I'm a threat to her. Of course she's wrong."

Ash laughed. "No, Ellie, you're wrong. Frances's days as the queen bee are numbered, and there's nothing she can do about it. Caro knows this, too, but she's not ready to accept it."

She watched him maneuver his team around a lady's phaeton before she replied, "The last time a queen bee took a dislike to me, I left the hive." She was thinking of Dorothea. "I won't let that happen again."

Ash grinned. "That's more like it."

If she was to take in the season, she had to dress for the part of Jack's countess, and that meant ordering a complete new wardrobe. Jack was happy to leave everything in Ash's capable hands. He was an authority on ladies' fashions, a subject on which Jack felt out of his depth.

Thus it was that Ellie found herself, a few days later, on her way to Madame Clothilde's, one of London's most celebrated modistes, in an open curricle driven by Ash Denison. Had she visited the modiste with any other gentleman, the dowager told her, tongues would have begun to wag. But Ash's advice was sought after. That he had offered to be her mentor was a coup for her.

Madame Clothilde's establishment was on the Knightsbridge Road. This was Ellie's second visit. The first time, she and Ash had selected various designs and fabrics for the garments that were necessary to see her through the season—morning gowns, afternoon gowns, walking gowns, carriage dresses, and, of course, the inevitable ball gowns. The list was endless. Ellie felt guilty for spending so much money, but it was all done with Jack's approval. He trusted Ash, he said, not to bankrupt him. Moreover, he found the topic of ladies' fashions a dead bore, and since Parliament was now in session, he felt obliged to show his face in the House from time to time.

Ash scoffed at this. He couldn't think of anything more boring than sitting in the House of Lords when the real work of Parliament was done in the Commons. He'd far rather dress a pretty woman.

They left the groom standing by the horses' heads while they entered the premises. Madame saw her clients by appointment only, so there were no other customers to be waited on. She was in her early forties and the best advertisement for the garments she sold. Her silver hair flattered her patrician features. Her slender figure was clothed in a long-sleeved gown of deep lavender. Though she was eager to please, she was not intrusive. And her French accent, faint though it was after many years in England, was pleasant on the ears.

She led them upstairs, where two of her assistants were

laying out a selection of garments that would see Ellie through the next few weeks, until the rest of her wardrobe was ready. There wasn't a gray gown in sight.

Ellie stood there entranced, her gaze moving slowly from one delectable creation to another. Ash, with a little help from Madame, had chosen the colors that suited her hazel eyes and auburn hair—shades of ivory, green, tawny brown, and gold. She had a vision of Jack following her with his eyes, struck dumb with admiration for the beautiful creature she'd become.

Ash was watching her intently. "I've arranged a little party," he said, "with Jack's grandmother and Caro. We're to meet them at the Clarendon for dinner. Don't worry about Jack. He'll be tied up at the House for hours."

"Dinner! At the Clarendon!" She knew the hotel by reputation. "Isn't that a bit risqué, Ash?"

"Nonsense. Didn't you hear me? The dowager and Caro will be there. Oh, I invited Robbie, too, but his friend Milton is in town and they're engaged to go to the theater with friends."

"What about Frances?"

"I didn't bother to ask. She's hosting one of her literary get-togethers, don't you remember?" His eyes were twinkling.

Her lips began to twitch. "How did you persuade Caro to join us?"

"I promised that Beau Brummel would be there. Why have you stopped smiling?"

"I'm not dressed for a dinner party."

"That," he said patiently, "is why we are here." He spoke to the modiste. "Madame, shall we begin?"

By the time they were ready to leave, Ellie's head was spinning. Ash and Madame had discussed and handled her as though she were a tailor's mannequin with no mind of her own. Her indignation was short-lived. How could a lady object when she heard herself spoken of in such flattering terms?

"It is a pleasure to dress someone who is so perfectly proportioned." That was Madame.

"This apricot shade is perfect on her. It adds a blush to that fine-pored complexion." That was Ash.

"Her hair is wrong. It's too long." Madame.

"I beg to differ. The style is too severe. Let's soften it a little around her face. Where are the scissors?" Ash.

"But . . . but . . . I've always worn my hair this way." That was Ellie.

"Ah!" That was Madame, when Ash let down Ellie's hair. "That color! So rich, so silky. Truly a woman's crowning glory. You are right, monsieur. It is not too long. I think it is her best feature."

This was all very heady for a lady who had spent the last number of years living in the shadow of brighter lights than she. Not that she had cared. Looks and fashion had never been highly prized in her family and she wondered what Papa and Mama would say if they could see her now.

She doubted they would notice the difference, but they would applaud her desire to be a credit to her husband.

Ash came to stand behind her at the cheval mirror. "All ready to make your grand entrance at the Clarendon?"

She was wearing a creamy tissue gauze afternoon gown in the current mode—low bodice, high waist, and puff sleeves. It was the attention to detail that lifted it above the ordinary. The neckline and hem were embroidered with tiny rosebuds in gold threads.

When she nodded mutely, Ash held out the apricot merino wool pelisse for her and she slipped into it.

Madame came forward with a high poke bonnet that tied under her chin with satin ribbons to match the pelisse.

"Tell me the truth, Ash," she said. "How did you get Caro to forgo Frances's literary get-together to have dinner with me?"

"I told you. The lure of meeting *the* Beau, what else?"

"You're an unscrupulous schemer," she scolded and laughed.

"I've never denied it."

Boxes were packed and stowed. The odd gown still had to be hemmed, but Ellie assured Madame that her maid, Alice, was a competent seamstress and could be trusted to do the task well. Thanks were expressed, then they were on their way to the Clarendon.

Chapter 16

Jack was in his study with Robbie's tutor when Ellie arrived home. He heard her lilting laugh and Ash's voice as they passed his door. He tried to pay attention to what Mr. Barrie was saying, but he could not drum up any interest in Robbie's problems with Greek grammar. He'd heard it all before. Besides, his mind was on other things.

He glanced at the clock. She wasn't expecting him to be home at this hour. He'd left the House early with some idea of taking Ellie to the theater, just the two of them, only to be told by his butler that no one was home with the exception of Frances, and she was hosting her literary soiree in the drawing room. He took that as a warning and shut himself up in his study to wait, with diminishing patience, for his wife to come home. And it was in his study that Mr. Barrie found him by chance when he came by with a book for Robbie.

She'd been with Ash for close to five hours. It wouldn't have been so bad if they'd come home when it was still light. But this was February. Dark came early. The candles were lit. Where had they been? What had they been doing? And why was he behaving like a sulky schoolboy? He'd sanctioned these outings. He knew they were innocent. What rubbed him was that Ellie was spending more time with Ash than she did with him. A husband ought to have a few private moments alone with his wife throughout the day.

They were never alone unless one counted their early morning rides in Hyde Park, but even then, they hardly exchanged more than a few words. Ellie spoke more to her horse than she did to him.

He had a base, salacious imagination. He would watch her pet Blackie as she bounced up and down on the saddle and the most lurid pictures would flash in front of his eyes. It didn't stop there. He would watch in fascination as she bit down on a piece of dry toast and delicately licked the crumbs from her lips. It went on and on. She wasn't to know that she was driving him crazy.

If he'd known that this is what came of celibacy, he would never have handed her that key, never have uttered those challenging words. He needed no invitation to enter her bedchamber. He was her husband, and a husband had rights.

He didn't want to exercise his rights. He wanted a warm, willing woman in his bed. And in spite of the lack of opportunity to be alone with her, he sensed he was making progress. She laughed at his jokes, listened to his opinions, and seemed genuinely pleased to have him around. Besides, he knew she was a woman of warm emotions. How long could she go against her own nature?

A paper fluttered in front of his face and he looked up at Mr. Barrie. He was a retired schoolteacher, came highly recommended, and was so much in demand that he could spare Robbie only an hour or two every day.

"Perhaps this will explain what I mean," said Mr.

Barrie. "If Robbie would only master the subjunctive, we could move on to the optative."

Jack looked at the paper that Robbie had completed for his tutor. He could barely remember the Greek alphabet himself, much less the conjugation of Greek verbs. He couldn't help pitying Robbie. This must be torture for him. If Ellie's heart hadn't been set on a university degree for her brother, he would have told Robbie to give it up. There were plenty of things he could do to earn a living without a degree. And Jack had influence. He would help him.

To the tutor, he said, "Leave it with me. I'll make sure Robbie does this over."

"He'll need help," replied the tutor dubiously.

"That won't be a problem."

He was aware that a new respect glowed in Mr. Barrie's tired eyes. The gentleman said, "Not many gentlemen keep up their Greek. It's gratifying to know that there are some who appreciate what we teachers have done for them."

"Quite so."

He saw no need to correct Mr. Barrie's false assumption or bring Ellie's name into the conversation, and with a haste he hoped was not unseemly, he showed the tutor out.

Before ascending the stairs, he stopped for a moment in front of a pier glass and studied his reflection. He scarcely ever thought of his clothes. That was his valet's job, but he wondered, fleetingly, if perhaps he was a tad too conservative in his tastes. That was what Ash thought.

Pushing that irritating thought aside, he began to climb the stairs. He thought Ellie might have gone to her room to tidy herself, but there was only one place Ash could be and that was in the drawing room. He was tempted to leave him there as punishment for keeping Ellie out so long, but his conscience wouldn't allow it. No one should have to suffer through one of Frances's tedious literary affairs.

When he entered the drawing room, he came to an uncertain stop. There was no sign of Ash or Ellie among the group of chirping ladies who were taking tea.

When Frances rose and came to greet him, the chirping died away.

"Jack," she said in her well-modulated voice, "what a pleasant surprise. Do stay and have tea with us. Mrs. Tuttle is about to share her latest piece on..."

She glanced over at a plump, disorganized lady who promptly replied, "The purpose of the chorus in Greek drama."

Greek again! Jack suppressed a shudder, politely declined the invitation, and said for Frances's ears only, "I thought I heard Ellie come home. Was I mistaken?"

Aqua eyes smiled into his. In a voice that carried to every corner of the room, she replied, "The last I saw of her, she went driving with Lord Denison, but that was more than five hours ago." She sucked in a breath. "I hope there has not been an accident."

The ladies behind her gave a collective gasp.

Five hours with another man. That was what Frances wanted everyone to know. He wanted to shake her. Instead, he feigned dismay.

"Good grief! I was to meet them at Madame Clothilde's. It slipped my mind. I suppose they are still there waiting for me." And like any distracted husband, he left them all staring.

He knew damn well that Ellie was in the house somewhere. He couldn't be sure about Ash. He might have slipped away while Jack was with the tutor. *Five hours alone with Ash.* Frances had done her work well.

He found them in the corridor outside Ellie's bedchamber. Ellie had a dreamy expression on her face and Ash was kissing her hand.

"Ellie!" said Jack in a voice like thunder.

She jumped back with a guilty start. Ash turned to face Jack, wearing his usual sardonic expression. "Talk of the devil," he said. "You're home early." He cocked his head to one side. "I can tell by the expression on your face that you're the bearer of bad news. Don't say we've declared war on France again!"

As sardonic as his friend, Jack replied, "Worse than that. I've been talking to Robbie's tutor, but we'll get to that later. If I'm home early, you're home late. Five hours is a long time to leave your horses standing out in the cold, Ash. I thought you were more careful of your cattle than that."

"My 'cattle'?" Ash frowned faintly. As enlightenment dawned, the frown vanished and he looked as though he was smothering a smile. "So that's it! I'm sure my horses will be touched by your concern, but it is quite unnecessary. You see, I sent them home when your grandmother offered to take us up in her carriage. We've been at the Clarendon, lingering over a scrumptious dinner. Time has a way of flying when one is enjoying oneself, doesn't it? But here we are, and no harm done to my horses."

"You were with my grandmother?"

"And Caro," said Ellie, color high on her cheeks. She was beginning to grasp that there was a subtext to this conversation, and she did not like it one bit.

Jack's gaze shifted when his grandmother and Caro appeared in the doorway to Ellie's room. Caro's eyes were shining. His grandmother's held a knowing twinkle.

Caro could hardly contain herself. "We met your friend, Mr. Brummel, and he promised to come to my ball. All my friends will be green with envy. And...and

Lord Denison has promised to take me to Madame Clothilde's to have my ball gown made up." Her voice became reverent. "Ellie's things are so lovely."

"And *expensive*," added the dowager with an air of satisfaction. "Only the best is good enough for our Ellie, though I'm not sure that marrying my clod of a grandson is the best she could do."

Jack said nothing. He was beginning to feel sheepish for having misjudged the situation.

"Grandmamma!" protested Caro. "Jack could have his pick of any girl he wanted." Her sunny smile vanished and she threw Ellie a resentful look.

Her ladyship snorted. "A girl who is there for the asking isn't the sort of girl a man wants. Take a leaf out of Ellie's book. She didn't want your brother at any price. No. No more debate. Let's leave these two children to settle their differences about…"—the twinkle in her eye became more pronounced— "…horses."

Ash said something indistinct. The dowager laughed. Shaking her head, she propelled her granddaughter along the corridor, Ash following in their wake.

Her spine as straight as a ramrod, Ellie marched into her room. Jack hesitated for a moment, but when she looked back at him with raised brows, he took that as an invitation. After entering her chamber, he shut the door.

There were opened boxes on the floor and garments in various fabrics and colors were draped over the bed and chairs. *This* is what he wanted for her, the finer things that had been out of her reach when she'd become the sole support of her little family. She deserved the best and he was determined that she should have it.

His eyes shifted to Ellie and his smile died. In the dimly lit corridor, he hadn't noticed what she was wearing, but several candles were lit around the room and he saw her in startling, scandalous detail. She looked like every man's deepest, darkest fantasy.

"Is that one of Madame Clothilde's creations?" he asked abruptly.

The reference to her new gown mollified her considerably. This is what she'd been waiting for—Jack's reaction to her transformation. She couldn't help preening.

"It is. Do you like it?"

His voice rose a notch. "You wore that to go shopping?"

Her smile trembled, then vanished. "I changed into it at Madame Clothilde's and wore it to the Clarendon. It was Ash's idea."

" 'Ash's idea'!" If his friend had been there, he would have had him by the throat. The bodice was so low that one little tug would have exposed her nipples. "I expected better of him, and better of you. The skirt is practically transparent."

These were not words she expected to hear. She said tartly, "Stuff and nonsense! Your grandmother said my gown was ravishing and Caro wants one just like it. Frankly, I don't understand you. This style is all the rage. Everywhere you go, you'll see ladies in these transparent gauzes."

"You're not every lady. You're my wife."

She threw up her hands in sheer frustration. "That's my point. I didn't ask for this." She swished her skirts. "You told me to trust Ash's judgment and I did. He says I'm an Incomparable. He says that my garments are in the height of fashion. He says that every lady will be green with envy when I enter a room."

It was what the men would think that set his teeth on edge. He knew his sex only too well. "I wouldn't believe everything Ash tells you."

He knew he sounded ungracious, but he couldn't seem

to help himself. He felt restless and edgy and was coming to regret that he'd agreed to allow Ash to bring Ellie up to snuff. He wasn't jealous. He knew Ellie and Ash better than that. What he objected to was that he, her husband, seemed to have been pushed to the far edge of her life.

Trying not to sound boorish, he said boorishly, "Ash is an inveterate flirt. He can't help himself. Don't let him turn your head with empty compliments."

This was adding insult to injury. The triumph she had anticipated when Jack saw the changes she'd made to make him proud of her had turned to ashes. Nothing of this showed in her expression. She said sweetly. "You should study Ash, Jack. Take a leaf out of his book. He knows how to treat a lady."

Tears of mortification were burning her eyes, so she turned away and began to fold the gowns on the bed so that she wouldn't betray how crushed she felt.

"Any fool can string pretty words together," he said moodily. "Even I."

She gave a soft, derisory laugh. "You're missing the point. It's not the pretty words that count, but the sincerity behind them. Ash understands that."

Too late, she realized that she was deliberately goading him. She should apologize at once.

And she would, when he admitted that he was a jackass.

When he advanced upon her, she took a quick step back and put out a hand as though to defend herself. There was a dark, brooding look in his eyes that told her her gibe had found its mark.

Now why did that please her?

His voice was husky. "You want sincerity? I'll give you sincerity. I don't care what you wear. In fact, I'd prefer it if you didn't wear anything at all. I want you naked in my bed. I want to make love to you. I can't speak plainer than that."

Her eyes were wide, her jaw was slack. "Wh ... what?" she stuttered.

Deliberately, he lowered his head to hers, delighting in the glaze in her eyes and the warmth of her breath on his lips. "If you were really mine," he murmured, "Ash wouldn't be a problem."

"He wouldn't?" she whispered.

"No, because he'd know you were mine." His voice took on a darker color. "A woman who finds pleasure in her husband's bed is a happy woman. She has a certain air about her. She's replete, satisfied, and it shows."

She was breathing hard. "I see. I'm to go to bed with you so that all your friends will know what a lusty roué you are!"

He was taken aback. One moment she was yielding; the next, she was on the attack. Aggrieved, he said, "You're twisting my words."

"Well, try twisting this." She poked him in the chest with enough force to make him wince. "I have never been more insulted in my life. When I go to bed with a man, it will be because I care for him, not to show off his prowess as a lover."

He combed his fingers through his hair. "I don't know what the problem is. You've loved me since you were a girl. Fine, now you can have me without compromising your scruples. Our union has been blessed by the church. What more do you want?"

She pressed the heel of her hand to her chest to ease her choked-off breath. Her dignity was crushed. Her pride was in ruins. Could she possibly be that transparent?

There was only one answer to such arrogance. "You've been listening to the gossips, Jack. May I remind you that we concocted that story to silence them? This marriage was forced upon us. Neither of us wanted it. We're both on trial. I suggest that you learn how to woo a lady and I'll do my best not to throttle you when you spout nonsense."

"'*Woo*' you?" He sounded more confused than angry. "Good God, woman, I married you."

Her shoulders stiffened. "In name only!"

"That's what I'm trying to tell you. We can change that here and now. The sooner the better."

Air *whoosh*ed out of her lungs. She hurried to the door and held it open. He took the hint, but halted on the threshold.

"I was right about that gown," he said. "You should look in a mirror." And with a lecherous grin, he sauntered off.

Ellie shut the door firmly behind him, when what she wanted to do was slam it. "*Prude!*" she said under her breath. He'd never complained about Aurora's dashing getup. Now that she had married him, everything was different. She wandered over to the cheval mirror to examine what had provoked his ire and what she saw made her gape. Madame Clothilde had warned her to be careful because not all the seams in her gown were stitched in place. That was obvious. The bodice hung open, revealing an indecent expanse of bare bosom.

She let out one horrified squeal, then stumbled to the bellpull and yanked on it to summon a maid. Having done that, she hauled the bodice up to cover her bare breasts.

She was completely mortified. Poor Jack. He'd tried to tell her and she'd instantly taken umbrage. She hadn't realized she was, literally, coming apart at the seams. It must have happened gradually, because she was sure the dowager would have said something before she embarrassed herself.

Jack had told her, so she'd taken umbrage and things

had gone from bad to worse. How could he be so dense? It wasn't compliments she wanted so much as a sign that he truly cared for her. Was *bed* all he could think about?

There was a knock at the door.

"Enter," she called out.

The maid who entered was one of the chambermaids. She was small-boned, with a quick intelligence in her bright eyes and a ready smile on her face.

"Meghan," said Ellie, "I need Alice to stitch up my gown. I'm afraid to move in case the whole thing falls apart. She'll know what to do."

Meghan's ready smile faded. "Alice is gone, mu'um," she said.

"'Gone'?" Ellie's brow wrinkled.

Meghan began to fidget. "She left the day before yesterday, before anyone was up."

"You mean, she crept away without telling anyone where she was going?"

Now Meghan began to look frightened. "No, mu'um. She was let go by Lady Raleigh."

"Which Lady Raleigh?" There were two of them, not counting herself.

"The mistress."

That rankled, though Ellie was careful not to show it. Meghan could only mean Frances. She said as gently as she could manage, "Why did Lady Raleigh let Alice go?"

If Meghan was restless before, now she was agitated. "I don't know. I can't say. Mrs. Leach said I wasn't to speak of it to anyone."

Ellie nodded. She didn't want to distress the maid, but she wanted to get to the bottom of this. "Does Webster know?"

"Yes, my lady. But she can't say anything. Mrs. Leach blames her for not seeing it coming."

"Did Alice steal something?"

Meghan's face registered shock. "No!"

"Was she rude? Impertinent to Lady Raleigh?"

"No, mu'um." Tears were swimming in Meghan's eyes.

A thought nagged at the back of Ellie's mind. Frances had called Alice "a ball of fat."

"Meghan," she said softly, "is Alice in trouble? You know what I mean. Is she in the family way?"

When the tears in Meghan's eyes spilled over, Ellie made a space for her on one of the chairs, pressed her into it, and gave her a handkerchief to blow her nose. It took her a few moments to remove her gown and slip into her dressing gown, then she came back to Meghan and kneeled in front of her.

"Now," she said, smiling encouragingly, "Alice has got herself in trouble and needs our help. I promise I won't say a word to Lady Raleigh. It will be our secret. But I must know what happened to Alice and where she went or I won't know how to help her. Do you understand?"

Meghan nodded, dried her tears, and told Ellie as much as she knew.

It was a common story. Alice had a young man. They were supposed to marry, but when Alice fell with child, her young man had taken off for greener pastures, promising to come back for her when he found work, and that was the last she'd seen or heard from him.

She'd tried to conceal her pregnancy as best she could, but as time passed, that became increasingly difficult. Mrs. Leach's eagle eye was impossible to fool for long. So Alice was turned off on the spot.

Her own family, decent country people, wouldn't have her back at any price. Disgraced, with no one to turn to and with very little money, she had taken lodgings with a family in Westminster while she looked for work. But work was hard to find.

The word "workhouse" hovered in the air.

Now Ellie understood why Alice was always teary-eyed. What a burden to bear by herself!

When Meghan came to the end of her story, Ellie's sympathetic manner became briskly optimistic. She would take care of Alice, she promised. She was a vicar's daughter, and had done this kind of thing before. And on that reassuring promise, Meghan's ready smile soon lit up her thin face.

When Meghan left, Ellie took the chair she had vacated and let her thoughts dwell on her conversation with the maid. She'd exaggerated a little. It was her mother who had helped girls in distress, not she. But with Mama's example to guide her, she knew where her duty lay.

Her circumstances were different from Mama's, of course. This wasn't a vicarage where the door was always open to people in need. This was a fashionable home in an exclusive part of the city. Alice could not stay here. She was a fallen woman. Decent women could not associate with her.

Stuff and nonsense! But such was the way of the world, and in high society, it was carried to extremes. Appearances had to be kept up, even among the servants.

Ellie was too much of a realist to think that she could change the world, but she was a resourceful girl. She would find a way to help Alice, with no one the wiser.

Chapter 17

The following day, Ellie set out for Westminster. Though she did not slip away in secret, she chose her moment with care. She had no wish to become embroiled in arguments or explaining herself, or in defending Alice. Her one aim was to assure the maid that she was not forgotten and that she, Ellie, would do everything in her power to help her.

She had brought with her a purse of money to tide Alice over and, what was more important, the offer of a job. Ellie had thought everything out. If Alice could not stitch her gowns in Park Street, then the gowns would be transported to wherever Alice had her lodgings. And this was only the beginning of what Ellie envisaged. One satisfied customer could lead to another, and she had many acquaintances who were in need of a seamstress. Perhaps Madame Clothilde could use Alice's services. But this was for the future. At this point, she did not want to raise false hopes. It was enough to make sure that Alice had the means to support herself for the next week or two.

She chose the hour before dinner to run her errand,

when the servants were downstairs in the Servants' Hall, eating their own dinner before serving their masters in the dining room. Jack was at his club and everyone else had letters to write or books to read. She wouldn't be missed for the next hour at least, and she intended to be back long before that.

She might have asked Meghan to go with her, but decided against it. If Frances got to hear of it, it could cause a great deal of unpleasantness for Meghan. The same could be said for Robbie. No. If anyone was going to incur Frances's wrath, it would be she and she alone.

With her umbrella tucked under one arm and her reticule dangling from the other, she set off at a brisk pace for Piccadilly where there were always hackneys waiting for fares. For this outing, she had chosen to wear her oldest coat. A lady of fashion would attract the wrong kind of attention where she was going. Besides, it was a cold, drab day with overcast skies threatening unrelenting rain if not sleet or snow. She wouldn't take the chance of soiling one of Madame Clothilde's creations.

Even before she reached the hackney that was first in line, she was unfurling her umbrella, and by the time she had given the driver directions to the Dirty Duck on Lucas Street, in the district of Westminster, the drizzle was turning into a downpour. The driver's face registered surprise, and she wondered why.

She thought she knew what to expect, but as the hackney left the environs of the Abbey and got closer to the river, she realized how wrong she was. The well-kept houses gave way to smaller, dilapidated buildings on narrower streets. She was nervous, but not alarmed. Meghan had told her that Alice had lodgings with a respectable family. That was what Alice had told Meghan, but Ellie was beginning to wonder whether Alice had been too proud to admit the truth.

When the hackney turned the corner into Lucas Street, her nervousness turned into an odd mixture of alarm and pity. No one should have to live like this. The foul stench of overflowing sewers made her stomach heave. The wretched dwellings looked mean and forbidding. Most of the pedestrians were hurrying to get out of the rain, or they were huddled under makeshift canvas awnings where hawkers were selling their wares. The whole scene was made all the more depressing because the light was fading and few of the streetlamps had been lit.

The hackney pulled up in front of a tavern that was in no better condition than the hovels around it. There was no mistaking the sign. A faded black-and-white duck stared her boldly in the eye. Her gaze moved to the house next door. According to Meghan, this was where Alice had taken lodgings.

She gave a start when a face appeared at the window of the hackney, then relaxed when she recognized the driver. He opened the door but prevented her from alighting.

"This is no place for a lady on her own, miss," he said earnestly. "Let me take you somewhere else. Back to Mayfair. It ain't safe here."

He was saying exactly what she was thinking. But she couldn't leave Alice here. The girl deserved better of her employers than to be cast off without a thought to her welfare.

She looked at the driver. He was younger than she, with a kind face and kind eyes. "There's someone here I must speak with," she said. Then, stretching the truth a little, "She has run away from home. Will you wait for me? This won't take long."

He looked up and down the street and shook his head. "The minute this rain stops, this place will be teeming like a rats' warren. They'll strip my hackney down before I can say my own name. I'll tell you what I will do, though. I'll drive around for a bit and pick you up here in say, oh, five, ten minutes?"

This kindness from a stranger brought a tickle to her throat. "What is your name?" she asked.

"Derek." He sounded surprised. "Derek Acton."

"Thank you, Mr. Acton. You are most kind," and she pressed his hand warmly when he helped her alight.

Her courage faltered a little when the hackney rattled over cobblestones as it lumbered down the street. She didn't look back and tried to blot from her mind the sensation of eyes watching her as she passed the entrance to the Dirty Duck. She heard snatches of bawdy songs and raucous laughter, but when this was followed by catcalls to the "pretty lady" on the pavement outside, her nerve broke. She picked up her skirts and went tearing up the stairs to the house where she hoped to find Alice.

The door was leaning off its hinges, so she didn't bother to knock. A few steps inside the building brought her to a halt. There were no lamps lit and she could hardly see her hand in front of her face. Her ears, however, rang with the din that seemed to echo from every wall— children shrieking, babies squalling, whimpers, shouts, voices raised in anger.

There must be some mistake. Alice could not possibly have taken lodgings here.

When a shadow moved in front of her, she gave a startled yelp.

"'Ere," said a coarse, feminine voice. "Who are you and wot are you doin' 'ere?"

Ellie put a hand to her face to dispel the fumes of gin on the woman's breath. After fanning it away, she said that she was looking for Alice Travers.

"'Oity-toity, ain't yer," said the shadow. "'Ow much is it worth if I takes you to 'er?"

On a matter of principle, she wasn't going to give the

woman money, knowing that it would only go to gin, but a masculine voice yelling from above, followed by sounds of a scuffle, made her change her mind.

"Sixpence?" she said meekly.

"Make it a shilling," said the woman, "and yer on."

This was robbery, but there was nothing she could do about it except knock on every door until she found Alice, and the very thought gave her the shudders. "You'll get your shilling," she said, "when I see Alice."

"This way, then, Madame 'Oity-toity."

The woman pushed past Ellie and led the way up the stairs. The fumes of gin, the smoke of tallow candles and odors that Ellie did not want to name, even in her own mind, wrapped around them like a fog. By the time they stopped at a door one floor up, Ellie had a hand over her nose and was breathing through her mouth.

"Fannie," roared the woman by her side. "There's summat 'ere that wants ter see yer, a fine lady with plump pockets."

A bolt was drawn back and the door opened. There was light coming from a smoky candle, but Ellie had to blink before she could see clearly. The woman who was standing before her looked more like a brawny blacksmith than a female, except that she was wearing skirts and a shawl was draped over her massive shoulders. Ellie decided on the spot that this was one lady she was going to treat with the utmost civility.

"How do you do?" she said. "I'm looking for Alice Travers. Would you happen to know where she is?"

From inside the room came a gasp, then the door opened wide and Alice herself was framed in the doorway. "Oh, mu'um," she cried, "you shouldn't be here."

"Neither should you," said Ellie, her eyes taking in the room behind Alice. The only heat came from a fire that had been allowed to go out and the smoking candle in the middle of a rickety table where several small children were making a meal of bread and tea. There was only one armchair and that was occupied by a man who had fallen asleep with an empty bottle clutched in his hand.

Her plans for Alice working from her home as a seamstress seemed ludicrous now. It wasn't a job the girl needed, but rescue.

"I wants me shilling," said the woman who had shown Ellie the way. "A bargain is a bargain."

As Ellie fished in her reticule for her purse, she said to the woman named Fannie, "I'd like to speak to Alice in private if you don't mind." Then to Alice, "Could we go to your room?"

This brought guffaws of laughter from the two women and an agonized look from Alice. "I don't have a room, mu'um," she said. She looked down at her shoes. "This is the only room there is."

Alice's words arrested Ellie just as she pulled a shilling from her purse. She said incredulously, "You mean, you live and sleep here? *All* of you?"

Alice bit her lip and nodded.

The shilling was snatched from Ellie's hand, not by her guide, but by Blacksmith Fannie. "You owes me that, Sal, for drinking my gin." She spoke to the guide and raised her fist threateningly to protect her prize.

The woman called "Sal" let out a howl. Her anger wasn't directed toward Fannie, but at Ellie. "That was *my* shilling!" she shrieked. "You let Fannie steal it! You had better give me another if you knows wot's good for yer."

Ellie was coming to the end of her tether. She didn't mind being taken advantage of, but this was abuse. More truthful than wise, she retorted, "Your quarrel is with your friend, not me. I brought this purse for Alice and no one gets a penny of it until I have a chance to speak to her alone."

The purse in question was clasped close to her chest. When Sal reached for it, Ellie beat her back with her umbrella. Sal let out an earsplitting howl. Alice moaned and retreated into the room, leaving Ellie to face Blacksmith Fannie alone. A martial light glinted in Fannie's eyes.

"Alice owes me a week's rent for board and lodgings," she said, "and I wants wot's due me or she stays 'ere."

"That's a lie!" cried Alice from behind the blacksmith.

With Ellie's attention momentarily distracted, Fannie lunged and knocked the purse from her clasp, spilling coins in every direction. Women and children, including Ellie, went diving after them. An elbow connected with Ellie's eye and she saw stars.

A sudden hush descended. When Ellie, who was crouched on the floor, blinked up, she saw Alice wielding a poker in one hand and clutching a bundle tied up in a shawl in the other.

"If anyone touches my mistress," said Alice in a voice that Ellie did not recognize, "I'll bash her brains out."

Silence. Even the squeals of the children died away.

Ellie got to her feet. "Thank you, Alice," she said. "Now, if you just give me a moment to collect my money, we'll be on our way."

Fannie's lips pulled back in a snarl. "Bert!" she yelled. "Wake up, y'drunken sot! They're stealing yer gin money."

"Wot?" said a masculine voice, then with more force, "Wot's that you said, Fannie? Me gin money?"

Bert was obviously waking from a drunken stupor.

"On second thought," said Ellie with all the dignity she could muster, "we'll wish you all a good day. Come along, Alice."

They walked sedately to the head of the stairs, but when they heard footfalls behind them, Alice threw down the poker and pushed Ellie ahead of her. "Run!" she cried. "They'll want the clothes off your back next!"

Ellie needed no further prompting and hurtled down the stairs with Alice at her heels.

Out on the street, people were milling about as though they had nowhere to go. It was just as Mr. Acton had said. Now that it had stopped raining, the street was teeming with people—hawkers selling pies and hot tea, children running wild, groups of adolescent boys looking for trouble. Ellie looked over her shoulder, but there was no sign of the hackney.

Alice spoke first. "Don't look back. Don't look around you. Keep your head down and follow me."

" 'Follow'? Where?"

"There's a doss-house one street over. We'll be safe there."

A doss-house, as Ellie remembered, was a lodging for people without homes and was only one degree better than the workhouse.

"Alice," she said gently, "you're coming home with me."

Alice shook her head violently. "No, ma'am. I know you mean well, but I'd rather be dead than face the shame of going back to Park Street. I mean it, and nothing you say will make me change my mind."

Alice didn't sound like the little maid Ellie remembered. She'd grown up in the few days she'd been out on her own. Just thinking about the lodgings she'd survived and the way she'd handled herself with Blacksmith Fannie gave Ellie something to think about.

Their hackney came round the corner just as a group of mean-looking adolescent boys surrounded them.

"Yer money or yer life," said the leader, half joking, half in earnest.

"Me mam could do with that coat," said another, fingering Ellie's coat.

Ellie raised her umbrella threateningly, but this only provoked the boy who wanted her coat. He wrested the umbrella out of her hands and would have hit her with it if Alice had not given him a hard shove, sending him into the gutter.

A whip cracked and the next instant, Derek Acton had jumped down from his box and was advancing upon the little group. Another crack of his whip sent the boys running.

"Get in the hackney," he yelled, "before they come back."

A hostile crowd was gathering. Ellie grabbed Alice's arm, dragged her to the hackney, pushed her in, and climbed in after her. Acton slammed the door behind them.

"Back to Mayfair?" he asked.

"No!" cried Alice.

Ellie said the first thing that came into her head. "Take us to the Clarendon Hotel on Bond Street."

That would give her time to decide what to do for the best for all concerned.

Jack arrived home to find a hackney stationed outside his front door. Assuming it was for Robbie, he barely glanced at it. He was running late and knew they would not start dinner without him. After dinner, he was to escort the ladies to the opera, not so much for the performance—which always left him in a stupor—but to mingle with friends and acquaintances and enjoy the pleasure of their society. That was the theory. For himself, he aimed to show Ellie off and demonstrate to the world that he was well pleased with his lot.

And that was a barefaced lie. He was anything but

pleased. He was confused. He didn't understand why Ellie continued to hold him off, or why he would let her, when the air between them would become charged whenever their glances met. He didn't know why he was turning into a sanctimonious old fogy. When had he ever objected to a beautiful woman wearing a revealing gown? Only with Ellie. And as for being jealous of Ash—he must be losing his mind.

Thoughts of Ellie evaporated when he heard raised voices coming from the drawing room. As he approached the door, his grandmother exited, white-faced and tight-lipped. When she saw him, she crossed to him at once.

"What is it?" he asked.

"Ellie," she said. "She sent a hackney driver to fetch clothes and money. She's putting up at the Clarendon with Alice. Frances is in such a taking, I think she'll have an apoplexy if she doesn't calm down."

Jack was bewildered. "Ellie at the Clarendon? Start over, Grandmamma, and speak slowly. Why is Ellie at the Clarendon?"

"Because Alice refused to come here. Look, talk to Robbie, or better still, talk to that nice hackney driver, Mr. Acton. They can explain better than I. I'm going to pack Ellie's things and see if I can find something that will do for Alice, too." She let out a sigh and managed a smile. "I'm glad you're home to take charge, because Frances has turned this unfortunate incident into a full-blown Cheltenham tragedy. You'd better get in there"—she pointed to the drawing room—"before Robbie throttles her."

With that, she turned and made for Ellie's chamber.

Jack's mind was buzzing. For one awful moment, he wondered if Ellie had left him. Sanity returned in the next instant. If ever she did leave him, she'd want to tell him to his face.

On that reassuring thought, he breathed deeply and entered the drawing room. When he shut the door with a snap, four people, all standing, turned to face him—Frances, Caro, Robbie, and a young maid whose name he could not remember. Since she was weeping into a handkerchief and seemed to be integral to the proceedings, he did not ask her to leave.

"Robbie," he said, "what's this about Ellie?"

Robbie opened his mouth, but Frances cut him off before he could say a word.

"Ellie has disgraced us all," she declared. "Without a by-your-leave or a word to anyone except"—she glared at the maid—"this wretch, she went off alone to the stews of Westminster to aid and abet that immoral slut I dismissed from our service not two days ago."

"What 'immoral slut'?" asked Jack.

His bewildered question had the young maid weeping again.

No one was listening to Jack. Robbie shot Frances a withering look. "Whom *you* dismissed without a penny to her name. Where else could she go but to the stews of Westminster or the workhouse?"

Frances's voice rose shrilly. "To put it delicately, the girl is *enceinte*. She deserves to be pilloried for her immoral behavior, not rewarded!"

Caro's hands flew up to cover her hot cheeks. "Oh, Jack," she wailed, "Ellie took Alice to the Clarendon! The *Clarendon*, of all places! What if someone sees her? What if they find out about Alice? There are so many fashionable people who go there. They'll be laughing behind our backs."

Robbie sneered at this outburst. "What a heartless girl you are! Can't you think of anyone but yourself?"

Caro's eyes glinted with fire. "And how like your sister you are!" she retorted.

This was too much for Jack. "Silence!" he roared.

Startled, everyone stared at him mutely.

Jack was beginning to make sense of all the fragments of information that were being tossed around, and it became clear to him that Caro had no business being there, a young girl of seventeen embarking on her first season. Too late now, to send her to her room. What was his grandmother thinking of?

As he well knew, his grandmother was not a stickler for propriety. Frances was, but not when she was bristling with self-righteousness. He supposed that most people would have agreed with her, but not Ellie. She had been raised by a different standard.

"I take it," he said, "that Alice is or was one of our maids?"

"She was a rather clever seamstress," Frances allowed, "before her fall from grace."

"I see." He let the thought turn in his mind. "How did Ellie find out?" He looked at the maid. "You told her?"

Meghan gulped and nodded. "Her ladyship wanted to help her."

"How?"

"*How* doesn't signify!" Frances's agitation could not be contained. She began to prowl the room. "It's *why* that matters, why Ellie does what she does." She pivoted to face Jack. "Your wife, let me tell you . . ." Whatever she saw in Jack's face made her trail to a halt.

Ignoring Frances for the moment, he spoke to the maid in the gentlest voice he could manage. "What is your name?"

Another gulp and a whispered, "Meghan."

"Well, Meghan, you did the right thing in telling her ladyship about Alice. You need not worry about your friend. Lady Raleigh would never allow any harm to come to her. Off you go, then. Get back to work."

Meghan darted a glance at Frances, then looked at Jack. "You mean, you're keeping me on?"

"Of course. Your position here is secure. You have my word on it."

Jack walked to the door and held it open. Meghan bobbed him a curtsy, sobbed out her thanks, and hastened from the room. Those who remained were perfectly still, their eyes fixed on Jack as he took a few steps toward them.

He spoke conversationally, but no one was deceived by his pleasant manner. His eyes betrayed the depth of his feelings. "You are quite right, Frances," he said. "It's the 'why' that matters. Why does Ellie do the things she does? I'll tell you why. Because she won't listen to reason; because she is stubborn." Robbie moved restlessly, but Jack paid no attention to that. "Because of the way she was raised. She's a Brans-Hill, and all the Brans-Hills are tarred with the same brush."

"I say, sir," began Robbie, stiffening, but Jack drowned him out.

"They're taken advantage of at every turn. They're easy pickings for anyone who comes to them with a sad story. They don't count the cost; they don't think of consequences." A smile touched his lips and he glanced at each person in turn. "So you see, Ellie deserves our utmost respect, and I intend to see that she gets it. Do I make myself clear?"

Evidently, he did. If a petal had fallen on the carpeted floor, everyone would have heard it. Satisfied that he had made his point, Jack left the room.

There was a footman crossing the hall downstairs. Jack called out to him, "There's a hackney outside. I want to speak to the driver. See to it, um—" He couldn't remember the footman's name.

Ellie would know it. Promising to do better in the future, he went to Ellie's room to have a few quick words with his grandmother before speaking with the hackney driver.

Chapter 18

Jack arrived at the Clarendon in a mild state of panic. Though the hackney driver, Acton, had assured him that Ellie was relatively unharmed, he'd been appalled to hear of the attack on her and her maid in a part of town that was inhabited by the dregs of humanity. "A plucky lady," Acton called her. "Reckless" was the word running through Jack's mind. He was sympathetic. He understood her scruples. One part of him admired her, but another wanted to give her a good shaking. A husband should have some say in the ordering of his wife's life. Ellie had too much freedom for her own good and he had no one to blame but himself.

He was out of the hackney the moment it stopped. Needless to say, he rewarded the driver with a generous gratuity for all his trouble. But Acton hadn't finished with him yet.

"Beggin' your pardon, guv'nor," he said, "but..." He stopped momentarily as Jack hefted the valise out of the cab, the valise his grandmother had packed with clothes and toiletries for Ellie and her maid.

"Go on, Acton. You were saying?" He tried not to show his impatience, because this young man had come to Ellie's aid, and he was grateful to him.

Acton gathered himself to say what was on his mind. "Go easy with her, guv'nor. She's had a bad fright. A bad shaking up, is what I mean. But I don't think she's hurt in any way that counts, leastways, not that I could see."

"I thought you said she was unharmed?"

"She is, she is!" Acton hastened to reply. "But she did take a bump on the head and she's acting a little odd."

Truly alarmed now, Jack made for the stairs to the hotel lobby and, in spite of the leather valise, took them two at a time.

A footman was hovering just inside the door. Jack wasted no time in asking him to lead the way to the countess of Raleigh's chamber. The footman, a stoic, elderly gentleman, gave no sign that the request was odd, coming as it did from the lady's husband, who had a luxurious town house at his disposal within walking distance of the hotel. He answered in the disinterested accents of one who has seen everything and is surprised by nothing.

"Your suite of rooms is upstairs, your lordship," he replied. "If you would be good enough to follow me."

A suite of rooms. Jack wasn't sure what to make of that, but a hotel lobby was not the place to show his ignorance. From the corner of his eye, he caught sight of acquaintances who, in the normal course of events, he would have been happy to talk to. But not now, not before he had a chance to speak to Ellie.

The footman led him up one flight of stairs, to where the best rooms the hotel had to offer were located, and stopped at a door halfway along the corridor. This floor was well lit by candles in pewter sconces on the wall. The carpet underfoot was luxuriously soft. Jack was pleased to note that the hotel's staff had recognized Ellie's quality and were treating her with every civility.

When he knocked on the door, there was no answer. The door was locked. "Ellie," he said urgently, jiggling the door handle.

The footman cleared his throat. "Might I suggest, your lordship," he droned, "that you use the key?"

Jack tried not to look sheepish. "The key," he said, and plucked the object from the footman's hand.

"Her ladyship asked me to give it to you. There are two keys to your suite of rooms. Her ladyship has the other."

"My suite of rooms?" said Jack. He left the question hanging. No need to show the footman that he was totally ignorant of his wife's arrangements.

The footman nodded. "Two bedchambers with an adjoining parlor. I believe her ladyship is in the parlor entertaining guests."

"Thank you."

The footman bowed and walked away. Jack used the key and entered the room. The only light came from a fire burning in the grate and from a door that was slightly ajar, the door to Ellie's private parlor, he supposed. When he heard her voice calling "Trump!" he was sure of it.

He threw the valise on a chair, then, smile fixed, he pushed open the door to the private parlor. One step in, he halted. Three gentlemen and Ellie sat around a table playing cards. It was evident who was winning by the pile of guineas beside Ellie's elbow. Now, why wasn't he surprised to find Ash here?

One comprehensive glance told him that his wife seemed none the worse for her adventure. Her cheeks were flushed, the result, no doubt, of the wine she was drinking. Apart from that, she seemed in fine fettle, cheerful even. But that could be because she was counting the money she'd won.

Since no one seemed to have noticed him, he shut the door with a snap. Ash was the first to react. Just as though he were still a soldier, he slipped his hand into his boot to retrieve his dagger and turned sideways in his chair to face the intruder. As recognition dawned, a big grin spread over Ash's face.

"Finally," he said, rising, "the cavalry has arrived. What kept you?"

"I wasn't at home when Ellie's messenger came calling." Jack's smile was unwavering.

He turned that icy smile upon the two sprigs of fashion who were also present—silly young jackasses, in his estimation, who were far too obvious in their attentions to his sister.

"Good evening, Mr. Plaisance, Mr. DeVane," he said.

They jumped to their feet. "Evening, Lord Raleigh," they chimed in chorus. His scrutiny brought blushes to their beardless cheeks.

Ellie was on her feet, as well. "Jack," she cried, "these gentlemen have done me a great service. Had it not been for Mr. Plaisance and Mr. DeVane, Alice and I would have been turned away at the door. They vouched for my identity and insisted I be treated with the utmost respect."

"Ah no, I h-hate to correct a l-lady," said Mr. Plaisance, stumbling over his words, "but it was Lord Denison who deserves the credit." He gave a forced laugh. "No one recognized DeVane or me, but everyone knew Lord Denison."

Jack could well imagine the scene in the hotel lobby. Had Ellie no sense? Didn't she care about her reputation? That thought led to another. Eyes narrowing, he said, "Where is your maid?"

The question brought Ellie up short, as though it had just occurred to her that a lady entertaining gentlemen with no chaperon present was no lady at all. She said feebly, "In her bedchamber. The excitement was too much for her. She wasn't up to company, I'm afraid."

Jack's focus was diverted when Ash thrust a glass of wine at him. "Drink it," said Ash, his face unsmiling, "before your blood turns to ice. The chill in here is becoming unpleasant. That's what comes from leaving all the doors open while we were waiting for you."

The reference was understood, but hardly made a difference. So all the doors had been left open to protect Ellie's good name. She shouldn't have been in this predicament in the first place. Had she confided in him, her husband, he would have taken care of everything.

Ash was smiling again. "Come along, gentlemen," he spoke to his companions. "Our usefulness is at an end. No, don't thank us, Jack. What we did, we did for your lovely wife." His smile slipped momentarily. "I should hate to hear that anyone had made so lovely a lady unhappy."

Plaisance and DeVane said much the same, but they did not try to emulate Ash when he pressed a kiss to Ellie's hand. With a wary eye on Jack, they bowed themselves out of the room.

Ash lingered for one moment longer. "Don't worry about the gossips," he said. "As far as anyone knows, there was an accident to Ellie's carriage. Her poor maid took a spill and cannot be moved until the doctor gives his permission. You'll note, Jack, I had the presence of mind to bespeak a suite of rooms in your name. Only the best, of course, because only the best is good enough for Ellie." He allowed himself a small smile—all for Ellie's benefit, Jack thought—then he went on, "I wish I could be there to see your face when you get the bill."

When he left, he shut the door carefully.

Ellie glanced at Jack. "You, sir," she said, "have the manners of a barbarian. How *could* you be so abrupt with these gentlemen whose only offense was to be kind to me? They helped me when I got into difficulty. I'm sure you were told that Alice wouldn't return to Park Street at any price. And who can blame her?"

He wasn't sure what he'd expected, but not this unprovoked attack. Her smiles and thanks were all for Ash and her two springs of fashion. No word of thanks to the husband who had rushed to her rescue and would have to pay the shot. Knowing Ash, he would guess that this suite of rooms was going to cost him dearly.

"And you, Madam Wife," he replied with equal force, "have the discretion of an unschooled puppy." To make his point, he walked to the door to Alice's room and closed it soundlessly.

For a moment, she looked crestfallen, but her expression cleared and she said in the same forceful tone, "We left it open to preserve the proprieties. That ought to please you. Besides, Alice is dead to the world. The excitement was too much for her."

"That's what you call propriety? Your maid asleep while you entertain three gentlemen next door? And playing cards, of all things!"

Her mouth flattened. "The money is for Alice. She's in need of it, as you surely were told by Mr. Acton. And it only amounted to a few guineas. Besides, these gentlemen are your friends. They could not have been more helpful."

And here was the source of her frustration. For the last little while, she'd come under a heavenly cloud of masculine admiration. Those kind young gentlemen, no more than boys, really, had treated her as though she were a princess. And they were kindness itself to Alice, a mere maid. That said a great deal about their character.

Then, when Ash arrived on the scene minutes later, she and Alice were whisked into a private parlor and feted with champagne and tiny sandwiches. Ash certainly knew how to please a lady.

Naturally, she had to account for the straits they were in, but she'd judiciously expurgated anything detrimental to her maid. She was willing to admit that things had turned out better than she deserved, but she did not think she deserved Jack's angry harangue.

What was he saying now? More on propriety?

"And do you think it proper to go off to the stews of Westminster without telling anyone, mind, on an undertaking fraught with danger?"

It was his tone of voice more than his words that hurt, and that hurt swiftly converted to temper. "I didn't know Alice's lodgings were anything but respectable. How should I? Had I known, I would have asked Robbie to go with me."

His voice rose. "What about your husband? You should have come to me for help."

"You were not there. Besides, I could not be certain that you would help me."

"That's my point!" Without conscious thought, he'd been edging closer to her and they were now toe-to-toe. "I said you were unschooled and this whole misadventure proves it. I'm your husband, but I might as well be a doorpost, for all the attention you pay to my wishes."

She stuck her nose in the air. "Oh, not a doorpost, Jack. Say rather a bell that constantly rings a peal over me."

He slowly lowered his face to hers. "Maybe you deserve it."

She'd always thought his eyes were the color of dark chocolate. For the first time, she noticed flecks of amber lurking in their depths, flecks that were glinting dangerously, turning his eyes a lighter hue.

If he was trying to intimidate her, it wasn't working.

She lifted her chin. "You did not forbid me to go to Alice's lodgings."

"Because you never asked!"

"And now you know why!"

She pushed past him, lifted the candle from the table, and marched into her bedchamber. After setting the candle on the mantel, she went to the valise and began to unpack it. He watched her from the open door.

Having found what she wanted, she marched with her bundle through the parlor and entered Alice's room. A moment later, she returned. He was still stationed at the door to her bedchamber.

"Would you mind?" she said, adopting her vicar's daughter mode. "My gown smells of the gutter and I'd like to change."

Her meaning was plain. She wanted him to leave. It was a challenge no self-respecting husband could tolerate.

"I won't stop you," he said. He took a step inside the room and shut the door with his foot.

Not a word from Ellie. She went to the valise, shook out a frock, and, preserving her silence, stalked to a tapestry screen in one corner of the room.

"Ellie," he said, "this is foolish."

He lost his train of thought when the gown she'd been wearing was tossed on top of the screen. His mind was filled with a vision of Ellie in her lacy underthings. The pleasant reverie vanished when it occurred to him that, for all he knew, her undergarments might be made of serviceable calico. A fine state of affairs when a husband did not know what his wife wore next to her skin!

His temper was spent, but not his determination to show Ellie the folly of her ways. Next time, she might not be so lucky. Next time, she might be taken up by scoundrels and wastrels, and not by gentlemen who followed a code of honor.

He tried to sound reasonable. "May I remind you, Ellie, you are not Aurora? You are not a woman of the world. You are my wife. What you do affects every member of our family. Our actions have consequences." He stopped and winced. He was beginning to sound like a pompous ass.

There was a flurry of movement behind the screen, then Ellie's head emerged. "Aurora!" she exclaimed. "Is that what this is about? You think I'm a wanton? You think I want to seduce every man I meet? Is that what you think Aurora is like?"

He stared in astonishment, then he began to laugh. Finally, when he could contain his laughter, he got out, "Ellie, my dear, I doubt that you've had a carnal thought in your life. You're not that kind of woman."

Strangely, this was the unkindest cut of all, because it touched on her deepest misgivings as a woman. She was twenty-eight years old and, in spite of her marriage, was an aging spinster with only a few heated kisses to her credit, and those with the man who so cruelly mocked her now.

If her chin was up before, now it jutted. "Don't be so sure of that. Aurora has had more adventures than you can dream of."

He frowned. "How many glasses of wine have you had?"

"Why must you always think I'm inebriated when I defend Aurora? One glass, two. What difference does it make?"

"That explains it!"

"Explains what? That I'm not the woman you think you know?" She stepped away from the shelter of the screen and advanced upon him with the sinuous grace of a cat. "Do you think ice flows in my veins? Do you think that I am not as other women? Do you think that passion and I are strangers?"

She had yet to put on a fresh gown and was wearing only her stays and drawers. Silk! She was wearing silk next to her skin? It clung to every feminine contour in a sinful embrace.

Candlelight warmed her flesh with a sheen of gold. Her hair was undone and fell around her shoulders in reckless abandon. She had the figure to torment the imagination of a saint, breasts that thrust against the edge of her stays, a waist that his hands could span, and hips that flared to a lush ripeness.

His mouth was dry. His feet were rooted to the floor. Ellie had turned into a siren.

"What's the matter, Jack?" she taunted. "Are you afraid that Aurora has taken over and you're in danger of being seduced?"

"No," he replied in deadly earnest. "I'm counting on it. Why don't you finish what you started at the Palais Royal?"

Chapter 19

She couldn't blink; she couldn't tear her eyes away. She was caught in his stare as though he held her in a spell. They didn't touch. Strangely, her senses were more acute. She could hear the rain dashing against the window-panes; she could feel the warmth from the fire in the grate. His breathing was harsh, hers was quick and shallow. Her instincts were giving her mixed messages. Should she run? Should she stand her ground?

Something moved in his eyes and the spell was broken. A sigh shivered through her. This was Jack. She had nothing to fear here. She could ask him to go or stay, and he would accept her decision.

She had never seen him look so uncertain. That look made her feel the power of her own femininity. It was a heady feeling.

She rested her splayed fingers on his chest. Her voice was husky. "You want Aurora to finish what she started in the Palais Royal?"

"I do." His voice sounded confident, but his eyes betrayed him.

She leaned closer. "Didn't you know? Aurora can't do anything without Ellie's permission."

He swallowed. "And what does Ellie say?"

"Ellie says, 'Kiss me, Jack.'"

When he remained there rooted to the spot, like a great oak waiting to be felled, she *click*ed her tongue. "I've waited for this moment half my life," she told him, "and nothing is going to take it away from me."

Then she felled him with a kiss. One moment he was standing there, eyes staring in disbelief, and the next, he reeled back on his heels—or was he pushed?—and went toppling over onto the bed. The siren pounced on him and, naturally, he was helpless to resist.

When they came up for air, he began to laugh, not in restrained chuckles, but in great whoops, with enough volume to raise the roof.

Ellie was mortified. "Will you be quiet? You'll waken Alice or the other guests."

"So?" he demanded with an indifference that shocked her, then he pulled back to look at her. A thought struck him. "Ellie," he said, "you're not tipsy, are you?"

"No," she replied solemnly. "I'm drunk."

He groaned. "In that case—"

Her arms tightened when he tried to roll off her. "Drunk with you, Jack Rigg. Don't ask me why. It's beyond comprehension. You're positively feudal in your notions about women, and the most unromantic man I know."

"'Feudal'?" he protested, though he wasn't offended. "I'm the most liberal husband I know. You don't think Ash would give you so much license if he were married to you?"

"No. Those charming, free-and-easy types often turn out to be ogres when they marry. I've seen it happen time and again. It's not that they don't trust their wives. They don't trust other men."

That she'd found fault with Ash in one small particular pleased him immensely. However, he prudently refrained from mentioning his own jealousy of Ash. "So I'm not an ogre. That's something. But I take exception to 'feudal.'"

His mind wasn't entirely on the conversation. He was trying not to fall on her like a ravening beast. He'd been celibate too long and the feel of her soft womanly contours so innocently molded to his rapidly hardening body was driving him crazy. With every ounce of will, he kept his eyes on her face and his hands away from her delectable breasts.

"Not feudal?" she scoffed. "Then what do you call it when a man is forced to take a wife against his will?"

"What man?"

"You, of course."

There was a silence as he absorbed her words. Is this what made her so prickly? His reluctance to marry her?

He gave her a gentle shake. "I married you," he said, "because I wanted to. Of course, the circumstances were not ideal, but I would have come to it myself sooner or later."

"A likely story."

He kissed the pout from her lips and smiled when she shivered. "We're more alike than you realize. Neither of us can be forced into doing what we don't want to do."

He couldn't help himself. His hands were moving over her, not possessively as he wanted to, but stroking, brushing, enticing.

She wriggled under his seeking hands. He knew he was making progress, but Ellie could never be distracted while something was on her mind.

"I've never had a lover," she pointed out, "while you've had legions. I hardly think that makes us alike."

"So you've been following my, ah, career?"

"Don't look so smug. I'd have had to stuff my ears with cotton not to hear about you. When you came into your title, you became grist for the gossip mill."

"I bet." It was beginning to register that there was more to this conversation than maidenly nerves throwing up defenses in a last, futile stand. So what was she really saying?

He dragged himself up on one elbow to get a better look at her. Her dark lashes veiled her expression. "Look at me!" he commanded.

Her lashes lifted. She looked, he thought, adorably vulnerable. It was not a description his capable wife would like, so he kept the thought to himself.

"We *are* alike," he said. "There never were legions of lovers. I was too busy fighting a war. I didn't know I was waiting for you to come along. All I knew was that most women bored me to tears. When you streaked into my life, then and only then, I knew what I'd been missing."

It wasn't a declaration of love, but she didn't expect it. After all, she didn't love him either. This was better than love. This gave them a common ground. Equals. She didn't want to be one among many. With this man, this one man, she wanted to make such an impression that all other loves would fade from his memory.

It was a forlorn hope. She hadn't a clue what to do or how to begin. Now that the moment was on her, all that feminine power she'd exulted in had vanished into thin air.

"What is it, Ellie?"

She looped an arm around his neck. "Promise me something."

"Anything."

"You won't be shy with me."

" 'Shy'?" He didn't know what she meant.

To his baffled look, she explained. "I have so much time to make up, so many things to learn. I'm only a novice. Perhaps you haven't had legions of lovers, but you're experienced. *Proficient*, is what I mean. I want you to teach me all you know."

Images flashed into his mind, each more lurid than the last. He closed his eyes against a wave of heat that suddenly raced from every pulse point in his body to pool in his groin. His heart was racing. His breathing was as choppy as the sea in a tempest. When he had gained control of himself, he looked down at her with a feeble smile.

She was looking up at him intently, as though she'd asked him to explain the intricacies of Greek grammar, and she was ready to take mental notes. One thing was certain, she would follow where he led.

Not that he would take advantage of her innocence. They'd get to that night of uninhibited passion he dreamed about, but they'd get there in easy stages. For now, he had to be patient and put a bridle on his own ravenous lusts.

"Making love," he said easily, "usually begins with a kiss. Here, let me show you."

He lowered his head and covered her lips with his. It was a gentle kiss, slow and undemanding. He drew back to gauge her reaction. "See how easy it is?"

She nodded. "But that's not how you kissed me before."

"How did I kiss you?"

"Let me show you."

He obediently lowered his lips to hers. She twined her arms around his neck. It was sweetly erotic until she thrust her tongue into his mouth. Then everything changed. Instant heat. Fire. His good intentions went up in flames. She wasn't helping. Her fingers were fisting and unfisting in his hair. She was arching, offering herself to him. It wasn't supposed to be like this. He was losing control. If he didn't get a grip on himself, he would ruin everything. She was a bride. He should be initiating her with the utmost restraint.

He dragged his mouth from hers with a harsh groan. "Ellie," he got out, "you're going too fast. This isn't a race. We're supposed to take time to taste and savor."

She looked crestfallen. "I didn't do it right?"

He waited until he had control of his breathing before he answered. "You're better than you know."

Her smile bloomed and her cheeks colored with pleasure. "Am I? Then why did you stop?"

He couldn't help laughing. She was as reckless in bed as she was out of it. He couldn't tell her that he stopped because, if he hadn't, she would have lost her maidenhead before he'd had a chance to remove his boots. A man of his experience should have more finesse than that.

She had that expectant look on her face, waiting for him to explain what couldn't be explained.

He tried anyway. "There are no rules. Don't rush things. Be natural, spontaneous. Let your instincts guide you."

Good God! He could tell from the intent look on her face that she was memorizing every word. It was his cue to stop talking before he got tied up in knots.

"Taste and savor," he said softly.

"I'll let my instincts guide me," she promised.

The mattress sighed as she nestled against him. He kissed her eyes, her brows, her throat, and nuzzled the lobes of her ears when he discovered a sensitive spot. He kept her hands in his, just in case. One never knew with Ellie what would set her off.

Her eyelids became heavy, her sighs became moans.

She found it hard to memorize sequences for future reference when her body was humming with new sensations. She was drifting in pleasure and that didn't seem right to her. She wanted Jack to feel what she was feeling.

What were her instincts telling her?

She came up on her knees and shook off Jack's hands. "I want to practice on you," she crooned.

She silenced his halfhearted protest with a kiss, then, brows knit in concentration, she suited action to words. From his brows to his throat, she left a trail of openmouthed kisses and laughed in sheer feminine pleasure when he began to moan. Eyes on his, she undid the buttons on his shirt and began to stroke the hard column of his throat, his shoulders, his chest, and where she touched, her kisses soon followed. Every muscle in his body was as taut as a tightrope. One wrong move and he would step into an abyss.

When she fumbled with the closure on his trousers, he batted her hands away. She was his bride, he reminded himself. He was going to initiate her in easy stages. Besides, he doubted she would be so bold if she knew where all this was leading.

She sat back on her heels. "What's the matter, Jack? Why have we stopped?"

They had stopped because he was belatedly trying to remember what he knew about virgins. Damn little, as it turned out. He had never initiated a virgin, had never wanted to. In fact, the very thought gave him the shudders.

Now who was the novice?

Just as though she could read his mind, she said, "Jack, you worry too much."

Laughing softly, she pushed him into the mattress and rose above him. Her fiery locks veiled her face and she tossed them back with an impatient hand. She looked, he thought, like some ancient warrior queen demanding surrender from a vanquished knight.

"Don't be shy," she said. "Remember what you told me. *Be natural, spontaneous. Let your instincts guide you.*"

He took her at her word.

When he pounced, she squealed and they went rolling on the bed. This time he came out on top. Her smile slipped a little when he removed her stays, her chemise and her drawers, but she didn't try to cover her nakedness and he marveled at her trust.

"I'll try to make this good for you," he said.

She smiled and reached for him. "I know you will."

He lowered his mouth to one bared shoulder and laved it with his tongue. When her breathing quickened, he smiled. He did the same to first one breast, then the other, laving her nipples, rolling them with his tongue, then sucking strongly when she began to moan.

His mouth was still playing with her nipples when his hand began to roam. She didn't take the hint, so he had to tell her to spread her legs. She was moving restlessly, her head thrashing on the pillow. He pulled back to watch her face as his fingers gently sank into her damp folds.

Her eyes were glazed with passion; her nails were digging into his shoulders. She would never be more ready for him than she was at this moment.

When he rolled from her, she tried to stop him. Eyes on hers, he began to undress, then he stood there in his nakedness, waiting for a sign that this was what she wanted.

Her eyes moved over him slowly, taking in the breadth of his shoulders, the hard muscular torso, the trim waist. But it was the solid shape of his manhood that had her eyes widening.

She knew what he wanted, but as her fever ebbed, so

did her confidence, and she looked around the room as though she didn't know how she'd got there.

"Don't turn craven on me now," he said.

He stretched out his hand and she automatically held onto it. "Jack," she whispered, "you told me to follow my instincts."

"And?"

"My instincts are telling me to hide in the closet."

He smiled faintly. "You decide, Ellie. Do we stop or do we go on?"

She rose to the challenge, as he knew she would. "My instincts were never any good. Let's go with yours."

She was everything he had ever dreamed of and more, generous in giving, voracious in taking. Each kiss, each brush of her hands made him wild to have her. This was Ellie, he reminded himself. He had to slow down, had to make this good for her. She wouldn't listen. She was intoxicated with her power, edging to orgasm and dragging him with her.

In a riot of sheets and bedclothes, he rose above her. He lifted her knees, positioning her for his entry. She showered kisses on his arms and shoulders.

"Trust me," he murmured. "I have to be cruel to be kind."

She was turning his words over in her mind when he drove into her. In one stroke, all her pleasure was submerged in pain. She gasped, she groaned. Bucking, shoving, she tried to throw him off, but her struggles only drove him deeper into her body, and the press of his weight pinned her to the bed.

She knew then that she had never been more deceived in her life. If she'd followed her own instincts, she would have been hiding safely in that closet.

When the pain receded and she stilled, she looked up at him. "*That,*" she said wrathfully, "was the most disappointing experience of my life, and I never want to repeat it."

He kissed her tears away. "Trust me. You'll change your mind. It's not over yet."

When he moved, she braced for the next wave of pain. There was none, only pleasure, a flood of pleasure, then heat building inside her, consuming rational thought. All she could do was feel. At the end, she cried out in rapture.

She awakened to a sense of dread. She wasn't disoriented. She knew where she was, knew that the man who was adding coal to the fire was her husband. She could hardly forget that they'd made love, not when she felt the soreness between her thighs. What preyed on her mind were the words she had cried out when she'd lost control and shattered into a thousand pieces.

I love you. She tested them gingerly and swallowed a groan. It was true. She loved him. How had this come about?

He hadn't said the words to her. She didn't expect them. But she'd wanted them to be equals. And now he knew. Would he gloat? Would he be amused? She wished she'd kept her mouth shut.

"Ah, you're awake."

His voice brought her out of her reverie. He had donned his shirt, but she wasn't wearing a stitch. She sat up and, as naturally as she could manage, tucked the edges of the sheet under her arms.

She thought his smile was smug and there was a confident swagger in his steps as he approached the bed. She wasn't given time to think. His hand cupped her chin and his lips took hers in a long, proprietary kiss.

There was a smile in his eyes. "How do you feel?" he asked softly.

If her body would stop humming, she might think of a suitable rejoinder. "Fine" was all that came to mind. "How do *you* feel?"

He kissed her again, then gave a lusty yawn. "Surprised," he said, "but deeply satisfied." He joined her on the bed. "I mean, I knew from the kisses we shared that you had a warm nature, but I couldn't be sure how far those kisses would take you. Had I known, I wouldn't have held off for so long."

He wasn't gloating. In fact, he seemed enormously pleased with himself. Her sense of dread began to ebb.

"And if I had known," she said, "that you had to be cruel to be kind, I would have held you off till Judgment Day."

He gave a whoop of laughter, pulled back the sheet, and slipped in beside her. Her humming nerves began to vibrate when his hairy legs brushed against hers.

"There was no fear of that happening," he disclaimed airily. "Aurora wouldn't have allowed it. I know, I know. You and Aurora are one and the same person. But I have to say that sometimes I don't know whom I adore more, Ellie or Aurora."

She was on the point of clouting him with her fist, but at the mention of "adore," her hand fell away. This was as close as he was likely to come to a declaration. For the moment, it would do.

He was staring at her quizzically. "What?" she asked.

He shrugged. "I was wondering about Aurora. Where did she come from?"

She sighed. He still didn't understand. "*I'm* Aurora, Jack. I always was. I tried not to be. A vicar's daughter doesn't enjoy the freedoms that other young girls enjoy. We're supposed to be an example to the daughters of our father's parishioners. Oh, don't think for a moment that my parents tried to mold me into a submissive little prig.

But we children of the manse soon learn that what we do reflects on our fathers. So, because we love them, we conform, as much as we are able. But that doesn't mean we don't long for adventure."

He felt a twinge of guilt. Her guileless words had put him squarely in the camp of those censorious parishioners who forced her to conform. There had to be a middle way. Aurora was adorable, but she terrified the life out of him.

He said doubtfully, "I don't remember you as a 'submissive little prig.' A 'prig,' maybe, especially when you were showing off your Latin and Greek grammar. But 'submissive'! Never!"

"That's because you always brought out the rebel in me."

"Aurora?"

She grinned. "Would a dutiful vicar's daughter arrange a clandestine tryst with a young rake under false pretenses?"

"I thought you were the miller's daughter!"

"That wasn't my fault. I didn't pretend to be Becky. You assumed too much."

She shivered when he drew the edge of his teeth along her shoulder. "I came close to thrashing you," he said.

"I know. You can imagine that after that, Aurora was put on a tight leash."

"How long did that last?"

"Until the circumstances were right for Aurora to emerge, and that didn't happen until I needed money to leave my Cousin Cardvale's house." She turned her head on the pillow to see him better. "Poor Aurora. She's lumbered with Ellie's conscience, and poor Ellie is lumbered with Aurora's sense of adventure."

He began to laugh. "Just when I think I understand, you confuse me again."

She frowned. "It seems clear enough to me."

He kissed her frown away. She kissed the column of his throat. "Jack?"

"Mmm?"

"I feel like you. Surprised. And deeply satisfied."

She could feel his smile against her brow. "I'm glad."

"And," she added innocently, "still looking for adventure."

He raised his head. "What?"

She gave a low, rich chuckle. "I told you. I have so much time to make up. Let's not waste a minute of it."

He had always known she was a quick study. She proved it here. Her phenomenal memory told her just where to kiss and touch to drive him mad to have her. Demanding, possessive, her hands brushed over every inch of him, leaving a trail of sensual heat wherever they touched.

It came to him that she was putting all her newfound knowledge into practice. Ellie couldn't help being Ellie. She was mastering him the way she would master a particularly difficult conjugation of a Greek verb. The optative, no doubt. That's not what he wanted from her. He wanted her wild and free and as adventurous as Aurora.

His mood swung between amusement and resolve. His little scholar had a great deal to learn about the ways of love. He pinned her with his weight and kept her hands clamped above her head.

"Memorize this," he said.

He rubbed his lips over hers but refused the offer of a kiss. Slowly, carefully, he tempted, he tortured, till she was bucking wildly beneath him. He wasn't satisfied yet. He turned her over and began the same process with every vertebra in her spine. When he kissed her bottom, she muffled her moans against the pillow.

He turned her onto her back.

Eyes wide and dazed, she gazed up at him. She said something, but it wasn't coherent, so he knew he had what he wanted. Ellie, not thinking, but feeling.

Only now did he take her the way he wanted to. At the end, her cry of rapture, mindless, abandoned, was everything he wanted for her and from her. No one else had given him this, only Ellie—or was it Aurora?

He drifted into sleep with a smile on his face.

Chapter 20

They stayed at the Clarendon for three more days. This was Jack's idea. If things had been different, he said, he would have taken his bride to Italy or Greece for their honeymoon, but with this being Caro's first season, they were obliged to stay in town. All they were doing was stealing a little time for themselves. Though he kept the thought to himself, what he had in mind was to make love to his beautiful wife every chance he got. In Park Street, there would be too many interruptions, too many claims on their time.

Ellie was more than happy to fall in with his wishes. She felt free away from the house in Park Street. There was no Frances to find fault with her and no sneering housekeeper to put her in her place. Just for a little while, she could forget all her troubles and enjoy being with Jack.

There was still the problem of what to do about Alice, but Jack arranged everything with a speed and efficiency that left Ellie breathless. Lodgings were found with Mrs. Mann in Henrietta Street where Ellie still kept on her rooms. Only, at Jack's suggestion, Alice had become Mrs. Travers and wore a thin gold band on her ring finger.

"It will make things less awkward for her," he said to Ellie. They were waiting for Alice to get ready to make the trip to her new lodgings.

Ellie beamed at him. "I had no idea you were so resourceful."

He replied obliquely, "Marriage to you, my love, has done that for me."

She laughed, but looked a little guilty. "Am I such a trial, Jack?"

A smile came into his eyes. "What you are is generous to a fault, though a tad too impulsive for my comfort." Before she could take umbrage, he went on seriously, "What happens when Alice has her baby? There are few landladies who will welcome infants in their homes."

She said with more hope than certainty, "Mrs. Mann is a kindhearted woman. She won't throw Alice into the street. And if things don't work out, well, we'll make other arrangements. There's plenty of time."

"When is the baby due?"

"I forgot to ask, but I'm sure it's not for a few months yet. She's hardly showing."

"What about the father of the child? Is he completely out of the picture?"

"I don't know. She's convinced that he will come back for her."

"And if doesn't?"

"Don't worry, Jack. I'll think of something."

He patted her hand. "*We'll* think of something."

It was a small room in the attic, but when they were shown into it, Alice behaved as if it were a palace.

"I don't have to share it with anyone?" she asked the

landlady. She was testing the bed, bouncing on the mattress.

Mrs. Mann shook her head. "No, dearie. I likes my lodgers to be comfortable, else they'll find rooms elsewhere." She looked at Ellie. "Have you decided what you want to do with your rooms in the basement?"

Jack's gaze focused on a smudge on his boot.

Ellie didn't have to think of her answer. It was the opposite of what she would have said a week ago. "I'm giving them up. Well, I have no need of them now, do I?"

Jack's smile almost blinded her. "Maybe Alice could have them," he said.

Mrs. Mann demurred. "After the break-in, I've decided to let them only to gentlemen. I wouldn't be easy in my mind if one of my ladies came face-to-face with a burglar, not after last time." To Alice, she said, "It would be different if Mr. Travers were here. When are you expecting your husband to join you?"

A look from Jack kept Ellie silent. He'd already warned her that, though Alice needed a helping hand, she did not need a champion. She was quite capable of answering for herself.

Alice gave the housekeeper a clear-eyed look. "He went up north to look for work. When he finds it, he'll come back for me." She moistened her lips. "Me and my baby both."

There was an interval of silence, then Mrs. Mann's rosy cheeks bunched in a huge smile. "A baby, you say? Well, we must take good care of you and see you're kept busy so you won't have time to mope."

They left Alice in the kitchen, helping Mrs. Mann with the mending and ironing while Jack and Ellie went to the basement to take inventory of the furniture she wanted to keep. Jack took the key out of Ellie's hand and unlocked the door. He entered first, looked around, then ushered her inside.

She was amused. "I'm not helpless," she said. "Why do gentlemen always open doors for women as though we don't know how to use a key?"

"Manners," he replied. "It's drilled into us when we're boys. And sometimes it pays to be careful, as you should know."

"You think I could forget that night? Never! I'm armed and dangerous now." She felt in her coat pocket and produced something shiny and silvery.

He looked baffled. "What in Hades is that?"

She held it up to the light. "A fork. I borrowed it from the Clarendon, and I'm not afraid to use it."

"Fine. After this, you can open the doors first and check to see there are no thieves hiding under the bed."

She laughed, threw off her bonnet, and looked around. It was still dark and airless, but everything had been put back in its place, and no one would have known that they'd surprised a burglar in the act.

It could have been so much worse. The things that mattered to her were untouched—her mother's mahogany dresser with the shiny brass handles, a highly polished drop-leaf table that once belonged to her Grandmother Brans-Hill, and a glass-fronted cabinet with her small library of books. She was as attached to her modest heirlooms as the Raleighs were to theirs, but she doubted that her precious objects would fit into the house in Park Street any more than she did. All the same, she couldn't bear to part with them. That's why she had found a permanent home for them when she'd parted ways with the Cardvales. Nothing less could have induced her to spend her hard-earned money on these dismal rooms.

"What are you thinking, Ellie?"

She tried to sound positive. "I'm wondering where to store my mother's furniture. I suppose there's room in the attics in your house?"

"*Our* house," he corrected. "And why in the attics? It's obvious that you're attached to all these pieces. Put them wherever you want."

"Thank you."

She doubted that she would, because she didn't want anyone sneering at them.

Jack said, "What about your private sitting room? 'The yellow room,' my mother used to call it."

"It's the blue room now," she said gently.

"I know. After Frances became mistress, she made a number of changes. I expect you'll want to do the same."

And she would, just as soon as she found the gumption to stand up to Frances.

She was moving around the room, examining bits and pieces, wondering if there was anything she could bear to sell or give away. She started on the books. One in particular caught her attention—her mother's recipe book.

After watching her turn pages for a goodly number of minutes, Jack took a chair. When more minutes had passed, he said, "Let's arrange to have everything moved to Park Street. I can see that you're not going to part with a thing."

She waved him to silence. "This is amazing."

"What is?"

She brought him the book and pointed. "Read this."

"Cardvale's punch," he read dutifully. He thumbed through other pages of faded writing. "This is a book of recipes. What's so special about that?"

She snatched the book from his hands. " '*Cardvale's punch*,' " she read, " 'from the kitchen of Jeanne Daudet.' "

When the name registered, he sat up straighter. "Let me see that."

He read it again.

"And there's more," said Ellie. "There's one for *Soupe de Poisson* and *Soufflé au Fromage*. And they're all from the kitchen of Jeanne Daudet. There's something else, something Robbie told me. The reason Louise took an interest in him wasn't because he was amusing or attractive or whatever. It was, so she said, because she and her mother came to live with us for a short time."

He was dumbfounded. "And you never thought to tell me before now?"

"I know I meant to, but other things crowded it out of my mind. So much has been going on. Besides, Mama was always helping people, and this must have happened a long time ago, because I don't remember them. Is it ... is it important, Jack?"

He thought for a moment. "Cardvale," he said. "That must have been your cousin's father."

"I suppose so. Or it could be my cousin. He was very young when he came into the title. Thirteen or fourteen, I think. Not that I remember. He's ten years older than I."

She kneeled in front of him and sat back on her heels. "I can't see how this helps."

He said slowly as the thought turned in his mind, "Well, it connects Cardvale to Louise Daudet, or at least to Jeanne Daudet." He smiled into her anxious eyes. "It's possible that Cardvale doesn't remember her, either."

She sighed.

"What?" he prompted.

"I thought we were free and clear. I thought the French authorities had discovered who murdered Louise. It's her dresser and her lover, isn't it? Can't we let sleeping dogs lie?"

"They're only suspects, Ellie. They have not been charged with the murder. And did I say that I was going to make trouble for Cardvale?"

"No. But I know you. Look how you came after me."

He gathered her in his arms and set her on his lap. His eyes glinted down at her. "Are you sorry that I did?"

She looked up at him sharply, then promptly blushed. He must know that she wasn't sorry, not after the night they'd shared. Just thinking about it made her bones go weak.

"No. I don't regret it," she said, "but I wish you would think kindly of Cardvale. He has always been good to Robbie and me. It was Dorothea who was hard to get along with." She pushed out of his arms and got up. "I don't want to part with a thing."

He got up, as well, and put an arm around her shoulders. "I promise not to go after Cardvale," he said.

She wasn't convinced. "There would be no point in it, and you might embarrass him. Perhaps there are things about his father he shouldn't know. And it's not as though a murderer is on the loose, stalking us. Apart from the break-in here, nothing out of the ordinary has happened. There's nothing to worry about, is there?"

"Absolutely nothing, except..."

She was losing patience. "Except what?"

"Except that I'd be easier in my mind if you got rid of that fork. People will think I've married a lunatic."

She laughed at his jest.

They spent the rest of the day in bed, rising intermittently to partake of the meals the Clarendon's footmen brought to their private parlor. It was close to midnight when, replete and sated, they finally fell asleep.

Jack wakened about an hour later, restless, his mind buzzing. There were so many things to think about, so many puzzles that invaded his dreams.

There's nothing to worry about, is there?

Nothing except who murdered Louise Daudet, who stole the Cardvale diamonds, and who broke into Ellie's rooms. And why did Cardvale's name keep coming into his mind?

Cardvale's punch. Could the thief have been after the recipe book? Could Cardvale be desperate to hide his connection to Jeanne Daudet? A moment's reflection convinced Jack that he was on the wrong track. The thief had barely touched the books. Then what was he after?

As for Cardvale, he could claim ignorance of the recipe book or having known either Louise or Jeanne Daudet, and who could contradict him? He might have known them once and forgotten them. The book was very old. He'd examined it thoroughly and there was nothing hidden in its binding or between its pages. All it pointed to was that Ellie's mother and Jeanne Daudet had once known each other.

One puzzle was solved. He'd never understood how a callow youth like Robbie had attracted the notice of the leading light of the Théatre Français. Silly young blighter! On the other hand, in Robbie's shoes, he might have exaggerated his appeal, as well. At that age, callow youths liked their friends to think they were far more worldly than they really were.

His mind kept coming back to Cardvale. Just because he didn't like Ellie's cousin didn't mean he was guilty of anything. In fact, his dislike was based on prejudice. He was, he grudgingly acknowledged, mildly jealous. Ellie had nothing but good to say of her cousin, a man who, in his opinion, had let her down badly.

All that was in the past. He was her husband now, and he would make damn sure that she never wanted for anything again.

She stirred in her sleep, sighed, and curled into him. Her trust humbled him. Her passion amazed him. And his driving need to possess this one woman and no other frightened him to death. She had become essential to his existence. How had this come about?

He didn't know and he didn't care. All he knew was that he felt more alive than he'd felt in an age.

He linked his fingers with hers and brought them to his lips. Her bones were delicate. She was more fragile than she liked to think. That was his undoing. She seemed so capable of handling all her troubles, then she would turn to him with that fragile look in her eyes. How could he resist?

He would do anything in his power to keep her safe. He wasn't going to relax his vigilance until he had the answers to his questions.

It was more than time he compared notes with Brand.

Chapter 21

Ellie arrived home from her Clarendon honeymoon on a wave of euphoria. Everyone could see the difference in her. Her eyes sparkled, a smile was never far from her lips, there was a spring in her step.

"There goes a woman who is loved," said the dowager to her granddaughter.

Caro said nothing. She merely looked miserable.

Her ladyship sighed. "Be happy for your brother, Caro. It's not everyone who finds love in marriage."

"But...but what does he see in her?"

Her ladyship knew who had put that thought in her granddaughter's head. She replied gently, "If you would give Ellie half a chance, you might find out."

Ellie wasn't as sure as the dowager that Jack loved her, but she was patient. After what they'd shared, she was sure he would come to it sooner or later. As for herself, she was a woman reborn. And now that she'd given up her rooms in Henrietta Street, she felt that she'd turned a corner. She had nothing to go back to. She had to go on.

With her newfound confidence came a purpose. She

had to get over her feelings of inferiority and make a place for herself in Jack's life. Something had to change, because she was not happy in this gloomy, stifling house. In short, she was going to make changes and turn this house into a home. Frances and she were fated to cross swords, but it would be at a time of her choosing.

The opportune moment arrived when she had the house to herself, except for Robbie and Milton, who were closeted in the library, working on their respective projects. Robbie's examination was fast approaching and Milton was writing a paper on Greek particles for some obscure journal. The ladies were making afternoon calls and Jack was meeting his friends at his club.

It was now or never.

She had a strategy, and it began with the butler. She found him counting the silver in the butler's pantry.

"Wigan," she said, "I want a word with you."

He looked surprised at the interruption, but said respectfully, "Yes, my lady. How may I help you?"

"I want the blue salon painted. A soft primrose yellow is what I have in mind."

"Yes, my lady. The furniture will have to be moved."

Clever Wigan. "Yes, and it won't be put back. You see, Wigan, I want my own furniture moved into that room. Perhaps you would see to that, too?"

He blinked as she gave him the slip of paper with Mrs. Mann's address, but apart from that, he remained his usual stoic self. "How shall I dispose of the furniture that is already there?"

"I leave it to your judgment."

"Thank you, my lady. Is there anything else?"

She breathed deeply before she uttered the words that were so hard to say. "I've decided to give a reception to mark my own come-out." There! She'd said the words and there was no going back. She took comfort from the fact that Wigan didn't look surprised or shocked, though he must have realized that she was stepping into Frances's domain. "Nothing too elaborate," she went on. "I don't want my reception to detract from Lady Caroline's ball. But it must be exceptional. Do I make myself clear?"

"Perfectly clear," replied Wigan serenely. "When is the reception to take place?"

"A week from today." If she left it any longer, she would not have the nerve to have it at all.

"'A week'?" Wigan's brows rose.

"Is . . . is that too soon?"

The butler's lips almost smiled. "If I may say so, my lady, we should have had this reception long before now. Leave everything to me."

It wasn't over yet. There was only so much a butler could do. The real problem was Frances and her cohort, Mrs. Leach. They could not stop her, but they could make things very difficult. She was certain that Jack would support her if she appealed to him, but her credit in the servants' eyes would slip by several notches. In fact, she might lose their respect altogether, not to mention her own respect. This was something she had to do for herself.

She spent some time in her chamber, rehearsing what she would say. It seemed absurd, but she found the housekeeper far more intimidating than the butler. Her strategy, she decided, would be to repeat what she had done with Wigan, more or less. Simple.

The housekeeper wasn't in her room, but one of the maids directed Ellie to the kitchens. Ellie heard Mrs. Leach's voice and followed the sound of it to the stillroom where she kept her supplies. That the housekeeper was livid with anger was never in doubt.

Ellie approached the open door, but froze in mortification when she heard Mrs. Leach's words.

"She's a slut, that's what she is. What decent woman goes off to a hotel with her husband when she has a perfectly comfortable chamber in her own home? It wouldn't surprise me if there had been an orgy. Well, we know Alice was there, and Lord Denison. And now Wigan has just told me that there's to be a reception here not a week away. I've a good mind to hand in my notice, except I wouldn't want to disappoint poor Lady Frances."

She came out of the door ahead of the cook, saw Ellie, and dropped the tea caddy she was carrying. The box broke open and tea leaves scattered in every direction.

As cold as ice, Ellie said, "I want you out of here within the hour. Settle up with Wigan. I'll tell him to be generous, but don't look to me for a character reference."

The housekeeper tried to have the last word, but by the time she had recovered her voice, Ellie was out of earshot.

They spent only a few minutes in Brooks. Brand wasn't overly fond of clubs since most of them, in his younger days, had excluded him from membership. He preferred the coffee shops in and around St. James's and, after a short consultation, they decided to move to Kenneth's Coffee Shop in Pall Mall.

"Where's Ash?" asked Jack.

"Where do you think? At his tailor, sprucing himself up to take in the season."

Both men chuckled.

After ordering coffee and buns, Brand studied his friend. "You look relaxed," he said. "Marriage must agree with you."

Jack smiled. "Do I detect a note of envy?"

"Hardly. Oh, I'm happy for you, but I'm quite content

with my bachelor existence. And believe me, if I see marriage on the horizon, I will barricade myself in the deepest, darkest dungeon till it passes me by."

"You're quoting my own words back at me," replied Jack pleasantly.

Brand was smiling hugely. "I couldn't resist the temptation. Ah, here is our coffee. Drink up, Jack. Coffee is good for you. It will sharpen your wits."

Jack swallowed a mouthful of the bitter brew. He was, he realized, deeply content. He'd known that one day, however reluctantly, he would have to marry and produce an heir, if only to keep the estates and fortune intact to provide for his dependents. He'd never expected to have the good fortune to marry someone like Ellie. She wasn't always easy to live with, but she made life interesting. That she had a passionate nature to match his own was the garnish that made the meal mouthwatering.

Suddenly realizing he had a stupid smile on his face, he frowned.

Brand said, "Now to business. Well, I was right. All our suspects have something to hide." He buttered his Bath bun and bit into it.

Jack watched him idly. He was interested, but there was no sense of urgency. If Brand had something urgent to report, he wouldn't have wasted time bandying words.

"You must understand," Brand went on, "that I haven't gathered *evidence*. What I have is only hearsay and gossip. If I were to publish what I've found out, I would be slapped with an action for slander."

Jack smiled quizzically. "Sounds to me that you've been listening at the keyholes of the very clubs you despise."

"I don't despise them. I'm indifferent. But they have their uses. I have paid informants who keep me abreast of the latest gossip, as well as highborn acquaintances who would be aghast if they thought that what they told me in confidence would be passed on to someone else. I'm a newspaperman, for God's sake. Nothing is confidential if I can prove its veracity. You would do well to remember that."

The last remark sounded like a warning. Jack's eyes narrowed. "Are you investigating Robbie?"

"No. I leave that to you. After all, you are in a position to gain the boy's confidence."

"He's told me everything he knows and I believe him!"

"Oh? I thought you said that his account of events and his friend's were a tad too pat for your attorney's comfort?"

"Well, I did, but…" Jack shook his head. "The worst I thought was that he was concealing the fact that he and Louise really were lovers, to protect Ellie's sensibilities. He wouldn't want to lose her good opinion."

In his distraction, he had bitten into a Bath bun before he remembered how much he detested them. He had to take a mouthful of coffee to wash it down.

"Why the face?" asked Brand.

Jack grinned sheepishly. "When I was boy, I picked one of the currants from the bun only to discover it was a dead fly."

"Is that all? I didn't realize soldiers were so squeamish." He took another healthy bite of his bun. "Now, where were we? Oh yes, Robbie. I doubt that he was her lover. Remember, she had a rich protector and was going off with him."

"Yes, I remember."

"Well, I think I know who our mystery man is."

Jack sat back in his chair. "Who is it?"

"Cardvale. Ellie's cousin."

They were all there for dinner that evening, including Milton, and Ellie hoped that the presence of a guest would make Frances mind her manners. She didn't know what to expect. She'd kept to her own room since she'd turned off Mrs. Leach, but she knew that the butler had seen the housekeeper off the premises and that Frances had taken the news of her favorite's dismissal very badly when she arrived home. The sound of her voice carried all the way to Ellie's chamber.

As she took her place at the head of the table, she could feel the tension in her neck and across her shoulder blades. She was beginning to feel like an interloper again, someone on the outside looking in. This family had managed for years without her meddling. They were set in their ways. What made her think she could change them? She was a fool to try. And she could see from the glitter in Frances's eyes that she would not escape unscathed.

She looked at Jack down the length of the table. He had arrived home with only minutes to spare before dinner was served, so there hadn't been the opportunity to tell him what a muddle she had made of things. She'd turned off the housekeeper. The furniture in the blue room had been moved out. In one week from today, they were to hold a reception. She hadn't even asked his permission.

She must have been out of her mind.

Robbie seemed to sense her nervousness and did his part to break the ice that gripped the table. "You have a very fine library," he said, looking at Jack. "Don't you agree, Milton?"

"Very fine," agreed Milton. He paused, rallied, and went on, "I'm finding a number of books to help me with my, um, paper."

There followed another long pause, then Caro asked Milton the subject of his paper.

"It's on Greek particles," he said. "No one really understands their significance."

"Some of us," said Caro lightly, "don't even know what they are."

Her jest was met with feeble laughter. Ellie sent her a look of heartfelt gratitude for making the effort to keep the conversation going. When Caro responded with a nod and a smile, Ellie almost fell off her chair.

Robbie spoke next, but this time more naturally. "Don't ask Milton to explain. You have to be brilliant to understand him. He doesn't have to study like us lesser mortals. I showed him my father's notes on particles and there wasn't a thing there he didn't already know."

"Robbie, please," said Milton in a strained tone.

Jack said, "I'm impressed. Ellie's father was a noted scholar. Tell me, Mr. Milton, what do you intend to do with your education?"

"Stay on at the university as a teacher, I suppose. It's a tradition in my family."

"He means," said Robbie, "as a professor. It won't be long before he becomes a master or a don."

Frances dabbed her lips with her napkin. "That seems rather tedious. I mean, spending one's youth learning, only to spend the rest of one's life teaching what one learned in one's youth."

"Oh, it is tedious," agreed Milton. "We scholars are not very interesting unless we converse with other scholars." He flashed Ellie a surreptitious smile.

After that, conversation became natural and dwindled only when footmen came forward to remove their soup plates. Ellie knew this harmony couldn't last. Sooner or later, Frances would reveal all. Everyone at that table knew it, except for Jack. If only she'd had time to talk to him alone. Since she hadn't, she had to take the initiative or hang her head like the coward she was.

"Jack." She took a moment to clear her throat. "I've decided to hold a reception, an informal affair, for our friends and family. Do you mind?"

The question seemed to surprise him. "Of course I don't mind. I'd say it's about time you started to show off that new wardrobe you ordered from Madame Clothilde's. By all means, let's have a party."

"I think it's a splendid idea," said the dowager. "And if I can be of assistance, you have only to ask, Ellie."

She shot the dowager a grateful smile. They were allies.

"What's the date of this party?" asked Jack.

"A week today," Ellie responded, but so indistinctly that she had to repeat it. "I know it's short notice, but if we leave it much longer, we'll be in the height of the season, and that's Caro's time. I don't want her to give up anything on my account."

"Nonsense," declared the dowager. "Caro is not so small-minded, are you, my dear?"

Caro had no option except to say that of course she wasn't small-minded.

"The more parties the merrier," stated the dowager. "In my opinion, this house is much too dull. Musicales and literary gatherings are all right in their way, but I like to see young people about me. I hope there will be dancing at your party, Ellie? It always makes things so much livelier."

She'd come to the sticking point, where she had to mention that she'd turned off the housekeeper. Everyone was looking at her expectantly. She opened her mouth, but Frances got there before her.

With a toss of her golden curls, she said in her sweetly husky way, "I hardly think we can hold a party a week from now without Mrs. Leach to direct things."

She looked at Jack, but he apparently had lost interest in the conversation and was conversing with Robbie.

Frances raised her voice and the sweetness was replaced by something more strident. "You must trust my judgment, Ellie. You have no experience in managing a household of this size. A housekeeper's services are indispensable. Who will supervise all the housemaids, order the supplies, stock the storeroom, the stillroom, and see to the table linens? Who will make the preserves, the cream syllabubs, the cakes, and sugar decorations? I think you were too hasty when you turned off the housekeeper. And really, she had given excellent service up to this point."

Ellie's head was reeling. She had no idea a housekeeper's job was so demanding.

Frances looked at Jack and frowned. He was still in conversation with Robbie. "Jack," she said, bringing his attention to herself. "What do you think?"

His expression was curiously blank. "I'm sorry," he said, "I was only half listening. We are short a housekeeper, I take it?"

Frances nodded. "Ellie turned off Mrs. Leach when we were all out visiting."

"In that case," he said, shrugging helplessly, "she had better find another housekeeper as soon as she can."

It was a victory of sorts, thought Ellie, but it left her feeling less than satisfied. She was forcing people to take sides, and that's not what she wanted. She wanted Frances to be happy...but preferably on some distant planet where their paths would never cross.

She felt sorry for Caro. Her loyalties were divided. She wanted to please Jack by liking his wife, but she was sincerely attached to Frances. For Caro's sake, she would be civil to the woman, even if it choked her.

She was dressed for bed, brushing her hair, when Jack

entered her chamber. Like her, he was wearing a warm, woolen dressing robe, but unlike her he was naked beneath it. The things one learned about men after marriage were truly shocking.

She put her brush on the dressing table and turned on the stool to face him. "You fraud," she said playfully, "pretending to be so innocent at the dinner table. You knew I'd turned off the housekeeper and had got myself in a pickle. I suppose Wigan told you."

"You couldn't be more wrong. I knew nothing, but as soon as I sat down, I sensed the charged atmosphere. Everyone seemed to be on tenterhooks, except Frances. I guessed it would be another episode like Alice, so I tried to keep out of it. I knew you could handle Frances without any help from me."

She reached up and pulled his head down for a long, lascivious kiss. Smiling into his eyes, she said, "You're not as dull-witted as I thought you were."

He took her hands and pulled her to the bed. They were sitting side by side. "Now, do you want to tell me about it?"

She told him most of it, but condensed the housekeeper's comments into one essential fact, that Mrs. Leach had insulted her in such a way that it was impossible to keep her on. A muscle in his jaw clenched, but he heard her out in silence.

Finally, she said, "It's not such a disaster as I thought it was. I had a word with Wigan before I came upstairs and he says that Webster would jump at the chance of taking over Mrs. Leach's position, at least until we find someone to replace her." She cocked her head. "What is it, Jack? You look...distracted."

He picked up her hand and pressed a quick kiss to her wrist. "It's hard to concentrate on problems with the domestics when I'm sitting on the bed with my beautiful bride."

She knew him better than that. "No, seriously, Jack. Something has happened and you're afraid to tell me. Is it Alice? I thought she was happy with Mrs. Mann."

"It's not Alice." He got up and began to prowl aimlessly around the room. "I met with Brand today. I may have told you that he is doing a little investigation on my behalf?"

"I understood you had decided not to go on with the investigation. What's the point?"

"The point is to make sure that Robbie's name is cleared. What if the dresser and her lover are found and have an unshakable alibi? The authorities will look at Robbie again."

She shivered. "So what has Brand found out?"

"All your friends at the Hotel Breteuil have something to hide, including Aurora."

He was making a joke of it, so she laughed. "What else?"

"That sweet little girl you were supposed to look after, Lady Harriet? She is secretly engaged to a young soldier who has been posted to Canada."

"They're not engaged, leastways I don't think so. Anyway, he is miles away. He was never a problem. What else did Brand find out?"

"Lady Sedgewick." He made a droll face. "She's an inveterate gossip, always sticking her nose in where it doesn't belong. The trouble is, she can't see what's in front of her nose. Or can she?"

He was watching her closely. "This is becoming rather sad, isn't it?" she said. "Your friend has discovered that Lord Sedgewick is not a faithful husband. Yes, I had my suspicions. I found him in the summer house once with one of Lady Sedgewick's friends. They both looked guilty, but I gave them the benefit of the doubt."

"Yes," he said slowly, "you would." Then, in an altered tone, "Did you find him with Dorothea?"

It took her a moment to make the connection. "No! Of course not! The Cardvales and the Sedgewicks met for the first time at the embassy ball in Paris. Sir Charles introduced Cardvale and Lord Sedgewick."

"Well, the Cardvales and Sedgewicks have become very close since then, especially Lord Sedgewick and Dorothea."

She shook her head. "I don't believe it. Brand must be mistaken. Dorothea would not be so stupid."

"Perhaps you're right. Brand says himself that he has no proof, only the word of informants he trusts. Sedgewick isn't Dorothea's only lover. There's also Paul Derby."

"Cardvale's man of business?"

"The same. And this is what's interesting. He showed up in Oxford, asking questions about Robbie. Shortly after, Robbie's room was broken into."

"Does Robbie know?"

"I think he must. Nothing was taken, so I don't believe he thinks it's worth mentioning."

She was following his train of thought. "I suppose Derby was looking for Dorothea's diamonds. She still believes that Robbie and I, between us, stole them from her." In the next instant, she sucked in a breath. "Do you think it was Derby who attacked me in my rooms? Do you think he was waiting for me, that he would have tried to force me to tell him where I'd hidden them?"

"I don't know." He shrugged. "We're looking for Louise's murderer. Something doesn't feel right about this. I can't see how Derby is involved when he wasn't in Paris."

Her shoulders slumped. "I wish we'd never started this! It's ugly. People have a right to their privacy." She looked at him as though she disliked him intensely. "How would you like it if someone started investigating you?"

"I should hate it. But we can't afford to be squeamish. These are the people who were close to you in Paris and are now here in London. We have to investigate them."

"How can these salacious details about people's private lives help us? Where's the motive? What about alibis? What...?"

She saw something in his face that made her words trail away. There was a heartbeat of silence, then she said slowly, "You haven't mentioned Cardvale. What did Brand have to say about my cousin?"

He sat beside her again and took her hands. "You remember Sir Charles told me that Louise was giving up the theater and was going off with a rich lover? Well, it's more than likely that that man was your cousin Cardvale."

"That can't be!" she said at once. "Robbie would have known if Cardvale was seeing Louise."

"Listen to me, Ellie. Cardvale was in Paris not long after the war ended. He and Louise were seen together then. This time around, he kept his head down. Well, his wife was with him. It could be that he was just being discreet."

"So what if he was seen with Louise? We know from my mother's recipe book that there is a connection between them. Maybe they're related. Maybe he was looking up an old friend. Why must you put a sinister shadow over everything?"

"Because," he replied forcefully, "someone must be behind all these incidents, and Cardvale is our best bet. Can't you see it? If he was Louise's lover, it gives him a motive for murder. Maybe he was jealous of Robbie. Maybe he set him up to take the blame."

Her spine straightened, her eyes flashed. "You'll never make me believe that!"

"I'm not finished yet!"

"Don't shout. I'm not deaf."

He lowered his voice. "He has a house in Hampstead that has recently been spruced up for a new occupant, a lady. Only, that occupant has yet to make an appearance."

She gave a disbelieving laugh. "You're on the wrong track. I know all about the house in Hampstead. He offered it to me the day I left Paris. Then again, just before our marriage."

"He did what?" he roared.

She instinctively cowered away from him, and that made her cross. "It was all very innocent. He was trying to be helpful. You're hurting my hands."

He dropped her hands and grabbed her arms. "If it's all very innocent, why didn't you tell me?"

She sucked in a breath. "You have a filthy mind, Jack Rigg!"

He gave her a shake. "And you, Miss Brans-Hill, don't know the first thing about a man's passions."

A fine thing to say to someone who was doing her best to learn! "And you don't know the first thing about women."

She tried to tear herself out of his grasp, and when that didn't work, she gave him a mighty shove. Caught off balance, Jack went toppling to the floor, dragging her with him. He took the brunt of the fall. She landed on his lap, her skirts hiked up to her hips, her legs splayed wide across his flanks. She had to clutch his shoulders for support.

They were both stunned by the fall. She came to herself first. Cursing him long and fluently, as only a lady knew how, she tried to rise to her knees.

With one powerful arm, he encircled her hips, preventing her from moving. "Will you stop squirming, woman?" he got out between gasps. "Give me a moment to come to myself."

She could feel his hard shaft rubbing against her belly. She stopped squirming and looked down. His face was clenched as if in pain. His eyes were hot on hers. She knew that look. She leaned close, so close that her breath fluttered against his mouth, but she did not kiss him.

"Now tell me I don't understand a man's passions," she breathed out, and she rubbed herself slowly, tauntingly, against his jutting sex.

She cried out when he shifted his position so that his back was supported by the bed. His hands cupped her bottom, holding her in place. His fingers spread, squeezed, caressed, and inched up under the hem of her gown till they found bare flesh.

The pleasure was intoxicating. She could hardly breathe. Her head fell forward on his shoulder, but when he adjusted her skirts, and his fingers brushed against the folds of her femininity, she came up on her knees and arched like a quivering bowstring.

He said something indistinct. She tried to focus, but her body couldn't be bothered with words when his clever fingers were driving her mad.

"What?" she panted.

His lips brushed her ear. "I said, 'Now tell me I don't know the first thing about women.'"

She couldn't stop now even if she wanted to. But he'd thrown down the gauntlet. Her pride was at stake. She had to pick it up.

"I'm not surrendering," she warned him.

"Neither am I," he got out.

It was part contest, part game. Where one led, the other followed, but going one step further. Each pushed the other to the edge, then pulled back. The game was torture, but neither wanted it to end.

Drunk on him, glorying in her own power, Ellie went too far. She brushed hot, lingering kisses from his throat to his groin and the game became a race.

He dispensed with their nightclothes with a speed that left her shaken. There was no part of her he did not want to kiss and touch. His hands took his fill of her, his caresses became more desperate.

And she gave as good as she got.

In one powerful lunge, he locked his body to hers. She flung back her head in sheer animal pleasure. Racked by sensation, they moved like lightning and went soaring over the crest. Her wild cry of release was muffled against his throat. He gritted his teeth as his body convulsed, spilling his seed deep inside her.

Weak and spent, they collapsed on the floor. Jack had barely enough energy to snag the coverlet and drape it over them.

Minutes passed, or maybe an hour. She'd fallen asleep and when she wakened, she was in Jack's room and in his huge bed, looking up at the ceiling. Jack was beside her, one arm draped around her waist, making escape impossible.

Now why had that thought popped into her head?

Remembering what they had just shared, made her face burn. What he had done to her! What she had done to him! She wasn't a prude. She enjoyed—what a tepid word—what they did in bed...or out of it. But this last bout, she could hardly call it making love, left her feeling strangely dissatisfied.

Not so strange when she thought about it. *You don't know the first thing about a man's passions.* Passion. Lust.

That's all a man wanted from a woman. If only he had told her that he loved her, she would be feeling on top of the world.

To be fair, she hadn't given him the words, either. But that was because she felt at a disadvantage. She'd compromised him. If he hadn't been dragged to the Hotel Breteuil to give her an alibi, he wouldn't have given her another thought. They wouldn't be married and he would be enjoying his carefree bachelor existence, just like his friends Brand and Ash.

She wasn't finding fault with him. He had made the best of a bad situation. He was a good man, an honorable man. But she couldn't help what she was feeling. Unrequited love left a bitter taste in her mouth.

This was childish and not like her at all. He gave as much of himself as he could give. It was churlish to expect more. But she couldn't help wondering if he had ever given those words she longed to hear to another woman.

Frances, perhaps?

She would never ask, of course.

He stirred, propped himself on one elbow, and gazed down at her. "What are you thinking?" he asked.

"I was just wondering..." She looked at him and looked away.

"Yes?"

She blurted out the words before she had time to think. "About Frances."

"What about her?"

She couldn't help herself. She really wanted to know. "Were you in love with her?"

He gave a mirthless laugh. "Believe it or not, I thought I was. But that was a long time ago."

Her smile was as mirthless as his laugh. "And I suppose you told her so? That you loved her, I mean?"

"That was my mistake. That's when she decided we were engaged to be married. I was a silly young cub then."

"And I suppose you've fallen in love with many girls since then?"

He was threading his fingers through her hair, and missed the dangerous glint in her eyes. "Dozens of them," he replied easily. "What man hasn't?"

Too late, he realized his mistake. She clouted him on the shoulder with her balled fist and scrambled from the bed. Her dressing gown was on the floor. She scooped it up and shrugged into it.

Jack combed his fingers through his hair. "You're surely not jealous! Those women meant nothing to me. A passing fancy, is all."

"Did you or did you not tell them that you loved them?"

His look of bewilderment was rapidly changing to one of annoyance. "I may have. What difference does it make?"

She gasped. "'What difference does it make?' I'll tell you what difference it makes. You have never said those words to me."

He had the gall to smile. "Ellie," he said, "this is foolishness. I was a boy then. I've learned since that romantic love doesn't last."

"So, if I were to tell you that I loved you, you wouldn't believe me?"

"Of course I'd believe you." He was yawning, stretching his arms above his head, showing off his powerful physique. "That is," he went on gently, "you're a female. That's how females think."

That was it? That was all he had to say to her? She'd bared her heart and he'd replied with inarguable logic?

He didn't believe in romantic love.

She was truly sorry for him. No she wasn't, she was as

mad as Hades, not only because he hadn't declared his love, but more especially since she had betrayed hers.

Head held high, she sailed into her own chamber.

"Ellie," he called out. "Come back here."

She waited until she heard his feet padding almost to the door before she turned the key in the lock with a gratifying *click.*

Jack glowered at the door, sighed, and padded back to bed. Arms folded across his chest, his back supported by pillows, he waited. He knew Ellie. She had a quick temper, but one flash and it was all over, then she'd want to make amends.

He didn't have long to wait. He heard the key turn in the lock, the door opened, and she tiptoed over to the bed. When he pushed back the covers and patted the mattress, she climbed in beside him.

"I've changed my mind," she said without the least rancor. "I don't want to hear those words from you, and I promise not to say them to you, either. What would be the point? When you've heard them and said them to so many other females, they lose their value. In fact, they're meaningless."

She yawned hugely. "You've done so much for me and Robbie. I'll always be grateful to you, Jack. I hope you know that."

He didn't want her gratitude, but he was happy to let things rest there. He was back in her good graces. That's all that mattered.

He blew out the candle and nestled down beside her. He'd never thought to ask her how many men had told her they loved her and, more importantly, how many men she'd loved in her turn. The thought kept turning in his mind until he drifted off to sleep.

Chapter 22

Ellie's little reception did not begin until ten o'clock. One hour later, it was obvious to everyone that the reception had turned into a ball. Because there had been so little time to plan for the event, no cards of invitation had been sent out. People were invited by word of mouth, and they turned out in droves.

The musicians, a quartet originally engaged to play a selection of quiet pieces that would not intrude on the chatter of the guests, were soon playing a lively selection of dance tunes at the request of the young people who were there. Carpets were rolled back. Another room had to be opened up, then another, to accommodate the crush of people. No one seemed to mind. Had they been invited to a formal ball, their measure might have been different. But as a reception, Ellie's informal party was proving to be a raging success.

Ellie wasn't aware of the general consensus. She was too busy responding to, as she saw it, one crisis after another. She was everywhere at once, and nowhere to be found. But Jack found her in the kitchens, outside the stillroom, wringing her hands as she listened intently to what her new housekeeper had to say. He hesitated. This was a woman's domain and he was reluctant to interfere.

Webster, or "Miss Webster," as she had to be addressed since rising in the world, was calm and reassuring.

"Everything is in hand, my lady. Cook and her helpers have spent the week restocking the storerooms."

"But," said Ellie, "there must be over a hundred people here. I only expected fifty."

"I'm not saying we can provide a sit-down supper. But the tables will be laden with enough delicacies to feed a small army. If you don't believe me, take a look in Cook's kitchen and the Servery."

Cook's kitchen was a hive of activity. The ovens were going full blast and Mrs. Rice and her kitchen maids were taking newly baked dishes from the ovens or putting the finishing touches to trays of savories and sweets that were so tiny they could be eaten in two bites. In the room beyond, the Servery, every table was laden with trays ready to be taken upstairs.

Cook turned as she felt the draft, straightened when she saw Ellie, and hastily dropped a curtsy. The kitchen maids stood and gaped.

Ellie went forward and, over Mrs. Rice's protests, clasped the cook's floury hand. "I do thank you, Mrs. Rice," she said, "and all your helpers, too." She acknowledged the maids with a nod. "Without your hard work, my first reception would be an unmitigated disaster."

Cook waited until the door swung shut behind Ellie. "Well," she said, "that's never happened before." She thought for a moment. "That's what I call a real lady." Then to her helpers, "Don't stand there staring. We has work to do. We're not going to let her ladyship down."

In the hall outside, Ellie came face-to-face with Jack. She was, he thought, looking none the worse for her labors. In fact, she was as lovely as he had ever seen her. That might have something to do with the gown she was wearing, one of Madame Clothilde's creations, a simple, white gauze with puff sleeves and a green satin sash knotted under her bosom. The ribbons threaded through her hair, now swept up in the current mode, matched the sash. There was a becoming flush on her cheeks. Her eyes were wide and bright, not in glad recognition at seeing him, but because she was harried.

He was coming to know her so well.

"Jack," she said, "did we order enough wine?"

He removed her hand and dusted the flour from his sleeve. "Ellie," he said, "there's enough wine in my cellars to supply several balls."

She let out a breath. "I should have known that I'd married a paragon."

"Yes, you should." He offered her his arm. "Shall we join our guests? If the host and hostess can't enjoy their own party, what's the point? Besides, I want to make amends to my beautiful wife."

His words intrigued her, but he wouldn't explain them. All became clear when they arrived at the improvised ballroom and the orchestra, at a signal from Jack, struck up a waltz.

"Let's pretend," he said, "we've just been introduced at the embassy ball. Miss Hill, may I have the honor of this dance?"

Eyes gleaming, she bobbed him a curtsy. "Oh, milord," she trilled, "I declare I am quite overcome with the honor you are bestowing on me. That I, a poor vicar's daughter, so far beneath your own estate—"

Her words were cut off when he encircled her waist and pivoted her into a series of fast turns.

"Vixen," he murmured in her ear. "Your tongue is still sharp."

"Toplofty lout," she riposted. "I couldn't believe the change in you from that boy I remembered."

"And now?"

"You improve on acquaintance," she allowed with a pert smile.

Her happy smile had him smiling, too.

Their progress was watched by Frances, who stood fanning herself at the edge of the dance floor. Caro was with her.

Frances said complacently, "Well, I did warn her, and just see the result. Nothing in readiness. Everything in a muddle. Can you imagine—guests helping footmen to roll up carpets? Second-rate musicians! Mind *you* don't dance the waltz."

Caro, who had been tapping her foot in time to the music, stopped and looked at Frances. "I don't see any harm in it. Besides, no one seems to care about rolled-up carpets. Everyone is having a good time."

"I daresay." Frances's voice had lost none of its complacency. "But think of the stories that will be circulating by this time tomorrow." She shook her head. "People will be laughing at her." She tapped her fan on Caro's arm. "You'll note that I did not invite any of my friends. They would be affronted to mix with this unruly crowd. Who are they? There are few faces *I* recognize. At your ball, we shall invite only the cream of society."

Caro stared at her idol for a long interval. Finally, she said in a choked voice, "Excuse me. I see Robbie and there's something I've been meaning to say to him." Head down, she hurried away.

If Robbie had known it was Caro bearing down on him, he would have taken to his heels. He considered her a sour-faced puss who looked down her long, patrician nose at anyone who did not meet her exacting standards.

But Caro, all dressed up for a grown-up party, was, as far as he knew, a stranger.

"Milton," he said, "who is that divine creature who is coming our way? Look. I think she knows you."

Milton followed the direction of Robbie's gaze. "Of course she knows me. It's Lady Caro. I hope she doesn't expect me to ask her to dance."

" 'Caro'?" said Robbie, crushed.

As she drew closer, the illusion vanished, and the dark-haired, dark-eyed vision in the silver tissue gown reverted to the sharp-tongued harpy he always tried to avoid.

"Milton," he said, but Milton had had the presence of mind to melt into the crush before Caro was upon them.

He didn't waste his charm on Caro, knowing she would only find fault. "I don't dance the waltz," he said.

Fire momentarily kindled in her eyes, but it was soon quenched. "I'm not allowed to dance the waltz, anyway, not until…oh, that doesn't matter. What I wanted to say is…"

She looked into his frowning face and rushed her last words. "I've been such a fool. I just want you to know that I think this is a lovely party."

Stupefied, Robbie watched her as she threaded her way to her grandmother's side. *Now what is that all about?* he wondered.

He didn't think about it for long. He was under his sister's orders to mingle and make sure there were no wall-flowers at her party, and Lady Harriet, Sedgewick's daughter, had just entered the room. He liked Harriet immensely. She didn't give herself airs or expect a fellow to act the gallant. More to the point, she didn't mind sitting out a dance. They could talk about horses or hunting or whatever took his fancy. Harriet was easy to talk to. She might even be interested in a little surprise they had planned for Ellie before everyone went home. Harriet would like that. She was very fond of Ellie. And she was a good sport.

He scanned the room. No sign of Harriet's mother. Good, because if Lady Sedgewick was there, he wouldn't be able to wedge a word in sideways.

It was close to three in the morning when Ellie stopped to catch her breath. The party was winding down. Some of her guests had left already. Others were waiting for their carriages to be brought round. She wasn't sure what the young people were up to, but they were within hailing distance, across the road in the park, ostensibly taking a last look at the night sky before their coaches arrived to take them home.

She sipped her iced lemonade, half concealed by the curtain of one of the window embrasures in the upstairs hall. She wasn't hiding; she was taking a moment for herself, enjoying her sense of accomplishment. Her expectations for her little reception had been widely exceeded. Over one hundred guests crowded into three rooms, and that did not include the library, which Jack had opened up for the gentlemen who wished to smoke.

The secret of her success was revealed when Ash and Brand arrived, bringing with them no less a personage than Beau Brummel. The realization that she wasn't the drawing card to her soiree, that word must have circulated that *the* Beau was expected, hadn't deflated her one bit, just the opposite. It relieved her of the horrible suspicion that she'd become a curiosity, like one of the performing bears in Astley's Circus, and that's what people had come to see.

The Beau wasn't the only one who had contributed to the success of her party. Ash and Brand rarely missed a dance and, along with Jack, managed to keep Frances purring—a heroic task, in Ellie's opinion. Robbie and Milton had been pressed into service. They drew the line at dancing, but they mingled with the young people and tried to keep them entertained. And she and the dowager did much the same with the older generation.

What she really wanted was to find Jack so they could gloat together. And she would, just as soon as she had done her duty by her Cousin Cardvale and Dorothea.

They'd arrived with the Sedgewicks, including Harriet, and she'd made a point of introducing them around, but other than a few stilted words of conversation, she hadn't known what to say.

That was Jack's doing. She was seeing them in a new light and it made her feel awkward around them. This was nonsense! As Jack said, all he had to go on was hearsay. The rest was speculation.

She knew that he hadn't confronted Cardvale with his suspicions, because he'd promised to wait until he had more to go on. She toyed with the idea of subtly introducing the subject of her mother's recipe book. It wouldn't work. She didn't know how to be subtle, and she didn't want to embarrass her cousin in front of his wife.

Better keep to a safe topic of conversation. The Cardvales' house was being renovated. It would do.

She found Dorothea in a quiet corner of the music room, talking in low tones to a group of ladies of varying ages who were following her words intently; Lady Sedgewick was there, as was Mrs. King, whose husband served on one of Jack's parliamentary committees; Mrs. Dearing, whose husband did something similar; and the Misses Honeyman, in their fourth season and enjoying themselves as much as if it had been their first.

There was no sign of Cardvale or Lord Sedgewick, and Ellie's overheated imagination pictured them fighting a duel. The Misses Honeyman put her right. One patted a chair, inviting Ellie to join them, then whispered in her ear, "Alas, we've been deserted by the gentlemen for the smoking room."

"But we don't mind," whispered the other. "All they talk about is politics. Lady Cardvale's story is much more interesting. Her diamonds were stolen in Paris, did you know?"

Ellie groaned inwardly. She'd thought she'd put this behind her. Evidently, these charming ladies had not made the connection between Miss Hill in Paris, and the Lady Raleigh who was married to Jack. Why couldn't Dorothea let it go?

She wouldn't let it go because she truly believed that Ellie and Robbie had stolen the diamonds. That's why Paul Derby had been asking questions. He must be the one who had broken into her lodgings in Henrietta Street.

She listened on tenterhooks as Dorothea related the events leading up to the robbery. Everyone gasped when she told how she'd practically caught the thief in the act. Ellie sighed with relief when no mention was made of Miss Hill and her little adventure. She was sure she had Cardvale to thank for that.

Mrs. King leaned forward in her chair. "And the thief was never caught?"

"No," replied Dorothea. Her eyes flicked to Ellie and slid away. "But we have our suspicions. All the doors were locked, you see, though one of the keys was missing. My own view is that it was stolen by one of the guests and given to an accomplice so that he could come and go at will."

"Why not simply force a window on the ground floor?"

"Because," replied Dorothea darkly, "all the windows have shutters that lock from the inside."

The lull in the conversation gave Ellie the opportunity

to lead everyone away from the topic of Dorothea's diamonds. "Mrs. King," she said, "I hear you're something of an herbalist. So was my mother, but I've lost most of her recipes. Tell me, where should I start? What should I plant in my herb garden?"

Not only did Mrs. King know her subject, but she was interesting, as well. For all that, Ellie found her mind wandering to the lost key. She had borrowed the key, of course. She had meant to return it, but in the excitement of being discovered and accused of robbery, she'd forgotten all about it.

What had she done with the key?

Her mind slipped back to the night of the riot in the Palais Royal. She'd arrived home alone, taken the key from her pochette to unlock the door, when someone opened it from the inside. The porter.

Then what?

Of course! She hadn't wanted the porter to know she'd taken the key, so she'd quickly slipped it into her coat pocket. But it wasn't her coat. It was Jack's cloak, the one his manservant had given her. And later, she had given the cloak to Lord Sedgewick to return to Jack as proof that she was Aurora. By that time, she'd forgotten all about the key.

So where was it now? She doubted that it would still be in Jack's cloak. A valet would empty his master's pockets before brushing his clothes and putting them away. Coates must know what he'd done with the key. Perhaps he'd given it to Jack.

It wasn't urgent. When she had a spare moment, she would ask Jack about it.

Her thoughts scattered when there was a sudden series of muffled explosions coming from the park, then light streaked across the sky. Some of the ladies gasped.

"Was that lightning?" asked Lord Stonebridge, suddenly coming to himself.

"A fireworks display, I think," said someone else.

Ellie's heart subsided. It seemed that the young people had decided to have their own party in the park. The neighbors would not take kindly to a fireworks display at three in the morning. Jack would soon put a stop to it.

People got up and wandered over to the windows. A shower of stars burst overhead. More pops went off.

"Those weren't all fireworks going off," said Colonel Howe thoughtfully. "I heard a pistol shot."

Down below, coachmen in vehicles waiting for their passengers had a hard time restraining their horses. Suddenly, light streamed onto the steps from the front door. Jack left the house, with Brand close behind him. They crossed the road and entered the park.

Ellie turned smartly and made for the door. Others were ahead of her and she could not get past them.

Ash was on the front steps, doing his best to keep people back. Ellie had to elbow her way through to reach him. She wasn't panicked. She was still hoping that this was nothing more than a prank that had got out of hand, and if Robbie was part of it, she was going to read him the riot act.

"You, too, Ellie." Ash's voice was stern and unrelenting. "Someone out there has a gun. No one is leaving this house until Jack gives the word."

His expression, his harsh tone, so out of character for Ash, had her rooted to the spot. Fear clutched her throat.

She cried out when Jack and Milton emerged from the park. They were supporting Robbie. His chin was lolling on his chest. There was blood dripping from his hand. Behind them were Cardvale and Sedgewick. Harriet was hanging onto her father's arm. Ellie scanned the crowd. A file of silent young people, all Ellie's guests as far as she could tell, were not far behind Jack. Caro was there, too, looking wild-eyed and bewildered.

Jack's face was as white as Milton's. He spoke to Ellie in a low, calming voice. "It's a flesh wound, nothing more."

"So much blood," she said, agonized. Now she could see the dark stain spreading over Robbie's jacket. She didn't believe Jack. This was serious.

Jack spoke to Ash next. "Get him to bed, then send for the physician. I'll be back as soon as I can."

"I'll see to it," replied Ash. The burden of Robbie was moved gently from Jack to Ash.

The dowager was there to take Caro into her arms. "Come along, dear," she said. "No, don't worry about Robbie. Ellie will look after him."

"Where are you going?" Ellie cried when Jack turned away.

"Back to the park. Brand is still there, waiting for the constables."

Jack entered Robbie's bedchamber to find Ellie sitting on a chair pulled close to the bed, spooning something from a cup into her brother's mouth. Robbie's eyes were closed and he was swallowing involuntarily.

The doctor was there, too. He came out of the dressing room, drying his hands after washing them in the washbasin. Bloodied towels lay on a chair.

"Dr. Blackwell?" said Jack.

The doctor looked up. He was in his forties, of middle height, with a slight build and a sprinkling of silver in his dark hair. He lacked charm or the soothing touch, but he knew his business and that meant more to Jack.

"A wound under his left armpit," said Blackwell. "The bullet did not lodge in his flesh, but it did take a bite out of him. I'd say he's a very lucky young man. There's a fresh scar here"—he pointed to his own left shoulder—"that still looks tender. A knife wound, is it?"

Ellie nodded. "He got that in Paris in a ... brawl."

"I see. A young man who likes to live dangerously."

Jack felt rather than saw Ellie stiffen. "Dr. Blackwell," he said, "a word with you?"

"Certainly." The doctor turned to Ellie with one of his rare half smiles. "No need to ask if you know how to dress the wound. Where did you learn your skill?"

She did not look up, but continued to spoon her brew, drop by drop, past Robbie's lips. "In my father's parish," she said. "I'm a vicar's daughter."

His brows rose. He flicked a glance at his patient, but all he said was, "Give him as little laudanum as possible. If he becomes fevered, send for me at once. Otherwise, I shall drop by tomorrow afternoon. No need to look so stricken. He's a young man; he'll mend."

In the corridor, Jack said, "Yes, he really is a vicar's son."

Blackwell colored. "I beg your pardon if I've offended."

Jack grinned wryly. "Not at all. My wife and her brother, for all their gentle upbringing, seem to attract danger. Believe me, it's hard to live with. Now, tell me, how lucky was he?"

Blackwell shrugged. "An inch to the right, a half inch, would have been the death of him. I could say as much about the knife wound. He may not be so lucky a third time."

"There won't be a third time," Jack replied. He thanked the doctor and had one of the footmen see him out while he went back to Ellie.

She'd set aside the cup and spoon and was bundling the bloodied towels, along with Robbie's bloodied clothes, into a wicker hamper. She seemed to be lost in her own thoughts. She was still wearing her party finery, now crushed and stained with her brother's blood. Her hair was coming undone. Her eyes were like crushed violets against the pallor of her skin.

He said helplessly, "One of the maids should do this."

"No. I want to do it. When he wakes, I don't want him to see a stranger's face." She looked up with a smile. "Did you think I was too delicate for the sight of blood? You should know me better than that."

He felt a wave of fury flood through him. That this brave and generous girl should have so much to bear! That even he, with all his resources, could not protect her! He didn't expect to go through life without sorrow. But this was different. They were pitted against a cunning, malevolent adversary, someone in the shadows who had a purpose they could not even guess. How could he fight such an enemy?

A fierce determination gripped him. They had been too complacent. He had deferred to Ellie's wishes. He would not make that mistake again.

"Let's sit down," she said, indicating chairs pulled close to the fire, "and you can tell me what happened. All Robbie was able to say was that he was responsible for arranging the fireworks display."

When they were seated, she looked at him expectantly. "Well?"

"Nobody really knows what happened. The constable questioned all the young people who were with Robbie in the park and let them go. They weren't much help. They were all looking up at the sky, at the fireworks display, when the shot went off. When they saw Robbie, they thought it was a joke, that he was playacting. When he didn't get up, they realized their mistake."

He reflected for a moment, then continued. "There was so much confusion at that point. A few panicked parents and God-knows-who else had crossed into the park to see what was going on. Someone cleared a path for Milton and me while Brand stayed in the park, waiting for the constable."

There was a long silence after that. Finally, Ellie stirred. "What does the constable make of it?"

He spread his hands. "That some enterprising villain saw his chance when the fireworks were going off and tried to rob Robbie."

She shivered and sank back against her chair. "To kill a man for the little he can carry in his pockets!" Then wildly and bitterly, "I thought the park gates were supposed to be locked at night!"

"It's easy to force locks," he replied simply.

Her fingers began to work at the knot of her sash. When she realized what she was doing, she stopped. After another reflective silence, she breathed out a long sigh and looked at him steadily.

"What are you *not* telling me, Jack?"

Their chairs were close together. He reached out and took her hands in his. "Do I have to tell you? Don't you know? I don't accept the constable's view of things. This is not another coincidence. This is a logical progression from the night Louise Daudet was murdered. I know, I know, it doesn't make sense to us yet, but, as God is my witness, we *will* make sense of it."

She pressed a hand to her eyes but remained silent.

He went on, "There was so much confusion in the park, so many people milling around, that I doubt we'll discover who shot Robbie. We have to go back to the beginning, to Louise Daudet. Her murder is the key that will unlock the mystery. Do you understand what I'm saying, Ellie?"

"You're thinking of Cardvale," she said.

She was only half right, but he did not correct her. "Yes, I'm thinking of Cardvale."

He knew it would be impossible to get her to leave her brother, so he did everything he could to see to her comfort. Most of the servants were already in bed, but his valet never went to bed before his master, so it was left to Coates to light the fire in Robbie's dressing room and find a maid to bring Ellie hot water to wash, a change of clothes, and a pot of tea.

While Ellie tidied herself, Jack stood watch over Robbie, a signal honor, as he well knew. And when Ellie returned, he settled himself in a chair beside the fire and had Coates bring him a glass of the best brandy he kept in his cellar. Then he sipped slowly, rarely taking his eyes off Ellie.

She sat quietly, trying to read by the lamp, but ever ready to put her book down when Robbie stirred or made a sound. The cup and spoon, now replenished, were on the table by the bed, and she made frequent use of them to quench Robbie's thirst.

"Only water," she answered to Jack's whispered query.

At intervals, she felt her brother's brow and checked his dressing, and seemed satisfied with what she found.

The house was stirring when she began to droop. That's when Jack insisted that she get some rest.

"I'm not banishing you to your room," he said over her protests. "The maid made up the trundle bed for you in the dressing room. We'll leave the door open if you like."

She gave in, but reluctantly. "I'll just lie on top of the bed and pull the coverlet over me. If there's a change in Robbie, you will waken me?"

"I'll waken you."

He went back to Robbie's room, leaving the dressing-room door open. Following Ellie's example, he felt

Robbie's brow, fed him some water, and checked the dressing.

All was well. He was young. When he wakened, he would feel the bite of his wound. But he was in good hands. He would soon heal.

He returned to Ellie. She was already asleep, the coverlet pushed back to her waist. On impulse, he spread his hand over her breast, not in a lover's caress, but to feel her life pulse in its slow, steady rhythm.

Some emotion he was reluctant to name tightened his throat.

He pulled the coverlet up to her chin.

Chapter 23

Jack was rarely away from the sickroom while they waited for the doctor to arrive. The patient was in some pain, but slept intermittently. Ellie had the burden of looking after her brother, and would not have had it any other way, but Jack was pleased to see that Caro tried to do her part.

She couldn't change dressings or do any serious nursing, she said, but she could make sure the bricks to keep Robbie warm were changed when they cooled; she could run and fetch and make herself useful. She could also sit with Robbie to relieve Ellie, should she want to go for a walk or rest.

Jack thought Ellie's response was apt. "Thank you," she said. "Coates and Miss Webster have been extremely kind and efficient, but they must get their rest, too. Besides, I can't confide in them, and I could do with some female companionship." She looked at Jack. "I'll be fine now that Caro is here. Go away, Jack. I know there are things you wish to do."

He tried not to smile. Caro looked as though a millstone had just been removed from around her neck. It was only now that he was beginning to understand how much Ellie might have had to forgive.

In spite of Ellie's permission, he waited till the doctor had examined his patient. By this time, Robbie was awake and lucid, but in a great deal of pain now that the effects of the dose of laudanum Ellie had given him had worn off. This was not the time to question him in detail. All he could recall of the shooting was that he'd been letting off fireworks when he'd felt as though a red-hot wire had become embedded in his side. He'd dropped to his knees. People had crowded around him until Milton ordered them back. He'd seen nothing and heard nothing but the fireworks going off.

"No infection and no fever," said Blackwell after examining the wound. "You'll be up and around in another day or two."

Jack did not wait to hear more. After a quiet word with Ellie, telling her where she could find him if anything untoward occurred, he left the house.

The sky was overcast, threatening snow, and the bite of the chill winds from the North Sea made Jack hug his coat close to his body. This bitter turn in the weather, had it come a day earlier, would surely have dissuaded Robbie and his friends from their jaunt in the park. This made him wonder about Robbie's assailant. If he was not a footpad, then he was a clever opportunist.

It was only a short walk to Knightsbridge where the Cardvales had rented a house and he took the shortest route, which was the route through the park. He did not delay or scout out the lie of the land where Robbie had been shot. He'd already done that earlier that morning with Ash and Brand. There were no clues—no abandoned pistol, nothing to point them in any one person's direction.

Lord Cardvale was not at home, the butler told Jack, then, when a look of determination crossed Jack's features, added hastily that his lordship was at his club.

At White's he learned that his lordship had put in a brief appearance, then gone off to inspect some property in Hampstead that he owned. This had Jack's ears pricking. This must be the house Cardvale had offered Ellie. Unfortunately, no one knew where in Hampstead the house was located. Jack debated whether he should return to Knightsbridge and question Cardvale's servants. Maybe Cardvale's coachmen could tell him what he wanted to know. On the other hand, he didn't want to rouse Lady Cardvale's suspicions, supposing she did not know about the house in Hampstead. In the end, he decided to take a hackney to the village and inquire of the locals whether they knew where the house was.

Dusk was gathering when he arrived. He was in luck. At the first place he tried, a hostelry on the edge of the village, the landlord, a hearty, portly gentleman, gave him directions.

His expression grew grave when he heard Cardvale's name. "Always kindly and polite, he is," said the landlord. "He's well thought of in these parts. You can't miss the cottage. It overlooks the heath, right by Kenwood House. Such a pity that his sister won't be joining him."

"Oh?" said Jack, trying not to show how interested he was. "What happened there?"

"He hasn't said, but we can all see the difference in him."

Jack was still mulling over the landlord's words when his hackney pulled up in front of a modest building that looked out on the heath. Kenwood House was a fair distance away, but there were no other houses close by. This had to be Cardvale's property.

He alighted and told the driver to wait.

This was no estate worker's cottage, but a two-storied building in prime condition that a city gentleman of means might well turn to as a rural retreat. There would be no hunting on the heath, but a nature lover would find much to interest him, and there were many fine walks.

Jack was beginning to have second thoughts. He could picture Cardvale here, but not the celebrated star of the Théatre Français, not Louise Daudet.

The door was answered by a servant who looked as though he'd come from the woodshed, a pleasant country fellow with no grandiose airs to intimidate callers. He ushered Jack into an oak-paneled hallway with a fine oak staircase branching off and told him to wait. He returned almost at once and led the way to the parlor.

Cardvale was there, on his feet, nursing a glass of brandy. "Lord Raleigh," he said, "don't tell me something has happened to Robbie!"

He seemed genuinely alarmed. "On the contrary," Jack quickly assured him, "he is on the mend. The doctor expects him to be on his feet in a matter of days."

Cardvale clutched the back of a chair for support. "Thank God for that." He took a moment to come to himself. "Then . . . how can I help you?"

Jack spoke slowly and distinctly. "Your name has come up in connection with Louise Daudet's murder, and the British ambassador to France has asked me to investigate, as a personal friend."

"Yes," said Cardvale. "I expected that someone would come to see me eventually. Shall we sit down?"

This mild acceptance of what was tantamount to an accusation of murder set Jack back on his heels. It was a moment before he moved to accept Cardvale's invitation.

When they were seated, Cardvale said, "Now, where shall I begin?"

"You can begin," said Jack, "by telling me about *Cardvale's punch,* and how Ellie's mother came to know Jeanne Daudet."

The manservant had added logs to the fire and they crackled merrily as Cardvale embarked on his tale. Jack had refused the offer of brandy. He had not wished to accept a man's hospitality when he had all but accused him of murder.

"Jeanne," Cardvale said, "called it *Cardvale's punch* after I came into the title. Before that, it was *George's punch.* I loved the stuff, you see. But my story begins before that. As you may know, I was an only child, born to parents who could not stand the sight of each other. I loved my father, but was deathly afraid of my mother. It was only when I was older that I came to see that my father feared my mother, too—her ferocious temper, her unceasing demands, the scenes…" He looked up with a feeble smile. "You may wonder that I married Dorothea, but when I met her, she seemed a sweet-tempered girl. And I would never have married Dorothea had I not wanted to make a home for Ellie and Robbie, but I'm getting ahead of myself.

"I was a lonely child, but there was one bright spot. Ellie's parents, my Aunt and Uncle Brans-Hill. I spent weeks at a time with them during school holidays, when my mother had taken to her bed with her nerves."

"Ellie never mentioned this to me," said Jack.

"She wouldn't remember. She was only an infant when my visits ceased." He took a sip of brandy before going on. "I had another home to go to in the holidays, as well—my Aunt Jeanne and her daughter, Louise Daudet."

Cardvale allowed himself a small smile. "That, of

course, was a polite fiction. Jeanne was my father's mistress and Louise was their daughter."

Jack was too shocked to say anything, and he reached for a glass of brandy that was not there.

"*Mistress*," said Cardvale. "What an ugly word. Aunt Jeanne was like a mother to me. This was her house. The heath was our playground, Louise's and mine. She was my little cousin, so I thought, three years younger than I, and I was her champion."

"She was your half sister," said Jack.

"I didn't know it then, not until after my father's death. I was only fourteen when I inherited the title. That's when my mother found out about Jeanne and Louise and the house in Hampstead. I'd never told her about my visits here because I feared she would put a stop to them. That's how she punished me as a boy. She would deprive me of whatever I loved."

He laughed, a hollow sound that filled Jack with pity. He knew what was coming next.

"Of course, my mother acted like the woman scorned when she found out. She wanted Jeanne and Louise to be thrown out in the street. I didn't know what to do. My guardian had control of my money and thought as my mother did. My father had made no provision for Jeanne and his daughter. He was taken so suddenly, and he was still young. I know he would have provided for them if he'd known his death was so near at hand."

It wasn't an uncommon story. Men thought they would live forever and gave no thought to providing for their dependents until it was too late. Jack had no patience with such fools.

After a long silence, Jack said, "How does Ellie's mother come into this?"

Cardvale blinked and focused on Jack as if he'd forgotten he was there. "I was desperate," he said. "My mother and guardian wouldn't listen, wouldn't lift a finger to help Jeanne or Louise. So I turned to the only people I knew would not let me down."

"Ellie's parents."

"My Aunt and Uncle Brans-Hill. And, of course, they were generosity itself. They opened their home to Jeanne and Louise."

"That doesn't surprise me," said Jack, remembering his own dismay at never knowing who would be sitting down to dinner at the Brans-Hills' table.

"And they provided enough money for Jeanne and Louise to return to France, where Jeanne had relatives. There's not much more to tell. I tried to keep up with them, but the war intervened. When I came into my majority, I sent money, but again the war intervened. I was there, in Paris, during the Peace of Amiens. By that time, Jeanne had died and Louise was making a name for herself as an actress. It was as though we had never been parted."

He smiled faintly, sadly, but there was pleasure there, too. "Louise was everything I was not—gregarious, fun-loving, and confident of who she was and where she was going. No one was too low to be beneath her notice. No one was too high. She never forgot a name or a face. If someone was in trouble, she was there to help. And she was fiercely independent. No one could tell her what to think or how to behave." He added with a chuckle, "But not always easy to live with."

He rolled his head on the back of the chair to look at Jack. "Ellie reminds me of her."

This was exactly what Jack was thinking.

"It's not surprising," Cardvale said musingly. "They were distant cousins, in the same degree as Ellie and I."

" 'Cousins'!"

Cardvale looked surprised. "Didn't I make that clear?

Ellie's great-great-grandfather and mine was the first earl of Cardvale. She is related to me on her mother's side of the family. That's why Louise was so taken with Robbie. He was her cousin, too."

"I see," said Jack, his mind working like lightning. Now he could understand why the Brans-Hills were so generous to complete strangers. They were not strangers at all.

Suddenly, Cardvale's voice turned savage. "Had it not been for that damnable war, I could have done so much more for Louise and her mother. When the war was finally over and I was in a position to help, it was too late."

Jack waited, then prompted gently, "I heard that she was retiring from the stage and coming to live in this house. Is it true?"

"Yes, it's true."

"But...why?"

Cardvale said heavily, "She was diagnosed with consumption of the lungs. The disease was in its early stages, but there is no cure. She wanted to spend whatever time remained to her in this house, where she had spent the happiest days of her life. She wanted to come home to die."

The fire crackled and sent sparks flying up the chimney.

"I'm sorry," said Jack, not knowing what else to say. At last he understood why Ellie kept saying that Cardvale was a changed man. He was grieving, was, in fact, consumed by grief.

He spoke as gently as he could manage. "Your last trip to Paris? Lady Cardvale went with you?"

"Against my wishes. I wanted to make arrangements for Louise to make the journey and see if she was fit to make it." His voice choked. "She looked so natural, so full of life, it was hard to believe she was ill."

"Yet no one remembers seeing you with Louise."

Cardvale shrugged. "I made sure they didn't. I was being careful. The last thing I wanted was for Dorothea to learn about Louise. I was afraid she would have treated Louise no better than she treated Ellie when she and Robbie came to live with us. And Louise, I know, would not have come to England if she thought it would cause trouble between my wife and me."

He passed a hand over his eyes. After a moment, he straightened his shoulders and looked at Jack. "When I heard that Louise had been murdered, I think I went a little mad. I went to the theater, but it was in darkness and the doors were locked. I went to the police, but they said it wasn't their case and sent me to another precinct. No one seemed to care." He gave a short laugh. "I didn't know what to do and I had no authority to investigate suspects. But I did have one friend who was highly placed and I turned to him for help. If it were not for Victor, I think the police would have dropped the case." His voice turned harsh. "To them, actresses are no better than streetwalkers, and not worth the time and effort they would expend if a so-called 'decent' woman was murdered."

Jack said slowly, "Who is Victor?"

Cardvale frowned. "Victor Jacquard of the French Ministry of Justice." He paused reflectively. "We met in Paris during the truce of eighteen two. I thought you were here because of him. He said that someone would probably want to ask me questions if the investigation bogged down. I assumed he had gone through the British ambassador."

In the interests of keeping things as simple as possible, Jack replied, "He may well have done so, but Sir Charles either chose not to mention it or it was an oversight on his part."

He was wishing that he had accepted that glass of brandy. He could feel his thoughts jostling one another inside his brain. It was hard to believe that Ellie's inoffensive cousin had shown such gumption. He wasn't a man of action, but in his own quiet way, he was making sure that the hunt for Louise's murderer would not grow cold.

He had never liked Cardvale, but now he was making adjustments to his thinking, and his estimation of the man's character increased considerably.

He breathed out a sigh. "What has Victor told you about the investigation?"

"Very little. Only that there are a number of suspects, but it takes time to gather the evidence to make a charge. He hasn't given me any names if that's what you think. It would be unethical for a man in his position to do such a thing. But I'm not a fool. I know Robbie must be on that list. Not that I believe for one moment that he had anything to do with it. There was no affair. All Louise wanted was to hear about England and his family, that's all."

Jack said quietly, "Did Victor ask you where you were the night Louise was murdered?"

"Yes. I was playing cards in the hotel salon with a few of the male guests. It's easy to remember that night. It was New Year's Day. The ladies had retired for the night." He paused, then added bitterly, "I played cards when someone was in the act of murdering Louise." He shook his head. "I thought I could make her last months happy. There was less time than we knew."

Jack looked into that ravaged face and felt another pang of conscience. Cardvale had deserved better than the faint contempt that he, Jack, had always felt for him.

"What can you tell me about Louise's dresser?" he finally asked.

"Rosa?" Cardvale looked bewildered. "Rosa adored Louise. I had a letter from her recently." He got up and walked to a heavy oak desk, opened the top drawer, and found what he wanted. When he returned to his chair, he handed the letter to Jack.

"She's heartbroken. Louise sent her home to Avignon because she had no need of her now that she was coming to England. Rosa was to be married and Louise gave her a handsome dowry before she left."

"Some things were missing—"

"Gifts to Rosa for her dowry, probably. I was there when she chose them. I can't remember them offhand, but if you were to give me a list, I'd know if something was out of place."

"I'll see to it."

Jack read the letter. It seemed genuine enough. Another door had closed.

There were other questions he might have asked Cardvale, but he decided to defer them to another day. He'd got what he'd come for. Cardvale and the dresser were no longer on his list of suspects. He wondered about Dorothea and Paul Derby.

His sense of frustration made him want to lash out and hit something. Cardvale had been his best bet. Where did that leave him now?

It left him, as he knew very well, with Robbie and Milton. He didn't suspect them of the murder, but he suspected they were hiding something. He might be clutching at straws, but what else did he have to go on?

He couldn't question Robbie in his weakened condition, but there was nothing to stop him questioning Milton. He wasn't sure where Milton lodged when he was in town, but he was in and out of the house on Park Street all the time. And if he wasn't in Park Street, maybe Ellie could tell him where to find him.

He was galvanized now by a sense of urgency, surer than ever that Ellie and Robbie were a threat to Louise's murderer. From now on, he wasn't going to let them out of his sight.

When he left the house, wisps of snow were drifting aimlessly in the wind. Jack huddled into his greatcoat and wished himself home with Ellie.

Chapter 24

Outside Robbie's window, the snow had turned into a mad dervish. Ellie looked at the clock on the mantel and wondered what was keeping Jack. She knew he had gone to see Cardvale, and that he wouldn't come home until he'd found him. But she couldn't help worrying. If Jack were right and Cardvale was the murderer, anything might have happened.

She put a brake on her runaway thoughts. She knew Cardvale better than that. Jack was wrong about her cousin.

Robbie laughed, a strained sound, but a laugh for all that, and that got her attention. Milton was there, sitting close to the bed, talking in an undertone, words not fit for a lady's ears, she supposed, but she forgave him. Now that Robbie was fully awake, he was proving to be a fractious patient. If Milton could get Robbie's mind off his pain for a little while, so much the better.

That put a thought in her mind, and on impulse she said, "Milton, you'll stay for dinner?"

When Milton hesitated, Robbie answered for him. "He can have a tray here with me. Keep me company."

"Now that I can't say 'no' to," responded Milton.

"There you are, Ellie. Milton will look after me. You've been cooped up here all day like a mother hen. It will do you good to have a little time to yourself."

"Thank you, Robbie," she said dryly, "but I promised the doctor I'd keep an eye on that dressing. And in case you've forgotten, you are only allowed gruel and milk. We'll have two trays sent up, one for Milton and one for me."

She made to rise, but Milton got there before her. He pulled the bellrope and a moment or so later, Jack's valet appeared at the door.

"Coates!" she said surprised. "You were up most of the night. I thought you would be catching up on your sleep."

"I'm an old soldier, ma'am," he replied. "I slept for an hour or two. That's all I need. We can't all sleep the day away."

Ellie understood. The servants should all have gone to bed after her party, but after the shooting, they had to stay at their posts while the constables questioned the guests. They must be working in shifts, and Coates must be relieving the butler.

She said, "Mr. Milton and I are having supper here with my brother. Would you be kind enough to tell Cook? Two trays only, Coates."

"Certainly, ma'am. Ah, may I, sir?"

The question was addressed to Milton, who had taken off his coat and thrown it over a chair shortly after he arrived. Coates picked up the greatcoat and waited for instructions.

"By all means," said Milton.

"Thank you, sir. I shall endeavor to have it warm and dry when you leave."

Seeing Coates with Milton's coat jogged Ellie's memory. "I've been meaning to ask you something, Coates."

"Yes, my lady?"

"I seem to have misplaced a key."

When she got up, Milton got up, too.

Robbie said crossly, "For heaven's sake! Sit down, Milton. No need to remember your manners here. It's only Ellie."

"I've always been taught to respect—"

"Your elders?" joked Robbie, then groaned when his laughter made his wound ache.

"Ladies," retorted Milton.

Ellie flashed Milton a smile. "On this occasion, my brother is right," she said. "No need to stand on ceremony here."

"Thank you," said Milton, and he took his chair again.

Ellie crossed to Coates, went into the corridor, and closed the door. She breathed out a sigh. Sometimes Milton's punctilious manners got on her nerves. And sometimes her brother's rudeness made her want to shake him.

Coates was waiting for her to speak. "As I was saying, I seem to have misplaced a key," she said, "and wondered if you had found it?"

"When was this, my lady?"

"The night of the riot in the Palais Royal," and she went on to explain, in sketchy terms, how her key came to be in Jack's pocket.

He nodded. "Ah yes. I remember very well. I beg your pardon, I had forgotten all about it until you mentioned it just now."

"Do you know where it is?"

"In the key cemetery—just my little joke! In a box in the laundry room where I brush and press his lordship's garments. There's quite a collection. The master seems to collect keys the way some gentlemen collect snuffboxes. Shall I bring the box to you?"

She looked at the door to Robbie's room. It was obvious that her company wasn't wanted. Two young gentlemen couldn't be natural when there was an older sister present.

She debated with herself and decided she was being too careful. Robbie was in his own house, surrounded by people who would protect him. And Milton was with him. Besides, she wouldn't be gone long.

"No. I'll come with you," she said.

The laundry room was in the nether regions of the house, as far from the kitchens as one could go. In the corridor right next to it, there was a door leading to a drying green where clothes could be dried in the summer or left open if the steam from the laundry and smells from the kitchen became too intense.

The laundry room was as orderly as her mother's herbarium. There was a lamp in the middle of a small deal table. Coates used the candle he'd brought with him to light the lamp, then spread Milton's coat on a chair, which he pushed close to the boiler. That was one thing she really appreciated about Jack's house. There was always plenty of hot water.

The box was on a shelf beside the flatirons. It was a plain box, and contained a disorderly collection of keys, some small, obviously for desk drawers or cupboards, others much more substantial, the keys to unlock solid front doors.

She looked up when Coates cleared his throat. "What is it, Coates?"

"It will only take me a moment to tell the kitchen staff to prepare two trays for Master Robert's room. With your permission?"

"Oh yes. Don't let me interrupt your work." She added,

as the thought occurred to her, "I know you must be working in shifts, but it seems excessively quiet down here. It's usually a hive of activity. Where is everybody?"

"There's not much to prepare today. There never is after a party. Nobody wants to eat. Those who do, don't want much and are quite happy with a cold collation."

One of the little bells on a board high up on the wall rang, its musical jingle setting Ellie's nerves on edge.

"I'd better find a footman to answer that," he said. "After last night, well, we're shorthanded."

She smiled to show that she sympathized. "Yes, shorthanded and short of sleep. Tell the servants not to worry. I'll make allowances. We can manage."

He smiled, bowed, and left her.

Ellie turned her attention to the keys. She discarded the smaller ones and set the others out in a row. There were five of them. Any one of them might have been the hotel key. It was hard to say which one. They were all big and heavy, with sets of ugly, uneven teeth at their ends. A guard dog would have envied those teeth.

One of the keys glowed in the lamplight. She judged that it wasn't as old or as heavy as the others. There was a small decoration on its ring, the letter "L." She thought for a moment, trying to visualize the key from the hotel. It, too, had a letter on its ring, the letter "B" for Breteuil. Not one of the keys had a "B" on it.

What was Jack doing with so many keys to unknown doors? She didn't like the answer that came to mind, that these keys had belonged to former lovers, and he'd simply forgotten to return them when the affair was over.

Having exhaled a sharp, exasperated breath, she examined the keys again. As far as she could tell, the key she'd slipped into Jack's pocket wasn't here. The only key with a clue to its owner was the key with the letter "L." She brought it closer to the lamp and turned it over in her hand. Something was engraved on its stem: *Louise Daudet, Théâtre Français, 1808.*

Jack and Louise Daudet? She entertained the thought for one moment, then discarded it. Jack would have told her if he'd known the actress. Louise Daudet was too closely connected to them for Jack not to mention it. All the same, finding the key unsettled her.

She looked at it from all sides, then she recognized what it was. No sensible person had their name engraved on a key to their door. If the key was lost and thieves found it, they could use it to enter one's house. This was a commemorative key.

She'd seen keys like this before, keys given by a father to a son when the son had reached his majority or accomplished some worthy ambition. Her own father had had a key like this. His uncle, another vicar, had presented it to him when he had completed a brilliant first year at Oxford. As far as she remembered, it was decorative, like a medal. It didn't open any doors.

How did Louise's key come to be here? She slipped it into her pocket with the intention of asking Jack about it.

This didn't help her find the key to the Hotel Breteuil.

She cast her mind back to the night she had last used it to leave the hotel. Milton was waiting for her on the other side of the door. With his usual punctiliousness, he'd taken the key from her, locked the door, and handed it back to her. Then she had dropped the key into her pochette. It was there when she returned to the hotel, only she'd never had a chance to use it.

Could one of these keys be the one in her pochette when she returned to the hotel? She supposed it could have come from Milton... if he had exchanged his key for hers. Why would he do such a thing?

Her mind was racing now. He'd left her in the Palais Royal while, he said, he would give Robbie's creditors the slip. The Hotel Breteuil was only five minutes away. He wouldn't have had to break in, not if he had her key. Within half an hour, twenty minutes, he could have stolen Dorothea's diamonds and returned for her. And if things had gone to plan, when he escorted her back to the hotel, he would have exchanged keys again, with no one the wiser.

The riot at the Palais Royal had foiled his perfect plan. He would not have been able to find her. What must he have thought?

She stood there transfixed as thoughts buzzed inside her head, then she gave a shaken laugh. She must be out of her mind! This was Milton, Robbie's best friend. All he cared about was his books. What would he do with diamonds?

Her hand went automatically to the key in her pocket. She withdrew it and studied it carefully for several moments. It seemed uncanny to her that Louise Daudet's key had turned up when she was looking for the key to the Hotel Breteuil.

Her hand was trembling. She curled her fingers around the key, not only to stop her trembling, but to get a grip on herself. All she had to do was talk to Jack and the mystery would be cleared up.

She slipped the commemorative key into her pocket again, put the others back in their box, and, after lighting a candle, doused the flame in the lamp. Flickering shadows seemed to leap at her from the walls. Her eyes flew wildly to garments that were hanging from a pulley. She was behaving irrationally, she told herself. She was in her own home. Cook and her helpers were not far away. All she had to do was call out and they would come running.

Only, she couldn't hear any sounds in that cavernous basement. Where was everybody?

With halting steps, holding the candle high, she left

the laundry room and walked the length of the corridor. Her steps slowed to a halt. Try as she might, she couldn't get her feet to move. There was a faint light coming from one of the kitchens, but that hardly encouraged her. The kitchens were at the end of that long, long corridor, and there were many doors between.

She jumped when a light appeared halfway down the corridor. Someone had just come out of the stillroom. It had to be Cook or one of the maids. Eyes straining, she tried to make out who is was.

"Mrs. Rice?" she called out, her voice weak and quivering like a string on a poorly tuned violin.

The light came closer. Not Mrs. Rice, but a man.

Milton.

Chapter 25

"Coates told me where you were," he said. "It's almost impossible to find you alone, and we have to talk."

Her heart was beating very fast. "Who is looking after Robbie?"

"Lady Caro. She was coaxing him to eat from a bowl of thin gruel when I left."

When he took a step toward her, she cried out, "Don't come any closer!"

He stopped, head cocked, staring at her. His voice was gentle. "So you've worked it out?"

"So it's true!" She was shocked and, at the same time, she wasn't surprised at all. "You stole Dorothea's diamonds!"

He began to laugh. "Is that all? Yes, I stole the diamonds, but I was sure you knew the rest. My dear Ellie, can't you guess? I murdered Louise Daudet."

Her ears were ringing. She forgot to breathe. As her heartbeat gradually slowed, she shook her head. "Is this some kind of joke?"

A thin smile curved his lips and his brows rose. "It's no joke," he said. "I killed Louise Daudet."

She believed him. The boy she knew was no longer there. He held himself with catlike grace. The eyes that were weighing her, measuring, were those of a predator. And the key in her pocket was beginning to make sense. This must be the key he had exchanged for hers.

The word that was screaming inside her head came out as a whisper. "Why?"

"Because I could. Because I wanted to." He laughed, the sound of a little boy who had done something clever and wanted approval. "You're looking for motive. What can I say? The opportunity presented itself, and I seized it."

"You're ... you're mad."

"No, Ellie. What I am is clever. Brilliant, in fact. Not that anyone thinks much of that. Do you know how galling it is to live in the shadow of stupid people who are taken up and fêted by people who should know better?"

His voice didn't sound so gentle now. She swallowed hard. "Is that what Louise did with Robbie?"

"Robbie!" He almost snarled the word. "He's a dolt! He'll never pass that Greek examination! It's pathetic! He tries to memorize everything by constant repetition. And you're no better, for all that everyone is impressed by your grasp of classics. I've watched you teach Robbie. You teach by rote. I'm bored with you and bored with Robbie. I see something once and I make connections. You'll never be my equal."

Why is he talking about Greek? her mind screamed. *Who cares if he is brilliant? Who wants to be his equal? He's a murderer!*

It was this last thought that kept her panic in check. He wouldn't be telling her all this unless he was going to silence her.

He was going to kill her.

Her mind had never worked faster as she plotted how she could escape. She had no doubt that if she opened her mouth to scream, he would have his hands around her throat before she emitted more than a gasp. And who would hear her? Where were Cook and her helpers? Where was Coates? And where, oh, where, was Jack?

A plan formed, but it wasn't much of a plan. She started to edge backward, inch by inch, so as not to provoke him. If she could only get to the laundry room, she could open the door to the drying green and run for her life.

"You murdered Louise because you were jealous of Robbie." It was a statement, not a question.

He made a violent motion with one hand and she could see what she had not seen before. He had a knife in his hand. Now she knew why he'd come out of the still-room. That's where the housekeeper kept her own supplies. By sheer force of will, she kept her eyes on his and her feet planted on the floor.

"Stupid!" he snarled. "Didn't you hear me? I murdered her because I wanted to. I murdered her because it satisfied my vanity, to show everyone that they were no match for me."

She didn't believe him, or at least it was only partly true. He'd chosen his victims because he'd been made to lose face, not deliberately, but because he thought Robbie had succeeded where he had failed. It came to her that if only Robbie had told Milton why Louise favored him, none of this might have happened.

But this wasn't, couldn't be, where Milton's envy had begun. This was the culmination of a lifetime's frustration. No matter how brilliant he was, in his own eyes he'd failed the test. So he blamed others for his failure.

It didn't matter. Milton had made his choices and

there was no going back. Her only choice was to run or fight him.

Or pray that someone would come looking for her. Sometime soon, surely her absence would be noticed. The servants would look for her, or perhaps Jack would. How much time did she have before he lost patience?

She had to keep him talking to gain a little time.

"You know, Milton, Louise didn't love Robbie." It amazed her that she could sound so natural. "She took an interest in him because her mother and ours were once friends. Robbie should have told you. The reason he didn't was, you see, because it suited *his* vanity to make his friends think that he was, well, more experienced than he was."

"You're lying!"

He looked like a child who had just broken his favorite toy.

"I'm telling you the truth. Listen to me, Milton. I like you. I've always liked you. I won't say a word to anyone about Louise. I won't say a word about the diamonds. You helped Robbie when he was stabbed . . ." She trailed to a halt.

He laughed and straightened. He'd recovered his equilibrium. "Have you just figured it out? I told you you were slow. I didn't help Robbie by choice. I thought I'd killed him, too. It gave me quite a shock when he stumbled out of the theater into my arms. I wasn't waiting for him. I'd just discovered that I'd dropped something in the struggle with Robbie and I was on my way back to get it."

"What?" she asked hoarsely.

"Louise's key. If I'd met him on the stairs, I would have finished him off. But there were too many people outside the theater. I had no choice but to help him."

Only one thing made sense to Ellie. Milton hated Robbie enough to kill him. The words were out of her mouth before she could think of their wisdom. "You must have had other chances to kill him before we left Paris. Why didn't you?"

He gave a short laugh. "Believe me, I would have if I thought I could get away with it."

She said with a sneer, "You mean, if he'd turned his back on you? What happened, Milton? Did you lose your nerve? Was Robbie getting stronger every day? Were you afraid that he could beat you in a fair fight?"

She stopped suddenly, realizing that she was goading him when she should have been placating him.

"Bitch!" he spat, and spittle sprayed from his mouth. "Do you think I'm stupid? He was holed up in his hotel. If anything had happened to him, I would have been suspected. Only tell me where the key is, Ellie, and I'll let you both go."

He must really believe that she was stupid. This time, however, she kept her mouth shut.

"Where is the key, Ellie?"

Air was rushing in and out of his lungs, and she knew time was running out. He was losing control. She began retreating again, edging her way to the laundry room.

She said dully, "It was you who broke into my rooms and lay in wait for me."

"At last, you're beginning to use that intelligence you take such pride in. I knew you had the key, but knew you didn't realize its significance or you would have mentioned it to Robbie."

She was sickened by what he was telling her, but beneath the revulsion, anger was beginning to simmer. She and Robbie had made a friend of this boy. They'd trusted him.

"You engineered the attack on Robbie in the park."

"Oh, the fireworks were Robbie's idea. As I told you before, when an opportunity presents itself, I seize on it.

And there have been too few opportunities since you and Robbie came to live in this house. I could never rest easy, you see, waiting for one or the other of you to figure everything out. And how right I was not to become complacent! First Robbie wants to clear the dresser's name, and now you have remembered a key you have misplaced. But another opportunity presented itself and here we are."

" 'Clear the dresser's name'?" she said, just to keep him talking. "What difference will that make?"

"I'll become a suspect, Ellie, and I can't let that happen. That's why I attacked Robbie in the park. He can no longer be trusted to keep his mouth shut."

Was it her imagination or was he enjoying himself?

"I searched everywhere for that key, Ellie—your rooms, your Uncle Freddie's house, this house—and could not find it. Where did you hide it?"

"I didn't have it."

"But you have it now or you would never have accused me of stealing the diamonds. In Robbie's room, you were your usual condescending self. Now you're afraid of me. You needn't be, you know. We can strike a bargain. Give me the key and I'll let you go. Then I'll be on my travels with the proceeds of the diamonds. I'll be far, far away, in Greece, viewing the ruins. You might even like to come with me."

He really must think she was a simpleton if he thought she would believe that. Once he had the key, there would be no reason to keep her alive.

Straining to sound as reasonable as he, she said, "I know you won't hurt me, Milton, because Coates knows you're here with me. And if anything were to happen to me, Jack wouldn't like it."

The strain was unbearable. She wanted to cry and scream and rage. She wanted someone to help her. But most of all, she wanted to drive a knife through his black heart.

He giggled, and that terrified her. "Ellie," he said, shaking his head, "give me credit for some intelligence. Coates doesn't know I'm here. I told him I was going out for a breath of fresh air and wondered if you'd like to come with me. He told me you were in the kitchens and I told him I wouldn't disturb you. Everyone thinks I've left the house. I opened the front door and called out a cheery good-bye. Then I shut the door and came to get you. And don't look for the servants to help you. They are delivering trays to various rooms. I took the liberty of locking the door to the basement. When I leave, I'll go by the back door. It's a mistake to underestimate me, Ellie. You see, I've thought of everything."

She knew he wouldn't kill her before he had the key, and that made her dangerously obstinate. "It's not that I underestimate you, Milton," she said. "It's just that you're hapless. You may be brilliant at Greek, but look what a muddle you've made of Louise's murder, not to mention the theft of the diamonds." Her voice developed a crack. "And why attack Robbie? What threat could he possibly be?"

He was advancing. She was retreating. "He knew about the key," he said. "Now the games are over. Give me the key, Ellie, or I'll use the knife."

One of the servants' bells jingled, cutting the silence like a clashing cymbal to Ellie's ears. Milton gave a start and looked up at the board. With sheer animal instinct, Ellie threw down her candle and gave him a hard shove. As he went reeling back, she whisked herself around and sprinted for the back door.

Jack arrived home, veering between temper and despondency, temper because coachmen had not slackened their pace though the ice made the roads treacherous, and despondency because Cardvale's disclosure about Louise Daudet's dresser brought them full circle. Robbie was back to being the prime suspect.

No one answered the door when he pulled the bell, and he had to search through his pockets to find his key to let himself in. Wigan was descending the stairs, shrugging into his coat.

"Where is everyone?" asked Jack, stripping off his own coat and handing it to the butler.

"The dowager and Lady Frances are resting in their rooms, and I believe that Lady Raleigh and Lady Caro are in the sickroom with Master Robbie."

"Not the family, Wigan. Where are the servants?"

Wigan's stoic expression cracked a little. "We're working in shifts, sir, to compensate for a sleepless night. As you may remember, the staff were kept busy attending to guests while the constable asked questions, and after the guests went home, the staff had to clear away. By the time we finished, we had to begin our next day's work."

Jack couldn't be bothered with this. "Thank you, Wigan. I wasn't finding fault. All I wanted was information."

He took the stairs two at a time. Caro rose when he entered. Robbie was sitting up, propped against the pillows, looking none too pleased with himself.

To Jack, he said, "I'm not eating that pap, not even if you pay me to. I want a tray like everyone else."

Caro said, "Dr. Blackwell told Ellie that Robbie wasn't to eat solid food for another day. I made him some thin gruel." She held up a bowl and spoon.

As with Wigan, Jack couldn't be bothered with this.

"Caro," he said, "I want a word in private with Robbie. Would you mind?"

He held the door for her. A look of alarm crossed her face, but she obeyed him just the same. He closed the door firmly at her back.

Robbie seemed puzzled. "What is it, Jack? What's happened?"

Jack took the chair Caro had vacated. He'd made up his mind to question Milton, not Robbie, but he saw no reason to stick to that plan. He felt a sense of urgency. Moreover, Robbie was here and Milton was not.

"How are you feeling?" he asked solicitously.

"I . . . Fine."

"No headaches? Fever?"

"No. Just this pain in my side when I move or cough."

"Good," said Jack, "then I need not treat you as an invalid." His gentleness vanished and he went on harshly, "I learned from Cardvale today that Louise's dresser—you remember the dresser? She was suspected of the murder—well, the dresser is no longer a suspect in the case. If Sir Charles doesn't know it yet, he soon will. You see what this means? We're back where we started. You're the prime suspect, and I don't know where to begin to clear you."

Robbie said nothing. He stared at Jack with eyes bright with alarm.

"Yes," said Jack, "you would do well to be worried." His voice dropped to a confiding whisper. "What is it, Robbie? You can trust me. What is it you know about Louise's murder that you haven't told me?"

Eyes fixed on Jack's, Robbie shook his head.

"Don't lie to me! I know you're hiding something, and I don't care if I have to beat you to get it out of you."

Robbie said quickly, "Why should I hide anything?"

"You would if you had done it and Milton was covering up for you."

Robbie shook his head. "No. She was dead when I entered that room."

Jack moved suddenly and grabbed Robbie by the shoulders. "Don't you understand anything?" he roared. "Someone tried to kill you last night! Someone tried to kill you when you found Louise in her dressing room. If you won't think of yourself, think of Ellie. He was lying in wait for her, too; yes, and might have killed her had I not been with her."

"I didn't know. She didn't tell me!"

"Well, you know now. You and your sister will be in mortal danger until we unmask this villain."

"It's only a little thing," Robbie got out. "And now that the dresser is cleared, it doesn't matter."

Jack's clasp relaxed and he let Robbie go. "I thought so." He sank into his chair. "So, you have been keeping something back. Go on. I'm waiting."

Robbie swallowed. "I told you that when I was attacked, I struggled with my assailant. Well, what I didn't tell you was that he dropped something before he ran off. It was Louise's key. Her name was engraved on it. I had it in my hand when I stumbled down the stairs and collapsed in Milton's arms."

Jack frowned. "The key to what?"

"It didn't open anything. It was a commemorative key. She kept it on top of her dresser. Someone gave it to her when she got her first leading role at the Théâtre Français."

Jack turned the thought over in his mind.

"Why would the murderer take that key?" asked Robbie.

"As a trophy," said Jack savagely, "a souvenir to remind

the murderer of his victim. Why didn't you tell me this before?"

Robbie shrugged. "Because it didn't seem relevant. Because I'd run off with the key and couldn't put it back. I thought it made me look as if I'd stolen the key, that it made me look guilty. But when I heard the dresser was suspected of the murder, because some of Louise's things were missing, I wanted to tell you that she hadn't taken the key."

"Where is the key now?"

"I gave it to Milton. He threw it in the Seine."

Jack was about to stretch his weary muscles. Instead, his jaw snapped shut. He looked at Robbie as though he were seeing beyond him.

"Jack?" said Robbie, when some moments had passed.

Jack focused on Robbie. "You gave the key to Milton and he threw it in the Seine. Did you see him do it?"

"No. I still don't know what you're getting at."

There was a moment of silence, then Jack said, "Did Milton want you to tell me that the dresser hadn't taken the key?"

"No. He said that it would convince the authorities that I was guilty." His voice turned bitter. "So I did nothing."

"I'm missing something." Jack was staring into space. "Correct me if I'm wrong. You and Milton went to the theater together—"

"Yes," said Robbie. "But we met at the Café de Foy. I was there first; Milton was late. As soon as he arrived, we went to the theater."

Jack was talking more to himself than to Robbie. "All this time, it's been staring me in the face. Why didn't I see it? Milton wasn't covering up for Robbie but for himself."

Robbie's jaw went slack. "What are you saying? That Milton murdered Louise? What motive did he have? She was hardly aware of him."

Jack ignored Robbie's questions. "Where can I find Milton?" he asked abruptly.

"He was here, not long ago. I think he went for a walk."

Jack's head snapped back. "He was *here*?"

"Yes."

"And where is Ellie?"

The urgency in Jack's voice made Robbie stare.

"Ellie!" Jack yelled. "Where is she?"

"I don't know. She went off with Coates."

Jack was at the door in two strides. "Coates!" he roared. "*Coates!*"

She pounded down the length of that corridor expecting at any moment to feel herself dragged back. There was no light to guide her, except for the odd glow of lamplight that came through the small basement windows from outside, but that wasn't light. It was merely a lighter shade of darkness.

She welcomed the darkness. It meant his candle had gone out, too. She couldn't see him, but he couldn't see her, either. If worse came to worst, she could hide herself in the warren of rooms that seemed to go off in every direction. She was wishing now that she'd spent more time in the servants' quarters getting to know the lie of the land. Some rooms led into others, but if she hid in one that did not, she would be trapped.

Her dash down the corridor left her gasping for breath. There was a stitch in her side. All that was forgotten when she threw herself against the back door. There was no key in the lock. Sobbing, she tried to think. Where, oh, where would they keep the key? Her panic subsided when she remembered that at the vicarage, the key was always attached to a hook on the doorframe.

She felt around the door lintel and found it, but in her

haste, she knocked it off its hook and it went clattering to the floor, then slid into the laundry room.

She went after it, dropped to her knees and with fingers splayed wide, groped to find it. It was impossible to see where it had fallen. As she became more desperate, her movements became less cautious.

When she heard sounds in the corridor, she went perfectly still. He was coming her way, opening doors as he advanced.

"I know you're here, Ellie," he said, his voice pleasant and faintly amused. "If you'd left by the back door, I would have felt the draft."

She cupped a hand over her mouth to stifle the whimper of sheer animal terror that bubbled up. This couldn't be happening! She was in a house full of people. There were over twenty servants. She was mistress here. She shouldn't even be in the kitchens. And a boy she would have trusted with her life was trying to kill her.

He'd succeed if she didn't get a grip on herself.

She needed a weapon to defend herself. A poker would do, a plank of wood, a knife. The only weapons at hand were laundry supplies and the lamp on the table.

She stifled another bubble of panic and rose soundlessly to her feet. He was approaching the door to the laundry room. There was no time to sniff at bottles for acid or lye or something to throw in his eyes to blind him. She found a bar of gooey soap, but that didn't inspire her confidence. She was feeling her way toward the lamp when she heard flint on stone and a watery light glowed from a small room on the other side of the corridor. He'd managed to light his candle.

Then she saw it. The key to the back door glinted at her from under the table. There was no thought of concealment now. If she didn't get the key, she would never escape.

She grasped it in her hand, darted to the door, and inserted it in the lock. Her fingers had never worked faster to turn that key. She heard the *click* as the lock turned. Her sigh of relief turned to a gasp of terror as his booted foot slammed into the door, closing it tight. She whirled to face him and in the next instant he lashed out, catching her a blow to the face, and she went reeling into the laundry room.

If she had not caught herself on the wooden tubs, she would have fallen to the floor. Her jaw was aching, her head was swimming, she tasted blood in her mouth. She watched in a daze as he set his candle in a holder on the table, then put down the knife beside it.

He *click*ed his tongue. "Why do you insist on defying me? I don't want to hurt you. See, I've put my knife down. Give me the key and I'll let you go."

At that point, she would have done anything to prolong her life except give him the key. She still didn't understand its significance, but she knew that once he had it, he would have no use for her.

She pointed with her finger. "It's over there." Her voice cracked with fear. "In that box."

He smiled. "Why don't you show me?"

She had to straighten her knees before she could move. He followed her to the shelf where she'd left the box of keys. He took it from her and, for one unguarded moment, turned his back on her as he walked to the table to examine the contents by the light of the candle.

That was all she needed, one unguarded moment. She reached behind her, grabbed a flatiron, and slammed it into his back. He went down on his knees, doubled over, retching as he tried to get his breath.

She could have used the flatiron again, to crack his skull. Thankfully, she was not put to the test. There was the sound of shattering wood and a moment later, light

streamed into the basement from the door to the upstairs.

"Ellie! Ellie! Where are you?"

Jack's voice!

She dropped the flatiron and hared down the corridor
to that welcome sound. She wanted to lose herself in the
comfort of Jack's arms, but he thrust her away from him.

"Where is he?" His voice was like steel.

"In the laundry room."

That was all Jack needed to hear. He started down the
corridor at a run. He hadn't got far when the back door
swung open and Milton disappeared into the night.

Jack's run became a sprint.

"Be careful!" Ellie cried out. "He has a knife."

Servants were streaming in, silent except for a few
whispers. Candles and lamps were lit. Coates tried to get
her to go upstairs. She hardly heard him. After a moment's hesitation, she went sprinting after Jack.

It had stopped snowing, but even though she scanned
the darkness, there was little to see but the outline of
bushes and trees, the houses next door and...

Footprints in the snow going round the side of the
house toward the street. She picked up her skirts and ran
to catch up with them.

Park Street was well lit. She had no trouble finding the
figures she wanted. They were running up the pavement
toward Piccadilly. Jack was gaining on Milton.

Milton looked over his shoulder, saw his danger, and
darted across the street toward the park. Ellie watched in
horror. He was panicked. He would never make it. A
coach and four bore down on him. The driver called out a
warning and tried to rein in his team, but it was too late.
Milton was swept away in a brutal tangle of horses and
wheels.

Chapter 26

A week later found Jack meeting with Ash and Brand in the coffee shop in Pall Mall. Brand had just returned from Bristol where he was covering the trial of a man accused of a particularly vicious murder and he had missed the gory conclusion to their own investigation. What irked him was that he could not print a word of it in his newspaper.

"I'm afraid not," said Jack. "There's no proof of anything except that key, and it wouldn't be enough to prove our case. Besides, Ellie and Robbie are quite happy to let the world think that Milton died accidentally. They want to spare his family's feelings, you see."

"What annoys me," said Ash, adding lumpy sugar to his coffee, "is that the villain receives a blameless, Christian burial while Louise Daudet gets nothing, not even an exoneration of her character. There was no rich protector waiting in the wings, only a heartsick half brother."

"Now that," said Brand, "is where I may get my story if Cardvale is willing to cooperate. He need not be flowery or emotional, just give a plain statement of fact, admitting that Louise Daudet was his half sister and that she was leaving France to take up residence in Hampstead. As for the rest, I won't mention any names, but there's nothing to stop me saying that both English and French authorities believe that the perpetrator of the crime killed himself when they were close to making an arrest. What do you think, Jack? Will Cardvale help me?"

Jack looked doubtful. "He may if he thinks it will clear Louise's good name."

Ash made a derisory sound. "Lady Cardvale might have something to say about that!"

"No," said Jack. "She won't be a problem. The Cardvales have decided to separate."

"*What?*" Ash and Brand spoke in unison.

Jack answered dryly, "He made it worth her while. The house in Cavendish Square becomes hers, plus an income to cover the style of life to which she has become accustomed."

"And what does Cardvale get out of it?" asked Ash.

"Peace of mind," replied Jack crisply.

He didn't elaborate, but he was thinking of Cardvale as he'd last see him, when he'd called on Ellie to tell her about the separation. Though Cardvale had tried to sound grave, they couldn't help seeing the change in him. It wasn't so much that he was happy, but content. His eyes were brighter, his voice was firmer, and he looked as though he'd shed ten years.

They'd shown him Louise's commemorative key and, as they suspected, it was he who had given it to Louise when she'd landed a leading role in the Théatre Français. He was grateful for its return. They thought it might make him sad, but it did the opposite. He spoke at length about the sister who had brought him so much happiness.

After he left, Ellie became lost in thought. Finally, she

said, "He's like the cousin I once knew. I'm not sorry he is leaving his wife. He is far too fragile to be married to someone like her. I don't know what my father would say, but I'm sure my mother would agree with me."

And that was that.

"What about the diamonds?" Brand asked. "How did Milton know about them?"

"We all knew about them," Ash pointed out. "Lady Cardvale made damn sure everybody knew how priceless they were. I used to wonder if she wore them to bed."

Jack smiled at this. "I think Brand means how did Milton know where to locate them. Ellie blames herself for that. She told Milton that when the Cardvales had arrived at the hotel, Dorothea had kicked up a fuss when she discovered she was assigned room 13. It couldn't be changed because the hotel was full. Milton had stayed at the hotel on a previous visit. He must have known about the staff staircase and the door into the dressing room."

"He must have had nerves of steel," said Ash.

"What he had," replied Jack, "was an arrogance that defies description."

"How did you find the diamonds?" asked Brand.

"Robbie told me that Milton stored his valuables in a wooden box that was made to look like a Greek lexicon. It was in his room at Oxford." He shook his head. "No one doubts that he was brilliant, but he wasn't very bright. I gave them to Cardvale along with other pieces Milton stole. Whether he returns them to Lady Cardvale remains to be seen."

"So you see," Ash added, exasperated, "Milton is still considered blameless."

The Bath buns arrived for Ash and Brand, plain scones with no raisins in them for Jack, and the next few minutes were taken up pleasurably in drinking coffee and buttering buns.

But Brand wasn't finished yet. Still chewing on a mouthful of bun, he said, "What gave him away? What made you realize he was the murderer?"

Jack gave a sheepish grin. "A lack of suspects. Paul Derby didn't really come into my calculations, not seriously, because he wasn't in Paris at the crucial time. I thought that if he was acting for anyone, it would be Cardvale. As it turns out, he was working for Lady Cardvale." He smiled grimly. "He and I had a short conversation and he told me everything. Dorothea wanted him to get her diamonds back, but they thought Robbie must have them, not Ellie. It was Derby who searched Robbie's room in Oxford."

"How many black eyes is he sporting?" asked Brand.

Jack didn't bother to respond. "So what it came down to was that I had one last clue to follow up—you know what I mean, Brand. You kept hammering home the point that my attorney thought Robbie's and Milton's statements were too pat and that they might be concealing something."

"Yes. But I suspected Robbie. I thought Milton was supporting his story because he was his friend."

"Deep down," said Jack soberly, "I was thinking along the same lines, though I wouldn't acknowledge it, not even to myself. It bothered me, though, that the killer hadn't finished Robbie off. It wouldn't be the first time someone had turned a knife on himself to establish his innocence."

"But surely," said Ash, "after Robbie was shot in the park, you were convinced of his innocence?"

"True enough. But I knew that he was hiding something and I was afraid that he might be attacked again." He gave a short laugh. "Robbie is a loyal friend, but that loyalty damn near cost him his life. He'd promised Milton he wouldn't say anything, and I had to browbeat him into telling me about the key.

"I was electrified. For the first time I began to think of Milton as a suspect. Then when Robbie told me they'd met at the Café de Foy before going to the theater, I could see how it was done. The café is only a few doors down. Milton could have murdered Louise while Robbie was waiting for him in the café." His voice hardened. "Then he came for Robbie, to lead him to the slaughter."

Ash shivered. "What I can't understand," he said, "is why Milton took the key in the first place. And why go back for it when he discovered that he'd lost it in the struggle? He could have got clean away."

"It's not uncommon," said Brand, "for murderers to want a keepsake of their crimes. I come across it all the time in the cases I cover for my newspapers. It's something to gloat over in their private moments. What I find interesting is the object itself. The key had Louise's name on it. I'm sure every time Milton looked at it, he would have remembered that Robbie wanted Louise and he'd taken her away from him." He looked at Jack. "I think he must have hated Robbie intensely."

Jack nodded. "Ellie thinks Milton was jealous of Robbie. Oh, he was a brilliant scholar, but Robbie was popular. Milton felt slighted. People never seemed to look up to him or take to him. Then they came to Paris, and Louise favored Robbie, too."

After a long silence, Ash said, "Then if Louise's key meant so much to him, why did he use it to fool Ellie? Why part with it? Why not use a key that could not be traced back to him?"

"We shall never know now," said Brand, "but in my experience, murderers never foresee that things may go awry or that they may make a mistake. If only there had not been a riot at the Palais Royal! If only Ellie had stayed where she was supposed to stay! If only he had used another key! It was sheer arrogance on his part, in my opinion, that made him take such risks. Even at the end, he took an appalling risk and paid for it with his life. At least his family is spared the knowledge that he was a murderer."

Ash said, "I would rather have seen him hanged. His death was too easy."

Brand smiled faintly. "What about you, Jack? How do you feel?"

"Oh," said Jack pleasantly, "I would rather have seen him hanged, drawn and quartered. You see, where my wife is concerned, I'm barely civilized."

Twenty minutes later, he arrived home and was met in the hall by Wigan, who informed him that her ladyship wished to speak to him.

"She's in the yellow parlor, my lord."

Was that a smile that flickered briefly on Wigan's thin lips? If so, it was an encouraging sign. This had been a house of gloom in the last week, largely because Ellie seemed despondent, and the servants took their cue from their mistress.

They all did—Grandmamma, Caro, and Robbie. He couldn't say about Frances, because she rarely left her room. Ellie did whatever was needful, but she was subdued and uncommunicative. She wouldn't share her feelings, not even with *him*. She rarely went out. She'd even lost interest in Robbie's progress in Greek, and that was more telling than anything.

No. The most telling sign that something was wrong was her lack of interest in their marital bed.

He entered Ellie's parlor to find her pacing and her fine brows drawn together in a ferocious frown. Oddly enough, this made him want to laugh out loud. The ice sculpture that Ellie had turned into was melting from the inside out.

"Ellie," he said softly.

At the sound of his voice, she turned and straightened her shoulders. That small gesture was another telling sign. When Ellie straightened her shoulders, she had something on her mind she had to get out.

She took a quick breath. "I have some bad news for you, Jack. Well, it's not all bad. There's good news, too."

He crossed to her and took her hands in a firm clasp. "Tell me!" he commanded.

"Frances has left us."

There was a challenge in her eyes that made him want to kiss her. He had his old Ellie back. "Go on," he said.

"While you were out, she packed her boxes, ordered the carriage round, and went off to be with her friend Mrs. Tuttle in Kensington."

He kissed her hand. "Is that all? Now tell me the bad news."

She missed his little joke. "Did you hear me? She says that nothing will induce her to return, that she intends to set up her own establishment in town and—"

"She can afford it!"

"—and mix with civilized society!"

So, Frances was responsible for bringing his wife out of the doldrums. He must remember to thank her.

"What brought this on?" he asked calmly.

The temper in her eyes cooled considerably. "That's the good news I was coming to. Alice's young man came back for her. Can you believe it? I feel so ashamed now for ever doubting him. But she never doubted him, not for one moment. He came in person to tell me that they're to be married, very quietly, tomorrow, then they leave the day after for Carlisle, where he has found work.

"Married tomorrow? They'll need a Special License and that costs money." And he was quite prepared to pay it.

She made a small sound of impatience. "They *have* money. Don't you remember that I won it for Alice when I played cards with Ash and his friends at the Clarendon?"

"Ah yes, *that* money. You're very farsighted."

The more he smiled, the more she frowned. "And," she went on, "we've been invited to the ceremony."

"I wouldn't miss it," he promptly replied. He knew there was more to come, so he waited patiently.

She rushed her next words. "I took it upon myself," she said, "to offer to hold the wedding breakfast in our home. Well, the servants will want to be there, too. What better place to have it?"

"I agree. Ah, I see. But Frances didn't. Is that it?"

"She called it the last straw. Thankfully, Alice's young man had left before I told Frances about the wedding breakfast. Grandmamma and Caro thought it was a wonderful idea, but Frances raged like a deranged woman. The things she said about Alice do not bear repeating."

She looked at him pensively. "I did not try to persuade her to stay. Perhaps that was unfeeling of me. This has been her home far longer than it has been mine. If you want her to return, you'll have to ask her yourself, and I will do my best to make my peace with her. But one thing I insist on. Alice is going to have her wedding breakfast here among her friends."

"Ask her to return?" His horror was genuine. "I am not so softhearted as you. She's right about one thing. This is the last straw. I've turned a blind eye to her conceit, her small-mindedness and her constant fault-finding, but a slight to Alice, after all you have done on the girl's behalf, is more than I can stomach."

Ellie said crossly, "You should have reined her in long before now. Why didn't you?"

"Because..." He had to think this through. "Because," he said slowly, "her faults were not so glaring until you were here to compare her to."

She cocked a brow. "Careful, Jack, you're coming perilously close to a declaration. But I won't tease you. I have a million things to see to for Alice's wedding breakfast."

He was left staring thoughtfully at her retreating back as she stepped jauntily from the room.

The wedding breakfast was held in the Servants' Hall. Alice was very self-conscious and looked as though she would shrivel if anyone looked at her the wrong way. She need not have worried. Every servant there knew that a wrong word or a wrong look would not be tolerated. Besides, a month ago, they were laboring under the heavy yoke imposed on them by Frances and her henchwoman. The new mistress and her housekeeper had removed that yoke, but their patience was not limitless. No one wanted to follow in the footsteps of Lady Frances and Mrs. Leach.

As the breakfast progressed, Jack became more and more mellow. Everyone seemed to be having a good time. It made him think of the time he had spent with the Brans-Hills. Their dining table wasn't very large, but there was always room for one more. He supposed a great many people would look back on the Brans-Hills with the same fond memories. Cardvale for one. Louise Daudet and her mother also came to mind, as did Sir Charles Stuart.

He knew there was a metaphor in his reminiscences, but he couldn't put his finger on it except... Ellie seemed to personify that dining table. No. The dining table personified Ellie and her family. Now he had it right. He knew one thing: He was going to make sure that he always had a place at Ellie's table.

It was time for the toast to the young people, a duty that Ellie had bestowed on him.

"Nothing fancy," she'd told him. "Just wish them long life and happiness."

At a nod from him, Wigan dutifully went from guest to guest with a tray of long-stemmed glasses filled with champagne. There were "oohs" and "ahs" from everyone when they discovered what was in the glasses Wigan had served. It was a grand gesture, something for Alice and Sam to remember fondly when they looked back on this day. They were so young, not much older than Robbie. He hoped to God time was kind to them.

His wife was making faces at him, telling him to get on with it, so he got up, cleared his throat, and began on the little speech he had rehearsed.

"Alice and Sam," he said, addressing the bride and groom, "I used to think that marriage was a trap for the unwary. I think most men do, until they meet the right woman. Well, look at me." There were a few encouraging titters.

"We men never think that women have the same apprehensions, but they do. Ask my wife." There were no titters this time.

He cleared his throat. "Some marriages get off to a bad start. What I mean to say is a less-than-perfect start. That doesn't matter in the long run. There will be hurdles to overcome. Don't give up on each other. Always remember that marriage is what you make of it. And you two young people have a head start. No one can doubt your love for each other."

The servants were staring at him with unblinking eyes. Caro and Robbie looked flummoxed. His grandmother was laughing into her handkerchief and Ellie was making a face at him again, telling him to cut his speech short and get on with it.

He obeyed. When he raised his glass, a collective sigh of relief went up. Everyone got to their feet.

"To Alice and Sam," he said. "Long life and happiness."

"To Alice and Sam," everyone chorused, and put their glasses to their lips.

It wasn't until they were clearing the table that he had a private word with Ellie. "I'm not very good at speeches," he said. "You should have asked Wigan to give the toast."

She gave him the sweetest smile. "No one doubts your sincerity. Words are cheap. Everyone knows how generous you have been to Alice and Sam. You were the right person to give the toast."

That made him feel much better.

He looked down at the table as Wigan came to clear the glasses away. "Well," said Jack, "everyone seemed to enjoy the champagne."

"Why shouldn't they?" intoned Wigan with a pained expression. "It cost forty pounds a bottle."

Jack gave a wry smile. "It was worth it," he said.

Ellie called out to him. They were seeing the young couple off. He felt in his pocket for the banknote Ellie had requested for their wedding gift. As long as Ellie was happy. That's what mattered.

When they climbed the stairs to bed that night, Jack had the candle, so Ellie had to follow where he led. This last week, he'd been sharing her with Robbie, and that was all right. They'd wanted to relive and retell how Milton had come to hate them so much that he'd tried to kill them. It wasn't easy to understand. But it was over. It was time to turn the page and start on the next chapter of their life. And this time, he was going to do it right.

She looked a little surprised when he passed the door to her chamber and led her to his own. He said in an undertone, "Your door is always open to anyone who wants a heart-to-heart talk. This time, it's my turn."

"'Heart-to-heart'?" Her brows lifted. "Now this I must hear."

As he dismissed Coates, who had been waiting up for him, she walked to one of the long windows and looked out. The park was in darkness except for lanterns that watchmen carried on their rounds, but Park Street, where Milton had met his end, was well lit. He hoped she wasn't reliving that night. He joined her and closed the drapes.

She smiled at the gesture. "I'm not going in terror of memories of Milton," she said. "If anything, I'm thankful that his family was spared the agony of a trial."

"Then what do you think when you look out at the park?"

She made a helpless gesture with her hands. "I feel sorry for a wasted life, but I feel more sorry for the life he cut off without a qualm, so it's not only Milton I think about when I look out the window. Cardvale said that Louise was hoping to meet me. That's what Milton took away from me. He tried to take Robbie, too. I'm not vengeful. I'm just glad it's over."

She put a hand on his arm. "What do *you* think when you look out the window?"

He remembered the rage that had consumed him when he had sprinted in pursuit of Milton. If he'd caught him, he would have throttled the life out of him.

"I try to be forgiving!" he said.

She gave a hoot of laughter, slipped off her stole, and perched on the end of the bed. "You mentioned something about a heart-to-heart talk," she said. "Was that it or is there more?"

He perched on the bed, too. This was harder than he

thought. "There's more," he said, and stopped. Her eyes were dancing.

"You know what I'm trying to say!" he reproved.

"Oh yes, Grandmamma told me. That convoluted toast you made to Alice and Sam was really meant for my ears."

"I wish my grandmother would mind her own business!"

"Now that was unkind. She means well." She rested her chin on one pointed finger. "I should have guessed when you mentioned a marriage trap. I seem to have heard those words before." She shook her head. "But, Jack, you said that bad word, you know the one I mean." She spelled it out for him. "L.O.V.E.—and that put me off the scent. I knew you'd never use that word to me."

"I suppose I deserve that."

Her humor vanished. "That's wasn't a reproach! That was a joke."

He put his hands on her shoulders and gave her a steady look. "Well, this is no joke. I mean it. I never knew what that word meant until I met you. When Milton tried to kill you, all I could think was that you would never know how much I loved you."

She covered his hands with hers. "Idiot," she said. "I knew, oh, not from your words, but from your actions."

"I didn't do anything!"

"Oh? Then who gave me an alibi? Who was there when Milton broke into my rooms and attacked me? Who married me to redeem my character? What about Robbie? Alice? I could go on and on. Face it, Jack, you betrayed yourself at every turn. I felt so useless. I knew how little the words meant to you, and I had nothing to give you in return."

"There is one thing you can do. Always make sure there's a place for me at your table."

"What?"

"And give me the words. From you, they mean something."

She wanted to ask him to explain about the table, but before she could get a word out, his arms closed around her and his mouth came down on hers. Blind instinct did the rest.

Another week went by when Jack and Robbie entered Ellie's little parlor to find her once again at the window, looking pensively out at the park. Jack cursed softly under his breath. Robbie did not notice. He was waving a paper over his head.

"Ellie!" he cried out. "Ellie! I passed my Greek examination. I can be back in Oxford for the Easter term."

Her pensive expression vanished as she was swallowed up in a bear hug. They were both laughing when they broke apart.

"Well done, Robbie," she said. "I knew you could do it. How do you feel?"

He was jubilant. "As though I'd climbed the Matterhorn! Where are the others?"

"They're in the house somewhere."

He was out the door in a few strides. "Caro!" he called out. "Grandmamma! Where are you? Coates! Wigan!"

Jack looked at Ellie and smiled. "No more talk about not graduating from Oxford," he said.

"No. It's funny what a little success can do. Robbie will do just fine."

He stopped her when she made to go by him. "Still gazing out at the park, Ellie? Still thinking of Milton? You must try to put all that behind you."

Puzzled, she glanced out the window. "Oh," she said finally, "I'm not thinking of Milton. Believe me, Jack, I was thinking of something entirely different."

"What?"

"I was watching the children playing. Their nurse-maids and mothers take them to the park from miles around."

Now he was puzzled. "So?"

She fingered his lapels and sighed. "You told me in no uncertain terms once what you thought of the marriage trap. I know you'll be honest with me. What do you think of the baby trap?"

It took a moment for him to make sense of what she was saying, then he reached for her and held on for dear life. That one gesture told Ellie what was in his heart. With Jack, actions would always speak louder than words.

"I love you, too, Jack," she said.

About the Author

Best-selling award-winning author Elizabeth Thornton was born and educated in Scotland, and has lived in Canada with her husband for over thirty years. In her time, she has been a teacher, a lay minister in the Presbyterian Church, and is now a full-time writer, a part-time babysitter to her five grandchildren, and dog walker to her two spaniels.

Elizabeth loves hearing from her readers.
If you wish to receive her newsletter, e-mail her at:
elizabeth.thornton@mts.net or visit her Web page at:
www.elizabeththornton.com.

Join Elizabeth Thornton in her next

spellbinding and seductive novel . . .

The
Bachelor
Trap

by

Elizabeth
Thornton

On sale June 2006

Read on for a preview . . .

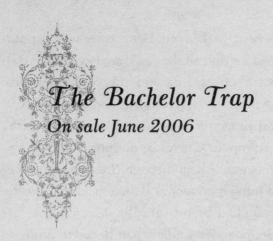

The Bachelor Trap
On sale June 2006

Longbury, October 1815

Edwina Gunn pushed through the back door of her cottage and quickly turned the key. There was a bar on the door, and she slammed it home as well. Her heart was racing. She was breathing hard. She'd been asking too many questions, poking her nose in where it wasn't wanted. All she'd achieved was to rouse a sleeping tiger.

"Get a hold of yourself, Edwina," she told herself sternly. "You're sixty years old. At this rate, you'll give yourself an apoplexy! You're not a threat! You can't prove anything. And after all this time, he is bound to feel safe."

When she had control of her breathing, she crossed to the window and, standing well back so as not to be seen, looked out. Her cottage was just outside the estate, and all she could see beyond her own small patch of gardens and the outhouses were stands of beech trees, hawthorns and oaks, the remnants of their winter foliage now bedraggled with the sudden downpour. There was nothing else to see.

She, too, was soaked through. She unfastened her coat and hung it on a hook beside the door. The fire in the grate had been banked by Mrs. Ludlow, her daily help, but Mrs. Ludlow had her own family to tend and always left in time to prepare their dinner.

She was alone in the house and her nearest neighbors were up at the Priory.

This last thought prompted her to make sure that the front door and all the downstairs windows were locked. It was something she was in the habit of doing every night, though, like most country people, she left her doors unlocked during the daylight hours. From now on, she was going to lock her doors during the day as well.

"Silly old woman," she chided herself. She'd probably run from a stray dog or one of the estate gamekeepers.

Feeling more like herself, she began to mount the stairs. It was a struggle and she had to use the handrail to haul herself up. She made up her mind, then, to move her bed chamber to the unused maid's room next to the kitchen. It was small but convenient for someone who couldn't manage the stairs. The very thought made her feel her age all the more keenly.

Once in her own room, she wrapped herself in a warm dressing robe, put on her wool slippers, then poked the fire to a cheery blaze. As she watched the flames licking around the small lumps of coal, she became lost in thought again.

She was thinking of Hannah, who would always remain young in her memory, Hannah who loved life and was fearless in how she lived it, Hannah who was the source of so much heartache.

Twenty years ago, she'd left this very house vowing never to return, and that was the last anyone had seen of her.

Where are you, Hannah? What happened all those years ago?

Had she been a younger woman and in better health, she would have posted up to London and consulted with Brand. He was as close to her as any son, and what she had to say was better said face-to-face. But she hadn't been well enough to travel so she'd done the next best thing. She'd sent a letter to Brand's office in Frith Street, giving him a brief sketch of what she'd discovered. That was more than two weeks ago, but there had been no reply. She wasn't finding fault. All that meant was that Brand hadn't received her letter. He was a busy man and traveled around a great deal. The letter would catch up with him eventually.

There was another letter she should have written, to the one person who might well solve the mystery at one stroke, her niece, Marion.

On that thought, she sat down at her escritoire and assembled her writing materials. After dipping her pen in the ink pot, she paused. This wasn't an easy letter to write. She hadn't seen Marion in over twenty years. Their correspondence had been sporadic, largely because she and her sister, Diana, who was Marion's mother, had had a falling out. Diana's tragic death from pneumonia the year before, followed so closely by the death of Marion's father, had brought she and her niece closer together.

She swallowed a lump in her throat. Not all her remorse and regret could make up for those wasted years. How could she and her sister have been so foolish?

She would not make the same mistake with Marion. But she hardly knew where to begin. After all, they did not know each other very well. If she started making unfounded accusations, Marion would think she was deranged.

She toyed with the idea of inviting Marion to come to Longbury for a visit, but soon discarded the notion. For one thing, Marion lived a good three days journey from Longbury. For another, she had her hands full taking care of her two younger sisters. Nor did she like the idea of bringing Marion into a situation that was fraught with danger.

If only Brand were here, he could advise her.

There was no harm, however, in corresponding with her niece. They could reminisce about the one and only time Marion had come for a visit. She must know what happened that night. She was there. Someone had seen her. Perhaps the memories were locked away in her mind and a little prompting would set them free.

She began to write. Not long after, she heard a floorboard creak. Her mouth went dry and she slowly got up. When the floorboard creaked again, she went to the fireplace and lifted the poker from its stand. In the corridor, she paused. All she could hear was her own heart beating painfully against her ribs. Nothing seemed amiss, nothing was stirring.

She walked haltingly to the top of the stairs and looked down. Nothing. Lowering the poker, she half turned to go back to her room and saw the face of her assailant before she felt the first blow.

It's the wrong person, was her last conscious thought before the darkness engulfed her.

The following morning, Mrs. Ludlow arrived at her usual time and let herself into the cottage. She had a package under her arm, a nice shank of mutton that she'd picked up from the butcher that morning, enough to make a big pot of soup with meat to go with it, and perhaps a little left over for her own family. Miss Gunn was a generous soul.

After removing her coat and putting on her apron, she got the fire going. The kettle of water for Miss Gunn's morning cup of tea was soon whistling on the hob. When everything was ready, she set the tray and carried it into the front hall. A few steps in, she halted. Her employer was lying in a heap at the foot of the stairs, her sightless eyes staring up at the ceiling.

It was an hour before the constable got to the house. There was no doubt in his mind that the old lady had fallen down the stairs. Only one thing puzzled him. There were ink stains on her fingers, but no letter was found, nothing to show for those inky fingers.

In his view, it was a small thing and not worth bothering about.

London, May 1816

It was only a small thing, or so it seemed at the time, but in later years, Brand would laugh and say that from that moment on, his life changed irreversibly. That was the night Lady Marion Dane stubbed her toes.

She and her sister were his guests, making up a party in his box at the theater. They hadn't known each other long, only a month, but he knew far more about her than she realized. He and her late aunt, Edwina Gunn, had been friends and from time to time, Edwina had mentioned her sister's family who lived near Keswick in the Lake District. In the last few weeks, he'd made it his business to find out as much as he could about Lady Marion Dane.

She was the daughter of an earl, but she had never had a season in London, had never been presented at court or enjoyed the round of parties and outings that were taken for granted by other young women of her class. If her father had not died, she would still be in the Lake District, out of harm's way, and there would be no need for him to keep a watchful eye on her.

Though he'd taken a sketch of her background, he could not get her measure. She was an intensely private person and rarely showed emotion. But in the theater, when the lamps were dimmed and she thought herself safe from prying eyes, she gave herself up to every emotion that was portrayed on stage.

The play was *Much Ado About Nothing*, and he could tell from her face which characters appealed to her and which did not. She didn't waste much sympathy on Claudio, or his betrothed's father, and they were, one supposed, cast in the heroic mold. Benedick she tolerated but the shrew, Beatrice, made her beam with admiration.

It was more entertaining to watch Marion's face than the performance on stage.

The final curtain came down, the applause died away and chairs were scraped back as people got up. Lady Marion was still sitting in her chair as though loath to leave. Her sister, Lady Emily—an indiscriminate flirt at seventeen—was making eyes at young Henry Cavendish; and his own good friend, Ash Denison, was stifling a yawn behind his hand. No affair such as this would be complete, for propriety's sake, without a chaperon or two, and doing the honors tonight was Ash's grandmother, the dowager countess, and her friend, Lady Bethune. The evening wasn't over yet. He had arranged for a late supper at the Clarendon Hotel where Marion's Cousin Fanny and her husband, Reggie Wright, were due to join them.

Everyone was effusive in their praise of the performance, but it was Marion's words he wanted to hear. She looked up at him with unguarded eyes when he held her chair, her expression still alight with traces of amusement. Then she sighed and said, "Thank you for inviting us, Mr. Hamilton." She was using her formal voice and he found it mildly irritating. She went on, "In future, when I think of this performance, I shall remember the actress who played Beatrice. She was truly memorable."

She got up, a graceful woman in lavender silk with a cool smile that matched her cool stare, and fairish blond hair softly swept back from her face.

Some demon goaded him to say, "In future, when you think of this performance, I hope you will remember *me*."

The flash of unease in her gray eyes pleased him enormously. Since they'd met, she'd treated him with all the respect she would show an octogenarian. He wasn't a vain man, but he was a man. The temptation to make her acknowledge it was becoming harder and harder to resist.

Recovered now, she smiled vaguely and went to join her sister. He had to admire Marion's tactics. It was seamlessly done, but very effective. She diverted young Cavendish's interest to someone in another box, linked her arm through Emily's and purposely steered the girl through the door.

Emily was an attractive little thing with huge, dark eyes, a cap of silky curls and a smile that was, in his opinion, *too* alluring for her tender years. There was always a stream of young bucks vying for her attention. And vice versa. Marion had checked her sister tonight, but that didn't happen very often.

There was another sister, Phoebe, a child of ten whom he liked immensely. Though she was lame, she was game for anything. She was also a fount of knowledge on Marion's comings and goings.

He was calling her *Marion* in the privacy of his own thoughts. If he wasn't careful, he'd be doing it in public, then what would Lady Marion Dane, cool and collected earl's daughter, make of that?

"She makes an excellent chaperon, doesn't she?" Ash Denison, Brand's friend since their school days at Eton, spoke in an undertone. "All she needs is one of those lace caps to complete the picture. Then every man will know that she's a confirmed spinster and he had better keep his distance."

The thought of Marion in a lace cap such as dowagers wore soured Brand's mood. All the same, he could see that day coming. Though she was only five-and-twenty, she seemed resigned to her single state. No. It was truer to say that she embraced it. All she wanted from a man, all she would allow, was a platonic friendship.

Did she know that she was setting herself up for a challenge? He let the thought turn in his mind.

"Careful, Brand," said Ash. "You're smiling again. If you're not careful, you'll be making a habit of it."

Brand turned to stare at his friend and made a face when he came under the scrutiny of Ash's quizzing glass. No one looking at Ash would have believed that he had spent the better part of his adult life fighting for king and country in the Spanish Campaign. Brand knew that those were brutal years, though Ash always made light of them. Now that the war was over, he seemed hell-bent on enjoying himself. He was a dandy and the darling of society.

Brand had neither the patience nor the inclination to make himself the darling of society. He knew how fickle society was. As the base born son of a duke, he'd met with prejudice in his time, but that was before he'd acquired a fleet of newspapers stretching from London to every major city in England. Now, he was respected and his friendship sought after, now that he could break the high and mighty with the stroke of his pen.

He knew what people said, that he was driven to prove himself. It was true. But he never forgot a friend or anyone who had been kind to him when he'd had nothing to offer in return. Edwina Gunn was one of those people. It was to repay his debt to her that he had taken Marion and her sisters under his wing.

Ash was waiting for him to say something. "The sight of a beautiful woman always makes me smile."

"I presume we are talking about Lady Marion? You haven't taken your eyes from her all evening."

This friendly taunt was met with silence.

"Is she beautiful?" Ash prodded.

"Not in the common way, but she has style."

"Mmm," Ash mused. "If she allowed me to have the dressing of her, I could make her the toast of the ton. I'd begin by cutting her hair to form a soft cap. We'd have to lower the bodices on her gowns, of course, and raise the hems. I think she would look her best in transparent gauzes. What do you think?"

Ash was known to have an eye for fashion and many high ranking ladies sought his advice. In Brand's view, their newfound glamour wasn't always an improvement.

"You know what they say." Brand moved to catch up with the rest of his party, and Ash quickened his step to keep up with him.

"What do they say?"

There was a crush of people at the top of the stairs and Brand felt a moment's anxiety. He relaxed when he saw Marion's fair hair glistening with gold under the lights of the chandeliers. Emily's dark cap of curls shimmered like silk. Then he lost sight of them in the crush.

"What do they say?" repeated Ash.

"One man's meat—"

The sentence was left hanging. A woman screamed. Some patrons cried out. In the next instant, Brand was sprinting for the stairs.

He shoved people out of his way as he thundered down those marble steps. He found her at the bottom, sitting on the floor, her head resting on her knees. Emily was with her.

"Stand back!" he flung at the group of people who had crowded round her. They gave way without a protest.

He knelt down and touched her shoulder with a shaking hand. He had not heard a shot, and there was no sign of blood. "Marion?" he said urgently. "What happened? Say something!"

She looked up at him with tears of pain in her eyes. "I stubbed my toes," she said crossly. "There's no need to fuss."

Then she fainted.